The Fuzzy CONUNDRUM

By John F. Carr & Wolfgang Diehr

Pequod Press

THE FUZZY CONUNDRUM
A Pequod Press Science Fiction Novel

Manufactured in the United States of America
First Printing 2016

V 10 9 8 7 6 5 4 3 2 1

ISBN: 978-0-937912-66-9

On the cover: Alan Gutierrez, The Fuzzy Conundrum
2016 (*www.alangutierrez.com*)

Pequod Press
P.O. Box 80
Boalsburg, PA 16827
www.PequodPress.com

H. Beam Piper Continuations Presented by Pequod Press

PARATIME

Gunpowder God
The Fireseed Wars
Siege of Tarr-Hostigos
The Hos-Blethan Affair
Kalvan Kingmaker
Great Kings' War
Time Crime

TERRO-HUMAN FUTURE HISTORY

Fuzzy Ergo Sum
Caveat Fuzzy
The Fuzzy Conundrum
Cosmic Computer
The Merlin Gambit
Space Viking
The Last Space Viking
Space Viking's Throne

ACKNOWLEDGEMENTS

Special thanks go out to our hard-working copyediting team, Victoria Alexander, Larry Hopkins, Dwight Decker, Mike Robertson, Dennis Frank and David Williams. And to Fred Patten for his help in keeping the continuity straight and true to H. Beam Piper's vision.

CHRONOLOGY

The Atomic Era is reckoned as beginning on the 2nd December 1942, Christian era, with the first self-sustaining nuclear reactor, put into operation by Enrico Fermi at the University of Chicago. Unlike earlier dating-systems, it begins with a Year Zero, 12/2/'42 to 12/1/'43 CE. With allowances for December overlaps, 1943 CE is thus equal to Year Zero AE, and 1944 CE to 1 AE, and each century accordingly begins with the "double-zero" year, and ends with the ninety-nine year—H. Beam Piper.

(All dates in the Chronology are based on Atomic Era dating. jfc)

28	First unmanned rocket, the *Kilroy*, lands on the moon.
30	The United Nations collapses.
31	Terran Federation formed.
31	The Thirty Days' War (World War III).
53	First human exploration of Mars; the *Cyrano* Expedition.
54 – 100	Further exploration of Mars, Venus, asteroids and moons of Jupiter.
92	Contragravity is developed.
95 – 105	First Federation begins to crack under strains of colonial claims and counter-claims of member states.
105	Venus secedes from the First Terran Federation.
106 – 109	World War IV (First Interplanetary War). Entire Northern Hemisphere devastated by nuclear bombardments.
110	First Terran Federation is re-centered in the Southern Hemisphere. Australia, New Zealand, South Africa, Brazil, Argentina, Uruguay agrees to abolish nation states, creating a completely unified world. This marks the beginning of a new civilization. Lingua Terra begins taking shape.

127	Reformed Second Terran Federation establishes a single-world sovereignty when Britain becomes the last nation to join.
172	Keene-Gonzales-Dillingham Theory of Non-Einsteinian Relativity developed.
174	Venus secedes from the First Terran Federation.
183	The First Terran Federation is dissolved and the Second Terran Federation is established. New Federation imposes system-wide pax.
183	Dillingham hyperdrive developed.
192	First expedition to Alpha Centauri.
200	Atomic Era dating adopted.
200 – 800	Period of exploration, colonization and expansion.
350	Marduk colonized.
399	Fenris Company chartered and Fenris settled.
409	Chartered Fenris Company goes bankrupt.
526	Native revolt on Uller against Chartered Uller Company.
629	Zarathustra is discovered and settled.
650	Poictesme is discovered by Genji Gartner and settled.
654	Fuzzy sapience is recognized and Zarathustra reclassified from Class III to Class IV world.
716	Svantovit discovered and Svants encountered.

DRAMATIS PERSONAE

Clarence Anetrou—Attorney for Hugo Ingermann.

Gustavus Adolphus Brannhard—Chief Colonial Prosecutor and Pappy to two Fuzzies.

Frank Carr—Mallorysport Chief of Police.

Johannes Chang—Scientist working on the Zarathustran climate mystery.

Michael Duncan Clarke—Zarathustra Native Protection Force (ZNPF) officer stationed at the trading post near the *Jin-f'ke* lands.

Darla Cross—Actress and romantic interest to Dr. Hoenveld

Cinda Dawn—Intern working on the Zarathustran climate mystery.

Piet Dumont—Deputy Commissioner of Native Affairs, former Mallorysport Chief of Police.

Max Fane—Federation Marshal stationed on Zarathustra.

Gunnery Sergeant James Fitzpatrick—Space Marine Gunny.

Thor Folkvar—Tall powerfully built chief of security for Morgan Holloway. Born on Magni, a heavy gravity world in the Federation.

Ned Foster—Assistant District Attorney under Gus Brannhard.

Enrico Garza—Businessman and financier of the expedition working on the Zarathustran climate mystery.

Victor Grego—CEO of the Charterless Zarathustra Company (CZC).

Captain Conrad Greibenfeld—Federation Space Navy intelligence officer.

Little Fuzzy—the first discovered Fuzzy, part of Jack Holloway's family.

Keezheekoni Helmut—Zarathustra Native Protection Force (ZNPF) officer stationed at the trading post near the *Jin-f'ke* lands.

Akira Hsu O'Barre Holloway—Morgan Holloway's wife

Jack Holloway—Commissioner of Native Affairs. Discovered the Fuzzies. Former Sunstone Prospector.

Morgan Holloway—Jack Holloway's son. Born on Freya and of half-Freyan ancestry. He has spent most of his adult life looking for Jack.

Patricia Holloway McLeod—Jack Holloway's older sister visiting on
Zarathustra.

Dr. Jan Christiaan Hoenveld—Head of the CZC Science Division and
arguably the premier scientist on Zarathustra.

Juan Jimenez—Division Head of Science Center Alpha.

Betty Kanazawa—Jack Holloway's love interest. Born on Terra,
immigrated to Zarathustra to work at the CZC.

Ahmed Khadra—ZNPF officer.

George Lunt—Major in the ZNPF.

Claudette Pendarvis—Head of the Fuzzy Adoption Bureau and wife of
Justice Pendarvis.

Chief Justice Frederic Pendarvis—Chief Colonial Judge on Zarathustra.

Tres Poe—Hired laborer for science expedition.

Bennett Rainsford—Colonial Governor of Zarathustra.

Douglas Rathbone—Member of a criminal organization devoted to
enslaving Fuzzies.

Jason Roberts—Former police detective from Terra turned private
investigator.

Ruth Ortheris Van Riebeek—Gerd's wife, former TFN espionage
operative working at the CZC.

Captain Ralph Osbourne—Captain of the *F.S.N. Hikaru Hatori*, a
Federation Navy Destroyer.

Gerd Van Riebeek—Division Head of Science Center Beta and former
Deputy Commissioner of Native Affairs.

Gregoire Rutherford—Scientist working on the Zarathustran climate
mystery.

Andre Sabahatu—Member of a criminal organization devoted to
enslaving Fuzzies.

Captain Shade—Captain of the *Pequod*, a large space yacht. Works for
Fuzzy slavers.

Clancy Slade—Restaurant and bar owner, local hero after killing Leo
Thaxter.

Rheiner Sostreus—Genetically altered Freyan, throwback to pre-mutated condition.

Johann Torseus—Genetically altered Freyan.

Starbuck "Buck" Trask—Federation Bureau of Criminal Investigation (FBCI) agent sent to Zarathustra from Terra.

Ray Trendell—Member of a criminal organization devoted to enslaving Fuzzies.

Joe Verganno—Computer programming specialist for the CZC.

Dmitri Watson—Scientist working on the Zarathustran climate mystery.

PROLOGUE

Suzanna Warren left her loft in Old Town Buenos Aires in a hurry. She had an appointment with her boss at 1400. Fortunately, she lived close enough to the Broadbill Tower to take a ground taxi to the office. Most of the residents of Buenos Aires lived in the contragravity towers that surrounded Colonial Old Town like a forest of glass and silver redwood trees. As she exited her building doorway, she noticed a crowd pressing upon a frightened woman and her pet—a small golden monkey or ferret—which was hanging onto her for dear life.

As Suzanna pressed forward to the street where her taxi was waiting, she could see the fear in the woman's wide eyes. She also got a better look at the animal she was holding—it was a Fuzzy!

No wonder the poor woman's attracted a crowd, she thought. The Fuzzies were the cuddliest critters since pandas, which had died out in World War IV, and the question of Fuzzy sapience had been the issue of the day on the news screens and talk shows about a year ago.

Suzanna had had her own difficulties with crowds. Her friends said she had star power; she just saw it as the ability to charm men with a "look" and a winning smile. It didn't hurt that she was half Freyan. She saw her taxi and immediately turned on the charm, waving to the crowd. Every male within a hundred feet turned in her direction.

She motioned for the Fuzzy lady to join her. The woman, the small Fuzzy cradled protectively in her arms, pushed her way through the crowd and joined her at the curb. "Thanks," she whispered, almost out of breath. "My name's Delia, by the way."

"Mine's Suzanna," she replied as they squeezed into the backseat.

"Where to?" the robo-driver asked.

"The Broadbill Tower," Suzanna replied. Turning to Delia, she added, "After I get out, the cab's all yours."

"Thank you, thank you. I was beginning to fear for my life, and that of F. Scott Fitzgerald."

"F. Scott Fitzgerald?"

"Oh, that's my Fuzzy's name."

Suzanna turned to F. Scott Fitzgerald, saying, "Hi, F. Scott. That's a pretty big name for such a little guy."

The Fuzzy shrugged. "It hokay. It my Big One name."

The little guy was so cute that Suzanna had to resist taking him into her arms and cuddling him. No wonder people were so crazy about Fuzzies. Maybe she could apply for one herself. "If you don't mind my asking, how did you obtain F. Scott?"

Delia reached over and put her hand on Suzanna's forearm. "You're our savior. For you, anything. I can't tell you how frightening it was to be the center of that crowd, and they were only getting more worked up…. Oh, but to answer your question, my husband and I were doing a tour of the outer worlds and one of the stops was the planet Zarathustra, the Fuzzy homeworld. The locals were in the middle of a big court case between the local chartered company and Federation lawyers regarding the Fuzzies' qualifications for alien sentience.

"As part of our tour, we visited the court and got to see some of the Fuzzies up close. I just had to have one! We ran into this rather unsavory man by the name of Raj who offered to sell us one." She paused with a sheepish look. "We didn't know—or care—if it was legal. We just had to have one of our own. For ten thousand sols, we were introduced to F. Scott and several other Fuzzies. He told us to let the Fuzzies decide who was going to accompany us."

Her voice rose. "And it was F. Scott Fitzgerald who jumped into my arms." She paused to ruffle his fur. "We've been inseparable ever since. But, after today, this is the last time I take him out in public. There was one man who looked like he was about to rip little F. Scott right out of my arms!"

"That's a good idea, Delia. I bet on the black market a Fuzzy would be worth a fortune."

Delia nodded. "My husband thinks we should hire some body-guards to make sure no one tries to steal him from us. I thought he was overreacting, but now—"

"Listen to your husband. Oh, here's my stop."

"Thank you, again, Suzanna."

"My pleasure," she replied, getting out of the cab. "Bye, F. Scott."

"Bye, Suza."

Suzanna took the antigrav lift up to the third floor where the law offices of her boss, Ansell Shawley were located. As soon as she reached her office, she was going to do a datastream search for Fuzzies for Sale.

I

Terra. August 5, 657 A.E.

Buck Trask settled into his chair and turned on the computer console. With the successful conclusion of his most recent case, the O'Gill murder, he was ready to get back to his unsolved caseload, which was substantial. Of all the worlds in the Federation, Terra had the highest crime rates and the lowest number of resolutions to those crimes.

Part of the problem, Trask had often thought, was too many people on too little land. Far too much of the planet was still a radioactive wasteland, despite efforts to reclaim the irradiated ground by importing processed guano from Yggdrasil and sterile dirt mined from marginally inhabitable worlds.

After three centuries of land reclamation projects, less than eight percent of the damaged real estate had been rejuvenated. Even as technology improved and hyperspace travel times shortened, the most optimistic estimate for total planetary reclamation was two millennia. Trask grunted as he scrolled through the cases on the screen. Not for the first time did he consider relocating to any one of the five hundred-odd colonized worlds and starting over. Smaller populations, lower crime rates, even fewer laws in many cases, made the idea of moving to a colony world very appealing. Sadly, for him, his sense of duty kept him rooted to the world of his birth.

He pulled up the Adoni Danggali case file. Danggali was charged with the second degree murder of his wife's illicit lover. The defense attorneys had managed to block every attempt to get Danggali questioned under veridication. That was another point in favor of the colony worlds—fewer lawyers.

"Terra to Starbuck! Are we reaching you, Starbuck?"

Trask looked up to see Abraxus Obispo standing in the doorway. "Sorry, Brax, didn't hear you come in. What's up?"

Obispo took a seat and feigned nonchalance. "The boss wants to see you."

"Colonel Springbok? What about?"

Obispo shrugged. "Beats me. I heard something about a big case that came up in South Africa. Maybe he wants you on it."

"We have enough investigators there to deal with things without calling me in all the way from Sydney. Well, I'll go see what it is and let you know if I can. It might be something all hush-hush, though."

Obispo rolled his eyes. "Hell, what isn't around here?"

Colonel Richard Samuel Springbok of the Sidney precinct of the Federation Bureau of Criminal Investigation was not the sort of man to stand on formality. In fact, he ran a fairly loose command as long as one rule was followed: The job got done.

Colonel Springbok heard the knock and looked up to see Trask standing in the doorway. "Ah, Investigator Trask, come in."

"You wanted to see me, sir?"

The Colonel pointed to a chair and Trask took the seat. "Buck, you mentioned to me once that you wouldn't mind taking a mission off-world. Is that still the case?"

Trask sat a little straighter in the chair. "It is, but my caseload—"

"Will be reassigned for the duration." Springbok tapped a button on his desk and the door to the office slid shut. "We have one Niflheim of a case, Buck. Last week the Johannesburg Precinct busted an illegal underground casino in Cape Town."

Trask tried to feign interest. Casino arrests were a near daily occurrence and he didn't see the off-world connection to it. "Oh? Find anything interesting?"

Springbok snorted. "Mostly what you would expect: gambling, drugs, prostitution, off-world art trafficking...same old, same old. Until they found the menagerie."

There it was. Xeno-critter trafficking, as Obispo would call it.

"Menagerie...like illegal animal imports?"

"Yup. Freyan kholphs, Ulleran graachatook, Sheshan kh'tch-in, Thoran tilbras, and something new that was discovered a few years ago. Zarathustran Fuzzies."

Trask mentally processed the list and stalled on the last item. "Wait... Fuzzies? Wasn't there something in the news about a year and a half ago about some big court battle that proved these...these Fuzzies were sapient beings?"

Springbok nodded. "Damned straight. And they were locked up in cages like animals under the casino. Lousy conditions, too. Moreover, they were being used as entertainment; dancing, mock duels, and some acrobatics."

"That's slavery and then some, sir. A bullet in the head for everybody involved." Trask read the Colonel's face and could see there was more to come. "What else?"

"A breeding program," Springbok said. "At least an attempt at one. Forensics has been poring through the computer files. No viable Fuzzy births while in captivity, so we can thank Ghu for that small favor."

Trask nodded, then an evil thought worked a slimy trail through his mind. "Ah...I hate to ask, and don't really want to know the answer, but...?"

"Were the Fuzzies being molested?" Springbok grimaced. "We haven't found any evidence of that...yet. Their size makes anything like that problematic, fortunately for them, but there are always a few deviants willing to press the issue. This case will be getting the full treatment and then some. That is where you come in."

"Yes?"

"I want you to go to Johannesburg and get briefed on everything they found, then you will go to Zarathustra to see if you can close the pipeline at the source."

"Why me and not somebody from Johannesburg? They're more knowledgeable about the operation than someone from our office."

Springbok shook his head. "Just between you and me, the Bureau Chief over there thinks he may have a rat in his house. This operation didn't just pop up overnight, and it went unnoticed for way too long. He wants somebody who couldn't possibly be compromised to work the case off-world. I owe him a few favors, and you mentioned you would be up for the trip—so here we are."

"What about the Federation Bureau of Colonial Affairs? Why aren't they involved?"

"The Chief of Colonial Affairs himself called me. There have been some problems on Thor, another native uprising. The Bureau is stretched too thin to send someone to Zarathustra. He asked for our help."

Trask thought it over. He had no problems with making the trip. Besides, he was one of the few FBCI agents without a family to hold him back. "Who is going with me?"

"Solo mission."

"Oh? What about the Bureau on Zarathustra?"

"Barely a presence. Up until the Charterless Zarathustra Company lost its charter, they were being watched by the Navy. An agent and a small staff were sent in about a year and a half ago, but I doubt they'll be of much help. So far, Zarathustra is considered too unimportant for a serious presence; only novices and sub-par agents have been assigned there."

He glanced at the ceiling as if making a supplication to a deity. This assignment was shaping up to be a career killer and he said so.

"A successful off-world assignment," the Colonel replied, "would bolster your chances for advancement."

Trask swallowed the sarcastic rejoinder that jumped into his head. "What is going to happen with the Fuzzies? Do they come with me?"

"The Fuzzies will be repatriated after we question them, give them a solid medical workup and let Mental Hygiene take a crack at them. That will take a few months, but afterwards the Federation Space Navy will handle their transport back to Zarathustra. You will go commercial as soon as you finish the briefing in Johannesburg.

"Let me warn you, this is a colony planet with looser laws than we are used to. The governor there is an appointee and had never served for any government office before getting tapped for the job. That might make him difficult to work with."

"Or easier," Trask countered. "Maybe this guy will be less worried about the politics and more about the Fuzzies."

"Or the opposite," Springbok countered. "Remember that mess on Loki from the history books? Or the one on Odin a decade or so back? Or the Baldur government conspiracy? The people running the planet are not above suspicion in this matter. In fact, until we know better, they are all persons of interest."

Trask felt the tension in his shoulders building and forced himself to relax. It was never good trying to bring down a corrupt government. "What do we know about the setup on Zarathustra?"

"Well, as you know, everything we have is at minimum six months out-of-date. They could have had another election, a *coup d'état*, deaths accidental or not, or people just plain skipping planet by now or even while you are in transit. Currently, to our best understanding, the Colonial Governor is Bennett Rainsford. Up until he was placed in charge by Commodore Napier, Rainsford was a naturalist with the Institute of Xeno-Sciences. He has an impressive record and set of degrees in anthropology, xeno-biology, crypto-zoology, natural science and a few other things. He has an equally impressive record in his fieldwork and is highly regarded as a top scientist in that area. No degrees in political science."

"I think I like him already," Trask smirked. "I hate career politicians on general principles."

Springbok agreed and said so. "Next is one Gustavus Adolphus Brannhard, the Colonial Chief Prosecutor. He was appointed by Rainsford almost instantly upon Rainsford coming to power. Brannhard also has an impressive record. However, it only goes back about thirty-five years or so. He appeared out of nowhere on, um, Freya is the best guess, and started up several law practices on a number of colony worlds until settling on Zarathustra about a decade ago."

"Sounds like he was on the run from something. Either us or the other side."

"Well, he is done running, now. But is that because he found a nice lucrative position running Fuzzies? Then there is John Morgan Holloway."

Trask had heard that name before. "Oh, right, he is the man who discovered the Fuzzies in his kitchen or something."

"One Fuzzy in his shower stall," Springbok corrected. "He was made the Commissioner of Native Affairs."

"The perfect job if you want to run Fuzzies. What do we have on him?"

"Quite a bit, actually. Third of ten children, left Terra in 614 A.E., bounced around from colony world to colony world. He has been arrested a few times but nothing ever stuck."

"Arrested for what?"

"Hmm... Assault and battery at least a dozen times, homicide on several planets, public intoxication, trespassing on tribal lands—"

"He sounds like a real anti-social type. How did he skip on the charges?"

Springbok scrolled down the file on the viewscreen. "It seems he was able to sell either self-defense, or defense of others in each case. More than once he was stopping another crime in progress—"

"And no charges can be brought against anyone acting to prevent a crime," Trask finished. It was the ultimate extension of the Good Samaritan Protection Act. "This Holloway is starting to sound like a good man. What about the other charges?"

"Mm...the trespassing was dismissed as a misunderstanding, but Holloway claimed he was escorted by a Sheshan who should have known better. Probably true. Sheshans are very antagonistic to each other and violating another tribe's holy lands would be par for the course. The public intoxication charge was on Fenris. All he said about it was that he had received some bad news from Freya and tried to drown his sorrows, and I am quoting here, 'like a damned fool.' Holloway paid the fine and left planet shortly afterward."

"Huh. We've all been there. At least this guy didn't whine about his troubles to get out of the fine." Trask found himself liking Holloway, too. That was bad for an investigator. "Anybody else of note?"

"Victor Grego, the CEO of the former Chartered Zarathustra Company. The Company lost its monopoly on the planet two years ago when the Pendarvis Decision smashed the charter, which is when it became the Charterless Zarathustra Company. Grego got back most of what he lost in a deal with Governor Rainsford—"

"Sounds like collusion, Colonel."

"It does. Holloway could supply the Fuzzies, Grego could use his connections with Terra-Baldur-Marduk Spacelines to get them off-world, while Rainsford could suppress any investigations into Fuzzy cases. But according to Commodore Napier everything is on the up and up."

"Which could be true, or Napier could be in on whatever is going on there. I'll have to veridicate a hell of a lot of people in the process, and most of them are in positions to prevent that. I could even find myself railroaded on some trumped up charges and imprisoned, or even killed outright. Nice assignment you handed me."

Springbok shrugged. "I thought you'd like it. Buck, this is a make or break career move. You are the best man for the job, though. Break the case and you'll likely find yourself on the short list for promotion."

Promotion? That would be nice, he thought. "For now, at least, I am expendable enough that I won't be missed for a year or two."

Springbok smiled. "There is that."

II

"Hi, this is Hal Huntington, inviting you to Huntington Dodge aircar and ground car headquarters in downtown Mallorysport. I'm Hal Huntington, and this is my Fuzzy, Spot. We've got aircars and ground cars for every need and wallet. I know we've got a lot of newcomers to Zarathustra, and I want to welcome each and every one of yawl.

"Everything on the lot, including my twenty-gallon hat is for sale; that is, except for my Fuzzy, Spot. I know a lot of you visitors want a Fuzzy for your own, so I suggest you visit Pappy Jack at the Fuzzy Rez on Beta Continent and tell him Hal sent you. And here at Huntington Dodge, we've got just the transportation you need to bring those happy Fuzzies home with you!"

Zarathustra, Jan. 23, 658 A.E.

The morning dew still sprinkled the grass and leaves as the bright orange sun cleared the horizon. Some wildlife stirred about seeking food or water while the more nocturnal members of the ecosystem nestled into their burrows or branches. Small furry quadrupeds competed with each other for the tastiest morsels in the foliage while staying alert for potential predators.

One such group that could be classified as predators stealthily moved through the thick high grass and considered their strategy for attacking several of the small mammals. These predators were known as Fuzzies to the Terro-humans who had settled on this world, and the small mammals were called goofers, though the Fuzzies had their own names for such things.

Goofers, so-named for their physical similarities to the Terran gopher, differed in some significant ways. Goofers burrowed only when nesting prior to giving birth and often traveled in groups of four, dubbed a gambol. They did not tunnel through the ground like their Terran counterparts. Aside from land-prawns, goofers were the preferred food animal for Fuzzies.

There were eight Fuzzies in the hunting party, which was about as large a group as anyone could hope to find this far east on Beta Continent. The gambol of goofers, four in number, would make for a good morning meal for all eight, provided they managed to catch them all.

Hidden from both the Fuzzies and the goofers other eyes watched the hunting party and their intended prey. The owners of these eyes were sapient beings from a world hundreds of light-years away. While the technology that brought these beings to this world was very sophisticated, the motives and intentions of the beings were not.

"Another few feet forward and we will be golden, Ted."

Ted, watching the viewscreen intently, nodded. "If they keep moving forward as a group, yes. Hunters tend to spread out and surround their targets when they can to reduce the chances of their prey from escaping. Especially when hunting for food and not just a trophy."

The other man shrugged and returned to watching the screen. The Fuzzies appeared to be in a discussion as to how to proceed. They all turned to one individual to settle the matter.

"That one with the auburn pelt must be their Wise One, Nick. See how they all look to him?"

"Looks like. I did some reading and sometimes there will be a member or two that decide they are smarter than the boss. If he or she tries to take over and fails, the group will become divided and go off in different directions. Then, assuming they survive, they will eventually meet up with another group and maybe join up with them."

"Right. That is why the language is more-or-less uniform. Wait, what about those Northern Fuzzies? They have a different language, or at least a different dialect."

Ted thought for a moment. "I think it has something to do with the geography. Fuzzies can swim in fairly shallow water, but they don't like it. The Northern Fuzzies are separated from the others by the wide rivers too deep for a Fuzzy to ford or swim across." Ted gave it some more thought.

"This group is separated from the rest of Beta by the mountain range. That means they might have yet another dialect or even fully developed language."

"Three languages on one continent? Seems like a lot—"

"Ha! You need to bone up on your history. Back before the Third World War there were countries with three or more established languages. In Belgium they spoke French, Flemish and in one quarter that had been annexed from Germany in the first Great War, they spoke German. Europe had something like ninety languages, and that was a landmass of about one fifth of Beta Continent. There could be dozens, if not hundreds of different Fuzzy tongues that have yet to be discovered, Nick."

Nick grunted. History was his admitted weak point. "Well, most alien species we have discovered tend to speak a single language, like Sosti or Sheshan. Even Terra is mostly mono-lingual, now. I would have bet that...wait, look! The Fuzzies are moving forward. Just a bit more... gotcha!"

Nick tapped a button on his console and on the viewscreen he could see the trap spring. The sides of the cage that had been carefully disguised with dirt and leaves sprang up and neatly enclosed the Fuzzies.

"Let's go out and collect them before they can try to climb out. Remember not to use sono-stunners. Dead or even deaf Fuzzies are useless to us."

"No worries. I tweaked the traps with anesthezine gas. Look."

Ted looked up at the viewscreen and saw gas shooting out from spheres at the top of the cages.

"When did you do that, Nick?"

"Right before I laid the traps. I wanted it to be a surprise."

Ted mentally wrestled with the thought for a moment, then said, "Good job, but no more surprises. Run any other ideas you might get through me first. Now, let's go bag us some Fuzzies."

*   *   *

Mallorysport spaceport was typically busy once a week for the purpose it was designed for: managing the ebb and flow of spaceship passengers. The rest of the time it supported itself with a maze of shops and bistros and not-too-overpriced hostels. When the ships were in, the port would be crawling with people coming in and heading out. This was one of those times.

Patricia Lorrain McLeod moved through the terminal with a baggage robot in tow looking for an exit through the sea of people moving in every direction. Where other women would have struggled through the press of bodies, Patricia's six-foot frame, backed by determination and confidence, easily powered through. When she finally made it outside she looked around for a taxi. She had to raise a hand to shade her eyes as the brilliant orange sun was midway through the sky.

"Would you be interested in sharing a ride?"

Patricia looked back to the voice and spotted a familiar face. "Hi, Buck. No, I don't think you would be going anywhere near where I am headed."

"Oh, that's right. You're headed to Beta Continent." Trask shook his head. "The locals really need to come up with some more interesting names for the major land masses." Trask looked around. "I thought I would see some Fuzzies as soon as I came outside, but there are none in sight."

"Fuzzies have very acute hearing, according to my brother's letters. I suspect the spaceport is too noisy for their comfort. I read in one of the pamphlets that there is discussion in the legislature here to rename Alpha Continent to Mallory Major or something like that. After the captain of the ship that originally discovered this planet. Anyway, I have to get over to Beta and see my brother, and I believe you have business here in Mallorysport...?"

Trask nodded. "I do, though I imagine I will be headed out to Beta in the course of my visit here. Gods, did you see all those ships up there?"

"And then some. I asked at the counter and they said that a lot of private companies are ferrying people here hoping to adopt Fuzzies."

"Adopt Fuzzies?" Now there was a good cover for taking Fuzzies off-world. "Did you catch where the ships were from?"

"Odin, Baldur, Isis, Poictesme, Imhotep, Marduk, Tiamat...you name it, they probably have a ship up there. Well, good luck with your business. Go ahead and take the first taxi. I'll bet I will have to go through a few before I find one willing to make the trip."

"Thank you, Pat. My best to your family. I hope we can speak again." Trask thought of something, "By the way, you never said what your brother's name was..."

"Jack Holloway. He's the Commissioner of Native Affairs around here." Pat waved and moved off to find transportation while Trask swore under his breath.

Trask went to the first taxi in the line while Patricia walked over to the second.

"Where to, lady?"

"A place on Beta Continent called..."

"Sorry. Too far with too little chance of a return fare. There is an airbus that makes the trip three times a week. Next trip is tomorrow morning—"

"Thank you, but I have waited long enough already. I'll try the next cab."

Patricia went to the next taxi in line, then the fourth, all with the same results. Before she got to the fifth she heard running feet heading her way. She glanced in the direction of the sound and spotted a young man headed quickly in her direction.

She smiled slightly, thinking, *I know this dance.* The man ran past as he reached out and grabbed Patricia's handbag. What happened next came as a complete surprise both to the purse-snatcher and the taxi driver who was halfway out of his aircar.

Patricia, still holding on to her handbag, gave a sharp yank backwards pulling the young man off of his feet and down to the pavement. Before he could regain his footage a very large pistol appeared in front of his nose.

"I am afraid, dear heart, this bag doesn't go with those shoes. Moreover, it was a gift from my husband, and I would hate to part with it, or get it all bloodstained, if you take my meaning."

He did.

The taxi pilot laughed so hard he had to lean against his aircar. "Bubbette, I am tempted to take you wherever you want to go gratis. In fact, if it is anywhere in town, I will do just that. This idiot has been robbing passengers for the last month and nobody was able to even I. D. him, let alone catch him."

"I'll settle for you calling a cop." Patricia glanced down at the mugger who looked like he was thinking about running. A solid poke on the nose with the barrel of the .38 Special changed his mind. "You try it and I'll slap you naked and hide your clothes."

"Already done." The cabbie jerked his nose at the air above. "Here they come."

Ten minutes, a sworn statement recorded with the portable veridicator globe an unwavering blue, and a thank you from the patrolman later, Patricia was ready to go.

"Beta Continent, eh? I see why the other cabbies rejected your fare, Bubbette. Ah, what the hell. Hop in."

"Are you sure, Bubba? It looks to me like you could do a lot of business today." Patricia indicated the crowd of people filtering out of the shuttle terminal.

The cabbie laughed again. "I could use a nice flight over the country. And the ocean, for that matter. And you are the first person on this planet in, well, ever to call me Bubba instead of asking why I call everybody else that."

Patricia smiled and said, "And, of course, you will expect a nice tip."

"I never expect a nice tip, Bubbette. But I do like to be surprised."

III

Red Fur was enjoying himself for the first time in many-many days. As the Wise One of many-many clans, he was always solving problems for all of the *Jin-F'ke*; that left very little time to go out and hunt on his own. From the Big One at the Trading Post, Red Fur learned about something called a 'day off' and something else called a 'deputy.' The deputy would run things while the Wise One took the day off. Sometimes the Big Ones had good ideas.

Red Fur spotted a land-prawn and ignored it. Unlike many of his kind, he did not like the taste. The goofer he spotted next was more to his liking. He crept up slowly on the creature and readied his chopper-digger for a strike when something else caught his attention. Through the tall grass he could hear the cries of one of the People.

Cautiously, Red Fur moved through the grass in the direction of the cries. In a small clearing he spotted a Big One forcing one of the *Jin-f'ke* into a cage. Red Fur's first thought was that the Big Ones had betrayed his people. He had no love for the Big Ones since the death of Sun Fur. Then he remembered his friend, Little Fuzzy, had told him about bad Big Ones. The good Big Ones would put the bad Big Ones in cages or make them dead.

Unfortunately, the good Big Ones weren't here. Red Fur stabbed his chopper-digger into the dirt and readied his bow. Unlike the chopper-digger, which came from the Big Ones, the bow and the arrows he carried were made by Makes-Things. While small, the arrows were tipped with the poison of the *net-zeetha*, a venomous lizard. The poison could kill a goofer almost instantly; hopefully it would stop a Big One.

Red Fur skirted the edge of the clearing in hopes of getting a clear shot at the Big One. Unlike many of the People, as the tribe's Wise One, he rarely had the opportunity to practice with the bow.

The Big One lifted the cage into the melon-seed shaped made-thing. Red Fur could not afford to wait. Drawing his bow, he took careful aim. He hoped to strike the leg; that way the Big One would be slowed by the injury even if the poison failed to work.

The arrow failed to strike the Big One in the leg. Instead, the missile went high and struck the man in the posterior. Red Fur did not understand the words that the Big One screamed out, but suspected they were some of the mean-nothing words they used when angry. Little Fuzzy had taught Red Fur some of them.

The Big One pulled the noisy weapon they all carried and swung it to and fro looking for the source of his injury. Red Fur backed into the tall grass to avoid detection. He took another shot, this time hitting the leg. Not the leg he was aiming at, but that was fine with the Fuzzy.

The Big One again screamed in pain and aimed his gun in Red Fur's direction. The Fuzzy quickly ducked and moved deeper into the grass. The man fired his pistol several times, once nearly hitting Red Fur. When the Big One paused to reload his weapon, Red Fur stepped out and took another shot at the man. This time the arrow hit the man in the shoulder. Red Fur used some of the mean-nothing words Little Fuzzy had taught him as he ducked back into the grass.

The Fuzzy considered his alternatives. He was alone, yet the noise made by the Big One's weapon might attract other *Jin-f'ke* in the area. It could also attract something more dangerous. Large predators, looking for food, might come to investigate. Worst of all, the Big One might get into his aircar and fly away with the captives.

Red Fur could not wait for help. Carefully, he moved out of the tall grass with his bow at the ready, then lowered it in relief. The Big One lay on his side on the ground with his eyes closed. Red Fur moved forward carefully; Big Ones were clever and this one might be pretending to make-dead.

Red Fur circled around and approached the body from behind. When the Big One showed no signs of life, he quickly snatched up the pistol and jumped back. The only thing the Fuzzy knew about the weapon was which end to avoid, so rather than attempt to use it, he stuffed it in his backpack.

Even without a weapon and wounded, a Big One could be very dangerous. From behind the prone body he could see no signs of breathing. Even Big Ones had to breathe, and so much more air than one of the People.

Calls from the aircar reminded the Fuzzy of his people trapped in cages. Red Fur inspected the cages. They were made of the same hard shiny material as the chopper-diggers the Big One, Pappy Jack, had given to the *Jin-f'ke*. He would not be able to cut the branches...no, *bars*...to get them out.

"Need shiny twig to open," a Fuzzy with silver fur said. "Big One keep in not-fur covering."

"Go-dam sunnabish!" The last thing Red Fur wanted to do was go near the Big One again. He jumped down from the vehicle and held his chopper-digger at the ready as he approached the body. He tried to imagine where the shiny twig would be hidden in the not-fur. Red Fur recalled that the Big One called Joe Quigley had holds-things places near his hips. Cautiously, the Fuzzy checked the man's pockets. He found a ring with many shiny twigs and started for the aircar when something grabbed his leg.

Red Fur used his chopper-digger to slash the hand and forearm of the Big One. Just as he feared he might also be put in a cage, the man's grip relaxed. Red Fur turned to face the Big One and saw him release a long gurgling breath. The Fuzzy let out a long breath of his own in relief. It was the last gasp of the bad Big One.

After numerous fumbling attempts, Red Fur finally found the right key and released his people from the cages. The Fuzzies rushed out, almost knocking Red Fur down, seized their weapons and stabbed at the Big One's corpse. The Fuzzy leader just sat and watched and thought. Little Fuzzy had warned him that some Big Ones were bad, but most were good. The Big Ones with the big shiny things on their chests were supposed to be good, and would stop bad Big Ones from hurting Fuzzies.

Red Fur nodded to himself when he came to a decision; he would go to the Big One trading place where they traded the goofer skins for the *estee-fee* and chopper-diggers. There he would tell the Big One with the shiny chest thing about the bad Big One.

*   *   *

The taxi set down in front of the Federation Bureau of Central Intelligence building, little more than a two-story walk-up, and Trask appraised the edifice.

"Are you sure this is the correct address?"

"Yes, sir," the taxi pilot answered. "I don't know what you were expecting, but this is a colony world. You want everything to be all big and fancy, either go to the CZC building or pick another planet, like Terra or Odin."

Trask recalled he had been warned about the conditions of the local office. He paid the cabbie, then entered the building. He was relieved to see that it was at least being properly maintained. The walls were clean, the floor swept, mopped and waxed and the lobby furniture more or less new, though covered in animal hides he didn't recognize.

Behind a wood desk, which would be worth a small fortune on Terra, sat a woman in her mid-twenties tapping away on a keyboard. Trask cleared his throat to get her attention.

The woman looked up with a surprised expression. "Can I help you, sir?"

"I need to speak with the...agent in charge, please." Trask had to think a moment to decide the best approach. An office this size would not have anything higher than a sergeant in charge back on Terra, but colony worlds played by a different set of rules. It wouldn't do to antagonize anybody by assuming the ranking structure incorrectly.

"Lieutenant Williams," the woman hesitated then glanced at her chronometer, "would be out to lunch. He should return in about ten or fifteen minutes if you care to wait, Mr...?"

"Trask. Yes, I will wait. Do you have a vending machine? I could do with something to eat, but I don't want to miss Lieutenant Williams when he returns."

"I am afraid not, but there is a bodega across the breezeway that has a pretty good inventory. You might like to sample the local foods there."

Trask thanked her and went to the bodega. It was not lost on him that the woman spotted him as an off-worlder almost instantly. That was good. It meant that at least one person in the local chapter of the FBCI possessed decent observation skills and deductive reasoning.

The bodega selection surprised Trask only in that it also carried off-world type snacks. Corn crisps and onion rings lined shelves next to dried pool-ball fruit and veldbeest jerky. His research before coming to Zarathustra underlined that it was a largely self-sufficient world. Apparently, self-sufficient did not mean they didn't get off-world products, only that they didn't really need them. Trask mentally shrugged. Luxury items and junk food were still the two largest imports on any given planet. Sadly, it was their recent exports that had brought him to this world.

After eating a sandwich washed down with a beer, Trask returned to the FBCI office. Ordinarily he would have waited in the lobby. Being on a different planet he decided to take a less-anxious looking approach. For all Trask knew, the local branch of the FBCI could be a rat's nest of intrigue and/or corruption. He wanted to take it slow and easy until he could scope out the situation before getting down to cases.

The secretary, or whatever her actual position was, spotted him as soon as he walked in.

"Lieutenant Williams just came in, Mr. Trask. His office is down the hall at the end. I will tell him you are on your way."

"Thank you, Miss...?"

"Kealamauloa."

"That one might take me a while to get right," Trask said with a sheepish grin.

"C.K. will do."

"Thank you, C.K."

Trask turned and headed down the hallway to a glass door with Lt. Williams' name etched in it. The door opened before he could hit the buzzer button. Williams was already standing when Trask entered the office. He stood about six foot three, with dark hair, a thin well-groomed mustache and old-style eye glasses, suggesting his myopia was untreatable by conventional medicine.

"Mr. Trask, my apologies for keeping you waiting." Williams extended a hand and Trask reciprocated.

"Lieutenant Williams."

"You can call me Roger," he replied.

"Call me Buck." Trask took a plastic card out of his jacket. "These are my orders."

"Orders?" Williams took the card and inserted it in a slot on his computer console. The viewscreen came alive with documents, all with the FBCI header on them. Two words in particular jumped out at Williams. The first was Fuzzy.

"For real? How many have been discovered...oh, here it is—my god!" Williams scrolled down a bit when the next word of significance jumped out at him. "*Captain* Trask?"

Captain? Springbok must have slipped that promotion into the orders. He must have figured I would need the clout.

"So you're here to investigate the Fuzzy abductions and assume command of this precinct," Williams summarized. "They don't trust *us* to handle this back on Terra?"

Ah, Nifflheim! Now Williams is going to be hostile. "Nothing like that, Roger. We simply have more information to work with."

Williams' expression made it clear that he didn't buy that. "Well, I suppose you will need my office since you will be in charge."

Trask had taken in the Lieutenant's office when he entered. One desk with a computer console, a couple of chairs, the picture window and one potted plant, presumably an indigenous species, and nothing else. "That won't be necessary. Any room with a desk will do, though I hope you can scrounge one up with ample elbow room. I expect to need the space."

"We have a lot of empty offices, sir," Williams replied, stiffly. "This is a new precinct and we haven't gotten the staff up to size yet."

Trask nodded. He had heard that colony world precincts tended to be understaffed at first. Part of the problem was the lack of qualified applicants. The other was the dearth of personnel on Terra willing to make the move on a permanent basis.

"We will also have to get you some different clothes and a sidearm you can wear openly. Right now you look like a tourist. You need to blend in more."

That was a change from working on Terra. Back in Sydney he was expected to stand out a bit from the crowd unless he was working undercover. The idea was to intimidate people. On a colony world, as Williams explained, intimidated people tended to shoot at whatever made them nervous.

"I appreciate any help you can give me, Roger. And forget the 'sir' business. Buck will do here in the office. Out in the field I will go with whatever rules of formality, or lack thereof, you think appropriate. I am not here to shake things up or tell you how to run your precinct. I am going to need your knowledge of the planet and experience in the field here on Zarathustra. I expect you to tell me when I am stepping on the wrong toes and keep me moving in the right direction. And when we bust this case, and we will bust this case, the credit will be given to the entire precinct, not just glory-grabbing me."

Williams digested Trask's little speech for a moment. "Okay, Buck. I think we will be getting along on this. Frankly, things have been too damned quiet around here. The last big case, Gus Brannhard's abduction and the Fuzzy slavers on Beta and in Mortgageville, were handled by the locals before we could get properly involved. But this, off-world trafficking of sapient beings, lands squarely in our jurisdiction. Not even the Governor is going to be able to keep us out of it."

Trask caught that last bit and rolled it over in his mind. "Did the Governor keep you out of the loop?"

Williams snorted. "To be fair, I don't think he is even aware we exist. When he calls for help, he calls on Marshal Fane or Commodore Napier. I did a background check on him and he never skirted the law, as far as I can tell, and spent all of his time out in the field working in his chosen vocation before getting roped into the governorship."

"Maybe, or maybe he doesn't want anybody other than his friends, possibly co-conspirators, getting involved in things."

Williams thought about it and shook his head. "I very much doubt Governor Rainsford would be involved in anything like Fuzzy kidnapping. He enacted some of the most bloodthirsty laws I have ever seen to protect Fuzzies. He even adopted two of his own."

"Or," Trask countered, "he set up those laws to make himself appear beyond reproach. And executing Fuzzy poachers is a good way to get rid of anybody who might implicate him. If Brannhard is in on it, anybody who gets caught could scream their heads off and nobody would ever know it. I accept nobody at face value until I get them in the chair."

Williams whistled long and low. "Putting a planetary governor in the hot seat can be very unhealthy, Buck. I don't know Rainsford beyond what I read in the datastream, but any politician that powerful can be damned dangerous to fool with."

Trask nodded. "True. But I will ask him nicely and gauge his reaction when he refuses. Cops went by gut feeling before the veridicator was invented. We can do it now if we have to."

IV

Among the known sapient species in the Terran Federation, only three were known to construct edifices that could properly be classified as castles. Terra, even after The Wars, could still boast a significant number of castles and palaces.

Next came Thor, a world whose sapient lifeform bore dog-like faces and a feudal society not unlike Terra's European Middle Ages, and held a number of castles that could be favorably compared to anything in Old Germany.

Then there were the Freyans, beings so similar to Terro-humans that they could viably interbreed. The Freyans raised the art of castle building to heights even Terrans never imagined. Designed both for security and esthetics, Freyan castles were among the most beautiful and functional in the Federation.

Jack Holloway paced back and forth in the most recent castle of Terran/Freyan construction. Dogging his heels was Little Fuzzy, quickly side-stepping when Jack pivoted and retraced his path. With him were Betty Kanazawa, Victor Grego and Diamond, with Sunstone, the new addition to the family, Gus Brannhard and his two Fuzzies, Allan Quatermain and Natty Bumppo, Thor Folkvar and his Fuzzy, also named Thor, and Johann Torsseus.

"You'll wear a trench in the carpet like that," Betty noted.

"I'll get him a new one," Jack said absently.

"Don't bother," Thor Folkvar said. "That is a Chartered Odin Company military-grade fibroid weave carpet. It will survive anything short of direct laser fire. Morgan doesn't scrimp on the home furnishings and he likes his things built to last."

"And, no doubt, he is heavily invested in that company," Grego ventured.

"So am I," the fluffy-bearded Colonial Prosecutor added. "Now that I think of it, I haven't checked into my holdings on Odin since I left."

"Where did you—" Grego stopped himself. He recalled Gus's confession of "liberating" millions of sols from a crime cartel in his youth on Terra. It would be impolitic to bring that up in front of people not in on that secret, especially since the secret itself answered the question he was about to ask.

"Why are you so worried?" Betty stood up from her seat and blocked Jack's path.

Jack stopped just short of bowling the woman over and looked at Betty with a worried face. "Morgan's mother died in childbirth. Even though the Freyans cheerfully accepted a lot of advancements from the Federation, they maintained their primitive reproduction rituals: No help conceiving and no help birthing beyond a midwife. It was like pulling teeth from an angry damnthing just to get them to accept pre-natal vitamins."

He jerked his jaw at the wall separating the birthing chamber from the waiting room. "Akira is in there with a Freyan midwife and nothing else. A lot can go wrong and I would have liked a doctor and some very fancy medical equipment on hand just in case."

"I vould not vorry so much, Herr Hollovay," Johann said. "Mine dotter ist an experienced mit-vife und vill take gute care of die mutter und kinder."

Betty pursed her lips and nodded. "See, Jack? Akira is in good hands. Besides, natural childbirth is common on many colonial planets. Akira is strong. So is Morgan, for that matter. I have to believe that their baby will be just as strong."

Jack winced and looked away as thoughts of possible catastrophes danced in his mind. *Umbilical cord around the baby's neck, breech, placenta prevaria, gestational diabetes, or even any number of unknown pathologies....* The list of possibilities of what could go wrong raced through Jack's mind. And that didn't even take into consideration the fact that mixed marriages had their own problems.

Betty read Jack's face. "Wait…are you worried because Morgan is half Freyan?"

Jack grunted then nodded. "Terro-humans and Freyans are the closest thing, biologically, ever discovered on different planets. We can interbreed and generate viable offspring, like Morgan. But…but…infant and mother mortality is higher among mixed pregnancies than either of the races when they don't mix. Federation medical science still doesn't know why. Hell, had I known that when Morgan's mother was alive I would have avoided having children with her."

"What? Did you tell Morgan that?"

"Several times, except the part about not having children of my own, of course. Akira, too. They still insisted on doing it 'the old fashioned way.'" Jack patted the dagger on his belt. "That is why I have this stupid ceremonial dagger. When the baby is certain to survive, I am supposed to prick his left thumb with this dagger and declare him fit to bear the family name." He patted the dagger with the plastic medical seal around it for effect.

Betty was shocked and her face showed it. "What? That's barbaric! The risk of infection alone—"

"That I attended to," Jack interrupted. "I sterilized this blade and sheath with everything from rubbing alcohol to gamma radiation at the CZC Science Center. No grandson of mine is getting as much as a case of the sniffles on my account. I also laser sharpened the blade so he won't feel a thing."

"But why do it at all? Can't you put your foot down…?"

Jack rolled his eyes. "You think I didn't try? You don't really know my son. Morgan is a member of the ruling class back on Freya. While he is happy to make his home here on Zarathustra, he was still born and raised in that society and adheres to the archaic customs of his homeworld, which means every non-optional ritual has to be observed. And not even for his own benefit!

"What if his son chooses to go to Freya? Terro-humans have enough trouble fitting in there. It is twice as hard for a half-breed. Just ask Morgan about that. The child will have to prove himself twice the man to get half the respect. So Morgan observes every stupid little custom and ritual that Freyan society demands. And, in all fairness, I think he got my gene for stubbornness in the mix, if there is such a thing."

"Not all of die customs are so stupid, Herr Hollovay," Johann interjected. He was not offended since that same Freyan society had also grievously mistreated him and his people. "Infant mortality ist high, *ja*, und vas even more so on Magni for mein people. But only die strong survive vit'out your Federetion science, und so ve stay strong as a people. Morgan ist strong. His Frau ist strong, und der kinder vill be strong. Besides, I understand dat dere are Terrans dat believe in natural childbirth."

"I meant no insult, Johann. I am just worried. Please accept my apologies."

"*Macht nichts*, Herr Hollovay. I t'ink some of die customs are a bit foolish, too."

"The Amish, Christian Scientists, backwoods types that never joined modern society," Gus provided, pausing from his financial discussion with Grego. "They also have an appalling infant mortality rate."

"Have they picked a name, yet?" Victor Grego said. He was hoping to change the subject to something lighter. "Maybe something suitably Freyan?"

Jack, Thor and Johann all chuckled.

"You don't know about Freyan naming conventions, do you?" Thor asked.

"Well, no," Grego admitted. "Am I missing something?"

"The first-born son, if he survives the birth, is named after the father. Always," Jack explained. "How do you think Morgan got my name when his uncle hated me so much? The mother tells the midwife, if she doesn't already know, and the midwife assigns the name. Uncle Orphtheor had no choice but to use it when he took Morgan in. If the child is stillborn, or dies shortly after birth, he is given a different name to be buried with, and the next son, if there is one, is given the father's name. Freyan immortality, in a way. The rule about renaming the child if he doesn't survive is what allowed Orphtheor to fool me with the fake birth, and death, certificates."

"Wait," Gus said as he held up a hand. "Then why did Morgan have such a hard time finding you? He already knew your name."

"He assumed that I might have changed it after running out on his mother, as Orphtheor had him believe," Jack said. "Besides, do you have any idea how many John Holloways there are in the Federation? It is almost as bad as John Smith was back in First Century AE." Jack considered something then shrugged. "And I did use some other names a time or two...for unrelated reasons."

"Say no more," Gus warned. "As an officer of the court I might have to take action if you reveal a past crime."

Victor Grego smiled. He had, in fact, read up a bit on Freyan society, especially since Morgan arrived on Zarathustra. "So, you are Jack, excuse me, John Morgan Holloway the Greater, and Morgan is the Lesser. What will the baby be?"

"Chohn Morgan Hollovay der Minor," Johann supplied.

Grego then asked, "Jack, are you the Greater until you die?"

"Not at all. On Freya, where life spans are a little shorter, I would already be in my dotage and relieved of any responsibilities. Morgan would then take my place as the Greater, and his son would move up to fill the role of Lesser. I would become John Morgan Holloway...uh...Emeritus is the closest translation from *Sosti* I can think of."

"*Ja, das ist gut,*" Johann nodded. "Sometimes, der Lesser vill challange der Greater to take die position. Dat vas in die old times before ve joined der Federetion."

"Really?" Grego decided his plan was working and wanted to keep it going. "Then what about the second son?"

"They are typically named after a great hero, an uncle with no children of his own, or after the godfather, sort of, if he has no children," Jack replied. "Sometimes the father's middle name, if he has one, will be given to the second child as a first name. Of course, that applies to the males. The females have a lot more discretion with the names."

Gus stroked his chin. "Say, who is the godfather for Little John going to be?"

"Dat has to be a person of high renk und great importance as Herr

Morgan ist of high renk," Johann said. "Die highest villing to accept der responsibility."

Gus glanced at Grego who shook his head.

"Our esteemed Colonial Governor got tapped for that job," Jack said.

* * *

Little Fuzzy joined the rest of his family in the corner of the waiting room where they were discussing what the Big Ones were up to.

"Waiting for baby," Little Fuzzy explained.

"Know that," Koko said. "Why in big house place...?"

"Pappy Jack say Big Ones not have baby outside. Not squat in field when baby come," Little Fuzzy said.

Mama Fuzzy nodded in approval. "Field bad place to have baby. Too open. Ha'py or screamer see you. Eat you. Better behind trees."

Everybody agreed with that.

"But why Pappy Jack look sad?" Mike asked. "Big house place safe from ha'py an' screamers."

"Not understand ever thing," Little Fuzzy admitted. "Pappy Jack worried that Mo'gan an' Akira have problem. Not know what."

"Big One babies born wrong?" Mitzi asked. "They not know how to fix like with Fuzzee?"

Cinderella snorted, a gesture she learned from watching Big Ones on the viewscreen. "Big Ones are very wise, know how to fix ever thing. Don' they?"

"Nobody know how to fix ever thing," Koko argued. "Maybe Big Ones have diff'rent problems with babies. Something we are not wise enough to understand."

Everybody nodded. Allan Quatermain and Natty Bumppo came into the waiting room dragging two land-prawns each and everybody forgot about what might be worrying Pappy Jack, even if only for a little while.

V

Deputy Commissioner of Native Affairs Piet Dumont pursed his lips and leaned back in his office chair. The portable veridicators were on back order, mostly due to the fact that nobody believed they were necessary for use on Fuzzies. With very rare exceptions—unique, in fact—Fuzzies always told the truth. Piet's argument that they needed the veridicators for the human trespassers had thus far failed to produce any results.

"Did you find the body?"

"Did I! There was no way I couldn't find it," Officer Helmut said emphatically. "I half-expected to go out there and do a lot of looking for nothing. Not because I didn't believe the Fuzzy, Red Fur, but because I anticipated somebody trying to clean up the mess. Like in the old flatties where somebody sees a crime, then the evidence disappears? Not here, Chief. When I got there I saw half a dozen Fuzzies guarding the body and aircar."

Piet raised an eyebrow. "Only half a dozen?"

Helmut nodded. "At first. Once we landed and Red Fur yeeked, then dozens more popped out of the high grass and shrubbery all armed to the teeth. I never even caught a glimpse of them from the air."

Piet nodded. Fuzzies who had problems with Big Ones wouldn't take any chances. Red Fur had to be a Fuzzy military strategist of some kind. "Where is the body now?"

"Awaiting transport back to Alpha for identification and autopsy," Helmut said. "Cobra-lizard venom is what they'll find for cause of death."

Piet looked up from the report he was holding. "You sure?"

Helmut shrugged. "Red Fur and his gang dip their arrows in the venom sacks of the *net-zeetha* for the big or dangerous animals they come across. Fuzzies seem to be immune to the effects of the venom in their food. I wouldn't know about a direct injection via bite, though. Anyway, the body is in pretty bad shape regardless. Fuzzies have a vindictive side when provoked."

"Don't I know it?" Piet tapped a few keys and checked the viewscreen. "Damn. The next scheduled transport is tomorrow at noon. I'll have to check with Jack and see if we have anything else we can use. Regs won't let us take a privately owned vehicle for something like this or I would do it myself."

Helmut glanced around the office. "Where is the commissioner, Chief?"

"Still at the castle waiting for the next generation of Holloways to appear."

Helmut looked confused until he remembered that Morgan Holloway had erected a castle-like structure near the lower edge of Jack's land grant.

The sound of excited *yeeking* could be heard through the open window. A moment later Piet and Helmut could hear the whine of a contragravity engine. Piet, looking for any excuse to get out of his office chair and stretch his legs turned to his secretary. "Irene, I'm going out to see who that is."

"Yes, sir."

"Come along, Helmut. It might be some more off-world tourists looking to adopt a Fuzzy. I wish somebody could do something about that."

"Here we are, Bubbette," the cabbie announced.

Patricia stepped out of the taxi and was immediately swarmed by curious Fuzzies.

"Don't worry about the Fuzzies, Ma'am. They are a lot friendlier than most of the native life forms," the cabbie explained. "I don't know if you heard, but these guys are legally adjudged as sapient beings."

"Oh, I heard." Patricia bent down to ruffle a few heads. "I got a letter from my brother about this a couple years ago. That's one of the reasons

I wanted to come to this planet."

"One of the reasons? Is there another?"

"Yes. To see my—"

"Hold that cab!"

Both heads turned to the sound of the voice to see two men in uniform running towards them.

"Looks like you might have a return fare after all," Patricia observed.

The cabbie looked at the two men and recognized one. "Hey, that's Piet Dumont."

"Al? What are you doing here?" Piet asked. "I haven't seen you since I let you off with a warning on that parking infraction."

"Al? What is it short for?" Patricia asked.

"Alistair Forsythe Witherspoon, Bubbette. My father had delusions of high class." The cabbie turned back to Piet. "Just dropping off a fare, Chief."

"Ah." Piet glanced at Patricia, decided she wasn't a tourist, nodded politely, then turned back to the cabbie. "We'll come back to that. We have an emergency fare for you."

"Really? Who am I taking?"

Piet explained about the dead Fuzzy poacher.

"Humph. I'm betting he'll be a lousy tipper."

"Look, we would take him back if we could, but all we have right now are privately owned vehicles...."

"...and colonial law allows for public transportation to be used in an emergency. And my taxi falls under that category. Can I at least stow this deadbeat—"

Helmut stifled a laugh at the characterization.

"...in the boot? I wouldn't want anything to leak onto my upholstery."

"It's in a fibroid weave body bag with magna-stripped vacuum seal and refrigeration lining," Helmut explained. "No muss, no fuss."

"The boot is fine," Piet added. "Easier to load, anyway. I'll make you up a chit for the fare with the standard ten percent bump for the inconvenience. That includes a meal voucher since you won't have time to eat before heading back."

Meal voucher. Al rolled his eyes. Cops and military types always had to include dinner with the deal. "Where at?"

"The Bitter End. We get a special rate there since Morgan Holloway bought it."

"Whoa! That's good eats. You have a deal." Al mentally tallied the points he would get from his wife if he took her with him that night. The last time he took her did wonders for his after-dinner activities.

"And Helmut will have to escort the body to maintain the chain of custody," Piet added. "Adjust your rate accordingly."

Al waved it off. "Both fares are together, starting and ending. All covered in a single rate, Chief. Number of bodies, breathing or not, don't matter. And this way I have somebody to talk with on the three-hour trip back to Mallorysport."

Piet nodded, then turned to Patricia. "Ma'am, I am Deputy Commissioner of Native Affairs Piet Dumont. How may I be of assistance?"

"I'm Patricia McLeod, Deputy Dumont. I am looking for my kid brother."

"Call me Piet. Your brother works here on the Rez? Then I should know him. I know everybody around here. What is his name?"

"His name is John Holloway. But you might know him as Jack."

Piet's eyes went wide. "Great Ghu on a goat! We have to get you to the castle! Helmut, get going, I'll escort Mrs. McLeod."

Patricia was taken slightly aback. "I appreciate the help, but this is hardly an emergency, Chief."

"The Niflheim it isn't. Jack's grandson is on the way and I'll bet he would want you there for that."

* * *

"No report in two days."

"Ted's always missing his check-in, Doug. He is kind of like a dog that way. He sees a pluirrel and goes running off after it."

Douglas Rathbone shook his head and reached for another beer from the cooler. He looked out at the countryside from his lawn chair. Just over the rise was the Rez; *Terran verboten* territory. "Pluirrels are on

Epsilon continent, not Beta. Yeah, Ted misses the occasional check-in, but not two days in a row. And Nick is almost pathological about checking in unless he is out in the bush. Then he forgets about the rest of the universe."

The other man shrugged. "They probably split up to cover more territory and lost track of time. Worrying won't change anything."

"No, but being prepared helps, Andre. Maybe we should start packing up the campsite and be ready to go just in case." Despite his voiced plan, Doug remained seated and took another drink from his self-cooling can.

Andre watched as Doug downed his beer then reached for a third. It was one of the new brands based on a Freyan ale recipe brought in by some big shot off-worlder and a hell of a lot stronger than any beer should be.

"Doug, if something did happen to Ted or Nick, then our best bet is to sit tight and act like hunters on holiday. We have two damnthing hides tanning in the sun, all the gear and supplies any normal hunter would have, and no Fuzzies around to say different. If Ted were caught, he knows to keep his mouth shut under veridication. Nick, too. If they're dead, we don't need to run and will look more suspicious if we do. Now toss me a beer before you drink it all. If the Native Affairs' cops come by, I want a skinful, enough to look harmless."

"Here ya go. Go easy, though; you don't drink like I can, and this Freyan stuff has quite a kick."

Andre got halfway through his first can when he heard the klaxon of a Police vehicle overhead. Doug started to reach for his rifle and Andre stopped him. "This could just be a routine inspection. Don't forget how close we are to the Rez border."

The patrol car settled on the grass a short walk from the campsite and two men in Zarathustra Native Protection Force uniforms stepped out. One kept his eyes on the campsite while the other scanned the area. Satisfied there was nothing presenting an obvious danger, they approached Andre and Doug.

"Good day, officers," Andre said lightly. "Fancy a drink?"

"Thank you, but we're on duty," said the taller cop. "Names, please?"

"I'm Andre Sabahatu and this is my partner Douglas Rathbone."

"We doin' something we should'n' be?" Doug slurred.

So much for his higher resistance to alcohol, thought Andre.

"That depends," the shorter cop replied. "Where did you bag those two damnthings?"

The heads, which had a single horn on their foreheads and one on either side of their lower jaws, were still attached to the mottled black pelts.

Andre jerked a thumb behind him in the opposite direction of the Rez. "About five miles that a way. We were real surprised to find two so close together."

The taller cop nodded. "It's getting close to mating season. These two bulls you brought down would have ended up fighting over a cow out there somewhere."

"We were hoping for a harpy," Doug explained, seeming to sober up a bit. "Haven't seen a single one."

"No, and you aren't likely to, either," The tall cop said. "Harpies are almost extinct on Beta Continent, and now you need a permit to go after the ones on Gamma. Governor Rainsford doesn't want them wiped out, just controlled and kept away from the Fuzzies."

"Have you seen anyone else since you have been out here?" the short cop asked.

Andre made a show of thinking it over. "A couple other hunters a few days ago. There was that prospector before that. Maybe two or three aircars too high up to make out any details on. We just figured that those were you guys on rounds. Is there some sort of problem?"

Both cops nodded and the shorter said, "Fuzzy poacher bought it yesterday. His body is being shipped back to—"

The taller cop cut off his partner. "We don't need to bother these nice folks with that kind of information, Mark."

"Quite right. Well, you two have a good time and be careful what you aim at. Fuzzies don't know the Rez from Niflheim and wander on and off of it all the time. I would hate to see you in trouble for accidently shooting one."

"Hell, Officer, I would hate to kill a Fuzzy, too," Andre said.

"I bet they taste terrible," Doug joked.

Nobody laughed.

The ZNPF cops returned to their squad car and lifted off. Andre glared at Doug in disgust. "That was completely uncalled for."

Doug shrugged and reached for yet another beer. "A bad joke can't get you arrested."

"No, but it can get you remembered. Now we pack up. One of them is dead so there is no reason to wait for him. The survivor will have to find his own way back. We can't risk being here if he is spotted coming off the Rez."

Doug finished his beer and tossed it into the waste bin; litter laws were medieval on this planet. "What about lookin' suspicious?"

Andre collapsed his chair and stowed it in the boot of the aircar. "The cops were already here, saw the hides and explained we won't be getting any harpies on Beta. We will just go back to Alpha Continent and apply for a permit to go to Gamma and bag a couple."

Doug finished his beer. "Great Ghu! We have to go to Gamma now?"

"No. We just have to make it look like we want to. And stow the hides, too. We'll want to sell them back on Alpha."

Doug looked at the hides and wrinkled his nose. "Why bother? The damned things stink to Gehenna."

Andre sighed. "Because no hunter would go to all the trouble of bringing down and skinning a damnthing and not keep a trophy or sell it. I am going to make a walking stick out of the horn from the big one, anyway. They're coming back into style again."

* * *

"Something was off about those two guys, Jamal."

"I know what you mean, but outwardly there was nothing to pin on them." Jamal thought for a moment. "Did you notice their reaction when you mentioned the dead poacher?"

"Yeah. Their faces went all blank, like they didn't want to give anything away. I think it might be a good idea to run their names and see if we can find any connection to this Theodore Kalkadunga that Helmut found."

"You read my mind, Mark."

VI

"So you name the rest of the boys after, what, godfathers?" Victor Grego asked. He was running out of ways to divert attention from the activities in the next room and was starting to repeat himself. He remembered his daughter's birth by his first wife and the tension in the air even with all the medical machines and the team of doctors in attendance.

Before anybody could answer, there was a commotion out in the hallway. Thor Folkvar, who had been standing near the doorway, looked out to see an elderly white-haired woman with Chief Dumont threatening the Thoran guards. Amazingly, the usually stoic guards were set off-balance by the woman.

Thor Folkvar went into the hall and addressed the newcomers. "Chief Dumont, nice to see you again. And who is your rather formidable companion?"

"Patricia McLeod," Pat said looking up at Thor's face. "Which part of Jotunheim did you come from?"

It took Thor a moment to recognize that the statement was a mythical, not planetary reference. Thor smiled at the implication that he was a storm giant.

"Lady McLeod, I am Thor Folkvar of Magni and chief of security for John Morgan Holloway's estate. Since you are here with Chief Dumont I assume you have some important business."

"Yes I do. My brother is expecting his grandchild and I am here to wait with him. I just travelled here from Terra and will not miss this, giant or no in my way."

"Pat?" Jack poked his head out the door and the rest of him quickly followed. "Pat! What are you doing all the way out here?"

"After forty years I decided it was time to see you in person. You could visit Terra once in a while, you know. And now I find out you are about to be a grandfather?" Pat smacked the back of Jack's head. "You never even mentioned that you were a father!"

The Thoran guards looked at each other, then Thor Folkvar for guidance. Jack hugged Pat then pulled her into the waiting room.

"Everybody, this is Patricia Lorrain McLeod née Holloway, my second eldest sister." Everybody introduced themselves in return. Patricia looked about and asked where her nephew was. "In the birthing chamber with Akira, in direct contravention of Freyan custom. He is named after me, by the way, but goes by Morgan to keep confusion down."

"Oh, dear. Is this his first child?" Patricia asked.

"As far as I know," Jack replied.

"I think we should get a doctor in here," Patricia said. "For him."

The delivery room was not very different from those in use by countless hospitals across the Federation: clean white walls, bright lighting, a table designed for maximum comfort, under the circumstances, for the mother, and the smell of powerful disinfectants. What was missing were the various machines designed to monitor the mother's blood pressure, heart rate, respiration and the child's heart rate. Also missing were the various implements used in the event of a difficult birth. Only the midwife and a disturbingly large knife were present with the mother and father to be.

"Do not push, yet, Frau Hollovay."

"It feels like he wants to make a break for it, Ghu damn-it!" Akira screamed. "How much longer?"

"You are not yet, ahh, dilated enough. You are only at drei, ahh, t'ree centimeters. If you push now, you hurt yourself und das Kinder. Be patient. Kinder alvays know vhen to come out."

"Thank you, Heidi. Just try to relax and work on your breathing, Akira," Morgan said as he took a silk cloth and wiped her brow. "Just like we practiced in that class you made me take."

Akira yelled, "You can trade places with me if you think you can do it better!"

Morgan, in an effort to stay alive, fought desperately not to laugh at the highly improbable suggestion. Federation medical science was capable of many miraculous things, but still failed to allow men to give birth. Not that many men expressed an interest in going that far. Akira, his wife, had the honor and behaved as women throughout history have done since time immemorial.

"Och! She is't at fünf. It von't be long, now."

"You did this to me!" Akira screamed at her husband.

Still in survival mode, Morgan refrained from mentioning that Akira had initiated the act that brought them to their current predicament. Instead, he tried to guide his wife through the breathing exercises while wishing he was on Freya until the birthing was over. It was a mild breach of Freyan protocol that he was even in the birthing chamber at all.

After several long minutes Heidi announced, "Das Kind ist crowning. Do not push, yet! You vill tear yourself und hurt die beby."

Morgan tried to comfort Akira. "Try to relax, Akira. It won't be long now."

"DON'T TELL ME TO RELAX!"

Morgan felt the pressure on his hand increase to the point he feared permanent injury as Akira gripped him with greater strength.

"Here he comes," Heidi said. "Now, you must push." With hands the size of pie-plates, she gently cradled the new being coming into the world. "Der Kopf...ehh...head ist clear...no umbilical entanglement... here come die shoulders...*sehr gut!*"

The midwife held the child by the legs and vigorously rubbed his back. Almost instantly the newborn's screams filled the room. "Such vind! Ve have a healt'y vun, here. He vill make a fine son, Herr Hollovay. Vould you like to cut die cord?"

Morgan's face went ashen at the suggestion, yet he still accepted the knife and carefully severed the physical link between mother and child. After a few breaths Morgan beamed with pride.

"A son, Akira." Jack was about to say something when a mountain of muscle entered the room carrying a small bundle. Patricia was a bit surprised by the midwife's appearance though she had the good manners not to comment on it. Besides, she had already seen Johann and had been told about the mutated Freyans.

"Heidi! Is that…?" Jack asked.

"I haff die privilege of introducing Chohn Morgan Hollovay der Minor."

Heidi gently handed the squirming bundle over to Jack. Jack carefully accepted the bundle and was quickly corrected by Patricia on the proper way to hold a newborn. Babies were not something Jack fooled with as a rule.

Everybody crowded around as Jack took a seat and beamed at his grandson. He had missed all of this when Morgan was born.

Betty cooed at the infant. "He's adorable. He looks like you, Jack. Oh! Are you going to use that dagger now?"

"Dagger?" Patricia had noticed the knife in its sheath but thought nothing of it since this was a colony world and everybody was expected to walk around with all manner of weapons.

"Not yet." Jack turned to Patricia. "There will be a small ceremony when Akira is strong enough to attend. I just have to carry this silly dagger around until then. At least I managed to convince Morgan to have a doctor in attendance for that!"

"Wait, as the 'Greater' Holloway, couldn't you just declare it unnecessary?" Gus asked. "You are the boss, after all."

"Actually, the 'Greater' holds the responsibility of upholding tradition in Freyan society. Even still, I don't make a habit of going around telling people how to raise their children and what traditions to follow. And the pinprick Little John here will get from this dagger falls well below a ritual circumcision some Terran cultures still do."

"Good point. I attended a Bris once," Gus said looking a little sick. "You can stab my finger with a knife any day of the week rather than go through something like that."

Little Fuzzy jumped up and down for attention. Jack allowed the Fuzzy to climb up for a better look. "He very small, like Fuzzee."

Before anybody could stop him, Little Fuzzy placed his hands at the sides of the infant's head and gently touched foreheads with him. The others started to move to intercept, but Jack shook his head.

"Little Fuzzy just initiated Little John into the tribe," Jack explained.

*   *   *

Ray Trendell checked the trap and grimaced in annoyance. It was the last trap and all had come up empty. The Fuzzies were getting smarter. One of the traps had been smashed open. At first Ray thought a damnthing had trampled it. Now he considered the possibility that a Fuzzy got caught and was rescued by his tribe. It was said that you never had to teach a Fuzzy anything twice. Word would have passed from Fuzzy to Fuzzy and that meant the traps would be useless in this area from now on. Maybe every area. A new kind of trap would have to be considered.

Ray swore in Sheshan and kicked the cage. A nearby bird that was pecking at something reptilian squawked in annoyance and flew off. Ray considered shooting the bird out of sheer meanness and frustration, then calmed down.

Rifle fire could attract attention from inimical wildlife, like a bushgoblin or damnthing, or even more inimical humans. He didn't want to announce his presence to any Zarathustra Native Protection Force patrols that might be about.

Ray collected the collapsible trap and stuffed it into his backpack where he had put the others. The idea was to keep moving the traps around, whether they caught a Fuzzy or not, to reduce the possibility of discovery. He would meet up with his partner and relocate to a new area and redistribute the traps there.

Ray had just finished collecting the last trap when he heard a rustling in the brush. *Probably just a hobthrush*, he thought, but it never paid to take chances out in the wilderness. Ray unslung his gun and flicked the safety off.

He heard the rustling again and cautiously approached the source of the noise. Something scampered off before Ray could see what it was. A quick examination of the ground showed hoof prints. *Damnthing, alright. Half grown.* Ray released the breath he hadn't realized he had been holding. Even a young damnthing was something not to be trifled with. A damnthing was as dangerous an animal as you could hope to meet on Beta Continent. Like a cross between a bison and a rhinoceros with a very bad mindset. Thick hide, long jutting horn, and one Ghu-awful attitude.

When the horn suddenly sprouted from Raymond Trendell's chest, the last thought to go through his mind was: *and sometimes they circle around their prey to take them by surprise from behind.*

It would be days before his body, or what was left of it, and the cages he carried, would be discovered by the Zarathustra Native Protection Force.

VII

The Two Moons Café, by virtue of a centralized location in Mallorysport and judicious kickbacks to certain taxi pilots, typically did a brisk business among tourists and newcomers to Zarathustra. Among these newcomers were six men who varied in age, occupation and temperament. One of which was attempting to impress a young local woman.

"...and while Zarathustra is larger than Terra, it is less dense, on the whole, hence the gravity is slightly lower."

"But why is it less dense, Professor?" asked the attractive young woman. A red lock drifted down over an eye and she flipped it back with a toss of her head.

"Well, far less nickel in the core than Terra, for one, and lower quantities of heavy metals like titanium could be among the causes. However, the primary reason is the lower ocean to landmass ratio. You see, large bodies of water compress the crust...."

At the next table sat the other five men who watched as the professor attempted to make an impression on the young woman. They had all observed this particular phenomenon play out many times before and often with the result the professor desired. Strangely, he had surprising success in getting the young women he lectured to, to engage in a liaison with him. Even more surprising was that his ultimate goal, in this instance, was something else entirely.

"How do you think he's doing?"

The second man snorted. "He pretty much has her knickers off already."

"No, he means the other thing," said the third.

The fourth man shook his head. "Probably not smart enough. He should go after interns at the colleges, not cafés."

"He wants interns that think outside the box," the fifth man said. "You know how he is: 'Give me a fresh thinker, not a drone who can recite facts from a book.' In spirit, I agree. Sadly, that kind of mentality is a rare thing these days."

"Besides, this world has yet to construct a university," the third added. "I read somewhere that the governor is working out a deal with the Charterless Zarathustra Company to erect one."

The first one pressed a series of buttons on the console in the middle of the table to renew their drink order. The server, human—not robotic—appeared quickly and distributed the drinks.

"They do make an excellent cup of tea on this world," the third man stated.

"Terran-introduced crops do very well on Zarathustra," supplied the second.

"Another oddity of interest, on most planets special seeding and fertilizing are required to make Terran crops grow well in an alien soil. Zarathustra cheerfully accepts all comers without alteration." He sipped his coffee. "Damn, that is good."

"Ah, well. At least he has fun," the first man chuckled, returning to the original topic as if it never shifted. "Oh, look. He's bringing her to join us. That's new."

The men at the table all stood.

"Gentlemen, may I introduce the lovely Cinda Dawn, a post-graduate in geological studies. She has let me ramble on for the past fifteen minutes explaining to her that which she already knows so well. Miss Dawn, this is Enrico Garza, Johannes Chang, Melvin Kepler, Gregoire Rutherford, William Sokoloski and I, as you already know, am Dmitri Watson."

Cinda bobbed her red head. "Pleased to meet you. Are you all vacationing together?"

Gregoire Rutherford smiled. "If you believe that—"

"Be nice, Gregoire," Melvin interrupted. "Miss Dawn, we are all scientists. Like you, my field is geology, though I also hold a degree in archeology. My rude friend here is a quantum physicist, which might explain his lack of social grace. Dmitri is an astronomer and astro-physicist, though he also dabbles in geology, as you may have surmised. William is a mathematician and computer science professor. Johannes is a hyperspace engineer and Enrico a businessman of some considerable means as well as our backer."

While Melvin spoke, Enrico pulled a chair from a nearby table for Cinda and everybody took their seat.

"Hmm. Oh, I get it," Cinda said with a smile. "You are all here to figure out why Zarathustra isn't just a big chunk of ice."

"Exactly," Dmitri cried. "As you must be aware, for a planet this far from its primary to maintain the extant temperatures, it should orbit a G0, or at least a G1 star. Freya, for example, is approximately .61 AU from its K0 primary, and manages a world climate comparable to pre-atomic Terra. Zarathustra defies the very laws of physics by being so hospitable to Terran life forms."

"And we are here to find out why," Johannes concluded.

"I am afraid you are not the first," Cinda replied. "Every other year or so another group comes through like yourselves, digs around, takes readings, runs a few experiments, then they either get frustrated and give up, or their funding runs out. Usually it is the funding."

Enrico smiled. "It would seem that Miss Dawn is very much in the know. How would you like a job, Miss Dawn?"

Cinda did a double take. "What?"

"As a paid intern," Dmitri explained. "We need somebody to help us get set up on this world and you are far more intelligent than many I have interviewed."

Cinda brushed aside the flattery and concentrated on the job offer. "Wait, we were having an interview before you introduced me to your friends? Now you want to hire me to run errands and get your dry cleaning?"

"They still use dry cleaning on this planet?" Gregoire asked in surprise. "With chemicals and such?"

"It's an expression," Cinda clarified with an eye-roll. "We use directed sonics like every other civilized world."

"No, no, Miss Dawn, that was me thinking about asking you out," Dmitri admitted, returning to Cinda's question. "But I think you would be well suited to the work we are doing. And no, you will not just be running errands, although your knowledge of the local culture does make you the best choice for that as well. This is a chance to take part in a serious scientific investigation, and maybe even get your name on a paper. If you want to seriously pursue a career in geological studies, you need to get out in the field and publish your findings."

"Publish or perish," William added.

It was a lot for Cinda to take in. "I...I will have to think about it...I am trying to save up enough money to go for my masters' degree...."

"By all means think about it and meet us at...um...what is the best place in Mallorysport for dinner and dancing?"

Gregoire and William passed a knowing look at each other.

"That would be The Bitter End on the edge of Junktown," Cinda said. "It used to be owned by some mobster, but was seized by the colonial government and sold to some bigwig from off-world."

Dmitri smiled and said, "There, you see? Already you are of tremendous help to us. The Bitter End it is, at say 1900 tonight? For dinner. You can give us your answer then."

*   *   *

The tip of the knife entered the delicate flesh of the newborn's left thumb. Tiny drops of blood emerged from the small wound as the blade was extracted. The infant didn't make a sound as the ceremony continued. In the back the Fuzzies softly yeeked among themselves about the display.

Little Fuzzy was particularly concerned; although he assured the others there was nothing to worry about. Pappy Jack would never do anything to hurt a Fuzzy or a baby Big One. Maybe this was like the vaccinations the Big Ones gave to all the Fuzzies?

The audience chamber was filled near to bursting with attendees to the ceremony, human, Fuzzy and Freyan and even some other sapient beings from planets far and near. Victor Grego, Gerd and Ruth van Riebeek, Thor Folkvar, George Lunt, Ahmed and Sandra Khadra, Pancho Ybarra, Captain Zeudin, Gus Brannhard, Leslie Coombes, Juan Jimenez and even Dr. Hoenveld with his fiancée Darla Cross.

Johann Torseus acted as Master-at-Arms while his daughter, Heidi, stood near the raised platform where Jack held his grandson. In the background stood the crew of Morgan's private yacht, including Kronkeenk, the Ulleran and the Thoran security team, the Lokian, and the Gimlian. Even a number of the mutated Freyans were mixed into the crowd. With the other aliens in the room, they barely drew a glance from the humans. Patricia, as an honored family member, stood by Akira's side on the small stage Morgan had set up for the ceremony.

"I now declare this child," Jack intoned, "John Morgan Holloway the Minor, a fit heir and future master of the House of Holloway, to defend the lands and fortunes of this family and its retainers, and one day further procure the future of the family through his sons to come."

Jack sheathed the dagger and collected the child with his hands. Carefully holding the infant up, he said, "I present my grandson, John Morgan Holloway, for all to see!"

The crowd, uncertain how to respond, waited for the Freyans in attendance to take the lead. Johann raised his massive arms into the air and started clapping. Following his lead, the rest joined in.

The Fuzzies, even though they didn't understand everything that was happening, enthusiastically followed the Big Ones' example, throwing in some *yeeks* for good measure.

Morgan stepped up and accepted Little John from Jack and returned the child to Akira. While Freyan culture required a show of strength in many ways, it at least allowed the new mother a seat during the proceedings. Akira accepted Little John and held him while Lynne Andrews attended to the infant's finger.

Morgan turned to the crowd of people and held up his hand. The crowd quieted down allowing him to be heard.

"This concludes the ceremony. We have a buffet set up in the main hall. I do hope everybody will enjoy the Freyan and local delicacies my staff has prepared for you all."

After a brief though enthusiastic applause, the people in the audience lined up to convey their good wishes before filtering out of the ceremonial chamber. After most of the humans came the Freyans, then the various other aliens. The militant Thorans pledged their allegiance to the new Holloway, swearing to defeat all enemies of the Holloway clan while the pacifistic Lokian simply nodded to the child. The Gimlian bowed so low his nose, or what passed for a nose, touched the floor. Kronkeenk pounded his chest so hard in salutation that Akira winced. Last to leave were Gerd and Ruth, with their new baby girl, and Lolita Lurkin.

"Very nice ceremony, Morgan," Gerd said as he clasped forearms Freyan style. "What kind of ceremony do they have for the girls?"

Morgan laughed. "I have no idea. The women do something that the men are not allowed to be privy to. Heidi will have to guide Akira through it should we produce female offspring."

"So, you do plan on having more children?" Ruth asked.

"Oh, yes. It is always desirable to have what the European nobility refer to as 'the heir and a spare.' If something should happen to the eldest, the next son assumes the position and property of the elder."

"Excuse me," Akira said. "I think I have something to say about that." She laughed at Morgan's stricken expression. "Relax, Freya Boy. I am all for a big family. Within reason. Just not right away."

"Good thing, too," Patricia said. "Big families run rampant through the Holloway clan."

"Don't scare her, Pat," Jack said, with a smile. "Excuse me while I speak with Piet."

Gerd's brow furrowed. "Doesn't that increase the risk of intrigue within the family?"

Morgan nodded. "It can, but while the bulk of the family money and property falls to the eldest son, the other brothers receive generous allowances and property of their own to administer. As Gus Brannhard would say, most of the benefits without as many headaches. Should one be involved in a plot against the Elder, and is caught, he forfeits his lands, all claims to any titles and is banished from the kingdom. These days it means being sent off-world never to return."

"Hmm. That doesn't seem really bad to me," Gerd said. "I haven't been back to Terra in years, and don't miss it a bit."

"You were never on Freya," Ruth countered. "A planet very much like pre-atomic Terra filled with beautiful people, especially by our standards. And, no offense, Morgan, but in many ways Freyans are still somewhat backwards technologically compared to Terrans."

Morgan smiled. "No offense taken. I have said the same thing many times myself, which is why I fought to be schooled on Mars instead of Freya."

"Thank you, Morgan," Ruth said. "Gerd, imagine being pushed out into a galaxy where you lack the social and technical skills to fit in. I think that is very close to a definition of Hell."

Gerd mulled it over and decided Ruth had a point. She was the psychology expert, after all. "Well, by all accounts, you are an only child, Morgan, so there is nothing for you to worry about, after all."

"Well, that is true as far as Freya is concerned, but my father was out in the galaxy for many years and I think we can all agree that he was hardly a monk."

Gerd was taken aback by this. "You think Jack might...?"

"Have other children he is not aware of?" Morgan returned. "It is a possibility. That is why I have agents out there looking into it."

"What!" Ruth's outburst disturbed the baby. "Oh, Shari, mama's sorry...it's okay."

Jack found Piet patiently waiting near the buffet table. "Is something wrong?"

Piet swallowed the Freyan pasty in his mouth, downing a beverage that tasted like a cross between an orange and a lemon. "Dead Fuzzy poacher from up north, Jack. The Fuzzies took care of him real good, so I sent the body back to Alpha for an autopsy and a background check. I also stepped up the patrols in that area. I doubt this mutt was working alone. The aircar was full of cages, empty now, and we seized it as assets in the commission of a crime."

Jack nodded. "Don't try to put it into service until forensics has gone over it and Judge Janiver gives the okay." Jack knew Piet Dumont understood way more about police procedure than he did and was more than qualified to handle the investigation. "More Fuzzy slavers. I thought we took care of that mess already. Do you think all that traffic in orbit up there is connected to this?"

Piet took a second to recall all the ships in orbit loaded with tourists, all wanting to adopt a Fuzzy. "By Ghu's gonads, I hadn't thought about that. If so, then Fuzzies might be getting dragged off-world, though I can't imagine how they would get past spaceport security—"

"With a shuttle from a hidden spaceport," Jack said. "There is a lot of empty land out there and it wouldn't be hard to hide a small setup."

Piet agreed. "I'll send a message to Commodore Napier through Pancho Ybarra. He'll want to perform some 'safety' inspections on that imbroglio up there."

Jack nodded. "Okay, Piet. It's all yours. I'll be back on the Rez tomorrow. Don't worry, I won't get in your way, but I do want to be kept in the loop. I may take a trip up there and have a talk with Red Fur and see what he knows."

Piet smirked. "He knows plenty. Red Fur's the one who killed the poacher."

Jack wasn't too surprised by that. Last year he had been taken hostage by Red Fur's tribe and had a chance to see how well organized the northern Fuzzies were. He also noticed that the Fuzzies up north dipped their arrows in cobra-lizard venom. It would still take a lot of hits from something as small as a Fuzzy arrow to take down something as big as a man, but would get the job done sooner or later.

"Jack, I would like to go along, if that is all right?" Patricia asked.

Piet was dubious. "Ma'am, I am not sure if it would be safe for a greenhorn up there, no offense intended."

Patricia smiled and said, "None taken."

"You don't have to worry about Pat," Jack said. "If there is a better shot with a pistol on Beta Continent, I haven't met him. I'll give her the five centi-sol tour of the training grounds first so she will have an idea what Fuzzies are capable of."

VIII

Chief Colonial Judge Frederic Pendarvis slammed down the gavel to stop the two attorneys from bickering. In his private chambers the report of the gavel was like a gunshot. Hugo Ingermann's lawyer, Clarence Anetrou, had managed to learn that Gus Brannhard would be over on Beta for a few days and had seized the opportunity to try for bail. It was a long shot, but he had to pull the trigger anyway.

Ned Foster, one of Gus's assistant district attorneys was fighting tooth and nail to keep Ingermann in lockdown. He planned on trying to stay civil in front of the judge while Anetrou did his best to antagonize him.

"Your Honor," Anetrou said, with a little bow. "My client has been in lockup for seven months without a trial. I request bail on a humanitarian basis. He is currently, in effect, serving time for crimes he has not been convicted of."

"Yet," Foster cut in. "Your client has stayed in lockdown because you have blocked every attempt to proceed with his trial. As for bail," Foster snorted, "three years ago, while in the process of stealing a quarter-million sols worth of sunstones, Ingermann amply demonstrated his willingness to flee this court's jurisdiction."

"My client did not steal any sunstones," Anetrou objected, "and there are no convictions on his record to say otherwise."

"My pardon, accepted stolen goods, and that is one of the charges being levied against him." Foster turned back to Judge Pendarvis. "Your honor, the man is a flight risk, plain and simple. The People of Zarathustra lost him once and only his own foolishness and avarice brought him back to us. Moreover, he further tried to avoid prosecution for past crimes by undergoing significant cosmetic procedures. Had we not managed to obtain his body scan while in the hospital, he would still be at large."

"I am challenging the procuring of that body scan and all other files related to his treatment, Your Honor," Anetrou countered. "There was no warrant issued allowing the police to acquire my client's medical files, especially while he was still under care. I intend to bring suit against the hospital, the police and the colonial government for this. I will also file papers to have those files barred from being used as evidence as they were illegally obtained and, hence, cannot be used in court against my client."

"Your Honor, I would cheerfully retract all charges against Hugo Ingermann provided the case we have against Ivan Dane remains in place." Foster smiled at Ane'trou. "We only have to execute him once, after all."

Judge Pendarvis quietly listened to both sides though he kept his gavel at the ready in case they got out of hand again. He had heard enough.

"Mr. Anetrou, your main contention is bail and your client's professed identity. Mr. Foster, was any DNA recovered at the scene of the crime?"

Foster retrieved his datapad from his briefcase and started scrolling through the files. "Yes, Your Honor. Blood evidence was recovered at the scene, processed and recorded. Standard procedure requires scans for blood-borne pathogens and DNA."

"Two men were shot that day. How can you be sure you processed the correct blood?" countered Anetrou.

"That is a fair point, Counselor," Judge Pendarvis said to Foster. "I am issuing a warrant to procure a blood sample from one Ivan Dane, currently held in Prison House awaiting trial. If the sample proves to be different from that acquired at the scene," he turned to face Anetrou, "I will entertain your motion for bail. However, if the samples match, then your client stays in lockdown and the previous charges against Hugo Ingermann will also be applied."

Pendarvis slammed down the gavel. "That will be all, gentlemen. We are adjourned."

* * *

Colonial Governor Bennett Rainsford leaned back in his chair, puffing his cigar. He was a gnomish little man, with a bald head and a scraggly red beard with streaks of gray running through it. His blue eyes were anything but comical, and were as focused as a laser beam. Few people who saw him in action underestimated him twice.

Outside, playing on the lawn, were his Fuzzies, Flora and Fauna. He had been plowing through the massive piles of paperwork on his computer and needed a break. He was still dealing with the aftermath of the illegal sunstone prospectors and the so-called Fuzzy rocket ship.

The ancient spacecraft had been taken off-world to an undisclosed location, most likely Xerxes, by the Terran Federation Space Navy and stamped classified. Ben had no idea where Commodore Napier scrounged up an interplanetary military transport so quickly. There must have been one on Xerxes kept under wraps, which made sense; one couldn't fight a ground war if all the troops were stuck on a moon. The rocket would stay hidden until the TFSN could send an interstellar military transport ship big enough to haul it away to an even more secret location.

Unfortunately, for Ben and Victor Grego, the local news services and crackpots were convinced the colonial government still had it hidden in a Charterless Zarathustra Company warehouse, somewhere, and even guided tours though the CZC storage facilities failed to convince them otherwise. Even with the former radio station B.I.N., now H.I.N.— bought out by Morgan Holloway, personally, and not as a subsidiary of the CZC—and no longer whipping up the public with stories of a government conspiracy—the rumors abounded.

Then there was the Hugo Ingermann situation. Even as the most hated man on Zarathustra, and even while in jail, he managed to stir up trouble. So far there had been three suspended court dates and a parade of lawyers filing writs of habeas corpus and demands for bail to be set.

Ben wasn't having it and neither was Gus Brannhard. Gus, or rather his ADA Ned Foster, argued before Judge Pendarvis that Ingermann was a serious flight risk and the judge agreed. Now that they had Ingermann, they were not going to let him get away. Still, Gus's people were being worn to a frazzle keeping up with all of the paperwork. Fortunately, Victor Grego allowed Leslie Coombes and his staff to help out, though it resulted in even more paperwork attacking the legality of a private corporation working hand-in-hand with the colonial government.

Ben was so busy trying to stay on top of things that he had to miss Jack's grandson being christened...or whatever the Freyan equivalent was. The governor didn't even have time to look up the ritual on the datastream to see what was involved in the ceremony.

The intercom bleeped and the voice of his assistant, Francine M'Bata, stated that Marshal Max Fane wanted to speak with him.

"Send him in, Francine."

Max Fane lumbered into Ben's office, closing the door behind him. Ben looked over from his viewscreen and took in the massive marshal, noting that his uniform, while picture perfect, was not as snug as it used to be. The last year had been hard on him as well. Max spent a lot of time testifying in court against Ingermann in addition to his regular duties.

Among those duties was chasing down any ersatz sunstones that might still be floating around. A few still popped up here and there from time to time. Sunstones were the financial foundation for the Zarathustran government and even rumors of faux stones could damage the value of the genuine article. As such, anything that threatened the value of sunstones also threatened the colonial government that survived on the interest from the sale of sunstones. It was no wonder Max Fane had started losing weight with that kind of responsibility weighing him down.

"Hello, Max. What can I do for you?"

"We found another one," Max said without preamble.

Confusion clouded Ben's face. "Another one, what?"

Max sighed and took a seat in front of the governor's desk. "We found a dead man in Northern Beta. He was poaching Fuzzies."

Ben was stunned. "How? We shot all of the members of the Fuzzy slavery ring months ago. You questioned them under veridication. Is this the start of a new ring or members of the original we didn't know about?"

"My guess? More of the original Fuzzy faginy ring. There was one man we didn't get to question."

Ben knew whom Max meant. The slaver Morgan Holloway killed when he and Jack stumbled upon the Beta operation.

"I believe this ring is operating in cells, with only the top man of each cell aware of the others." Max shrugged. "I could be wrong and a whole new crew of vermin has entered the picture, but after that public display we had for the executions for the last bunch, I have a hard time imagining anybody new taking such a risk. My gut says this is the same group as before, just a different cell, or cells, since we didn't know how many more were involved in the operation. We might know more when the body gets here from Beta. It is coming in by air taxi with ZNPF Officer Helmut."

"Oh, Niflheim," Ben muttered. "Max, technically, this is a Zarathustra Native Protection Force case since the body was found on the Reservation, but I would like for you to stay in the loop. Last time they transported Fuzzies to Mortgageville. If it happens again, that is your jurisdiction."

Max refrained from rolling his eyes. He had been doing his job since long before Ben Rainsford became the colonial governor. He knew good and damned well what his jurisdiction was, but it would be impolitic to point that out to his boss.

"I'll get right on it, Governor. Piet Dumont will likely take the lead on the investigation at the Rez. He is a good cop and will be a great help to Jack Holloway."

Max thought it over for a second, then added, "I'll send a couple of my own men over to liaise with Piet. Chief Carr will handle that."

"Good. By the way, do you know which of his men took down the Fuzzy poacher?"

Max fought to keep the smile off his face. "That would be Chief Red Fur of the *Jin-f'ke*."

Ben stood up then sat down. "A Fuzzy! How?"

"Poisoned arrows and a lot of determination is Piet's guess. I already clued-up the coroner to run a toxicology screen on the body when it gets in. This should be in about an hour or so." An evil grin crept across Max's face. "Governor, should I arrest Red Fur for murder?"

Ben laughed. "Federation colonial policy is pretty specific about reservation law. The native inhabitants can make and adjudicate their own laws within the confines of the reservation. Red Fur is the closest thing to a national leader the northern Fuzzies have, so his word is pretty much law as far as the Federation is concerned. There, I said it and now the Fuzzies are covered if the poacher's family tries to make trouble. Besides, even if this happened off the Rez, Fuzzies have as much right to defend themselves as anybody else. And no action can be brought against anybody acting to prevent a crime. Red Fur is certainly well within his rights to stop Fuzzies from being abducted."

The intercom on Ben's desk beeped.

"Yes, Francine?"

"Governor, there is a Mr. Trask out here who says he needs to speak with you and Marshal Fane on an important matter."

"What now?" Ben asked out loud. He considered having the newcomer sent away with instructions to make an appointment, then changed his mind. The man wanted to see Max, too, and that might mean something else bad was in the air.

"Max, think we should see him?"

"I guess. It takes some kind of stones to barge in here like this. I wouldn't mind meeting the man who owns them."

Ben stifled a laugh and told Francine to send the man in.

Mr. Trask entered with a solemn expression and a rumpled suit. The style of the suit said 'cop,' while the creases suggested it had been pulled straight from a suitcase without the benefit of ironing.

"Governor, Marshal, my credentials." Trask held out a leather wallet that displayed a badge and an identification card that declared him to be Starbuck Trask of the Federation Bureau of Criminal Investigation.

"I apologize for barging in, but I do have an urgent matter to discuss with both of you."

"Have a seat, Mr. Trask." Ben gestured to the other chair next to Max.

Trask took the seat. "Feel free to call me Buck."

Max smiled. "Was your father a Herman Melville enthusiast?"

Trask looked to the sky with an exasperated expression. "You have no idea. I missed being named Queeg-Queeg by a nanometer."

Ben and Marshal Fane laughed.

When he'd recovered his composure, Ben said, "I have heard stranger names, Buck. One of my friends has a niece on Terra named Kandi Barr. Now, what is this urgent issue you needed to speak with us about?"

Trask cleared his throat before speaking. "About eight months ago on Terra, the FBCI busted an underground casino in South Africa. It had all of the usual trimmings: prostitution, gambling and illicit drugs. It also had something I had never seen before. Trained animals doing tricks on stage."

Ben and Max glanced at each other.

"And?" Ben prompted.

"The animals were from off-world and highly intelligent."

Ben felt a chill run through him. "Not animals. Fuzzies?"

Trask nodded. "Yes. It took the branch office a few days to realize that these were the new sapient beings that were discovered, what, three years ago? Once we put it together we slapped everybody within a mile of the casino into a veridicator and questioned them extensively." Trask let out a long breath. "There is at least one, possibly two, Fuzzy slavery rings. One in South Africa for sure. We don't know who yet, as they are very cagey and operate in cells. Nobody knows anybody outside of their cell, so we didn't get very far. When our investigation hit a dead end, I was sent to the source of the Fuzzy pipeline to see what I could dig up."

"And that brought you to us," Max said. "I think we have a body you will be interested in."

Trask turned to Max with a raised eyebrow. "Body! Human?"

"Human. Death by Fuzzy. I don't know what you may have heard back on Terra, but Fuzzies do not take well to being grabbed up and stuffed into cages," Max explained. "How many Fuzzies did you liberate?"

"Twenty-three adults, no juveniles or infants. We did find some documentation that suggested a breeding program was in operation, but with poor results. It would seem that Fuzzy reproduction is hampered by something on Terra."

"Under the circumstances, that is a plus," Ben said. He scribbled a note to look into the effects of hyperspace travel and Terran conditions on Fuzzy reproductive health.

"Do you have any idea how the Fuzzies were smuggled to Terra? The CZC controls all legitimate space travel on Zarathustra, and as far as I know there are no other space ports, legal or otherwise."

"Actually, a smaller hyperspace vehicle, say a yacht, could do a soft landing out in the wilderness," Max ventured. "The question then becomes, how did they slip through the signals and detection grid that covers the planet? That is managed by the Terran Federation Space Navy."

"Buck, you will have our full cooperation and assistance in this matter." Ben wanted to slam a fist on his desk for effect. He refrained as it might make him look silly in front of the Terran. "What happened to the Fuzzies and the people who enslaved them?"

"They are all, Fuzzies and slavers alike, being sent here by military transport and should arrive in a week or so," Trask explained. "The Fuzzies for further questioning and repatriation, the slavers for trial. It is the Federation's position that they broke your laws first and should be dealt with here. We do reserve the right to handle any others we catch off-world, though. We want to make a firm statement about what happens to slavers."

Ben grimaced. "I could not agree more."

"Glad to hear it," Trask said. "Now comes the awkward part."

"Awkward part?" Ben and Max said together.

"Yes, sir. I realize this is an imposition, but I would like to question your and the Marshal here under veridication. To rule you both out, of course."

Max smiled ruefully. "Of course."

"Why me? Or Marshal Fane?"

"After the trouble we had on Loki years ago, then Odin not so long ago, we like to cover all the bases," Trask explained. "In your positions, you could both get away with murder if you chose to. I want my people sighted on the correct objective and not have any suppositions about you two clouding their minds."

Ben thought it over for a moment, then agreed. "As long as you keep on point and my attorney general is on hand. Is that fine with you, Marshal?"

"Sure. Something like this, you can expect my full cooperation."

Trask was surprised and tried not to show it. "Very good, gentlemen. Would you prefer I bring one here or would you care to come out to the FBCI precinct? I do not want to cut too much into your schedule."

"We have one downstairs," Max said, "in the Marshal's quarters. You can have one of your people test it to be sure it hasn't been tampered with."

These people are just a little too cooperative, Trask thought. He began to wonder if they would simply arrange for an accident if he got too close to something. "That would be fine, Marshal, if only to dot the i's and cross the t's. Procedure, you know."

"Oy, don't I know it," Max said. "I served four years with the FBCI back on Terra before the Gypsy in me got the better of me."

Ben did a double take. "You were in the FBCI?"

"Yup. And the Odin Guard, the Baldur Secret Police and the Yggdrasil Police Force. I landed on Zarathustra fifteen years ago; joined the Marshal's Office as a captain and worked my way up. Colony life isn't for everybody, but promotions come fast as a lot of people decide they want to get back to civilization."

Trask made a mental note to do a background check on Marshal Fane when he got back to the FBCI precinct and see if there was anything off. "Well, shall I return at 1400 with my technician? The sooner we get this out of the way the sooner we can get to the bottom of things." Plus, that would keep them from having second thoughts.

Ben checked his schedule and told Francine to reschedule his 13:30 appointment to 15:00. "That should take care of it. See you at 14:00, Buck."

IX

After most of the invited guests had made their farewells, Morgan escorted the rest to his dayroom. Unlike most of the castle, this room was designed along Terran esthetic lines. It had an automated bar as well as the Lokian attendant, memory foam couches covered in damnthing leather hides, voice-activated lighting, a viewscreen that took up a three yard section of wall and several small tables that could retract into the wall or floor.

Morgan once explained that business contacts were more impressed by the high tech than the Freyan furnishings since he hailed from a mostly backward world, by Terran standards.

Akira sat in an overstuffed chair nursing Little John while the rest took seats a discreet distance away. Everybody made small talk until Akira finished and gave Little John to Heidi. Heidi took the infant to the nursery, allowing Akira to join the party.

"So, what are we talking about?"

Patricia patted the empty spot on the couch next to her. "I was just getting ready to fill in your husband about the family. You married into a rather large one, you should know."

Akira accepted a non-alcoholic drink from the manservant, if that was the proper term for the Lokian butler. "Thank you, Nerroohilan. How big a family? Mine was pretty big, too."

"Well, the eldest would be Virginia, then me, then James, Jack, Leila, Linda, Brenda, Dean, Paula and Diana. When I dig the photo album out of my luggage I can show you all of the cousins and their children." Patricia accepted another sweet tea before continuing. "The family has spread out quite a bit since Jack left about forty years ago. Jim is retired on Odin, Virginia moved to Thor, Paula and Diana went to Baldur and

Brenda is on Loki. Dean has been running the family business back on Terra since he left the Army."

"What kind of business?" Victor Grego asked.

"Planetary imports and exports. I am technically a silent partner in the business, as are most of us. I worked as an archivist in Australia for the last twenty years."

Gus started to reach for a cigar, then remembered that Morgan was a non-smoker and Freyan custom was to keep tobacco away from new mothers for fear it would damage them in some way. "Patricia—"

"Oh, call me Pat, Gus."

"Pat, Jack has been very tight-lipped about his life on Terra before running off to space. Do you have any juicy embarrassing stories?"

Patricia laughed. "A few, but Jack managed to avoid any serious embarrassment in his otherwise misspent youth. Being the shortest of the boys, he learned to be a real scrapper in short order and never took any guff from anybody."

"Jack is the shortest?" Betty couldn't believe it. At six foot two inches Jack wasn't a giant by any means, but he was still above average. Then she looked at Patricia again and estimated her height at six foot. If the women in Jack's family were that tall....

"Oh, yes. James was the tallest at...lets see...six foot six I think, followed by Dean at six-three. Except for Kandi, all of Jim's children are all over six foot. My boys run large, too, as does my daughter."

Jack chuckled, "If my wife wants an embarrassing story, tell her about the time Jim called you 'Patsy.'"

Patricia related how she hated that name and when James made a point of calling her that, she hit him so hard he flew over the couch.

"And now you know who taught me how to fight," Jack finished. "Pat also taught me how to shoot. Well, pistols, anyway. I learned how to handle a rifle from Pa."

Patricia laughed. "He was always practicing his quick draw as a child. He would watch old Westerns and try to copy them when they had a shootout scene."

"All that practice paid off," Ruth said. "I saw him beat up Leonard

Kellogg one second, then spin around and put three in Kurt Borch's chest in the blink of an eye."

"Don't forget that Kurt drew first and would have shot Jack in the back," Gerd added.

"Jack, you left that part out of your letters," Patricia chided him. "When did that happen?"

"That was before the Fuzzy Trial. I wrote to you about that. I guess I just neglected to mention what started the whole mess." Patricia wondered aloud what other fights Jack neglected to mention.

"Pat, if I wrote about every little scrape I had ever been in, I wouldn't have time to get into those scrapes!"

Everyone laughed.

"Well at least tell me about the last one you were in."

Both Jack and Morgan looked a bit embarrassed. Akira explained about the duel they had. "We can replay the duel on the viewscreen if you like. It was a real media event for a while."

"Little Fuzzy tried to kill me in the hospital," Morgan added.

Away from the Big Ones, Little Fuzzy turned away from the construction set he and the other Fuzzies were working on, decided he wasn't being called, and returned to assisting Baby Fuzzy in installing a support piece.

Patricia glanced at the small sapient beings, then looked quizzically at Morgan.

"Fuzzies are not the least bit vicious," Jack explained, "but fight like rabid Thorans when they or their families are threatened."

"They more often than not try to run from danger as it is usually too big for them, but when cornered, watch out!" Gerd added. "Little Fuzzy attacking Morgan was unusual as Morgan was not threatening anybody at the time, but he had shot Pappy Jack and, as we have learned, Fuzzies can be vindictive when provoked."

"No wastebasket is safe when a Fuzzy's ire is raised," Juan Jimenez laughed. That brought on a new round of explanations about when Jack's Fuzzies had been brought to the CZC before the trial.

They talked for a while, bringing Patricia up-to-date on things Jack had neglected to put into his letters.

"Oh, it is getting late and I need to find a hotel here on Beta."

"Hotel? As the sister of my father you are entitled to all the hospitality I can provide, Aunt Patricia. Nerroohilan, have the staff make up a guest room."

"Don't argue, Pat," Jack cautioned. "It's a Freyan thing."

Outside of the castle, Little Fuzzy and the rest of the clan played with a plastic throwing disk. Baby Fuzzy was particularly good at catching the high throws. As they played, they discussed the newcomer.

"What is sister?" Koko asked.

"Is family for Pappy Jack," Mike said as he caught and flung the disk.

"Are we Pappy Jack's sisters?" Mitzi asked as she caught and threw the disk.

"Pappy Jack says we like his kids," Little Fuzzy ventured. The disk flew over his head and went to Mama Fuzzy.

"Kid is baby zaragoat," Baby Fuzzy said. "Pappy Jack thinks we are zaragoats?"

"No," Mama said as she threw the disk to Cinderella. "Is not-so thing Big Ones say. Pappy Jack says we like his babies." Mama grew thoughtful. "To Big Ones we are like babies because we are not big. Baby for Mo'gan an' Akira near as big as us."

"Not babies," Little Fuzzy argued. "Not teach Big One babies how to make fire until big. Not let have gun. Fuzzee taught to make fire, use gun, go hunt. Big One's babies not learn until big-big. Fuzzee not baby."

"Or zaragoat," Koko added. "But what is sister?"

X

"Before you start your internship, I think we should bring you up-to-date on what we already know," Dimitri Watson said.

Cinda Dawn nodded and stayed fixed on Dmitri in spite of the activity all around her. It was early in the evening for The Bitter End, yet it was already filling up with customers intent on drinking and dancing as well as dining. She had expected all six of her prospective employers to be in attendance. It made her a little nervous when only Dmitri Watson had showed up.

Watson noticed the look of concern on Cinda's face and mentally sighed. "The others will be along shortly, Miss Dawn. This isn't a casting couch and I have no intention of chasing you around a desk. We want you for your mind, not the lovely vehicle that carries it."

Cinda relaxed a little but maintained her guard. "Okay, good. So, please, bring me up-to-date."

Dmitri ordered drinks before starting. He noted that Cinda accepted something non-alcoholic. Non-drinker or still guarded, he wondered.

"Okay, first the basics, though I suspect you already know this," Dmitri started. "Zarathustra orbits a K0 star. The star is at the extreme upper range, temperature wise, for a K0, but still well below any G class star. For a planet to support humanoid life as we understand it, this world should be approximately .62 astronomical units, give or take, from its primary in a K0 system. Freya is a textbook example of that and has the closest ecosystem to Terra's known to the Federation."

"Except for Zarathustra," Cinda added.

"Exactly! Zarathustra is nearly twice as far from its star as Freya. Further than Terra, even. Yet climatic conditions are, in some ways, even better for our kind of life form than Terra itself before the atomic wars.

Tell me, can you think of any reasons why this might be?"

Cinda thought it over before answering. "Well, a higher background radiation level would explain some of it, but Zarathustra has the lowest background radiation level of all the Federation planets, so that wouldn't be it. The axial tilt of the world is about half that of Terra, so there is less climate change with the seasons, but that would just make Zarathustra a more uniformly cool climate, except for the equator, maybe. Greenhouse gases caused by the methane from wildlife droppings and volcanic activity would help to trap in the heat from the sun, but how would that life have evolved in the first place if Zarathustra started out as a ball of ice?"

Dmitri nodded as Cinda spoke. She was brighter than he had initially guessed. He paused to fill his pipe with the local leaf, tamp it and then light it.

"Zarathustra has far fewer thunderstorms than Terra or Freya," she continued, "due to the lesser axial tilt. Less wind movement between climates. I would have to check, but the ozone layer could be significantly thinner, allowing more solar radiation in through the atmosphere."

Dmitri's eyes widened for a moment. "I will admit that I did not think of that. I suggest you make notes on your observation and maybe do some research on it. There could be a publishable paper in it for you."

Dmitri gave Cinda's idea some thought. Mild axial tilt, plus greenhouse gases and thin ozone layer, would account for some of the temperature levels, but not all. Still, it bore investigation.

"Anything else, Miss Dawn?"

Cinda fidgeted a moment, then said, "Um, well, the planetary magnetic shield is a little weaker than Terra's, but not enough to allow a significant amount of extra radiation through. If it was, the planet would have higher background radiation."

"Excellent. You are very up-to-date on this area of study," Dmitri said, with a smile.

"Oh, I read all of the articles that the previous researchers published."

Dmitri raised an eyebrow. "You did? When?"

"Right after I left the Two Moons Café. I wasn't sure if I wanted to accept the position and did some research of my own to help me decide."

"Is that where you got the idea about the ozone layer?" Dmitri had hoped Cinda came up with that on her own as proof of her ability.

"Oh, no. That was all mine," Cinda said. "I remembered something from history class about the ozone layer on Terra being damaged back in the 1st Century AE and how it was connected with global warming in that era. It made sense, to me anyway, that the same thing could happen here."

Dmitri was relieved. "I agree. You must join us as our intern—"

"Cinda? Fancy seeing you here."

Cinda and Dmitri turned to the source of the voice.

"Al? What are you doing here? You must have pulled in a big tip. Is your wife here, too?"

Alistair Forsythe Witherspoon shook his head in negation. "Naw. Turns out it was her Bunko night. Even dinner here couldn't drag her away from that. I'm here with a ZNPF guy. He's over there ordering for us. Who's your friend?"

Dmitri stood up and held out his hand. "Dr. Dmitri Watson, sir. Geologist among other things."

"Just call me Al, Bubba. Hey, Cinda, where's Jim and Sarah?"

Dmitri looked to Cinda in confusion. Was she a mother?

"Dax is Fuzzy-sitting for me tonight. I am here with Dr. Watson to discuss an internship with his research team."

"Dr. Watson," Al chuckled. "I'll spare you the Sherlock Holmes jokes if you buy this young lady a good meal. The eats here are great."

"I will be sure to do that, um, Al." Dmitri wondered who Sherlock Holmes was and made a note to look it up on the datastream when he returned to the hotel.

Al kissed Cinda on the cheek and went back to his table with Helmut.

"Is he friend or family?" Dmitri inquired.

"He was the taxi pilot who picked me and my family up from the space port when we first arrived on Zarathustra. Gave us some very good advice on what hotels to stay at, areas to avoid and where to go for the best dining. We used his taxi so many times we all became friends. If you need dependable transportation while on Zarathustra, he also chauffeurs. He owns the taxi outright and is privately licensed. He mentioned once that he had a larger transport for bigger jobs, too."

"Hmm...I think you may be on to something there. Your friend sounds very enterprising as well as personable. So, you have Fuzzies of your own?"

"Oh, a lot of people on Zarathustra do," Cinda explained. "Mine are named James Hutton and Sarah Balfour."

Dmitri recognized the names. "After the father of geology and his mother? I look forward to meeting them. Now, how soon can you start?"

Cinda considered. "I will have to find somebody to look after James and Sarah for a while. Where would we go first?"

Dmitri smiled. "Well, I have to do a little research of my own before deciding that. Delving through archives, rummaging through the tombs, as it were. Zarathustra's climate is something completely unprecedented, so a lot of backtracking will have to be done. I have all of the published works of those who came before us, up to two years ago, so that saves a lot of guess work. Eventually, I think we will go to Beta Continent."

"Beta? Why there?"

"Well, we read a paper by a Dr. Hoenveld about the adaptive evolution of the Fuzzies and the NFMp hormone. He conjectured that the hormone was a mutation that allowed the Fuzzies to survive some sort of change in the climate or environment. That change might have something to do with why Zarathustra is so much warmer than it should be."

Cinda had another thought that danced away for a moment, then jumped back into her frontal lobes. "Dr. Hoenveld? The one who is engaged to the actress, Darla Cross?"

Dmitri looked confused. "Engaged to an actress? Maybe we are talking about somebody else. The paper I read had to have been written by a stodgy old man with a mind for science and cleanliness in the workplace. The exactitude he used in the paper suggested somebody a creative person would find dreary and unapproachable."

Cinda laughed. "Yes, that would be him. I saw him in an interview on 'Tuning in with Tuning' last year. Dr. Hoenveld was defending the position that Fuzzies are native to Zarathustra. That was where he must have met Darla Cross. She was another guest on the show. He works at the CZC Science Center. You might be able to see him there."

"He is still on Zarathustra?" Dmitri became excited. "Yes, I would love to meet him. I will speak with the others about this. We should definitely speak with Dr. Hoenveld before we travel to Beta Continent."

"When we go to Beta, I would like to take Jim and Sarah along. They would love to see their friends on the Rez."

"I do not see a problem with that. And maybe you could find us some manual labor types to help with the grunt work while we are there." Before Cinda could answer, the rest of Dmitri's colleagues arrived. "Gentlemen, I have been assured that 'the eats here are great.' Let us test that theory along with our new intern."

Cinda was barraged with welcomes from the newcomers. She hoped she'd made the right decision.

XI

It was 13:57 when Trask returned with his veridicator technician. Marshal Fane arranged for an officer to escort him to the Marshal's Quarter, so called because it took up one fourth of Government House. Trask offered to check his weapon as he did when he came to see the governor, only to have Max tell him to keep it. "We're all cops, here," the Marshal explained.

Ben met them at the interrogation room and shook everybody's hand. The tech, Udo Jorgenson, was a little flustered over meeting the governor in person.

"Um...we'll need a...test subject...sir."

Trask had planned in advance. "That will be me."

"You?" Ben said in surprise.

"Sure. It seems fair, since I want to interrogate you that you should be allowed to check me out." In actuality, Trask wanted to be certain the veridicator had not been tampered with; he was the only person he knew on the planet that he could use to verify the device's reactions.

"Sounds good," Max agreed. "Have a seat."

Udo opened a panel and checked this and that, then nodded to Trask. Trask sat down and allowed Udo to lower the head-piece, then attached some electrodes to key locations. Trask noted the model was an older one. Back on Terra the veridicators used head-pieces little larger than a skull cap, and the electrodes were wireless. Still, older model or not, it would be just as effective if it had not been tampered with.

Udo turned to the marshal. "Sir, would you care to do the honors?"

Max nodded. "Please state your name and age."

"Trask, Starbuck U. Age thirty-two." The globe over his head remained blue.

"What does the U stand for?"

"Ugg-lug." The blue-lit globe flickered, then changed to red.

"Heh. Having fun with this, I see," Max observed. "Now answer truthfully."

"Ulysses." The globe returned to blue.

"Your father must have had a real passion for the classics."

"Actually," Trask countered, "that was my maternal grandfather's name. But yes, dad was a literature enthusiast." Blue.

"What is your mission here on Zarathustra?"

"To find and apprehend the Fuzzy slavery ring, or rings." Blue.

"Give me three false statements."

"I am an Yggdrasil Khooghra, I never touch alcohol, and I keep a bag of pixie dust handy to help me fly when my aircar is in the shop." Red, red and red.

Max chuckled. "Now give me three true statements."

"I am currently working for the FBCI, I am an expert with rifle and pistol, and I had a tail surgically removed at birth." Blue, blue and red.

"Aha. I see you are testing the veridicator...and us."

"Yes." Blue.

"Have you ever accepted a bribe?"

"No." Blue.

"Have you ever engaged in criminal activity?"

"Yes." Blue.

"Explain."

"When I was a kid I stole a candy bar from a local store. My father found out, took me back to the store, made me apologize and pay for the bar, then bought an entire bag of chocolate and made me eat the whole thing. I was sick for three days and never stole another candy bar." Solid blue all the way through.

Max nodded. "I am satisfied if you are."

Trask waited for the electrodes to be removed and the head-piece raised before he stood up. "You could have gotten more information out of me, you know."

"If we will be working together on this," Max said, "we will have to be able to trust each other. I know all I need to know for now."

Max turned to Ben. "Governor, would you like to go first, or shall I?"

Ben looked at the door then back to Max. "Gus isn't here, yet, for some reason, so I would rather wait. I may decide he isn't needed, though. We'll see."

Max nodded and took the seat. He had to struggle a bit to fit his bulk into the chair. Udo hooked him up then stepped back.

"Marshal, I will just go after what is pertinent, here," Trask said. "To speed things up, I will be blunt. As my only interest is my current case, anything I learn about other misconduct will be ignored. Understood?"

Max tried to nod but the head-piece wouldn't allow the movement. "Agreed."

"Name?"

"Maximilian Ivanovich Fane." Blue.

"Age?"

"Fifty-seven."

"Have you ever accepted a bribe?"

"Never." The globe moved towards purple until Max clarified that he had not done so since entering law enforcement and the globe settled back to blue. Trask decided not to pursue it.

"Have you ever intentionally placed a Fuzzy in danger?"

"No." Blue.

"Have you ever benefitted financially or otherwise from the sale of a Fuzzy or Fuzzies?"

"No." Blue.

"What would you do if you saw a man about to harm a Fuzzy?"

"Shoot the summich in the head." Blue.

Interesting, thought Trask. "Why the head?"

"Aiming any lower would place the Fuzzy at risk of being accidently shot." Blue.

"I see your point. Okay, now the sixty-four sol question; are you now, or have you ever been involved in the illegal capture and/or sale of a sapient being?"

"Never." Blue.

Trask made a note on his datapad then nodded at Udo.

"That clears you in my book, Marshal. Governor, I will ask you much the same questions. Do you wish to proceed or wait for your chief colonial prosecutor?"

An evil grin spread out over Ben's face. "Actually, I would like to ask the Marshal a few questions."

"What? Now wait a second, Governor—"

"Why did you leave the FBCI, Max?"

The Marshal fumed as he answered. "I became involved with the sector chief's daughter. He didn't like it and threatened to destroy my career, so I quit and left the planet." Blue.

"And what happened to the girl?"

"Married her." Blue.

"Why did you leave the other positions?"

"There was no opportunity for advancement in the Odin Guard, Baldur was too quiet a planet for me, and the food was terrible on Yggdrasil." Blue, blue and blue. "Um, I gained most of this weight after Yggdrasil, if you are curious."

Ben nodded. He had been to Yggdrasil and suffered through the food there. "Last question; do you think I interfere too much in your work?"

Max hesitated only a moment before answering. "Yes." Blue.

"Damn. Juan Takagashi was right. Okay, Max. I'm done abusing you."

Max vacated the chair and looked at Ben quizzically. "Why didn't you ask what I thought of you as a governor when you had the chance?"

Ben smiled. "When Napier appointed me to this position he warned me I would be respected, hated and looked upon with suspicion no matter how well I did the job. I would rather not know what the people I work with every day thought."

Before Max could respond, Ned Foster entered the room. "Governor Rainsford, I came up to tell you that the Chief Prosecutor won't be back for some time. Is there anything I can do for you?"

Ben thought a moment then took the seat. "Let's get this over with. Here is what is going on, Ned...."

* * *

Gus Brannhard opened the hatch and two Fuzzies leapt out of the aircar. Once settled on the floor of the parking structure, they patiently waited for their pappy to join them.

"You two shouldn't jump out onto the parking deck like that," Gus admonished them. "The duracrete is much harder than even rock. You could hurt yourselves."

"Hokay, Pappy Gus," Natty and Allan said in unison. Natty added, "We go Fuzzee Club now?"

"Sure. Be back by eighteen hundred."

Allan and Natty nodded then scampered off to the lift that would take them to the surface walks. Gus smiled as he always did when around his Fuzzies. They filled a gap in his life he hadn't even realized was present.

On the way down to his office he passed Ned Foster. Foster updated him on the last attempt by Ingermann's lawyer to procure bail. "Judge Pendarvis shut him down real nice."

"You did good, Ned, but don't count too much on the judge. Pendarvis strictly adheres to the letter of the law and he was on the fine edge issuing that warrant for ol' Hugo's blood." Gus chuckled. "Had it been anybody but Ingermann, I don't think he would have allowed it. But he is on solid, if thin, ground."

"Well, just to be on the safe side, I plan on shoring up the judge's order with as many precedents as I can find," Foster said.

"That shouldn't be too hard," Gus added. "You can find a precedent for almost anything in colonial law." Gus glanced at his chronometer. "I need to go see the governor. We'll talk later."

"Sure thing, Boss. Oh! You missed his interrogation earlier."

Gus stopped. "What interrogation?"

Ned turned around when he realized Gus had stopped walking. "Off-worlder from the FBCI came in and questioned Marshal Fane and Governor Rainsford under veridication."

"What about?" Gus rumbled.

Foster started to get a little nervous. "Fuzzy poachers with off-world connections. This FBCI guy, Trask, wanted to rule out the governor and marshal. The governor was anxious to get it done and over with and asked me to supervise in your absence. I suggested they wait for you, but you know the governor."

Gus closed his eyes and counted to ten. It wasn't Foster's fault, after all. "Did you advise the governor that he was under no legal onus to allow himself to be questioned?"

"I did. If it helps, none of the questions were the least bit damaging to the governor or government, and he answered every question truthfully. None of the questions were even actionable against him unless he was, in fact, involved with these new Fuzzy slavers. Max has a copy of the interview since they used his interrogation room where he records everything."

Gus resumed walking though he changed his destination. "And I thought my biggest headache today would be all those off-worlders coming to adopt Fuzzies. Thank Ghu for small favors. I am going to go have a chat with our esteemed governor and warn him about the pitfalls of setting unfortunate precedents."

"Gus, I really do not see the problem, here," Ben Rainsford argued. "Trask is looking for Fuzzy slavers, not me."

"Governor, Trask is looking for a promotion, like all FBCI people, and bringing down a corrupt politician is the fastest way to get there," Gus said, barely controlling his voice. It wouldn't do to yell at the governor, old friends or no. "Cops—no offense, Max—can bend the facts to suit them and get people sent to jail regardless of guilt or innocence. And the veridicator is no true defense, either. Why do you think I didn't let Jack take the seat when he was on trial? Because Coombes could have brought up previous scrapes with the law, especially all the people Jack killed over the years, and make an argument that he killed so many people that he no longer sees it as anything other than self-defense."

Ben looked confused. "Is that possible?"

"I very much doubt it, but juries don't know any better. Then there is the precedent you set by agreeing to be veridicated in the first place. What happens when the next cop or even news reporter wants your statement under veridication? You either spend all of your time in the hot seat answering questions instead of running the planet, or people wonder why you answered one guy's questions but not this other guy's. Now, if this gets out, every time you refuse to be veridicated people will assume you are hiding something."

Max had stayed quiet. Now he nodded and agreed with Gus. "I should have insisted he get a warrant before allowing you to be questioned."

"And no judge would have issued said warrant in the absence of hard evidence showing your involvement," Gus finished. "Great Ghu, I want a drink right now! Look, I will have a talk with Mr. Trask and ask him to keep the interrogation hush-hush. We will probably have to make some sort of concession to get him to agree. We can't have your cooperation in this matter get out." Gus glanced at his wrist. "It's getting late, so I will beard this lion in his own den tomorrow."

"Gus, I want to work with this man to stop the Fuzzy slavers," Ben said. "Try not to step on his toes."

"I'll take him out for beer and pretzels if he agrees to keep that interview off the datastream."

Outside on the terrace, Flora and Fauna overheard everything. It was often overlooked that, aside from dogs brought back from Terra, Fuzzies had the best ears on the planet. Fauna picked up his chopper-digger and started toward Ben's office. Flora stopped him.

"Pappy Gus not make fight with Pappy Ben," Flora said. "They have...um...argument, like Fuzzies in tribe do."

"Why fight? Pappy Ben is Wise One for Big Ones. Pappy Gus help Pappy Ben. Why unhappy?"

"You not listen? Bad Big Ones want to hurt Fuzzee. Pappy Ben wants to help, an' Pappy Gus wants Pappy Ben to not make trouble for him."

Fauna was skeptical. "How make trouble for Pappy Ben? Big One Trask ask question, Pappy Ben answered. Why Pappy Gus mad?"

Flora shook her head. "Is so much we not know about Big Ones."

XII

"This is the archery range. That one shooting at the target with all the arrows in the bull's-eye is Maid Marian, our champion archer. Archeress?"

"Archer, Jack. You know, most male-female distinctions in titles died out long ago," Patricia admonished Jack. She looked around the Fuzzy Reservation and spotted something interesting. "What is that group doing?"

He followed the finger to where a furry of Fuzzies were throwing something at another target. "Throwing stars. Fuzzies take to almost any weapon requiring hand-eye coordination. It took a while to get them to grasp the idea of throwing the weapon at a target. You throw your weapon away, you don't have it anymore, basically. Then we pointed out that it was no different from shooting arrows and they understood. They are also very good with throwing knives."

"Didn't you say that these Fuzzies had the same mentation as a twelve year old?"

"According to Dr. Mallin, the CZC Fuzzyologist."

"And you trust them with all these weapons? What if they turned on you?"

He was about to say it would never happen, then remembered Red Fur and his gang in the north. "Well, as a rule, Fuzzies don't like to hurt people or animals. Only for food or self-defense. The crowd I will take you to see up north is a bit different, though. They had a very bad first contact with our kind and now they dislike all Big Ones on general principle. I don't blame them a bit, either."

Patricia took a seat on a nearby bench. "Jack, did something happen between you and the northern Fuzzies? Piet seemed more than a little concerned about going up there.”

“Well, that is a bit of a story.” He related the account of his capture and being held as a hostage, then the brief war between the Fuzzies and the subsequent treaty. “Red Fur is okay with the Fuzzies on the Reservation. Fuzzies don’t hold grudges, at least not with each other. But the *Jin-f’ke* do not like us Big Ones one little bit. It will take a long time to win their trust and this new crop of Khooghras is putting a very large spanner in the works.”

She thought for a moment, then said, “Maybe you should ask the *Jin-f’ke* for their help. Nothing brings people together like a common enemy.”

Jack shook his head. “If we were talking about Thorans or even Sheshans you would be right. Fuzzy psychology works a bit different. Either they like you or they don’t. Now, they can be convinced over time to change their minds, provided you didn’t hurt them too badly, like with Juan Jimenez who only put them in cages. But Big Ones killed one of their own and that is not forgiven easily. To the *Jin-f’ke* all Big Ones are all alike. It took several months—and a lot of help from Little Fuzzy—just to get them to accept the trading post slash guard shack at the edge of their territory. They trade furs for Extee Three and chopper-diggers, some of them, and that is as much contact as they care to have with us. Red Fur knows that what we make is better than anything his people can put together, but he doesn’t have to like us for providing it.”

They stood up and walked a little further and came to the Fuzzy smithy. The Fuzzy working the hammer and anvil was called, unsurprisingly, Smith. Patricia watched in fascination as Smith pounded out a flat piece of metal into what looked like a sword.

“Have you considered moving a bunch of Fuzzies into that area to teach the *Jin-f’ke* what they have learned?”

Jack shook his head. “No need. Any Fuzzy that wants to come here and learn is free to do so. Red Fur doesn’t put any restrictions on his people. I am not sure he could if he tried.”

He looked around until he spotted a group of Fuzzies practicing with pugil sticks. “See those Fuzzies there? The big ones are from Red

Fur's tribe. They come down, learn whatever interests them, then they go back and share what they know. Occasionally, one or two decide to stay and join my mob down here. They don't allow themselves to be adopted out, though. The Northern Fuzzies still don't trust us that far. Many of them become instructors, while the rest work as hunter-gatherers bringing in fresh meat and such."

"So the *Jin-f'ke* are larger?"

"Oh, yes. Two to four inches taller and about five pounds heavier. Like the difference between Old Chinese and Western Europeans in pre-atomic times. We think it is due to better nutrition. Before the southern Fuzzies found us, some of them were in bad shape—even starving. Now, the adolescents down here seem to be growing a bit larger than Baby Fuzzy when he first came to live with me. I give it a generation and my crowd will catch up with the *Jin-f'ke*. Maybe even surpass them with all the Extee Three they eat."

Patricia wrinkled her nose. "Gawd, how can they eat that stuff?"

Jack shrugged. "How do some Terro-humans eat hundred-year old eggs? Or drink turtle's blood straight from the source? There's no accounting for taste. Besides, the titanium that the Terran Federation Space Forces Emergency Ration, Extraterrestrial, Type Three contains is an essential item in the Fuzzies' diet. Without the titanium it contains, they are unable to reproduce successfully."

"Don't their usual foods contain any titanium?" Pat asked.

"Only the land-prawns. The Science Center is still working on the mystery of why the Fuzzies are so titanium dependent when it's such a rare element on Zarathustra. They've come up with some interesting hypotheses, but no firm answers."

She decided to change the subject. "Will it just be you and I going to see these northern Fuzzies or will we have a guard detail?"

Didn't she just ask this? "Just the two of us and my Fuzzies. Less is more in this case. We don't want Red Fur to feel threatened. I have seen firsthand how dangerous a Fuzzy can be when provoked.

"Now let's have a look at the weavers."

"Weavers?"

"Yes, these Fuzzies can work a loom and make blankets. We provide the yarn and they go to town on it. Some of the blankets in Morgan's castle were made here."

Patricia guffawed. "Like little hairy Amish."

Jack chuckled. "You know, I wish we had some Amish on this planet. I am surprised a bunch didn't come in during the attempted land grab."

"Really? Why?"

He waved an all-encompassing hand. "All of this that we are teaching the Fuzzies is meant to make them self-sufficient. That means low tech. Fuzzies can farm, hunt—boy, can they hunt—work a smithy, make arrows and simple bladed weapons and all kinds of good things.

"Victor Grego set up a few businesses where Fuzzies can make jewelry, polish small sunstones, paint and even do minor repair work where a human might be too big or clumsy. Fuzzies learn incredibly fast and have excellent hand-eye coordination; better than humans, in fact. But they need people who can teach them the things they need to know for surviving without us. Very few of us Big Ones know how to do these things anymore. Most of what we are teaching them, we had to look up in old books to learn how to do it. Little Fuzzy can fletch an arrow far better than I can, and I am the one who taught him from a book.

"If we had some Amish, or other low-tech society members, I could expand our teaching curriculum. Sure, I know how to make most home furnishings thanks to Pa. But I don't have the time to teach a class on top of my other duties."

"Jack, you could get a swarm of Amish out here with the promise of a few thousand acres of farmland," she said. "Here on Zarathustra, you've got a wonderful climate, lots of fertile land and open spaces as far as the eye can see. Just cover the cost of transportation and freight and the few left on Terra would stampede to get aboard."

Jack thought it over. "I wonder if I can get the Charterless Zarathustra Company to cover the costs?"

"Why not ask Morgan to use that yacht of his?"

He shook his head. "Too small for the people, equipment and animals that they'd insist on bringing. He does have a full-sized cargo carrier, though. And I'll bet I could get Ben to cover the costs out of the Fuzzy sunstone profits since it would benefit the Fuzzies."

"Now you're thinking like a Holloway, Jack."

"Now that I think about it, there is a good-sized parcel of land bordering the Rez that Grego doesn't plan to develop. It is about the size of... um...Rhode Island, I think. That should hold a fair amount of farms."

"And make them your neighbors," Pat said.

His voice began to rise. "Fuzzies could go to work on the Amish farms and learn all they have to teach." Jack was getting excited about the possibilities.

"And bring up the population of this planet in process," Patricia added. "A colony world isn't considered a civilized planet until it reaches 20,000,000 warm and breathing bodies."

"And not everybody raised Amish stays with that life," Jack said. "That means over time, more people for city jobs that will grow as the planet does."

Patricia smiled. She had hoped for something she could do to help Jack before she had to depart.

* * *

Morgan applied the adhesive strip to the edge of the diaper, then examined his work. He nodded in satisfaction and picked up his son, making sure to properly support the head.

"Well, Little John, it looks like your father isn't completely useless in the nursery, though it took some practice. I wonder what Heidi will say about it?"

"She vill say a man's place ist not in der nursery, Herr Hollovay."

Morgan turned and saw the mountain of muscle that was his son's nanny. To look at her one would doubt her qualifications for such a job. Her brutish appearance and powerful build made her look, to most humans, to be ill-equipped for the gentle nature of her position. Morgan knew better. Those powerful arms that could bend inch thick iron bars ended in hands capable of surprising gentleness.

"Heidi, on Terra, and even on Freya, men often share the work of caring for their young. In some cases, as single parents."

Heidi shook her ponderous head. "T'ose men are not part of Freyan nobility. You have far greater responsibilities."

"There is no greater responsibility than to one's own family," Morgan countered. He sat in a sofa chair and gently rocked Little John back to sleep. "I missed being with my own father when I was growing up. There were a lot of years when my only goal was to kill him for abandoning me, until I learned the truth of what happened. Little John, excuse me, John Morgan Holloway the Minor, will not suffer for the lack of my attention. As for the Freyan nobility, well, they have ostracized me ever since I fought for your people's compensation for what was done to you and your ancestors. I am barely tolerated on Freya and not tolerated at all at court. If being a proper father to my son would offend them, all the better."

Heidi bared her teeth in a manner that would frighten anyone who was unfamiliar with her people. Morgan knew the expression for what it was: a broad smile. "You make me proud. You make all of us proud. Und dat ist vhy ve vant you to be our king."

Morgan shook his head. "This is not Freya. The Federation frowns on self-styled royalty. They accept it on the worlds they discover, since they have rules against interfering with the governments they find on those worlds, but anybody setting up their own little fiefdom will find themselves in very deep, very hot water—faster than a kholph could eat a Terran banana. I am not interested in being a king in any case, here or on Freya."

"Ve are Freyans, no matter die vorld beneat' our feet. Our system of government has been in place long before Freya joined der Federation. You are vhat die hoomans call a beron already. Vit' die property you own you vould be a...um...a duck."

"Duke," Morgan corrected with a chuckle. "A duck is a Terran water fowl much like a *morlid*."

"Dyook, den. Can you not be our *dyook* here on Zarat'ustra? Mein fat'er could be your bürgermeister on Zeta continent. You vould represent us in court beck on Freya."

Morgan thought before saying anything. A dukedom was certainly impossible. In order to be elevated to such a title, he would have to petition the royal court, give a full account of his lands and holdings and even pay tribute on all of it, on and off-world. That would come to a great deal of money, enough that even Morgan would feel the pinch. And even still, King Noreek would not be kindly disposed to the man who had embarrassed the whole of Freyan nobility and even extorted compensation for the enslaved Freyans from Magni.

Yet, Heidi was right in that her people needed representation on the home world. One day her people's children might choose to return to Freya and reclaim their place in that society.

"I will have to discuss this with Governor Rainsford, Heidi. And Leslie Coombes and Gus Brannhard. I don't know what the legal issues involved in such a thing would entail. Now, let me spend some time with my son while I think things over."

* * *

Darius, the inner moon, hung low in the orange sky as the morning sun cleared the horizon. Little Fuzzy pressed his nose to the shatter-resistant glass as the contra-gravity vehicle made its descent. Once grounded, Jack told everybody to stay close to the aircar.

"Are you worried about something, Jack?" Pat asked.

Jack nodded. "Like I said before, these Fuzzies are very different from my crowd down south. More advanced in terms of weaponry and social development, and they do not—underlined, italicized and in big red letters—*not* like Big Ones sticking our oversized noses in their business. They had a very unfortunate first contact with our species and you never get a second chance at a first impression."

"Ha! Pa used to say that all the time."

"Paul Morgan Holloway said a lot of things. Most of them very true and well worth remembering." Jack scanned the surrounding area before advancing to the trading post. "Don't make any sudden moves in case the officer here is a new hire and doesn't know me on sight."

Jack mentally cursed himself for neglecting to check the duty roster before flying up. He had been making mistakes like that more often of late.

Little Fuzzy lit his tiny pipe as they approached the trading post. The door opened and a ZNPF officer stepped out. He was a large, heavily muscled man with very dark skin and a bald head. He spoke with a deep resonating voice. "Commissioner. I was not informed of your visit."

"Relax. This isn't a surprise inspection, Officer." *Though maybe it should be*, he thought. *I don't remember ever meeting this agent before. Maybe the Zarathustra Native Protection Force is just getting too damn big.*

"Clarke, Michael D., sir. I am covering Keezheekoni Helmut's shift while he is in Mallorysport."

"Anything new to report?"

"I have been speaking with Red Fur," Officer Clarke said. "Red Fur still doesn't like us Big Ones, of course. However, he recognizes the need to work with us to keep bad Big Ones away from his people. Red Fur has organized patrols to look for other poachers and I have been showing them what to watch out for and what to avoid. Deputy Dumont has said he will be sending more men out as soon as he can reorganize. The Fuzzy Reservation spans a lot of territory and even with aircars we can only cover so much ground at a time."

Jack nodded. "True. Do you think I can go and speak with Red Fur without catching arrows in my backside?"

Clarke smirked. He knew about the Commissioner being taken hostage the previous year as did most of the citizens of the planet. "I anticipated you might be out eventually, and told Red Fur as much. I got the impression that you would be welcome and he would enjoy seeing Little Fuzzy again." Clarke hesitated, then added, "You might have to jump through a hoop or two. Red Fur likes to keep us on our toes."

That was just like a Fuzzy, Jack thought. They had a little war here last year, and now everybody was friends. It was hard to stay mad at a Fuzzy; even for another Fuzzy, but they still tended to be wary of anything new and strange."

"Good. You can remain at your post. I remember the way."

Clarke's dark face looked distressed. "Sir, do you think it wise to bring a civilian along?"

Jack understood Clarke's dilemma. Civilians were *verboten* on this part of the Reservation. "Officer Clarke, this is Patricia McLeod, my sister. In all likelihood, she is a better shot than either of us and knows to keep her hands to herself in strange territory. If you have an objection you are within your rights to document it in your log. I will accept responsibility for her while she is here."

Clarke nodded. "Understood, sir. Ah, sir, I am required to inspect any parcels being carried onto the Rez...."

Jack was confused for a moment until he recalled that Patricia had brought along a shoulder bag. While he could easily order Clarke to ignore the rules, Jack disliked petty bureaucrats who thought themselves above the laws they were supposed to enforce. He also respected officers not afraid to hold their own bosses to the same standard. Jack made a mental note to have Piet keep an eye on the big man; Clarke had serious potential.

"Of course. Pat, would you mind?"

"Not at all." Patricia opened the shoulder bag for the officer to inspect. It was full of yarn and a pair of knitting needles.

Jack found himself curious. "What did you bring that for?"

"Well, habit, mostly. I did a lot of knitting on the voyage from Terra. I was thinking I could teach some Fuzzies how to knit while I was up here. They could make their own blankets and such."

Jack had to admit it was a good idea and wondered why nobody thought of it before. His bunch down south had mastered the loom, but it wasn't exactly portable.

"We'll have to discuss that idea on the way back. I'll have to tell you about zarasheep and the problems with domesticating them. For now, keep those needles down in the bag. To a Fuzzy they would look like atl-atl spears."

"They know what an atl-atl is?" Patricia glanced at Little Fuzzy and the rest. As usual, they all had on their backpacks and chopper-diggers, all made by Big Ones. "I thought you and the government gave the Fuzzies everything they use."

"Yes and no. Little Fuzzy, the first to meet a human face-to-face, got the first chopper-digger when I made it for him, but that was before we knew for certain that Fuzzies are sapient. Yet he still taught Baby Fuzzy how to make his own from natural materials. Baby brought it to me to trade for a metal one. That one is in the Fuzzy Museum in Mallorysport, now. We teach the Fuzzies everything we think they can handle: like a blacksmith working an iron smithy, and making chopper-diggers all by themselves. We have weavers, yarn and basket variety, fletchers, candlemakers and even tanners. There are Fuzzy villages that are largely self-sufficient."

Patricia was visibly impressed. "Did they build the houses or tents or yurts or whatever they live in?"

"Log cabins, mostly. A few still prefer to sleep under the stars and erect lean-tos when the weather gets bad," Jack explained. "Come with me and you can see how the other half lives. Oh, most of the Northern Fuzzies have never seen a female Big One, or even a Big One at all. Most Fuzzies were nomadic in nature until we started adopting or training them. Up here, some still hold to that life style."

"Do you think any of these will ever want to be adopted? There are a lot of people in orbit hoping to take a Fuzzy home with them."

Jack snorted. "Not this crowd, not in this lifetime. Maybe it's time I placed a moratorium on Fuzzy adoptions until we can be sure that nobody in that throng orbiting overhead is involved with the slaver operation."

"Sir, if I do not hear back from you in thirty minutes," Clarke interrupted, "I'll be coming out to see why. I hope this is acceptable to you."

"And if it isn't?" Jack asked.

"Then you can fire me when I come out."

Jack smiled. "You were trained by Harry Steefer at some point, weren't you?"

Clarke nodded, an impressive feat considering the thickness of his neck. "I served two tours in the army under him. In fact, I was with him when he was injured and forced into medical retirement from the army. When I learned he had moved to Zarathustra, I decided to follow him when I demobbed. He suggested I apply to the ZNPF when I arrived two years ago."

"I'll have to thank him for that. Thirty minutes will be fine and your job is secure, Officer Clarke."

Jack and Patricia walked over the hill to Red Fur's village. Patricia took in her surroundings. There were no log cabins, or even yurts or tents. She did see some thatch dwellings that didn't quite qualify as huts and some corrals for animals she didn't recognize. She didn't see anything to suggest these Fuzzies did any farming.

"Do the southern Fuzzies on the Reservation do any agriculture?"

"Some, out in the villages. But only after we salt the earth with titanium dust. It makes them less dependent on us Big Ones for Extee Three. This crowd up here is still in the hunter-gatherer stage, though they are taking a stab at domestication. Strictly for food, not as beasts of burden or transportation."

Patricia noticed there were no dogs around. She also realized that as primitive as the conditions were, the grounds were clear of debris and everybody looked industrious and, as far as she could tell, happy. That is, until they spotted the Big Ones. It was rare to see hostility on the face of a Fuzzy. Now almost every face they saw showed naked hatred.

Jack nudged Patricia's arm. "Be on your best behavior, Pat. Here comes the welcoming committee."

Several Fuzzies armed with chopper-diggers, some wood, some metal, ran out to block the path. One of them, holding a wooden chopper-digger, yeeked at them.

Little Fuzzy stepped forward and placed his chopper-digger flat on the ground then placed a foot on it. This gesture told the *Jin-f'ke* that he was here to talk and make friends. Little Fuzzy yeeked, listened to more yeeking, then turned to Jack.

"Fuzzee want to know why we here. I say we go see *Bal-f'ke*—Red Fur—make talk about bad Big Ones. *Jin-f'ke* say we follow."

"Okay, Little Fuzzy. We follow." Jack explained to Patricia as they went that Little Fuzzy could speak the language of the Northern Fuzzies and made an excellent translator. "I picked up some of the language when I was taken hostage, but since the Fuzzies here don't much like Big Ones, we're better off with Little Fuzzy doing the talking, anyway."

The *Jin-f'ke* surrounded Jack and Patricia as they were escorted to Red Fur. Patricia half expected the village leader to be seated on some sort of primitive throne. She was half right. Red Fur, while seated, rested on a log along with several other Fuzzies. No special treatment or deference was in evidence. In fact, if not for the deep scarlet hue of his pelt, Patricia would not have known which one was Red Fur.

"Pappy Jack, Wise One for Big Ones," Red Fur said. His voice was pitched to the human register allowing the two Big Ones to understand his speech.

"Red Fur, Wise One for *Jin-f'ke*," Jack replied. "I come to offer help."

Jack never saw a Fuzzy snort in derision before. Red Fur did a pretty good imitation of it. "Again we have big-big trouble from Big Ones. Why?"

Jack understood Red Fur's ire. His contacts with the Big Ones had been less than stellar. *Maybe a visit from Diamond and the CZC gem heist Fuzzies might help. They understood the difference between bad Big Ones and good Big Ones.* "I am here to help you with these troubles."

Red Fur considered it. He did not like the Big Ones on general principle. Big Ones killed Sun Fur. Big Ones' noisy made-things hurt Makes-Things ears. Still, the Big Ones also gave his people the hard shiny *shoppo-diggo* and taught anybody who wanted to learn new things. Little Fuzzy said that there were good Big Ones and bad Big Ones, and that Pappy Jack was the best of the good Big Ones.

Finally, Red Fur nodded. "We make talk."

XIII

Not for the first time, Juan Jimenez noted that the work environment at Science Center had become significantly more pleasant in the last several months. An outsider might speculate that the new equipment, on loan from Morgan Holloway, might have something to do with the improved mood of the employees. Certainly, the new holographic display unit and the DNA decrypter drew a lot of attention from the staff. Still, Juan had his own theory as to what made his people happier to come to work.

Darla Cross, or more to the point, the effect she had on Dr. Hoenveld. Ordinarily, the good doctor made a nuisance of himself micromanaging his people. He was also a fanatic about keeping a clean workplace, normally a laudable trait, to the point where he brought many an intern to tears by berating them for their sloppiness. Since he had started dating the local actress, much to the surprise of everybody, Hoenveld had mellowed and even became personable on occasion. Darla Cross's appeal was obvious; Hoenveld's was not, unless the actress was attracted to intelligence.

Not that the doctor was unattractive. He was of average height and average build, with mousy-brown hair streaked with gray. Even his face, while not ugly, was unexceptional. Only the piercing blue of his eyes stood out when meeting Hoenveld for the first time. His social skills, on the other hand, tended to be lacking, at least until Darla Cross entered the picture.

This morning marked one of his personable occasions. Hoenveld was looking over the results of one of the intern's projects using the holographic display. Floating in the air was a three-dimensional representation of a Fuzzy. After a moment Juan recognized the Fuzzy as Zorro, who had been brought in several months earlier to determine why he didn't like Extee Three.

As Juan approached the holographic display, the intern tapped a few buttons on the console and the furry exterior of the Fuzzy vanished to reveal the internal organs, musculature and skeletal structure. Juan's heart missed a beat in his surprise. "What the Niflheim are you doing there?"

Hoenveld and the intern looked back at the Division Head. "Doctor Jimenez. Good morning. Lars here just came up with a clever way to combine the functions of the DNA decrypter and the holographic display."

"Indeed?" Juan looked over the display. "It looks like the middle of a horror movie to me."

"Um, actually, sir...uh...Dr. Jimenez, this is for a diagnostic plan," Lars stammered out. "The DNA decrypter is able to map the biology of the Fuzzy to tell us what he should look like, inside and out. The data is converted into holographic imagery and displayed here. Then we compare it to medical scans of what he looks like now. That data can then be input to give a three-dimensional representation of anything going on inside of the Fuzzy. This would be a great way to identify malformations and pre-existing genetic conditions."

Juan looked over the display with new respect. He could see the heart pumping blood through the Fuzzy's system. Lars had found a humane way to vivisect a Fuzzy.

"Wait, how do you get the medical scans to match up with that level of detail?"

"The scan data is overlaid on the hologram. A simple X-ray can provide enough information to show a break on a bone, for instance." Lars tapped out a series of commands and a fracture appeared on the right humerus. "From there, the computer can extrapolate the secondary and even tertiary injuries caused by the break. Any wound we can get a decent scan of can be duplicated on the holographic image."

Another series of commands healed the break and created a stab wound from a chopper-digger. Juan could even see where the blood would pool under the dermis.

Juan tried to find pitfalls in the idea. "What about the effect of diseases or toxins? That wouldn't show up on this display very well."

Hoenveld turned to Lars with an arched eyebrow. Lars tapped in a few more commands and the display enlarged the area around one of the veins. The vein wall became transparent and Juan could see red and white corpuscles racing by. Another keystroke and the motion slowed to a crawl.

"We can input the results from a blood test to view micro-organisms in the blood and the computer can extrapolate the effects of anything we have on file. New diseases would be a problem, but I think a serum of nano-cams injected into the patient could give us a real-time display of what the bugs are doing."

Lars looked both proud and nervous. For an intern, explaining himself to the Division Head was a bit like a new priest having an audience with the Pope. Make that a Cardinal—Victor Grego would be the Pope. Juan remembered the first time he met Leonard Kellogg. Whatever Kellogg's faults, and they were legion, he had tried to put the young Dr. Jimenez at ease. Juan decided in that respect the former Division Head should be emulated.

"This is good work, Lars. Very good work. I suggest you patent your idea quickly before I steal it for the Company," Juan said half joking. "This has some very far reaching medical applications, and not just for Fuzzies."

"I already suggested that, Dr. Jimenez," Hoenveld said. "May I suggest you order another set of machines like these? Mr. Morgan—oh, wait, that's Mr. Holloway now—will want this pair back before his yacht spaces out next month."

To where? Juan wondered absently, *and what did he need this equipment for in the first place?* "I will do that before end of shift. Do you have any idea why he even has devices like this?"

"He didn't say," Hoenveld said, "although I suspect he used these in his search for his father. The DNA decrypter's function is fairly obvious and the holographic display has an age progression application that might help him identify anybody from an old picture. Young Lars here found a number of images in the stored memory."

Lars, taking Dr. Hoenveld's statement as a cue, brought up several images of an elderly man. Some were thin, fat, average, balding or shaggy and several had the look of having had cosmetic surgery. The men in the pictures all had one thing in common—the eyes.

Juan nodded. "That makes sense. No telling what kind of changes a man could go through over thirty odd years. Age, strain, weight gain, weight loss. That one looks a bit like Chief Steefer. The shaggy one could almost pass as Gus Brannhard. The really overweight one could pass for Max Fane from the right angle. Clearly, Morgan Holloway was on a mission and willing to go to any lengths to accomplish it. A man like that would be a good friend to have, or a very bad enemy." Juan turned to Lars. "I would be very careful with this equipment. I wouldn't like to see Morgan upset with you."

"I...I will be very careful, sir." Lars looked a little shaken.

"Ah, any particular reason why you used Zorro for the display?"

"Oh, well, I had his DNA handy after I examined him last year," Hoenveld explained. "I also have the DNA profile of his mate, Lolita Pulido. While both Fuzzies are outwardly healthy, and Zorro does not have the NFMp hormone to interfere with his reproductive process, he and Lolita have failed to sire any young. According to the scans I took several months ago, Zorro should be more than capable of fathering offspring. Fertility tests on Lolita suggest she is quite capable of conceiving as well. But a recent test shows that Zorro is suddenly sterile. I do not know if this is a temporary or permanent condition, or what caused it."

"That reminds me, I was speaking with Mr. Grego earlier and he wants a study done on some two dozen Fuzzies coming in from Terra in a week or so. Governor Rainsford was informed of sterility problems and would like it checked out."

"I was unaware that so many Fuzzies had traveled to Terra," Hoenveld stated. "I only knew of Mr. Coombes' family making that journey. Maybe we should start doing workups on them to get started. Zorro is the first homegrown case I have found. I'll do more workups on him as well."

Juan thought it over. One Fuzzy suddenly becoming sterile was disconcerting, but hardly a catastrophe...except for the Fuzzy. "Have there been any other cases?"

Hoenveld nodded. "Of the thirty Fuzzies we brought in, three were sterile. We only brought in Fuzzies we had previously examined and had medical records on for comparison."

"Great Ghu, Chris! If this is a contagious viral infection—" Juan left the statement unfinished. Discovery of the NFMp hormone and its effect on Fuzzy reproduction was well documented. The discovery of a long chain molecule in the digestive tracts of land-prawns led to an effective treatment for the condition. But what if something new was inhibiting Fuzzy reproduction, and even worse, could be transmitted to Terro-humans? "What have you learned thus far?"

Hoenveld tapped some buttons on a nearby computer and brought up the file containing Zorro's medical history. "Blood tests have failed to reveal any viral or bacterial infections. Medical scans show no recent injuries that could account for the lack of spermatozoa production, and his diet, while bereft of the usual intake of Extee Three is still in keeping with the promotion of good health in a Fuzzy. And, like all Fuzzies, he is active and energetic. I should add that he is a non-smoker, as well. We should take such good care of ourselves."

Juan looked over the screen and wondered if the same thing could be happening to other Fuzzies on the Reservation, or if only the Fuzzies who lived with humans were affected. "Dr. Hoenveld, this gets top priority. If this is something big, maybe we can get ahead of it before it becomes a serious problem. I suggest we quarantine Zorro and Lolita, along with the other affected Fuzzies, until we can determine what is wrong with them, or at least whether or not they have a contagious pathogen."

Hoenveld smiled slightly, which for him was the equivalent of a toothy grin. "Already done. I have them in one of the environmental studies biomes. It isn't as good as being outside, for them, but it is fairly roomy and equipped with enough Zarathustran flora to feel homey. I am also having some land-prawns and goofers brought in for them to hunt, and a viewscreen to watch. For now they have plenty of educational toys to keep them occupied."

Of course Dr. Hoenveld would go for educational toys, Juan thought.

"We should get some more Fuzzies in for examination," Juan said as he watched the image change back to a fully furry Fuzzy. "Some from Mallorysport and others from the Reservation. And we will need a control group as well."

Hoenveld nodded. "The cause could be environmental. By adopting Fuzzies and bringing them into the city we could be causing more harm than we tried to prevent. For testing we should initially use Fuzzies that already have healthy offspring," He added, "If we accidently sterilize any of them, I don't want it to be a childless couple."

"How will we get the informed consent?" Lars asked. "From what I understand, if you tell a Fuzzy you want to make some tests, they will ask if it is good to eat."

"I can see you don't have a Fuzzy of your own," Juan observed. "Fuzzies are smart. Scary smart in some ways. After three years of living with Big Ones, Fuzzies have learned a lot, especially about medical tests. We have put them through enough examinations that some of them know the routine by heart. And one thing a Fuzzy *really* knows well, is whether they can make babies or not. That was a big problem before they joined up with us. Anything that can help protect their ability to reproduce will bring a swarm of volunteers. The risks involved might scare some off, but the smarter ones will stick around to help."

"Oh. Well, okay. As long as there are no objections, I'm in."

Hoenveld scratched his chin thoughtfully. "I think the real hurdle will be getting this past Jack Holloway."

Juan mentally slapped his forehead. Hoenveld was right, and it would be Juan's job to discuss the matter with him. The Fuzzies would be subjected to a series of tests, many of which would be invasive, and some potentially harmful, though Juan would work to keep the risks minimal. While he didn't seriously believe Jack would shoot him for suggesting such a thing, he made a mental note to update his will—just in case.

"By the way, where is the funding for all of this coming from?" Hoenveld asked. "I understand the new CFO, Morgan Holloway, put a stop to the Company's expenditures of this nature."

Juan nodded. "True, but only because the Fuzzies can afford to pay for it themselves from the Yellowsand sunstone mine payments."

*   *   *

"No way!"

"Yup! Saw it myself."

Betty fell backwards on the cushions laughing. "I...can't believe it! John Morgan Holloway the Lesser, Freyan nobleman and richest man on Zarathustra...changing diapers!"

"Not only that, but he was terrible at it," Akira laughed. "It took him three tries the first time he did it."

"Ha! I could have taught him a thing or two. I had a younger brother and two sisters to practice on." Betty giggled for a moment then sobered. "I wonder if I will ever have any of my own."

"Have you and Jack gotten that far...um...I mean, has he...?"

"We haven't discussed anything like marriage, yet. After what happened with his first wife, I think he may be a bit gun-shy." Betty sighed. "I don't know about his biological clock, but mine is definitely ticking away."

"Do men even have biological clocks?" Akira wondered. "Well, Jack does already have a son and may not feel the need for more. Especially with all of his Fuzzies around."

"Oh, I know. And if we had a child he or she wouldn't be an adult until Jack was in his eleventh decade. He may not even feel up to the rigors of child rearing at his age."

Akira rolled her eyes. "This isn't pre-atomic Terra, Betty. Jack could live to 140, assuming he avoids another duel with Morgan. Seventy is the new thirty, as they used to say."

"Oh, I know that, too. And while he was in the hospital Morgan had Jack 'overhauled,' as he calls it. Jack says he hasn't felt this good since he was in his actual thirties."

Akira giggled. "I think you have more to do with that than any medical procedure. Look, if Jack isn't willing to make the leap, then move on and find somebody else. Or just have an insemination and go it alone."

Betty sighed again. "Three guesses who I would want for the donor."

Akira got up and poured another glass of wine at the bar for Betty and Freyan ale for herself. "As long as it isn't Morgan, go for it."

Betty accepted the glass and wrinkled her nose. "Do you actually like that stuff?"

"The ale? It's growing on me. Heidi insists that I drink it to help lactation. I checked it out on the datastream. They used to do that on Terra back in pre-atomic and the early part of 1st Century AE. Lynne Andrews said it should be safe enough as long as I don't overdo it or drink any too close to John's feeding time. Now, what are you going to do about Jack?"

Betty thought for a moment. "Jack isn't the kind of man you can push into something he isn't ready for. Ha! You should have seen his face the first time he woke up next to me. I pretended to still be asleep and almost hurt myself trying to keep from laughing."

"Wasn't he under the influence of a drug interaction?"

"Under the influence or not, he knew his way around the landscape." Betty winked.

"Oh, eww! That's my father-in-law you are talking about. I don't need that kind of mental image dancing in my head the next time I am with Morgan." Akira took a long drink of her ale. "Are you using contraception blockers?"

"No, I stopped that a few months ago. And no, I don't intend to trap Jack with a pregnancy. If he doesn't put a ring on my finger, then I hope to have that child I want. I am starting to wonder if Jack can come through on that, though."

Akira rolled her eyes. "Again, eww! And Jack might be taking blockers, too."

"Oh, I hadn't thought of that. He is probably old-fashioned enough to want to be married first, assuming he wants children at all."

Akira nodded. "Look, you and Jack need to have a long talk about where you two are headed. It might be he isn't sure you want to settle down with a man his age. Don't pussyfoot around. Tell him where you stand. I think he will respect that if nothing else."

Betty looked thoughtful. Akira did have a point. "What about Morgan?"

"Betty, Morgan has no say in Jack's personal life. Ghu, there's the mental image I was hoping to avoid. Anyway, I am sure he would welcome a younger brother or sister. You just worry about you and Jack. I'll take care of Morgan."

XIV

The flight over to Mallorysport took roughly three hours by contragravity aircar. When approaching any town or city of any significance, it was necessary to slow down to subsonic speeds in order to prevent damage to glass and hearing from sonic booms. Otherwise, the trip would take half an hour less.

Most of the Fuzzies, Mike, Mitzi, Ko-Ko and Cinderella, watched as the ocean turned into land through the portals. Little Fuzzy, Mama Fuzzy and Baby Fuzzy wrestled with the new notion that Auntie Pat tried to explain to them.

"Not unnastan.' What is sister? What is brother?" Little Fuzzy tried to grasp the concept with little success.

Patricia turned to the aircar pilot. "Jack, can you help me out with this?"

"You opened this can of worms, I should let you try to stuff them back in," Jack said, with a laugh. "Part of the problem is that for a very long time, Fuzzies had a low birthrate. What successful births they had often ended badly. Stillbirths, malformed fetuses, high mortality rate...it was rare for any pair of Fuzzies to have even one viable offspring. I have never heard of a second successful birth by the same parents until about eighteen months ago, thanks to the Extee Three. So the concept of a sibling hasn't had the chance to take hold for them, yet. And don't even try to explain the idea of cousins."

Patricia was horrified and her face showed it. Being second of ten children in her family, and the mother of four, the idea of growing up without a lot of siblings bordered on being an alien concept. "But you said that Victor Grego's scientists found a cure for that condition almost three years ago."

"Not a cure, a treatment," Jack countered. "And there have been a lot more births since then. In fact, I think Mitzi might be with child. While we're in Mallorysport, I plan on having Lynne Andrews give her a look-see. But I haven't heard of any other Fuzzies working on a second child, yet."

"Do they have mating seasons?"

Jack laughed again. "Only if every other hour counts as a season. Fuzzies go at it like rabbits. Ben Rainsford thinks it is in response to the low viable birth rate before finding us Big Ones."

"Then why aren't they building bigger families?"

That was a damn good question. Jack thought it over for a moment. "I'll speak with Ben and Gerd. It might be that the reproductive urge shuts down for a while until the offspring grow enough to not need constant supervision. And, frankly, they have only been treated for the NFMp for the last three years or so. Maybe the family situation will take care of itself over time."

This time Patricia laughed. "Lucky for us that shutting down the reproductive urge isn't a human trait, or you and I wouldn't be here." She turned back to Little Fuzzy, Mama and Baby. "Hokay, you,"—she playfully poked Baby Fuzzy in the belly—"are baby to Mama Fuzzy, yes?"

Baby Fuzzy nodded.

"Good. If Mama Fuzzy has another baby, it would be your sister if a girl, or your brother if a boy. Jack, please tell me they know the difference between girl and boy."

"As well as you or I."

"Mama Fuzzy not have another baby," Baby Fuzzy declared. "That not-so thing."

"Is not-so thing like Little Fuzzee say Pappy Vic give him sunstone?" Little Fuzzy asked.

Jack shook his head. "Is different not-so thing. Not a lie..." Jack struggled to come up with a comparison and floundered.

Patricia was about to try to explain the concept of using imagination when she decided to try another tack. "Pappy Jack and Auntie Pat have the same mama and papa. So, I am Pappy Jack's sister, and Pappy Jack is my brother."

Little Fuzzy and Mama Fuzzy continued to wrestle with the concept, but Baby Fuzzy brightened up. "Like birds have many eggs an' become more birds. They all brother an' sister. Is so?"

"Very good, Baby Fuzzy!" Patricia turned to Jack while Baby explained the concept to Little Fuzzy and the other Fuzzies. In a whisper, she asked, "Does Baby Fuzzy belong to Little Fuzzy?"

"You mean is he Baby's father?"

"Right."

Jack shook his head. "Little Fuzzy was the wise-one of his tribe and took care of Mama and Baby Fuzzy. Something bad must have happened to Baby's father. Fuzzies don't dwell on bad news. Before they ran into us, the southern Fuzzies were in a heap of bad trouble. Birthrate dropping, population declining, they were headed straight for extinction. To cope, they learned to accept death as a daily occurrence.

"Nor are Fuzzies typically monogamous, although they are before and after childbirth. The father and mother usually stay together until the child can fend for itself, then they go their separate ways. However, this observation may be due to the crisis state the southern Fuzzies found themselves when we discovered them. I should probably get Gerd or Piet to do a study of the northern Fuzzies to verify this conclusion."

Patricia noticed that Baby Fuzzy was trying to listen in. She raised her voice, "Baby seems to speak Lingua Terra better than the other Fuzzies I have heard."

"Baby came to live with me at a much younger age and was able to learn the language better than an adult. You know how it is; a child can duplicate almost any sound he hears while an adult can only make the sounds he learned as a child."

"Like second-generation immigrants who grow up speaking the local tongue better than their parents." Patricia looked at Baby again.

"Exactly," Jack nodded. "I would bet my largest sunstone that the next generation will be able to speak Lingua Terra like Terran natives. They might even start getting nine to five jobs like the rest of us."

Patricia couldn't decide if Jack was joking, then wondered why somebody like Baby Fuzzy couldn't do exactly that, once he was grown and properly educated. "Do the young Fuzzies attend school with the human children?"

"Not yet, but we are getting there. The concern is that human children might bully the Fuzzies. Humans do enough of that to each other as it is."

Jack adjusted his flight path as Mallorysport appeared on the horizon. "We're almost there, Pat. Get ready to meet the most powerful man, outside of the Charterless Zarathustra Company, on the planet. But, first we'll drop by the adoption bureau. Ruth told me that lately they have been having some problems."

*   *   *

The Mallorysport Fuzzy Adoption Bureau had a line going out the door and down the block. The vibrant clothing and lack of visible weapons declared that almost every person in the line came from off-world. Every one of them reeked of wealth and affluence and entitlement. One of them in the crowd spotted Jack, Patricia and the Fuzzies.

"Look! It's Commissioner Holloway with some Fuzzies," one woman with silver hair and an extra fifty pounds shouted. The line broke up in the immediate area and swarmed around them.

"Commissioner, are these some of the Fuzzies up for adoption?"

"How soon can I get a Fuzzy?"

"How much is the application processing fee?"

"Will it take long to get a Fuzzy?"

"Do we get to choose our Fuzzy or is there some sort of lottery?"

Jack was starting to feel cornered until one man stepped on Koko's foot. Koko let out a yeek, probably something profane he had learned from the Big Ones back on the Rez, and moved his chopper-digger into a defensive position.

Jack's reaction was very similar to Koko's, with one exception; having no chopper-digger in hand, he sent a vicious punch into the face of the offending foot's owner. The man didn't fall back due to the press of people pushing him up, allowing Jack to get in another shot at him.

"Hey, he attacked that man!"

"Grab him and hold him for the police!"

The mob lurched forward. Jack, surrounded by uncountable people couldn't get to his gun. His own shock was just as great as everybody else's when a gun fired right next to his ear. Panicked, most of the mob backed away.

Jack looked about for the source of the gunshot and saw Patricia holding her .38 Special high in the air. She lowered it and aimed it pointedly at the crowd.

"The next Khooghra to lay a finger on my brother will end up with more holes than Freyan cheese," Patricia shouted.

She turned to the man who stepped on Koko, "As for you, I hope when you get home your mother runs out from under the porch and bites you in the leg!"

Three men in uniforms, one MPD and two ZNPF, pushed their way through the crowd.

"Commissioner, come with us and we'll get you inside."

The tourist with the flattened nose, cried out. "Arrest that man!"

Helmut put his hand up. "How would you like to spend the night in jail, Mister? There are laws against hurting Fuzzies."

The man quickly disappeared into the crowd.

"Thank you, Ahmed," Jack said. "The woman with the gun is with me. What you probably heard was her warning shot."

"Ma'am, you can put that gun away. If anybody needs shooting, we'll handle it."

"Yes, Officer." Patricia returned her pistol to the purse, then scooped up Koko. "This one was assaulted by that man there. The one with the bloody nose."

"Understood. Helmut, would you do the honors?"

Officer Helmut smiled. "My pleasure." He turned to Patricia. "He's gone now and I don't believe he'll be coming back. I never heard anybody called a son-of-a-bitch so poetically. My respects, ma'am."

"You should hear me when I am really mad," Patricia said.

"No, he shouldn't," Jack said.

Jack, Patricia and the Fuzzies were quickly, though respectfully, escorted through a side door that required a security card. As they entered Jack recalled hearing about Helmut before. "Shouldn't you be back on Beta by now?"

"I would have been, but when I saw this mob outside the Adoption Bureau I called the Chief and asked if I could help out here."

"Good thinking," Jack said nodding. "In fact maybe we should have Piet send a few more...and maybe a tank and some Marines."

Inside the building, Jack made a beeline for the office. There he found Claudette Pendarvis and Ruth Van Riebeek talking at Claudette's desk and little Shari asleep in a crib.

"Jack, thank Ghu you are here," Ruth said. "No doubt you saw that mess outside."

"Saw it? I was in it until I was rescued by Ahmed, Helmut and that local cop...I didn't catch his name...?"

"Jacob Marley," Ahmed Khadra supplied.

"You have got to be kidding," Patricia said. "Like from the Dickens book?"

Khadra shrugged. "It's a big galaxy, there were bound to be a few out there walking and breathing. In my time I have met three Mohammed Alis, two William Batsons and even a Bruce Wayne."

Jack chuckled. "There are over a trillion people out there. We can't all have unique names." He sobered and turned back to Ruth. After a quick introduction he asked, "What's the story with those people lined up outside?"

"Those are just some of the off-worlders who want a Fuzzy to take back with them," Mrs. Pendarvis said. She tapped a stack of papers. "These are the applications we have received so far. Most of them just want one Fuzzy, occasionally two, to take back home to whatever planet they hail from to show off to their friends."

"Fuzzies are becoming a status symbol for the über-rich," Ruth added. "Something to rub their rivals noses in."

"We don't even know if a Fuzzy can adapt to life on a different planet," Jack almost growled. Adrenaline was still working his metabolism on overtime after the confrontation outside. He was about to say something when a large red-faced man in tourist garb pushed his way into the office chased by two more ZNPF officers.

"What is going on?" the man demanded in a loud stentorian voice. "I've come a long way to get to this backward planet. Why hasn't anybody let me adopt a Fuzzy, yet? I'm a busy man; I don't have time for this nonsense!"

"I'm sorry, Commissioner," said one of the officers. Jack recognized him as Dakota Brown. "He just forced his way past us."

Jack quickly sized-up the man; five foot eight, a good three hundred pounds, all muscle. *Must be from Magni*, he thought. Dakota and Bart would have to shoot him to slow him down. "Mister, I advise that you go back outside and wait in line like everybody else."

"To Niflheim with that. Do you have any idea who I am?"

"Not a clue, nor do I care," Jack said, trying to keep a lid on his temper. "Helmut, would you say this man has committed a crime by forcing his way in here like this?"

"Ah, trespassing at the very least. Maybe assault since he forced his way past 'Kota and Bart, here."

"Ahmed, what is the law concerning good Samaritans who act to prevent a crime in progress?"

"No legal action may be taken against anybody acting to prevent a crime," Khadra quoted.

"Good. Then if I shoot this idiot, I am in the clear?"

"Yup."

"Works for me," Helmut added.

"Aim for the forehead," Ahmed put in.

Jack drew his pistol and pointed directly at the man's face. "Now, I will give you just one chance, and one chance only, to leave. You have until the count of five. One...four..."

The man quickly spun about and rushed out of the office, followed by Dakota and Bart.

"Jack, I can't believe you did that," Patricia said.

"What? Pa always said the direct approach works best."

"No," Patricia said. "That you didn't let me threaten him. I am better at it."

Jack smiled. "True. Next time. Ruth, we are closing the Fuzzy Adoption Bureau until further notice. No Fuzzies will be given to any person or persons who intend to take them off-world until we have scientific proof that doing so will not harm them."

"At the very least, taking a Fuzzy away to a place where there will be no other Fuzzies would be very damaging to them psychologically," Ruth explained.

"Good point," Jack nodded. "Keep that one in your holster and draw it as needed. I'm headed to see Ben next. He'll have a thing or two to say about all this."

XV

Governor Rainsford flicked off his viewscreen and poured himself another coffee. He glanced at the wall clock and saw it was 10:00 a.m. Z-Time. For the colonial governor that was the equivalent of lunch time as he had been in the office since six. He had to do something about his schedule. Flora and Fauna never complained, but it was getting pretty clear that they missed spending more time with Pappy Ben.

Gus Brannhard, Max Fane and even Victor Grego had been pushing him to put more responsibility onto Deputy Colonial Governor Juan Takagashi. Takagashi had run against Ben in the last election, which he had actually expected to lose and be rid of the headaches of being in charge of an entire planet. Privately, Ben admitted to himself that he liked the job and the paycheck that came with it, although he would gladly step down if that was the best thing for Zarathustra and, especially, the Fuzzies.

He had taken Takagashi on as his deputy once he was certain that his own position was secure and the Legislature would accept him. Now, Gus, Max, Victor and even Jack were telling him to put the deputy to better use.

"Fine," Ben grumbled to himself. He buzzed for his secretary and told her to send for Takagashi. The deputy governor appeared so quickly that Ben suspected he had been in the outer office waiting for his call. "Did you find the secret to instantaneous spatial transposition, Juan?"

"No, just the quirk of good timing, Governor," Takagashi said with a smile. He had a good smile; the kind that looked good on the viewscreen or a billboard. Ben still couldn't understand how he had beat him in the last election.

"Okay, Juan, I know why I called for you, but what did you want?"

"Ah, I prefer that you go first, Governor."

Ben mentally sighed. "When it is just the two of us, call me Ben. Please. I am 'governored' to death all day. As my second in command, you can use my first name. That sort of thing seems to work for the CZC. Or would you rather I call you 'Deputy' all day?"

"Okay, Ben," Takagashi said with a grin. "You win. Now what did you want to see me about?"

He thought over what to say and how to say it, then just settled on speaking plain. "I would like for you to take on more responsibilities. Some of my responsibilities to be precise."

A look of surprise covered Takagashi's face. Then he broke out in a loud hearty laugh. Ben started to wonder if his deputy governor had taken leave of his senses.

"Gov...Ben, I was coming up to speak with you about exactly that," Takagashi said, when he recovered his composure. "Since you added me to your cabinet, I have been little more than a tourist attraction...and Zarathustra doesn't get much by way of tourism, yet. I officiated the re-opening of the Fuzzy Museum after the *Jin-f'ke* wing was added, cut the ribbon at the opening of that new aircar dealership opening, something the more civilized worlds stopped doing a century or so ago, by the way. I shook a lot of hands and kissed a lot of babies, so to speak, and only handled such paperwork that was too small of importance to be brought to you. That is not what I signed up for."

Ben nodded. "I...you have my apologies, Juan. I have been at this job for three years now, and I still don't believe I have gotten the hang of it."

Takagashi waved that off. "Actually, your background is a point in your favor, Ben. Most career politicians become either jaded or corrupt after a while. Do you recall what I did before coming to Zarathustra?"

Rainsford nodded. When Takagashi ran against him in the last election, Gus Brannhard did a thorough background check on him. It was extensive and impressive.

"You graduated summa cum laude with a degree in law from New Harvard in Australia back on Terra. You traveled to Odin and opened up a legal firm there. You were rather successful until you were selected for the governor's cabinet. You served under Governor Kirby until his stroke, then under Governor Martin until his impeachment and subsequent imprisonment. You then went to Thor and opened another law firm, which failed to thrive. Finally, you immigrated to Zarathustra and opened another firm, this one somewhat more successful."

Takagashi nodded. "The Marshal does good work."

Ben decided not to correct his Deputy.

"Governor Kirby was a decent man and a competent leader. Martin was as corrupt as they come. One thing they had in common, though, is that they knew how to delegate. Kirby had his fatal stroke while hunting, enjoying himself, not hunched over his desk doing work that should have been done by a clerk on his staff."

"Okay, Juan. Clearly you have more experience with government than I, and know the workings. What say we hunker down and work out something we can both live with?"

"Agreed," Takagashi nodded. "And the first thing you need to do is take a vacation."

Ben's eyes widened in surprise. "What? With the problems facing this world and the Fuzzies?"

"In your position there is no such thing as a good time to take a break. There will always be a crisis of some kind to deal with. You have not had a vacation since you took the governorship. That's three years' worth of headaches, high blood pressure and damned little sleep."

Rainsford shook his head. "Back in 1st Century AE there was an American president who took vacations right and left at taxpayer expense. I do not want to get his kind of a reputation."

Takagashi looked to the ceiling as if seeking help from a deity. "Would you rather be known as the governor who worked himself into an early grave? Let's just go over everything you heaped onto your plate, delegate where possible and set policy for the rest. Then, you take a break and let me have the headaches for a couple weeks. If it gets to be too much, I'll call 'uncle' and you can come bail me out. And besides, we don't have taxpayers on this planet, remember?"

Ben chuckled at that, then sobered. "Did you hear about the off-world FBCI agent that came in here earlier?" Takagashi admitted he had not and Ben brought him up to speed. "I would like for you to cooperate and allow him to question you under veridication. Max and I have already had a turn in the hot seat so I am not asking you to do anything I haven't done."

Takagashi rolled his eyes. "Ben, do you have any idea what kind of precedent you have set?" He drew a deep breath and let it out slowly. "I can't believe Gus let you do that."

"Gus wasn't here so I had Ned Foster sit in on the interrogation." Ben leaned forward and put a hand on Takagashi's shoulder. "Juan, I know this is a lot to ask, but we need to get ourselves clear on this. To protect the Fuzzies."

Takagashi grunted. "Fine, but we keep this all on the QT. Your friend...Trask, was it?...has to agree to keep even the fact of the interrogation strictly confidential. If this gets out to the news services we will both be in for a bad time."

Within thirty minutes Ben and Takagashi had worked out a more realistic workload for the governor. Several items were delegated and the actual work divided between the two men, effective upon Ben's return from his vacation. They were just wrapping up when Ben's secretary buzzed in to inform him Jack Holloway and guests had arrived.

"Send them in." Ben straightened his neck cloth while Takagashi took a different seat off to the side of the great desk.

"Hi, Jack. Ma'am."

"Ben, this is my sister, Patricia McLeod," Jack said. "You would have met last night if you had made it to the naming ceremony."

"The duties of state, Jack. Mrs. McLeod, it is an honor. Jack, you know Juan Takagashi, don't you?"

Jack shook his head.

Takagashi stood and offered his hand, which Jack accepted. "Sir, Ma'am. I have been working with the governor to open up his schedule a bit. Maybe he won't miss as many special occasions in the future."

"You pull that off, you'll have my vote when Ben decides to step down," Jack said with a smile.

"It is a pleasure to meet you both," Patricia said. "And call me Pat."

"Then you will have to call me Ben."

"And me Juan."

"Oh, you must be from South America back on Terra. Juan is the most common name from there," Patricia observed.

"Australia, actually. But my mother was from Brazil. We have quite a few Juans here on Zarathustra, too. In fact the head of the CZC Science Division is another Juan," Takagashi said with a smile.

"Oh, yes, I met him last night."

"Juan, could you entertain Pat a few minutes while I speak with Jack in private?" Ben pulled Jack out to the terrace before Takagashi could reply. Outside, Ben quickly told Jack about Trask, the Fuzzy slavery on Terra and, as an afterthought, about his vacation.

"You are going on vacation now?" Jack couldn't believe his ears.

"Yes, to be free to work with you and Trask to bring down the slavers," he answered earnestly. "I'll be more useful out from behind that damned desk and out in the field with the rest of you. Besides, Juan has more experience working in a governor's office than I do. Now, we need to get you and Victor cleared so Trask can concentrate on whoever is really poaching Fuzzies. You in?"

Jack paused to fill and light up his pipe. He didn't like being questioned under veridication anymore than anybody else. Not having anything to hide was beside the point. Still…. "Yeah. I'm in, and so is anybody on the Zarathustra Native Protection Force who wants to keep their jobs." Jack pulled out his pipe and began to fill it with tobacco. "Now I have another headache for you; these damned tourists wanting to adopt Fuzzies."

"The Fuzzy Adoption League is what Gus calls them," Ben said. "Yes, he told me about them. However you want to handle that mess, you will have my support. Personally, I am against letting Fuzzies be taken off-world, but we did allow the precedent for that with Leslie Coombes' Fuzzies three years ago. I fear that in the confusion of those times a few more might have left Zarathustra with tourists."

Jack groaned inwardly. "Yes, I was against that then—and still am. I'll admit that CZC Home Office and the rest of the crowd back on Terra needed to see some live Fuzzies up close, but I am still concerned about long-term effects they might have from that visit; pathogens, residual pollution, radiation hot spots, even just being surrounded by giants and having no place to escape to if they were threatened...physically and psychologically. Coombes took a very big risk. Well, I think it is past time to start a long-term study on the environmental effects of alien worlds on a Fuzzy."

Ben thought it over. "It sounds like a good idea, and we can put a moratorium on Fuzzy adoptions. It will allow us to keep the Fuzzy Adoption League at bay for the time being. How do we study those effects?"

Jack had been giving that some thought since leaving the Fuzzy Adoption Bureau. "Juan Jimenez has a bunch of artificial environments called biomes that can be used to simulate almost any planetary conditions. We'll ask for some Fuzzies to volunteer to be the guinea pigs with the understanding that they can be released from any study they don't like. When they do, we list the environment as hostile to Fuzzies, and any world matching those conditions will be Fuzzy *verboten* territory. Yggdrasil is automatically out since the Fuzzies couldn't survive on anything they ate in the wild there."

"Nor would they want to. The food there! Biomes...hmm. I like it. I will ask Juan Takagashi to make the funding available. I don't see too much resistance for this plan coming from the Legislature, either."

Jack snorted smoke from his nose and almost choked. "Gak...Ben, saying things like that just proves how little you know about politics. There is always somebody willing to fight any cause for no better reason than to get his picture on the news services or the datastream."

XVI

Piet was just thinking about lunch when the communication screen beeped. *This job makes it pretty easy for me to keep the weight down,* he thought with some amusement. He flipped on the screen to find his boss staring back at him.

"Commissioner! Calling for an update?"

Jack smiled. "Piet, you can call me Jack like everybody else, you know."

"Familiarity breeds disrespect," Piet quoted a line from the Army officer's manual. "I am afraid there hasn't been anything new on the Fuzzy slaver case. I have people going over every square meter of the Reservation, but nothing has turned up yet."

"Keep me apprised of any changes on that. What I called about is to give you a heads-up that the CZC Science Center will be looking for some Fuzzy volunteers for some medical checks. Nothing too dangerous, mind you. We are just trying to get the jump on the next disaster."

Piet's brow furrowed. "What kind of disaster?"

Jack explained about the sterile Fuzzies and Hoenveld's concerns.

"Kind of jerking the trigger, aren't they? I am no medical expert, but something like that happens to Terran-type humans all the time. Maybe this Zorro is just past his reproductive age?"

Jack admitted he had not thought of that, but doubted it would be the case. "We really have no way of knowing the age of a Fuzzy when they come in from the wild since they don't track years the way we do, but I doubt they get the chance to get old enough to suffer from geriatric sterility. It is a hostile world for a Fuzzy out there and only the young and strong survive in it. And three out of thirty is a pretty high percentage. That suggests something else is happening and we should try to get ahead of it. Mention your idea to Juan Jimenez when he comes out, though. It might be relevant."

"Okay, Boss. Anything else?"

Jack turned away from the screen for a moment, then turned back. "It seems that Little Fuzzy needs to speak with Maid Marian about something. Can you get her in?"

Piet laughed. "Yeah, she should be easy to find. More likely, she'll be at the archery range practicing. When she isn't hunting, eating, sleeping or um...socializing...that's where she spends her time. I'll send a man out to fetch her."

Piet pressed the call button. "Mike is on the way now. Should I call you back?"

"No need. Just keep the connection open and fill me in on anything I missed while I was out. Oh, I almost forgot; Marshal Fane is sending out a veridicator on loan. He will also be sending a technician to set it up and test it. I will be back in time to try it out on some of the men. I'll fill you in on more details when I get there."

A veridicator? Not just a portable model but the deluxe edition? Something is up and the Commissioner is being cagey. "Sure thing, Commissioner. I have wanted one for a while."

*   *   *

Businessmen on colony worlds have been said to be a breed apart. Unlike the office dwellers on Terra who grow old and die of boredom on golf courses, these were men who worked the nine to five grind in the larger settlements, then headed out to the open country at every opportunity. To suit this lifestyle, many of the more successful men and women maintained an apartment or home within the city limits to facilitate easy access to the businesses they worked at or owned, and then another dwelling out in the country where they could pursue other interests more to their liking. Since Terra no longer provided any kind of decent countryside, they migrated to the various worlds not yet bogged down by too many members of species *Homo sapiens terra*.

In many ways Morgan Holloway identified with such people. He preferred to be away from the big city, though small villages appealed to him as they reminded him of his holdings on Freya. For this reason, he maintained a penthouse suite in Mallorysport in addition to his castle-like home on Beta Continent. While Akira recovered, Morgan elected to take time away from his business dealings and spend time with his growing family.

Having no use for the penthouse while away from Mallorysport, he offered it to Jack whenever he was in the city. Jack appreciated the offer, while worrying about getting Fuzzy hair all over the place. It was in the penthouse that Juan Jimenez located the Commissioner of Native Affairs.

Jack filled Juan in on the latest developments with the Fuzzy Adoption League and their worries about Fuzzies taken off Zarathustra to live on other worlds, as well as the moratorium on Fuzzy adoptions. "…just do what you need to, Juan. Within reason, of course."

"Thanks, Jack," Juan Jimenez said with some relief. "I will keep you in the loop."

The two men made their goodbyes and Jack shut off the screen. Patricia looked up from her breakfast at the dining table. The Fuzzies sat around a second table scaled down to their size.

"First the slavers and now this," Jack grumbled.

"Your friend wants to do some medical tests on the Fuzzies?" she asked.

"Some of the Fuzzies here in Mallorysport came up sterile and he is worried it might have something to do with their association with us," Jack explained as he took a seat at the table. The plate holding his breakfast rested on a self-heating panel on the table.

"Didn't you say there was a problem with that a couple of years ago? I thought your friend Victor solved that," Patricia said as she studied the river pig bacon. The home fries and eggs were made from Terran introduced potatoes and chickens, but the bacon looked flat-out wrong to her.

"Dr. Hoenveld discovered the treatment," Jack corrected his sister. "Victor found a way to efficiently produce it in quantity. You really should try that bacon. It's made from river pig and tastes better than the Terran variety, believe it or not. It is also leaner and higher in protein."

"But it's yellow!" Patricia took a small bite, then ate the entire strip. "Not bad. Why don't you export this to Terra like you do with the veldbeest meat?"

"I think it is because river pigs haven't been successfully domesticated, yet. They don't breed in captivity and gain weight very quickly. The fat changes the taste in a very bad way. What we are eating right now had to have been hunted down in the wild in the last week or so."

"Hmm. What does a river pig look like?"

"Like a cross between a wild boar and a hippopotamus, about the size of a large St. Bernard."

"This *is* a lot leaner than the bacon back on Terra," Patricia said as she examined another strip. "If the Fuzzies were already treated for their reproductive problems—"

"This is something new," Jack interrupted. He moved his food around on the plate with his fork then set it down on the table.

"Are you worried about the Fuzzies?"

"Well, yes. Although a few cases of sterility in otherwise healthy Fuzzies is a long ride from potential species extinction. I think Juan may be overreacting a bit."

Patricia stared at Jack for a moment then put her own fork down. "Jack, you can get away with that whole stoic, unworried act with a lot of people, but not me. You're hoping your friend is overreacting. You really do care about these Fuzzies, don't you? I never saw you this worried about anybody or anything since Pa died over forty years ago. Well, except for Adonitia. I think that is when you really closed yourself off from the universe. Until now. Or rather three years ago when you found Little Fuzzy in your shower."

Jack started to say something but Patricia put up her hand for silence.

"Jack, you treat these Fuzzies like they are your own precious babes. Don't worry, that is a good thing. And it is okay to be concerned. From what you told me in your letters, these little guys were on the brink of extinction when you first met them. A new threat to their existence, no matter how seemingly minor, should be investigated and dealt with. And a ten percent sterility rate in the tested group is by no means minor!

Remember what German measles did to the Freyans and everybody thought that was a minor disease until people started dying from it."

They both sat quietly for several seconds, then Jack chuckled softly. "Pat, you and Lee were always the smart ones in the family. Yes, I guess I did shut myself off from the universe after Morgan's mother died. She was really something. You would have liked her. After she passed, I hurt worse than I thought possible. I never wanted to feel like that again, so I buried myself in work. I jumped from planet to planet taking jobs so dangerous most people wouldn't touch them. I told myself I was just a thrill seeker, but maybe I was purposely putting myself in harm's way. Finally, I just became tired of it all and decided to retire on a barely known backwater colony planet. I found a bit of peace here, carved out a comfortable niche for myself and started marking time.

"Then I met Little Fuzzy. It was like I started breathing again. At first I just thought he was a clever animal, like a Freyan kholph. Then his sapience was proven, in a court of law, no less, and it was like having a family again. Hell, he is family. And when something threatens your family, you do everything you can to protect them. Thanks, Pat. I couldn't talk about this to anybody around here, except maybe Betty and I doubt she would understand."

"Now don't you go underestimating Betty. She's all but roped and branded you."

Jack just shook his head in bemusement.

At the smaller table Little Fuzzy had listened to everything Pappy Jack had said. Moreover, he understood it.

* * *

Commodore Napier was bored. This was a common condition among military personnel of his rank and position, and the leading cause of retirement among his peers. Back when he first joined the Terran Federation Space Navy as a candidate in the Officers Training Academy in Pretoria, he rarely had the time to get bored. Training, combat, more training, transfer to the next assignment. Training kept his mind and body active. Combat, as any war veteran knew, was ninety-eight percent boredom, while waiting for the enemy to try something, and two percent terror, where the body fought for survival on trained reflexes and adrenalin. But that was a different kind of boredom, the kind a man could even look forward to during a skirmish.

After his field commission to second lieutenant, Napier was kept busy getting and giving orders. There was always one more hill to take, and take them he did, though not without losses along the way. He still remembered the names and faces of every man and woman who had ever died under his command.

When he was given command of Xerxes base he expected things to be quiet, yet still be interesting. Spying on the Chartered Zarathustra Company and the intrigues that went with it carried its own challenges. Then the Fuzzies were discovered and things really started popping. The CZC lost its charter for a Class III uninhabited world while he lost his two best operatives, Ruth Ortheris and Henry Stensen. Ruth retired from the service and married Gerd van Riebeek while Henry Stensen simply devoted more time to his cover job as a craftsman. Both lost their effectiveness as covert operatives after Ruth testified in open court and Victor Grego found the bugs Stensen planted in places where only he had had access.

A subject who knows he is being spied on, and by whom, is almost impossible to gather information on.

After the Fuzzy Trial, as the locals referred to it, things settled down, at least where the Terran Federation Space Navy was concerned. The Fuzzy Sunstone caper, Little Fuzzy getting lost at Yellowstone, Gus Brannhard's abduction and even Hugo Ingermann's bid to take over the colonial government all fell outside of his jurisdiction. At least the so-called Fuzzy rocket made things interesting. The rocket was still stored on Xerxes awaiting military transport off-world to a secure facility.

For the last several months things had been quiet and dull. Base commanders, while shouldering the responsibilities of those under their command, have very little to occupy themselves as a rule. Most of the paperwork is handled by subordinates, as are the personnel themselves. The sergeants and petty-officers did all of the real work while the officers set policy and shuffled papers. As the commodore, Napier rarely ever saw the men outside of inspections and parades. Officers and enlisted men were not supposed to fraternize. There were minor exceptions, but only in the lower officer ranks where they had to deal with the men on a daily basis, and even then they walked a thin tight line.

Napier considered calling a staff meeting, but everything that needed to be covered had been addressed at the last meeting a week earlier. It wouldn't do to invent an excuse to bring the senior officers together just because he felt bored.

"Great Ghu, I almost wish somebody would start a war!" Napier reached for a cigar, a special stogie designed to use very little oxygen and produce even less smoke, important modifications on a base situated on an airless moon. Before he could light it, his communication screen beeped. Napier dropped the cigar and toggled the screen controls.

"Yes?"

The Marine sergeant in the outer office came on the screen. "Sir! Colonial Governor Bennett Rainsford on line one. Sir!"

If I am lucky, he thought, *Rainsford just wants to shoot the bull. If I am really lucky, he has a problem for me to fix.* "Put him through, Gunny."

After a quick "Sir, yes, sir," Ben's face filled the screen. The Governor held up his clasped hands and shook them on the screen and Napier responded in kind.

"Governor, what can I do for you?"

"Commodore. I want to let you know that Deputy Governor Juan Takagashi will be assuming my post for the next two weeks."

Commodore Napier smiled. "Finally taking that vacation?"

Ben smiled back. "Now don't you start. There is another matter I need to discuss with you, but I would rather do it in person. I can come up there if you'd like...?"

"I'll be down in three hours, Governor. Should I bring Pancho Ybarra with me?"

Ben looked off-camera for a moment. "Yes, I think that would be a good idea. Will you be bringing your usual security attachment?"

"Regulations. I can't leave base without them."

"Then we will arrange for accommodations for everybody. See you soon, Commodore."

Napier blanked the screen then considered the call. *We?*

XVII

Juan Jimenez stepped out of the transport to find himself surrounded by hundreds of Fuzzies. That was not really unusual as the Fuzzies tended to swarm whenever a visitor came out to the Reservation. Juan smiled as he looked out at the sea of small furry bodies, then his smile melted away. The Fuzzies were not clamoring for attention or yeeking as was normal. Instead, they all looked silently at him with somber faces. Juan became very worried.

One of the Fuzzies stepped forward. Juan vaguely recalled her name was Marian something. "You Unka Juan?"

"Um...yes?"

"You here to make help for Fuzzee? Find why some Fuzzee not have baby?"

Juan was stunned. Somebody had told the Fuzzies why he was coming out. Between the Fuzzies' small size and relatively simple grasp of Lingua Terra it was easy to underestimate their intelligence. Juan reminded himself of what Victor Grego was fond of saying: "No bet on what a Fuzzy couldn't do was safe."

"Yes. That is why I am here. I need some volunteers." *Do Fuzzies know what that word means?* "Humm..."

"You want Fuzzee to make test. Many many Fuzzee."

I couldn't have put it any better. "Yes. If you want to help."

"We go with you," Maid Marian declared.

"What...all of you?" Juan did some quick calculations in his head and determined he could only take about three dozen. "I can't take all of you—"

"Let me know how many you need, Dr. Jimenez. I can arrange for some transports."

Juan spun around to see Piet Dumont walking over. "Deputy Dumont. Nice to meet face-to-face again. I think the last time we did so was when Marshal Fane brought you and some police into Company House looking for Jack's Fuzzies."

"Call me Piet," he said, shaking Juan's hand. "Actually, it was at the wedding reception, but you had downed a few Freyan ales, so the memory lapse can be forgiven. Anyway, I have some off-duty troops that have volunteered to use their own vehicles to help you take as many Fuzzies back to the CZC as you need." Piet pulled a datapad out of a shirt pocket. "I also have the medical records you requested."

"Thank you, Deputy...Piet. Call me Juan."

"Juan—like the Deputy Governor, eh?"

"Yes. But really, we don't need all of these Fuzzies; Science Center can only house so many at a time. I was planning on going through the medical records for the best candidates. Oh, and I have a veridicator for you from Marshal Fane. Since I was coming over anyway Mr. Grego thought it would be more expedient if I played delivery man, too."

"I'll have a few men come out and unload it." Piet didn't detect a trace of petulance in the Science Center Division Chief's voice. Back on Terra he knew petty bureaucrats who would scream bloody murder at the thought of playing courier. "Come inside the office and we'll put the records up on the main viewscreen."

Piet escorted the flustered Juan through the sea of Fuzzies to the main office. "Sorry about that disturbing welcome outside. Little Fuzzy spoke to Maid Marian on the communication screen about your visit and everybody is anxious to help. Having babies is very important to Fuzzies."

Juan took a seat in front of the viewscreen. "Do they even understand what I am hoping to do?"

"They understand enough. Fuzzies are a lot more sophisticated, I have learned, than they were three years ago. I remember Dr. Mallin claiming that a Fuzzy's mentation compared favorably to that of a Terran twelve-year old. Under veridication in open court, no less. Well, as a cop I can tell you that a twelve-year-old can be very smart and even dangerous under the right circumstances. Fuzzies have been around us soaking up all that we can teach them, watching the viewscreen, talking to Big Ones and asking questions. Lots and lots of questions. And don't forget their life before we came along was no picnic. Fuzzies are smart and learn fast. Baby Fuzzy barely has an accent anymore and understands more than the adults fresh from the wild. I would bet in another generation they could work side by side with us Big Ones with as full an understanding of Terran culture as you or I."

Juan mentally kicked himself for not realizing how far the Fuzzies had progressed. Piet was only a cop, but even cops had a basic understanding of psychology and human interaction. More so than the average human, in fact.

"So, the problem won't be getting volunteers…it will be in only taking the ones we need?"

"Bull's-eye," Piet said as he nodded. "Every Fuzzy of mating age wants to have children. Before we came along it was all hit and miss…mostly miss…then we brought in Extee Three and the viable birth rate more than quadrupled. Now there is a reason, admittedly small at this point, for them to worry about not having babies again. So, yeah, Fuzzies want to help."

Juan placed the datapad on an alcove in the viewscreen console and tapped a few buttons. The viewscreen lit up displaying a directory of the medical records on the pad. "You have been reading up on Fuzzies."

"You betcha. This is my job and I like to do it right. Since Jack hired me on to replace Gerd van Riebeek I have been reading everything Gerd and Ruth wrote about the Fuzzies, as well as Dr. Mallin's—even your papers on Fuzzies. By the way, I think you and Mallin could benefit from more field work here at the Rez."

Juan felt a bit chagrined at the suggestion from a layman, but suspected Piet was correct. Lab studies only went so far. "Actually, Gerd was handling that until he accepted the position as head of the Beta Center. Has he been brought into the loop on this?"

"You will have to ask Jack…and maybe your boss," Piet admitted. A thought struck him. "Um…how do you plan to get the…the samples for testing from the Fuzzies?"

"You mean blood draws? Same as you or I. The needles are as close to painless as we can get them..."

"No...the other samples."

Juan turned and noticed that Piet had reddened a bit. "Oh! That. Same way as we did with Zorro. Initially we were going to draw samples with a needle but Dr. Hoenveld, if you can believe it, objected. So I asked Entertainment Division to make up a short film explaining the process. They can do some very realistic stuff with computer graphics. We then showed the film to Zorro, after clearing it with Leslie Coombes and Gus Brannhard to make sure we wouldn't be charged with anything like faginy. Zorro was confused as it seems that Fuzzies do not pleasure themselves as most species do...Dr. Mallin thinks it might be a reaction to the low birthrate...but he performed and produced the necessary sample."

Juan chuckled. "It was the first time I ever saw a Fuzzy look embarrassed."

"Huh." Piet thought it over and realized that Fuzzies weren't prone to the social stigmas that cause embarrassment as a rule. "Well, let's hope we don't start a trend that results in a new reproductive problem."

"Dr. Mallin says that the drive for self-gratification can't be taught. Only the mechanics, and Fuzzies are less inclined than humans to pursue it once learned. He is doing a separate study on the phenomenon in the hopes of publishing a paper on the subject."

"That one I'll leave off my reading list," Piet said as he rolled his eyes.

Juan smiled slightly as he scrolled through the records. A few years ago sexual inhibitions were at a high in Terro-human culture. The pendulum tended to swing to both extremes in fifty- to sixty-year cycles, much like what the history tapes called "The Roaring Twenties" when sexual expression was at a relative high only to be followed by the more repressive 1940s and 50s, then back to the 1960s and 70s. Piet was a product of his times, while the younger generation was already chafing and breaking away from the repressive mores of society at large.

Thorans went through similar transitions, as did the Gimlians. In fact, only Ullerans seemed to stay in a single stage, no doubt due to their hermaphroditic biology which carried its own cultural stigmas. *Maybe one day the Fuzzies will go through the same societal shifts?*

"Will you be giving the Fuzzies the 'Talk?'"

Juan broke out of his reverie at the question. "The Talk?"

Piet chuckled. "Yeah, the 'where do babies come from' talk."

"I dare say Fuzzies know good and damned well where babies come from, Piet."

"They know that Tab A goes into Slot B and makes Product C. Not what goes on inside Slot B that causes Product C. Every Terran twelve-year-old knows how it works. Maybe the Fuzzies should be educated as well?"

Juan uttered a profanity. *What the hell did I get myself into, now?* "I think Dr. Mallin would be better suited to that particular job."

* * *

The first official day of a new job was always a tense time for Cinda. More so since she had been hired right off the street to work in the field she had studied for at the university. After dropping off her Fuzzies at the Kimberly Slone Daycare Center for Fuzzies, she took her aircar, a used model she found through an online listing, to get five coffees and one tea, then she was off for the Hotel Mallory.

Hotels on Zarathustra differed from other large businesses in that instead of aircar ports on the roof or open levels between floors, it had what was called on pre-contragravity Terra, *parking lots*. This was to keep the more sensitive guests from being disturbed by the whine of the contragravity engines coming and going during quiet hours. The more affluent guests could reserve a spot or two close to the hotel entrance.

Cinda set down in one of the two spots reserved by her new employers. The other would be used by Al when he started ferrying the scientists around. Cinda collected up the self-warming thermo-box containing the beverages and her map bag, then headed for the main entrance. On the way in she spotted the plaque that declared this hotel was the first to cater to Fuzzy guests below an engraved representation of several Fuzzies. Presumably, the larger Fuzzy in the forefront was Little Fuzzy. Cinda smiled as she walked through the automatic doors.

Cinda started for the help counter when she spotted her employers filing out of the elevator. Dmitri Watson spotted her, glanced at his wristwatch, then smiled.

"Miss Dawn, I see that punctuality is a virtue not lost on you," Dmitri said. "We were just headed to the hotel cafeteria. Please join us."

"That would be nice, Dr. Watson—"

"Please call me Dmitri. I would rather not have people start with the 'elementary' jokes."

"Elementary?"

"Ah, you are unfamiliar with the works of Sir Arthur Conan Doyle?" Dmitri shook his head. "I am afraid that is a point against both of us, Miss Dawn. I looked it up on the datastream last night and even read a few short stories."

"Call me Cinda, Doc—Dmitri." Cinda recalled reading some of the Sherlock Holmes stories after Al suggested them back when her family first arrived on Zarathustra, but decided to play dumb. It never paid to one-up the boss. "Outside of the Company, we tend to be informal on this world."

"I think that is an excellent idea for us all. No point in being formal out in the field," Greg Rutherford said.

"That works for me," Enrico Garza added. "As the only one here without 'doctor' in front of his name, I won't stand out as the odd duck. Cinda, please feel free to call me Rico."

"I can answer to Hans," Johannes Chang said.

"Bill," William Sokoloski said with a nod.

"Humph. I always hated my given name, but I'll accept Kep, as I was called back in University of Montevideo," Melvin Kepler said with a dour expression.

"Excellent! Now that we have finished with the name game, I am anxious to try out some of the local cuisine," Dmitri said with a flourish. "Cinda, do you have any suggestions?"

"Well, we do have Terran chickens here on Zarathustra, though you can get banjo bird eggs if you want something more exotic. Riverpig sausage and bacon are as good as anything you will find on Terra, and is accepted as kosher when prepared properly. Pool-ball fruit is nice—"

"Pool-ball fruit," Bill interrupted. "That is the fruit that tastes different depending on the color, yes?"

Cinda nodded. "Botanists have been going crazy trying to explain how fruits from a single tree could vary so much in color and flavor. I am partial to the orange ones. Oh, and the breads and pancakes and such are made from Terran introduced wheat, rye and pumpernickel. We have yet to cultivate any native cereal crops for mass production, though the CZC is hopeful with willowgrass from Gamma continent."

As the party moved in the direction of the cafeteria, Rico asked, "What about coffee? Any native brews?"

"Mostly introduced crops. There is a chicory-like plant that some people favor, but that is as close as this planet gets. Which reminds me, I brought this coffee and tea from the café. The Mallory is famous for its food and infamous for its coffee."

The group took seats around a table and tapped on the console at the edge to bring up the holographic menus. After ordering, discussion turned to the day's planned activities.

"I brought some maps that I thought might be helpful," Cinda said as she passed out the coffee and tea. "Old-style paper and an electronic tablet. I also have a list of planetary wonders that you might be interested in."

"Like what?" Rico inquired.

"Well, there is an extinct volcano on southern Zeta. The Company punched a tunnel in the side, back when they were exploring the planet. They didn't find anything particularly valuable there, but it looks a lot like Carlsbad Caverns on Terra. On the west coast is New Crater Lake where luminescent algae create rainbow swirls on the surface at night. On Beta—"

"One second, Cinda," Kep interrupted. "I think the volcano might be a good place for us to start. At least until we download the notes from prior expeditions."

"Oh, I have that." Cinda pulled another electronic tablet from her bag and handed it over to Kepler. "I accessed the Company archives last night and pulled all the data I could find on all exploration and scientific investigation done on Zarathustra in the last twenty-eight years. There are about three-hundred Exabytes with pictures and video files. I have a friend dredging the datastream for the Federation exploration information before the planet was sold to the CZC."

Greg looked over the information on the tablet and nodded. "Rico, how much are you paying this brilliant young woman?"

"About now, I am thinking around half what she is worth." Rico looked over at Cinda. "Consider that oversight corrected. And if you ever decide to return to Terra, there will be a position for you."

"Don't forget to have your friend submit a chit for his time," Dmitri added.

"Look at this!" Greg turned on the holographic display application on the tablet. "This is the volcano that Cinda was talking about. Is that natural lighting?"

"Yes. Some from test holes punched at the top of the caldera, the rest from bioluminescent wingworms."

"An enclosed caldera? Fascinating!" Dmitri pulled out his own tablet and accessed information on the extinct volcano.

"Wingworms?" Hans prodded.

"Invertebrates about three inches long with an expandable membrane that allows them to form wings and glide around the cavern," Cinda explained. "They subsist on the local equivalent of lichen. The lichen feeds on the moisture in the cavern, some sediment on the rock and the light generated by the wingworms. Unlike Terran lichen, this is a single organism, not a symbiotic one."

"Now how do you know all of that, Miss Dawn?" Dmitri said with mock imperiousness. "You said your field of study was geology."

"That sort of thing is covered in advanced geological studies, Dmitri," Kep said. "Anything that could cause changes to the rock has to be understood. Like the rock-eating bacteria, or lithotrophs, used for micro-mining on Terra. Lithotrophs are generally capable of utilizing inorganic compounds as their primary energy source. The compounds can be, quite often, the mineral components of actual rocks. In fact, lithotrophs represent a major environmental force contributing to the weathering of rocks in nature on almost every Terra-like world, though no evidence of this has been found on Uller...yet. There are a significant number of lithotroph species, though the most commonly known are the sulfur-oxidizing bacteria, such as Thiobacillus and Sulfolobus."

"No points for showing off in your own field, Kep," Bill chided. "Or do you want me to recite pi to the thousandth decimal point?"

Cinda was relieved that Kepler had cut in. She did not want to admit she studied up on the volcano when she thought the scientists might want to go there. While she did take the advanced courses Kepler pointed out, Odin University did not cover Zarathustran flora and fauna. It took a while for even the best universities to catch up with all of the new discoveries on colonial worlds.

"The volcano it is," Rico declared. "Now, let us drop the discussion until we have dined or I may find myself giving Miss Dawn another raise. Two wage increases on the first day before breakfast could start a trend even I couldn't afford."

"Agreed." Dmitri looked to Cinda. "What time could your friend Al get here?"

Cinda looked at her watch. "If I call him now, he might be here by the time we are done eating, provided he hasn't already headed out with his taxi."

"Excellent. I leave it to you to negotiate his fee, Cinda, as you have a much better idea of what will be considered a fair rate on the world," Rico interjected. He turned to the others. "Will we need some muscle for this foray?"

"It wouldn't hurt," Kep replied. "I have a lot of equipment and we don't have a contragravity platform to haul it with, yet. Cinda?"

"I can call Dax and Tres. Dax is an artist with lots of free time and Tres just had a son, so he will be looking for some extra income until he gets that promotion at the Company warehouse. If we need more bodies, there is a job board at The Soup Kitchen in Junktown. I am afraid all we can count on is mostly unskilled labor types, though, as we don't have a university to draft student interns from."

"Then by all means, make the call." Rico noticed that a serving robot was headed towards the table loaded down with the breakfast orders. "Best be quick, though. Breakfast is served."

XVIII

Douglas, startled awake by the alarm clock, smacked the top and rolled back over intending to return to his slumber. It was not meant to be. Just as he started to drift off, he was startled anew by Andre lumbering into the room.

"Doug, wake up. We got problems."

Douglas rolled over and sat up on the edge of the bed. "Whas up? Since when do you make like the early bird?"

"Early? I just got in. I was out all night bar hoppin'. Ya gotta love a colonial planet that hasn't gotten around to passing laws against a pub being open all night. That's where I was when I saw the news."

"Let me get some caffeine in me first. I prefer my bad news when I am wide awake and able to properly appreciate it."

Douglas got up, stretched and walked over to the coffee dispenser. While the hotel they stayed in barely rated two stars, it managed to have fresh hot coffee in every room via the mini-vending machines. Doug dropped a fifty-centisol coin into the slot and gratefully accepted the pick-me-up in a cup.

Half a cup later, Douglas was ready to hear what Andre had to say. "Okay, shoot."

"They found Ray," Andre said without preamble.

Douglas did a double take. "Alive or dead?"

Andre shook his head. "Dead. Damnthing got him according to the CZCN news."

Douglas gave the matter some thought. With Ray dead, he couldn't talk under veridication and spill what he knew about the operation. It was like watching your mother-in-law crash into a mountain in your brand new aircar; a little good in with the bad.

"Well, at least he can't implicate us."

"The ZNPF found the cages, too," Andre added.

That was less good. More like the weird uncle at family reunions that everybody liked in small doses instead of the mother-in-law doing the crash up. Still, Ted had been caught red-handed, by Fuzzies, so it wasn't a secret that there were poachers on the Rez.

"I'll have to get a message to the Boss," Douglas said. "He might want to pull the other teams in before they get caught."

"Can't you do that?" Andre asked.

"No, because I don't know where they are or even who they are," Douglas said testily. "Only the Boss has that information. That way nobody can spill his guts under veridication, and why we were not all caught up when that group on Beta was discovered. If you were sober you'd remember that."

Douglas glanced at his watch. "The next check-in won't be for a few hours. I might as well get in a shower and some breakfast while you sleep it off."

Two hours later, washed, fed and treated to the cacophony of his partner's snoring, Douglas attached a small device to a portable communication screen and tapped a button on the side. The screen came to life with a kaleidoscopic splash of color. After a moment the screen image cleared to a masked figure. It was disconcerting to see a damnthing staring back at him from the screen.

"Is this line secure?"

"Of course." Douglas barely stopped himself from rolling his eyes. The device he attached to the communication screen had two functions, scrambling the tele-signal and automatically calling the masked man's screen code. Douglas couldn't call at all without the scrambler device as he didn't have the Boss's screen code without it.

"Report," the masked figure ordered.

"Ted and Ray are dead."

"I watch the newsfeeds. What is your status?"

"After a visit from the ZNPF, we closed camp and returned to Mallorysport to file for a permit to hunt harpies on the preserve."

"Harpies?"

"I tried to convince the cops Andre and I were after trophy kills. Fifty sols for a permit is worth it if it keeps us off the police blotter."

"Did you collect some damnthing hides first to keep your stories intact?"

"Already done. I know it isn't my place to say, but you might want to pull any other teams from Beta until things cool off."

"You are correct; it is not your place to say," the damnthing-masked man said sharply. "Still, you might be right. I will discuss it with the Top."

The Top? The boss over the Boss. But wasn't he, or she, or they, back on Terra? It would take a year for new instructions to come in. Unless...?

"He's here?"

"Not your concern. If your permit is approved, go to Gamma continent and bag enough Harpies to look legitimate, then return to Mallorysport for new instructions. If not, find something else trophy worthy to hunt. Take a week or two. Hunters do not rush their hunt, nor should you. You will find additional expense money deposited to your account by tomorrow morning. Good hunting."

Before Douglas could respond, the screen went dark. "Well, that's just slap-up dandy," he growled. He hated hunting.

* * *

Jack Holloway was in his office poring over the Fuzzy birth records when his viewscreen chimed. He hit the reply button.

"Hello."

"Hi, Jack. This is Dr. Dyson over at the Mallorysport Hospital."

Jack felt his stomach drop. Had something happened to Betty? All he knew was she was in Mallorysport with his sister shopping.

"No, it's nothing serious," Dyson answered, after seeing Jack's stricken appearance. "It's a problem case."

"What kind of problem, Doc?" Jack asked.

Dyson shook his head in exasperation. "I've got a really tricky case here in the hospital—"

"So what does that have to do with me?" Jack interjected.

"My patient is a Fuzzy," he snapped back. "Sorry I yelled, but this is the damndest case I've yet run across. We don't get many Fuzzy accident victims—"

Jack's stomach dropped. "Was it anyone I know?"

"I don't know. The victim is a female Fuzzy named Emily Dickenson."

Jack shook his head. "No one I know. I can ask Little Fuzzy if he's heard of her, but he's not around."

"That's fine. I just wanted to run this by you. Emily was in a ground car accident with her adopted parent, Cherise Lemont—head librarian at the Mallorysport Library. Some damn drunken tourist, a Terran I believe, ran into their car. A head-on collision. Cherise was killed instantly, massive chest and head wounds. Emily came out okay, except for a bump on the head and a sprained wrist; you know how damn adaptable Fuzzies are. She must have curled into a ball just before the impact. I saw the car afterwards; I don't know how anyone came out of the vehicle alive." Dyson shook his head in wonderment.

"That's a real tragedy, but what does it have to do with me?" he asked.

"Well, Cherise Lemont was a spinster, in her late fifties. No relatives on Zarathustra. No one to look after little Emily."

Jack threw out his hands. "I've got scads of off-world visitors, as well as locals, just dying to adopt a Fuzzy. But, we've had to put a moratorium on Fuzzy adoptions. Too many off-worlders and no time to check their bona fides. Plus, we still don't know if Fuzzies will thrive off-world. We've got lots of room, so Emily could stay here with the rest of the Fuzzies at the Reservation."

"That's not the problem, Jack. Her head injury had an odd side effect."

"Side effect?"

"Yes, she lost her ability to speak the Fuzzy language."

"Nothing at all, Doc?"

"No, not even a yeek! However, she can speak fluent Lingua Terra. Like I said, it's the damndest thing!"

"That is one for the books," Jack said. "It's unheard of for an adult

Fuzzy to be fluent in Terra Lingua—why's that?"

"Well, when we were kids, Cherise was what we'd call an "Old Biddy"—very set in her ways. I've kept in touch with her over the years since I use the library a lot. I hate those goddamned data books—they're even worse than the talking ones! Anyway, I got to know her fairly well; she was very old-fashioned and set in her ways. Almost the archetype of the old-maid librarian. I was surprised when she up and adopted her own Fuzzy. I asked her about it: she said it was her duty as a good Christian Woman to help bring enlightenment to one of God's blessed creatures."

Jack shuddered. He couldn't stand people who believed it was their duty to enlighten the kindest and sweetest beings in the known universe. Not a one of them even came close to a Fuzzy for caring about their fellow beings.

"Cherise felt it was her Christian duty to teach Emily, who she named after her favorite poetess, a 'real language.' She did a good job. I met Emily several times before the accident and she spoke better Lingua Terra than any Fuzzy I've ever met, including Little Fuzzy."

"I hope she did this by legal means," said Jack through gritted teeth. More often than not, those holier-than-thou types resorted to sticks and switches to bring their messages to their charges.

"Don't get me wrong, Jack," Dyson said. "She was inhibited, overly-religious and closed-minded, but—at heart—she was a kind person. That's one of the problems. Emily is all broken up about losing her Big One."

"That shouldn't be a problem," Jack replied. "Once the adoption moratorium has been lifted, I'm sure I can find her a new parent with the same qualities. There's no lack of qualified Big Ones these days, to say the least!"

"No, she doesn't want another Big One. Not for now, at least. She wants to be with other Fuzzies."

"Well, that's not a problem. Betty's in town with my sister Pat. I can screen her and have her pick up little Emily and bring her back to the Fuzzy Reservation this afternoon."

"Maybe that'll be the best thing," Dyson said, rubbing his forehead.

"I'm just not sure she'll fit in."

"What do you mean, Doc?"

"Well, she doesn't speak a word of Fuzzy lingo. I'm not sure how the other Fuzzies will take to that, Jack."

Jack nodded, pausing to light up his pipe. He took a puff of tobacco smoke and let it settle, then exhaled. "That's a problem that's never come up before. I know just what to do. I'll have Little Fuzzy keep an eye on her. He's good at that, and very protective. You should see him around Little John."

"Okay, but please keep an eye on her. She's really a pretty little thing, and if I was ever at home, other than to sleep, I'd adopt Emily myself. It's been crazy days here at the hospital ever since all these Earthers started shipping in, looking for their own Fuzzies. Half of them don't know how to drive and the other half are either getting into fights with the locals or drinking themselves to death. For some reason they think the minute they're off-Earth all the old rules go out the space chute!"

Jack smiled knowingly. "I've seen that problem on other worlds, too. Relax, Doc, we'll take good care of Emily."

XIX

"What Pappy Jack want Little Fuzzee make do?" Little Fuzzy asked.

Betty had just dropped Emily Dickenson off at the Fuzzy Reservation, and told Jack that if Emily had any problems there, she would adopt little Emily herself. Jack had to agree; she was one of the cutest Fuzzies he had ever seen.

"I want you to watch over a new Fuzzy here at the Rez," Jack said.

"New Fuzzee wild one, Pappy Jack?"

Jack pointed out his office window to the courtyard in front of the office where twenty or so Fuzzies were talking to each other or playing with their chopper-diggers. "See that Fuzzy with the white bandages wrapped around her head."

Little Fuzzy nodded. "Her look like that Mummy from the flattie you show me."

The other week Old Movie Channel had been playing classic horror films. The Fuzzies called the old black and white films flatties because they lacked depth of the Tri-D movies. Little Fuzzy had enjoyed the festival a lot; his favorite movie was Lon Chaney, Jr.'s *The Wolf Man*. He called him the "Big Bad Fuzzy."

"Yes, she does look a little like the Mummy, or at least her head does. Her name is Emily Dickenson and she was hurt in a bad ground car accident. Her Big One died."

Little Fuzzy's eyes widened.

"I want you to watch over her."

"Hokay, Pappy Jack."

"There's another problem, Little Fuzzy."

"What problem?"

"When she hurt her head, it affected her speech." He realized he was getting into deep water for a Fuzzy, even with Little Fuzzy. "To put it simply, Emily can no longer talk Fuzzy-speak."

Little Fuzzy frowned and grew serious. "Make trouble with other Fuzzee. Fuzzee not like to talk Big One when talk to other Fuzzee."

"That's what I thought," Jack said. "That's why I want you to watch over her. I know the other Fuzzies won't hurt her, but they might shun her."

"Shuun… What is shun, Pappy?"

"Shun means the other Fuzzies might refuse to talk with her or play with her. Maybe even ignore her, like she is dead one."

"Oh. Fuzzies not like Fuzzies who talk only Big One talk. But this not Emily fault. I will point my nose in her direction."

Little Fuzzy looked out of the window again at the girl Fuzzy with the mummy bandages, as Pappy Jack called them. She was pretty, at least what he could see of her was; her fur was a tawny golden brown and her body was lithe and trim. He also noticed that the other Fuzzies were keeping their distance.

Maybe it would be good for him, too. Now that Pappy Jack had his son and sister around he didn't have much time for his old friends. Little Fuzzy had been feeling lonely these past few turns and maybe taking care of another Fuzzy was a good thing.

As he walked out of the office, two of his friends sidled up to him. "Where you going, Little Fuzzee?

"I go to see new Fuzzee. One with the white stripes on her head."

"Oh, her, high fur," Ko-Ko said. "She won't talk with us. So we won't talk to her."

"That right," echoed Mike.

"Not her fault," Little Fuzzy explained. "Her in bad crash—aircar go BOOM! Her Big One die."

"Oh, no!" Ko-Ko gasped. "Bad thing, very bad thing."

"Her head go bang!" Little Fuzzy mock-banged his head against a nearby pool-ball tree trunk. "Hurt bad. No speak Fuzzee now."

"No speak Fuzzee?!" Mike cried out like that was the worst thing he'd ever heard of.

"Right, Mike. She make only Big One talk."

Ko-Ko cringed. "Bad-bad thing."

The other two Fuzzies wandered off as Little Fuzzy approached Emily. "Hi," he said.

"Hello, Little Fuzzy," Emily replied.

"You know me?"

She smiled shyly. "No, but you're the most famous Fuzzy on Zarathustra."

Little Fuzzy shrugged. "Why you speak Big One talk like Big One?"

"My Big One was a librarian—You know what they are?"

"Yes, book watcher."

"Very good. She thought it was important that I learn to speak like other humans and she only allowed me to speak Lingua Terra."

"You still make talk like Fuzzy?"

"Yes," she replied. "But there were no Fuzzies in our apartment so I rarely met with other Fuzzies. But I still could speak our language, until the accident." Her face grew sad. "Now the other Fuzzies won't talk with me. Why is that, Little Fuzzy?"

"They not like to make Big One talk with other Fuzzee." He puffed out his chest and said, "I talk to them and"—he paused to find the right word—"'splain why you no make Fuzzee talk."

"Thank you, Little Fuzzy," she said with a smile that lit up her face. "That is so kind of you."

"Have idea for…um…make help other Fuzzee on Rez."

"What is that?" she asked.

"You teach Big One talk to the young Fuzzee, like Baby Fuzzee. Young Fuzzee need Fuzzee—" He paused to search for the right word.

"Teacher," Emily interjected.

Little Fuzzy smiled. "Hokay! Need Fuzzee teacher. You make do?"

She smiled. "Yes, I would love to. It will give me something to while away the hours."

Little Fuzzy liked seeing Emily happy; it gave him a warm feeling in the pit of his stomach. He suddenly decided he wanted to spend more time in her company, and an idea came to mind. "You teach me to make better Big One talk?"

"Why?" she asked. "You already speak it better than all the other Fuzzies." She used her arms to encompass the courtyard.

He nodded. "Little Fuzzee not make talk like Big One. Emily talk good-good Big One. Little Fuzzy want"—he stumbled for the right word—"to learn."

She grinned and took his paw in her own. "It would be my pleasure, Little Fuzzy. You're very gallant."

Little Fuzzy felt his face grow hot. He wasn't sure what "gallant" meant, but by the tone of her voice it was a good good thing. He liked that.

*　*　*

The communication screen activated automatically to reveal the face of a damnthing. Sitting before the screen console sat a man wearing a simple hood. "Report," said the hooded figure to the screen.

"All three ships at twenty-three percent capacity," the masked man replied. "At the current rate of acquisition we should be at full capacity by the end of the next month. We may need to suspend acquisition activities in northern Beta. That area is compromised."

The hooded figure said something under his breath before responding. "That is our best location for getting uneducated Fuzzies. The *Jin-f'ke* are isolationists, at least where humans are concerned. That keeps them away from most Federation protections. The rest of the Fuzzy Reservation is heavily patrolled by the ZNPF. Ninety percent of our current stock was gathered from northern Beta. This will put our timetable at risk."

The damnthing mask bobbed up and down on the screen. "There's no helping for it. Two members have been found dead up there along with their cages and trapping equipment. The operation is blown in that area—for now."

The hooded man swore again. This time in Sheshan. "We may have to take a more aggressive approach."

"That would be ill-advised. There is the Federation Space Navy post on Xerxes. We have neither the manpower nor the weaponry to take on a company of Space Marines," the damnthing said.

"We have four hyperspace yachts. We could do a snatch and grab, and then space out before they could even get organized."

The figure in the screen gave the idea serious consideration, then shook his head. "We would have to attack a location with enough Fuzzies present to meet our demands, grab them up, possibly while under fire, while trying not to damage any of the natives we are trying to collect. We'll have to keep that plan as a last resort. I will give it some work and see what we can put together. In the meantime, I advise that we step up operations in the other areas and warn the men to take extra precautions."

"Very well," the man wearing the hood said. "Do so and contact me when you have something new to report. Use signal Omicron with a two minute advance warning in case I am with other people."

"Understood. One last thing: the fourth ship claims supplies are getting low. We will have to dispatch a team to Mallorysport."

"Hmm..., the hooded man said, "send a two-man team and have them hire locals to do the acquisitions. It will draw less attention."

The screen went blank and the hooded man leaned back and relaxed in his seat. He took no offense at the suddenness of the call's termination; calls were scheduled for a time when communications were at the highest level to avoid tracking, and kept brief for the same reason. Pleasantries were overrated, anyway.

XX

Victor Grego awoke, as he usually did, to Diamond and Sunstone bouncing on the bed. After three years he had no idea how Fuzzies knew it was time to get up without the benefit of an alarm clock. He was just sitting up when the alarm started beeping.

Grego turned off the alarm clock, then ruffled Diamond's and Sunstone's head fur. "Maybe I should just toss the clock and let you two handle the wake-ups, huh?"

His Fuzzies nodded, then yeeked.

The three went into the kitchen and Grego started the coffee maker. While he waited for the pick-me-up to finish brewing, he opened two tins of Terran Federation Space Forces Emergency Ration, Extraterrestrial, Type Three and put them on small plates with a miniature fork. Grego was trying to teach his Fuzzies how to eat like civilized people.

The coffee maker beeped and automatically filled a cup. Seconds later there came another beep; breakfast was sitting in the dumbwaiter fresh from the chef. Grego preferred not to have people puttering around in his quarters while he slept, so he set up a breakfast schedule that had the food sent directly to his quarters each morning. The order changed from day to day according to a menu he selected well in advance. The tray included fresh juice for the Fuzzies as well.

Breakfast was quiet time. Grego scanned the news on a small viewscreen set on the table while the Fuzzies softly yeeked at each other. Two more cups of coffee and breakfast was done.

"What do you two have planned for the day?" Grego asked the Fuzzies. Diamond was long past needing a sitter while Pappy Vic was at work and he could be trusted to keep Sunstone out of trouble.

"Go to school. Practice arch'ry," Sunstone volunteered. She wasn't catching on to Lingua Terra as quickly as Diamond had. "After we go to jewl-ree place and polish sunstones."

With so many Fuzzies being adopted it was necessary to set up a second school on Alpha Continent. It gave Fuzzies a place to continue their education and spend their time when their Big Ones were at work. The jewelry place was a CZC sub-department where low-grade gemstones were cleaned and polished. Many of the stones, too small or low quality to sell on the market, were turned into jewelry for the Fuzzies. In fact, the Fuzzies made the jewelry themselves.

"Good idea, Diamond, Sunstone. Education is important." Grego was about to say more when the comscreen beeped. "One second, kids." Grego tapped a button on the console and Leslie Coombes appeared on the screen in his housecoat. "Good morning, Leslie. Checking up on me? I promise not to play hooky today."

"Good morning, Victor. And I am afraid that I am checking up. I wanted to be sure you were back in time for the board meeting. Remember, you're wearing two hats until Morgan comes back."

"That's right. Well, he promised to come back to work in a month—"

"Terran or Freyan month?"

"Zarathustran," Grego corrected. "Our new Chief Financial Officer wants to do his due diligence as a father before running back to the office. Not to worry, Leslie. I held down both the CEO and CFO spots long before Morgan showed up."

"And you talked him into taking the position to reduce your workload." Coombes noticed Diamond and Sunstone waving at him from behind Grego and waved back. "When does Morgan return to his duties?"

"Next month after the baby is big enough to travel. He and Akira will be staying in his penthouse in Mallorysport during the work week, and scooting back to the castle on weekends. At least, that is the plan. Now, remind me what is on the docket for the meeting. I don't want to be surprised by anything I should already know."

Coombes nodded and reached for a datapad off screen. "The biggest issue will be the lease-back deal with the Colonial Government for one thousand hectares of land on Alpha continent. You intended to lease back the property for one sol per hectare per year, which the governor will then lease to the Federation Navy at a considerable markup. Why not just lease the property to the Navy yourself and pocket the profit for the Company?"

Grego thought for a moment, then remembered his plan. "A few reasons. One, the military is disinclined to rent property from a corporation. Something to do with some age-old problems they had after the fourth world war. Two, we didn't exactly make a lot of friends in the Navy with the events leading up to the Pendarvis Decision. I don't know if Commodore Napier holds a grudge, but I would bet many of his subordinates do. Three, Ben Rainsford will not hold the reins of power forever and I want the government and the CZC to be good buddies long after he and I are gone. Letting the government collect rent from the Navy on property we don't need makes us look good. Besides, as the population grows, the interest on the banked sunstone sales may not be enough to sustain the government. This will provide an alternate source of revenue and keep this world tax-free. We all benefit from that."

Coombes considered it and agreed. "I don't imagine you'll have any difficulty getting board approval. Next is the appropriation of funds for Science Center to look into the latest reproductive problem."

Grego snorted. "I didn't tell you? All Fuzzy-related research and development comes out of the Fuzzies' Yellowsand mining royalties. Ben signed off on that a few weeks ago. No out-of-pocket cost to us; and the CZC helps the Fuzzies, which makes us the good guys. There is still a lot of bad sentiment from the Lolita Lurkin fiasco, even though we had nothing to do with it directly. And the money we do occasionally put into the research is chickenfeed to the Company."

"I agree, but you might consider pointing out that whatever affects the Fuzzies might affect us, too," Coombes said. "With so many people on reproduction blockers, they might be sterile without knowing it."

"Great Ghu, I hadn't considered that. I'll get a hold of Juan and have him look into it. He can check with the hospital and discreetly inquire if there has been a rise of sterility among Terro-humans. Good catch, Leslie. Anything else?"

"Just the usual. Oh, yes, Peterson is going on about a major stockholder starting businesses in competition with the Company."

"What?" Grego thought a moment, then said, "Oh, Morgan buying out the B.I.N. radio station. That's a plus. The Federation doesn't allow any one company to control all of the media on any one planet. If somebody has to own the competition, I am glad it is Morgan."

"I believe he might be skirting the very fine edge of that law, since he is a stockholder in the CZC, Victor. I'll look over some precedents on that. One last thing: are you going forward with the urban renewal project for Junktown?"

"Absolutely. Clancy Slade brought the plan to me when I bumped into him during one of his shifts. He pointed out that most of the people in Junktown were former CZC employees and that the place is a breeding ground for criminals. He thinks we will benefit in the long run by cleaning it up. I had been considering something like that for a while, anyway."

Coombes pondered the name for a moment then recalled that Slade was one of the security staff. He had also taken down Leo Thaxter during an assassination attempt on Hugo Ingermann, of all people, and had received a significant reward for this. "Victor, he still works for the Company? With the reward money on Thaxter I would have thought he would open his own business or something."

"He opened several: Clancy's Bar and The Soup Kitchen, one here in Mallorysport proper and one out in Junktown. His wife runs most of it. I have eaten at the Mallorysport location a couple of times. Nothing super fancy, but still very good food. And he keeps a job board up for people that need work. McVie from Human Resources told me he gets a lot of his temps from that board."

Coombes' confusion came through the screen. "Then why is he still working in security?"

"I believe he's running The Soup Kitchen on a shoestring budget and keeps his job here to stay solvent. Harry Steefer says that Slade never misses a shift, is always on time and is available for overtime if offered.

And the Junktown branch of his Soup Kitchen is a payment optional operation. I offered a donation to the Junktown chapter, but he says it should stand or fall on its own merits."

Grego turned, then said. "I have to cut this short if I am to make it to the meeting on time. I'll see you there, Leslie."

Leslie Coombes leaned back in his chair and thought about Clancy Slade. Something was off about him. Opening one restaurant with the reward money he received after shooting Thaxter was one thing. Two restaurants were a bit much. Granted, Clancy also received a significant amount of money from the people who arranged for him to take Thaxter's place. Maybe that was it. Still...?

He tapped a few keys on his console and brought up a list of new businesses and their owners. Clancy also owned a bar in Mallorysport. A liquor license cost 10,000 sols. That was a Federation standard. Two restaurants and a bar would be very pricey on any planet, more than Clancy's finances should have been able to support.

He entered the CZC Bank's databases using his authorization codes. Few people in the company, and none outside of it, would be able to access the kind of information he would be privy to.

Coombes quickly scrolled through the list of accounts until he found Clancy Slade's. His bank balance was 26,398.67 sols! Well, lots of people borrow even when they have money in the bank. On worlds with income tax there were tax breaks and other incentives to do so. Clancy was fairly new to Zarathustra and might be using old business strategies out of habit. A quick check with the loan department showed no business loans, or any other kind. If Clancy borrowed the money, he didn't get it from a bank since the Company ran the only one on Zarathustra.

That meant Clancy either got the money from loan sharks or had an alternative source of revenue. Loan sharking was pretty much dead on Zarathustra, at least for the moment. Leo Thaxter had been the biggest loan shark on the planet until he was arrested in relation to the Fuzzy Faginy ring. Raul Laporte, the heir to the throne, had been murdered several months before that, and the people who had tried to take over his interests were all either dead or in prison.

It was possible a new loan shark had popped up that hadn't been identified, as of yet. For that matter, Clancy could even be the new shark in the pool. The reward money would certainly have been a good setup stake. The Soup Kitchen would make a great cover for his operations.

Ordinarily, Leslie didn't involve himself in the activities, criminal or otherwise, of people outside of the Company's upper echelons. But with Victor Grego becoming involved with Clancy Slade, he felt it necessary to look into things. Grego, normally a shrewd judge of character, might be taken in by a potentially dangerous Clancy. Clancy Slade would have to be checked out. Discreetly.

* * *

Jack Holloway came into the office and saw Piet Dumont sitting at his desk, hunched over a viewscreen.

"What are you looking for, Piet?"

"I'm just going over the Fuzzy Applicant List."

"Yeah," Jack said, as he took out his tobacco pouch. "What about it?"

"Did you know that we've received over twenty-five thousand applications to adopt a Fuzzy! Most of them coming in within the last month."

Jack rubbed his forehead. He felt the beginning of another headache. "I knew there were a lot of them, but not so many. I remember Morgan mentioning how the tourists were becoming a problem; he said they were swarming Mallorysport like a bee colony."

"That's right, tourists are coming from Terra, Odin, Baldur, Marduk, Isis—even as far away as Poictesme! But they all have one thing in common...."

"What's that, Piet?" Jack asked, as he lit his pipe.

"They all want to adopt a Fuzzy. Sheesh!"

Jack nodded. "It makes sense, if you think about it. It's been over two years since the first Fuzzies left for Terra. I suspect they made quite a flash there. Some probably reached Odin, Marduk and Baldur before then. We've put a moratorium on Fuzzy adoptions; that'll work in the short term. But, long term, we're going to have to do something about this...."

"I agree, Jack. But what? I can't even fill a thousandth of these applications; there aren't that many Fuzzies on the Rez. How many are living on Beta Continent?"

Jack shrugged. "Before we discovered the Northern Fuzzies, I would have put their number at less than twenty thousand. Now, maybe twice that. Although, none of the Northerners have any desire for human companionship."

Piet laughed. "To say the least! Those Northerners'd rather wrestle with a bush-goblin than cuddle with a human."

"It's no laughing matter. How many Fuzzies do we have on the Rez looking to be adopted?"

Piet looked thoughtful, then frowned. "Maybe a hundred, a hundred and twenty-five.... We did get that new female Fuzzy, Emily. She lost her Big One; maybe she wants another one."

"She's the one that Little Fuzzy's been keeping an eye on."

"What's that all about?" Piet asked.

"Emily was orphaned in a car crash. She was in the ground car when it crashed and took a bad bump on the head. She lost all capacity to speak Fuzzy, and the other Fuzzies were ostracizing her—"

"What! I've never heard of Fuzzies ostracizing anyone before."

"Piet, I fear they might be picking up some of our bad habits. However, we don't know enough about Fuzzy social interaction to know anything for sure. So I asked Little Fuzzy to take her under his wing."

Piet nodded. "He's done that. They seem to be doing everything together. It's probably a good thing."

"What do you mean?" Jack asked, setting his pipe down.

"You didn't notice?"

"Notice what?" Jack asked, his voice growing strident.

"Little Fuzzy's been kinda lost lately."

"Lost? Why?"

Piet let out a sigh of exasperation. "Jack, if you haven't noticed, it's because you haven't been spending much time with Little Fuzzy lately.

First there was Morgan, and then the new baby, to occupy your time and attention. Now you and Betty are spending so much time together, the poor little guy probably feels abandoned."

"That's ridiculous," Jack snapped. Then he paused, *maybe there's some truth in Piet's words. I've been awfully busy lately; I can't remember the last time Little Fuzzy and I spent any non-work time together. Now, with Pat in the picture.... Well, maybe the little fellow is feeling neglected....* "You may have something there, Piet. I'll have to spend some more time with him."

"I think it'd be a good idea. Now, back to this Fuzzy adoption thing. What are we going to do about it? We've got a thousand applicants for every available Fuzzy. Once this moratorium is over, how are we going to choose who gets whom without a riot?"

"Are you serious?"

"Think about it, Jack. How would you feel if you spent six months, or a year inside a cramped spacecraft coming to Zarathustra to adopt a Fuzzy, only to learn, after your arrival, that only a very few were available? And most of those were going to the locals."

"I'd be pissed as Hell," Jack said, nodding.

"Who would you be maddest at?" Piet asked.

"The SOBs who are doling them out. Not the idiot newscasters who had broadcasted their availability."

"Correct," Piet said. "Especially, if the few Fuzzies they had weren't doled out in a fair manner—most of them going out to the locals."

"Phew. We've got an atomic bomb in our lap! Maybe we ought to outlaw the deportation of Fuzzies off Zarathustra."

"You're not thinking this through, Jack. This adoption moratorium is bad enough. Outlawing off-world adoptions would look an awful lot like local favoritism, then we'd really have a riot on our hands. We're going to have to be damn careful how we treat this thing."

Jack agreed. "Kid gloves all the way. I'm going to contact Ben and the rest of the gang. We're going to need their input. Maybe Commodore Napier's, too."

XXI

Prison life did not sit well with Hugo Ingermann. Everywhere he turned there was nothing but enemies. The guards hated him on general principles, which was to be expected. There was a time when prison guards could be bought, bribed or threatened into providing special favors. The introduction of the polyencephalographic veridicator had put an end to all of that. Guards were randomly interrogated under veridication weekly, so anybody providing special considerations for the prisoners would soon be found out and either discharged or jailed themselves. Fortunately, while Ingermann could not bribe the guards to provide him with extra protection, the other prisoners couldn't bribe them to arrange for a fatal "accident."

The other prisoners hated Ingermann for more personal reasons. Many had been left high and dry with pending court dates when Ingermann had skipped planet almost three years earlier, resulting in a lot of easy convictions. Others disliked Ingermann for his connection to the Fuzzy Faginy racket; even most criminal types liked Fuzzies, and convicts were inclined to treat inmates that hurt Fuzzies the same way they treated child molesters…very badly.

Again, only the threat of the veridicator protected Ingermann from violent reprisals from the other inmates. If Ingermann ended up dead, everybody in Prison House, from the warden on down, would be questioned under veridication until they found the guilty party who would then, most likely, be executed after a short trial. A bullet to the back of the head was a powerful deterrent.

Hugo Ingermann was safe as far as being murdered was concerned. Sadly, for him, such protection did not extend to the occasional "accidental" bump in the corridors, tripping on the stairs, or even a fight among inmates. Ingermann's body was covered in bruises as a result of these numerous "accidents." The warden couldn't veridicate prisoners for every minor scuffle, or he would never have time for anything else. Ingermann believed that the warden was only too happy to let him take the lumps anyway.

Today, like almost every other day, Ingermann's lawyer, Clarence Anetrou, was in to discuss his case. Privately, he knew it was a lost cause. Thaxter had ratted him out for absconding with 250,000 sols of CZC sunstones under veridication and on camera three years earlier. Quigley, elder and younger, had spilled their guts about his involvement with Ingermann's plan to distribute ersatz sunstones, among numerous other improprieties, after being arrested in exchange for a reduced sentence for his son. The list of charges against him included theft, illegal mining, conspiracy, murder, fraud, racketeering, extortion, bribery...the list went on and on, and that was just what he had done since returning to Zarathustra. The best Ingermann could hope for was a bullet in the back of his head.

The legal games Ingermann played were simply a means to delay his eventual execution for as long as possible. Thus far, he had added nine months to his life span through legal maneuvering that kept delaying his trial. While he hated prison, it was better than the grave, if only marginally.

"Somebody from off-world wants to question you under veridication," Ingermann's lawyer said without preamble.

Ingermann snorted. "Hello to you, too, Clarence. Where from?"

"Terra, I believe."

Ingermann shook his head. He hadn't been to Terra in almost a decade, aside from his brief visit where he had never even left the spaceport before hopping the next outbound ship. "What are they trying to get out of me now?"

Clarence Anetrou pulled some papers from his briefcase, more for effect than any useful information they might provide. "They wouldn't say. I was under the impression that they are fishing for something unrelated to any of the charges currently leveled against you."

"You blocked it, of course," Ingermann said. He internally debated how he might parlay this new element into staying alive a bit longer. Even Rainsford's administration wasn't stupid enough to execute a potentially valuable source of information.

"Easily. Until and unless they are prepared to tell us what they want to ask about, they won't even get you into the same room as a veridicator. Federation law, as you should well know, provides protections against this sort of ambush."

Ingermann mulled it over in his mind. "Whatever it is, it must be pretty big and they want to keep it quiet."

"I suspect it has to do with an ongoing investigation into something Terra-side, but still connected to Zarathustra." Clarence shuffled the papers dramatically. "You didn't get into anything unsavory before returning here, did you?"

Ingermann glanced around. While he was in a closed room with only his lawyer, there was always the possibility that the room was bugged. Procedures varied from world to world and Zarathustran law hadn't evolved to the point where defendants could be assured of total privacy when consulting with their attorneys.

"Relax. The jammer in my briefcase has been on since I sat down. It can't block any video feeds, but the audio is completely countered." Clarence moved around more papers for effect.

Ingermann nodded. "Yeah, I got into some things while off-world, but nothing that would have followed me here; certainly not all the way from Terra."

"Are you certain?"

Ingermann thought hard; nothing came to mind. "Yes. And there hasn't been enough time for it to track me here anyway. In fact, anything coming from Terra after my arrest wouldn't catch up with me for another three months." Slow communications between worlds worked to a criminal's advantage. By the time some infraction caught up with them, they could be on another planet far away. "Forestall any attempts to get me into the seat, but try to keep them interested. If they think I have something useful, they won't be in a hurry to shoot me in the head."

"Or they will put you in an iso-cell until you decide to cooperate. Remember, each world has full autonomy when it comes to prisoner treatment. Federation law will only go so far on a colony world."

Ingermann thought over Clarence's warning. Iso-cells were total sensory deprivation units. Intravenous feeding, so there was no sense of taste, controlled antigravity preventing him from touching anything, total darkness, no sound and no scent. The warden could keep him in there for hours, even days. Strong men had been completely broken by the iso-cell in less than a day. It was usually reserved for the most violent of offenders.

Ingermann mulled it over, then said, "Rainsford doesn't have the stones for something like that. If Grego or Brannhard were running things I would be worried. Their buddy Holloway would just shoot me outright, from everything I have heard about him."

Clarence leaned back. "You may be right. But what about Juan Takagashi?"

Ingermann's face screwed up in confusion. "What about him?"

"It was on the news feed this morning. Governor Rainsford is taking his first vacation since he took office. Takagashi is running things for the next two weeks."

All Ingermann knew about Takagashi is that he ran against Rainsford in the last election, then was brought in as the deputy. "Okay, we play it by ear. With any luck the deputy governor will be against the iso-cell. If not, well, maybe we should plan our legal strategy accordingly. We can fight it on the basis that it is torture and hence illegal...."

* * *

"Looking at the system map again, Dmitri?"

Dmitri looked up at Rico and nodded. "It never hurts to go back and take a second look."

"Or twenty-second, in this case," Melvin added.

Cinda, operating the aircar, turned on the auto-pilot and turned in her seat. "Do you think something else in this star system accounts for Zarathustra's climate?"

"Not really, but it never hurts to verify." Dmitri turned to Cinda. "What do you know about this system, my dear?"

"Not much," Cinda admitted. "K0 star, two moons and my studies into the planet itself."

Dmitri shook his head. "Do not fall into the trap that so many other scientists have. Expand your field of study to include other areas. You would be surprised how much it could improve your understanding of your chosen field."

"Oh, just tell her about this system, already," Hans said. "You're dying to show off, anyway."

Dmitri feigned innocence, then held up his datapad. "Cinda, if you look here you can see the other planets in this system. The closest to the primary is a planet roughly the size of Mars in an orbit just a bit further out than Mercury. It is called Freni. Then there is a Terra-sized planet in a Venus-like orbit known as Pourucista. Now, these planets are very necessary to Zarathustra as their gravity helps to stabilize this world's orbit, just as Darius stabilizes the axial tilt. Just like Mercury, Venus and Luna do for Terra."

Cinda admitted she hadn't known that.

"Then there is a little ball of iron and rock a little further out than Mars is back in the Sol system about the size of Mercury. Mmm...Hvōvi by name. Now things get more interesting. The next planet is a gas giant twice the size of Jupiter with over two hundred satellites of its own called Pourušaspa Spitāma. This is a very important world for Zarathustra's survival. The intense gravity sucks in rogue asteroids that might otherwise wander in and cause an extinction-level event. The same goes for the Neptune-sized gas ball, Dughdova, after it. The planets and dwarf planets after the two gas giants have precious little effect on the continued survival of this world."

"I read someplace that there are things called brown dwarfs that generate a lot of heat, but don't quite ignite like a star," Cinda said as she looked at the screen. "Is that the case here?"

Dmitri refrained from laughing. "I am afraid not, Cinda. Pourušaspa Spitāma would have to be five to ten times larger than it is to achieve brown dwarf status. And at that size it could destabilize the orbits of the nearer inner planets."

"Oh. Well, then how could this planetary arrangement affect Zarathustra's climate?"

Dmitri sighed. "That is what I am trying to determine. Aside from the effects I have already outlined, I see nothing here to explain the warm temperatures."

The aircar console beeped and Cinda returned to the controls. "We are coming up on Mallory's Volcano. Say, isn't Pourušaspa highly radioactive?"

"It is." Dmitri tapped a few commands into his datapad. "So much so that even robotic mining isn't feasible at this time. But three hundred and seventy million miles is a long way for radiation to travel from a planetary body. The fact that Zarathustra has a lower than average background radiation would tell you that little, if any, radiation is making it this far."

"What about the rotation of Darius?" prodded Kep. "Why isn't it tidally locked like most moons?"

"Off the top of my head two things could cause that," Dmitri explained. "A glancing blow from another astral body could increase the rotation rate, though it would gouge a significant chunk off of the moon in the process. Darius has the usual collection of pits and craters, but nothing remotely large enough to suggest such an impact. The other, more likely possibility is that it is a recent capture."

"Recent capture?" Cinda thought about it. "Oh, a rogue asteroid that got captured in Zarathustra's gravity."

"Very good. Darius probably got captured four or five million years ago. A few more million years and the rotation will eventually slow down until it becomes tidally locked like Luna is to Terra."

Another beep from the console, this time from the communication screen. Cinda turned it on to see a shadowy figure.

"Aircar, please identify yourself."

"This is Cinda Dawn. I am bringing some guests to see Mallory's Volcano."

"Miss Dawn, vere you unave're dat Zeta continent ist now privately owned?"

Rico arched an eyebrow. "German accent all the way out here? I didn't know anybody even spoke that as a first language anymore."

"My apologies. I did not know that. Would it be possible to apply for permission to see the volcano? My friends are here for scientific purposes."

"Vun moment, *Fräulein*...eh...Miss Dawn." The screen went blank.

"I am sorry, everybody," Cinda said. "I didn't know that the continent was under private management. My understanding was that it was leased from the government by the Charterless Zarathustra Company for a zillion years, but tourism was allowed."

"Backroom treaty," Rico surmised. "I suspect there was a private deal between the local government, the CZC, and whoever these people are. They might have kept it out of the news feeds to avoid backlash from the general public. Your ignorance is forgiven, Cinda. But see if you can sweet talk these folks into allowing us to see the volcano. The readings could be important."

Bill snorted. "We could always download the data from the previous parties. That volcano had to have been analyzed a hundred times by now."

"There is no substitute for hands-on analysis, Bill," Greg argued. "You never know what the other guys missed or got wrong. Not to mention the possibility of an accidental discovery that everybody else missed."

Bill doubted it but kept quiet rather than argue. Besides, he wanted to see the volcano whether it proved important to their studies or not.

The screen came back on. "Miss Dawn, you vill be permitted to visit der volcano, but please confine your visit to dat area. How long vill you need to be dere?"

Cinda looked back at her employers. "Two days minimum. A week tops. Are there guest facilities we could avail ourselves of?" Greg said.

After a pause the voice from the screen said, "Ja, dere ist und abandoned bed und breakfast near dere. If you haff your own food supplies, you may stey dere for die lengt' of your visit. If you require any assistance, contact us on dis frequency."

"Thank you, sir."

"Haff a pleasant stey. Der volcano ist currently quiescent, so you should haff no problems. *Auf wiedersehen.*"

The screen blanked out and went silent.

"Somebody bought an entire continent?" Dmitri shook his head. "What does a continent go for these days?"

"It depends on the availability of land on a new planet, the desirability of the environment and the population density of that world," Rico observed. "Do Fuzzies live there?"

Cinda thought for a second. "Not unless the new owners brought them there. Fuzzies are native only to Beta Continent. All the Fuzzies on other landmasses were brought there by their adoptive parents or moved as part of Commissioner Holloway's Fuzzy village project."

Rico made a note to look into the village project later. "So where did these, ah, Germans come from?"

Cinda shrugged. "It has to have been from off-world. And they had to have thrown around a lot of money to not only buy the continent, but pay off the CZC as well."

"Pay off the CZC?" Kep prodded.

"Yeah. The Charterless Zarathustra Company worked out an agreement with the Colonial Government. They work the sunstone mine on Beta and pay the Fuzzies so much per carat, which is administered by the government. The interest on the banked funds pays for the colonial government so they don't have to tax the citizens. The CZC also agreed to maintain the planetary services, like power, water, the prison and the hospitals. But mostly, they got a 999-year lease on all of the unseated lands when Zarathustra was declared a Class III inhabited planet. Whoever these new owners are, they also had to pay a buyback or lease fee to the CZC to get the land."

Greg was impressed. "You certainly know a lot about this, Cinda."

"Al was very chatty when my family first arrived on Zarathustra, and that was still the hot topic of conversation."

"Al?"

"The taxi pilot we will be engaging after this excursion," Dmitri said. "I met him at The Bitter End. Nice fellow."

"This is his transport we rented," Cinda added. "Oh, that must be the B&B. I'll land there."

"What is the local time, here?" Bill asked.

Cinda consulted the readout on the console. "Twelve hours earlier than Mallorysport."

"Ha! We have arrived at the time we left," Dmitri quipped. "We have a lot of daylight left to us gentlemen. I suggest we stretch our legs, have a meal, then get to work. We will have to awaken our assistants when we land."

"Better let me do that," Cinda cautioned. "Dax can be testy when he first wakes up. I'll wake Tres first."

Nobody wanted to risk annoying a six-foot-four, six-hundred pound Daxion if they could avoid it.

"Ah, it isn't really any of my business..." started Rico.

"Why is Dax so big?" Cinda finished. "There is something off in his metabolism. His mother was from Terra and his father from Magni. Under all of that fat is a lot of solid muscle, but no matter how hard he exercises or diets, he can't shake the weight. Even medication has no effect. He told me the doctors think it is related to the lower gravity of Terra and Zarathustra; his body simply isn't stressed enough to use all the fuel."

"Wouldn't moving to Magni fix that?" offered Kep.

"It might have, before he got too big. Magni gravity would probably overload his cardio-pulmonary system now; so, he lifts weights, takes long walks and works jobs that require a lot of strength and activity to keep from getting heavier."

Kepler glanced at his own paunch and made a mental note to start walking more. He didn't want to undergo another fat reduction procedure.

XXII

It is a little-known fact that private investigators are scarce on most colony worlds. Low population means limited prospects for clients. Legal dueling further restricts the potential client base. A man who thinks his wife is being unfaithful is more likely to get a dueling license than hire a P.I. Colony worlds owned by a chartered company are the worst for a private detective. Such companies tend to be very guarded with their secrets and even actively encourage those who make a living by ferreting out such secrets to leave the planet—sometimes by unpleasant means.

Jason Roberts arrived on Zarathustra just over a year after the CZC charter was smashed by the Pendarvis Decision. Roberts, a former police detective on Terra, had taken early retirement after being severely wounded in the line of duty. After a year of doing nothing, he decided he would leave Terra and go see the universe.

He was at the spaceport in line to buy an off-world ticket to Thor when the news feed on the big board announced the discovery of a new sapient species on Zarathustra. Roberts immediately changed his destination. When he arrived on Zarathustra six months later, Roberts hadn't planned on becoming a private detective.

His goal had been to hunt, carve out a piece of land for himself, and just enjoy his retirement. He even adopted a Fuzzy, who he dubbed Mike Hammer, in honor of his favorite detective stories' author.

Mike Hammer surprised Roberts in many ways. Within three months the Fuzzy started reading, first with children's books, then juvenile fiction such as comic books, then young adult fare and finally anything he could get his tiny little hands on. In short order the Fuzzy had worked his way through Roberts' complete collection of Mickey Spillane books, and then had started on his Sherlock Holmes novels.

Mike had little trouble with words and their meanings. Context proved to be more challenging. And, of course, the Fuzzy had trouble wrapping his mind around the idea that people would do bad things just to get pretty things and money. Roberts took it upon himself to teach the Fuzzy the sad truth about the human condition.

Roberts, already bored with retirement, rented office space on the edge of Junktown and hung out his shingle. He knew better than to think he would get a parade of customers, or even more than one or two a month. He didn't care. Roberts just wanted the occasional case to break the monotony of retirement and maybe show Mike Hammer what Big Ones were really like.

Two weeks after opening his office, he got his first case—a missing Fuzzy. Amazingly, Mike Hammer tracked the missing Fuzzy straight away to the home of another Fuzzy in one of the villages. She had found a mate and was torn between returning to her Big Ones and staying with her new mate. The situation was resolved when both Fuzzies went to live with the Big Ones; Jason Roberts received a modest fee and Mike Hammer proved himself to be a good tracker and detective.

The pair went on to enjoy some success as The Fuzzy Detective Agency. Roberts moved the office from Junktown to an office near the spaceport. This opened a new area of investigation: finding missing persons, runaway children, errant husbands, lost wives...the list went on. Most cases resulted in the person not being on-planet. A runaway with the options of an entire Federation to run to was only limited by the funds he or she had on him. There were several worlds between Terra and Zarathustra that were cheaper and more civilized than the relatively new colony world.

One of the more interesting cases involved an off-worlder from Freya. Roberts had been trying to instruct Mike Hammer on how to use the computer to search the datastream. Mike understood the mechanics well enough, but kept being sidetracked by the colorful advertisements and pictures.

"Mike, you have to ignore all of that and concentrate on the information we need."

"Hokay, Pappy Jay."

So intent had Roberts been on the Fuzzy, he missed hearing the door to the office open and close. He caught movement in the corner of his eye and spun about with one hand on his gun to face the newcomer.

"Mr. Roberts?"

Roberts quickly appraised the man before him. Mid-thirties, athletic build, expensive clothes designed to be stylish and durable. Buttons instead of a zipper or mag-seal suggested he had spent considerable time on Freya where buttons were the style.

"That would be me, Mr...?"

"Morgan. John Morgan."

Roberts indicated a seat in front of his desk and both men sat down. A quick glance out the window told him a taxi was waiting outside. Since this wasn't the usual taxi zone, Roberts assumed it was waiting for John Morgan.

"I think we should skip the usual pleasantries and dancing around and get to your business here, Mr. Morgan, or that taxi will run up quite a tab."

"That is not a problem, Mr. Roberts."

"You can call me Jason."

"...Jason, then, and you can call me Morgan without the mister." Morgan smiled. He had a good smile. Something about it seemed familiar to Roberts, though he couldn't place it. "I am looking for my biological father, Jason."

"Lost parents are far from unusual," Roberts noted. "Do you have a name? Any pictures or last known whereabouts?"

"At the time he disappeared, he went by the name John Morgan Holloway. Here is the picture." Morgan handed over a faded photograph.

"Hmm..." Roberts mumbled. "John Holloway isn't the most common name, but it is still up there. There would be a lot of them out in the Federation. I can think of at least two here on Zarathustra. One is a small-time thug currently doing time at Prison House, the other, assuming Jack is his nickname, is the Native Affairs Commissioner. This would take a lot of digging. This also assumes—"

"That he hasn't changed his name or altered his appearance," Morgan finished. "Yes, I have tracked down a number of men based on their name and appearance, thus far without success."

"Hmm...I assume you have been to several worlds in your search." Morgan listed off an impressive number of planets. "Whoa! Either your sire had some serious Gypsy in him, or you followed a lot of blind leads to dead ends."

"Both, I think. I am here to follow-up on four more leads. I know where to find these four men on Zarathustra. I need your help to obtain their DNA samples for comparison to my own."

Roberts considered the case. Buddying up to four men long enough to get some DNA could be time consuming and even hazardous. However, he didn't have much else going on.

"Do you have plans to meet these men personally? Normally, I would discourage this as you might scare them off."

"Yes, I expect to meet every one of them, but I will be circumspect."

Roberts thought for a moment, then reached into the bottom left drawer of his desk where he normally kept his scotch. He rooted around a moment then pulled out a small device. "This is an old DNA comparison device. It is outdated compared to the swab model, but works just as good. You place the suspect's sample in this compartment, here, then the comparison samples in the other four compartments. In this case, your hair, here, and whatever you can find from the other men here, here, here and here. I suggest you go for stray hairs. That is the easiest to get, if your target still has any, and you will get the best results. Since you are going to meet these men anyway, this is what I suggest. Meanwhile, give me the names and whatever background you have on the rest and I will run down what I can."

Morgan accepted the DNA scanner. "You trust me to do this alone? Shouldn't you try to dissuade me and do the job yourself?"

"Morgan, clearly you have done this dance on several other worlds with other detectives. No point in reinventing collapsium. You have been chasing this man since, what, college? You clearly have money"—Roberts threw a glance at the taxi waiting outside—"and resources. I suspect you have faced several prospects and are still here to tell of it. Either you are good with a gun, or you are very, very sneaky. If you decide you can't collect the samples without being found out—and you seem smart enough to know that, then I will use other methods. Before you go, let me show you a couple tricks for collecting hair samples. Given the likely age of your father, this should prove fairly simple."

Morgan found his father and engaged in a highly publicized duel with him. Both survived and seemed to work out their differences. Roberts got his DNA analyzer back, along with his fee and a substantial bonus. He also received some referrals that boosted his business.

Leslie Coombes entered the office and took in his surroundings with a glance. With the exceptions of the coffee maker and the computer, the office looked like it was cut whole cloth from an old detective movie, circa early 1st century AE. Coombes approved of the décor. It took money to decorate a place like this, and that spoke of success. If you want to hire a private investigator, a successful one was the only way to go.

At the desk where one would normally find an attractive young woman acting as secretary in the movies was instead a Fuzzy with two books. One was a Mickey Spillane novel. The other was a Lingua Terra to Lingua Fuzzy dictionary. Presumably, the Fuzzy was reading the novel and referencing the dictionary when he came upon a word he did not know. Given the sophistication and complexity of Lingua Terra, Coombes couldn't imagine how the Fuzzy translations could hold up. He made a mental note to check one out and possibly pass them out to his own Fuzzies.

The Fuzzy looked up from his books and said, "May I help you, Pappy Lessee?"

"Yes, I would like to speak with—" Coombes froze in shock. The Fuzzy had addressed him by name. "How...how did you know who I am?"

"We watched recordings of the Fuzzy trial," came a voice from the next room. A man stepped into view through the open doorway. "Mike, here, can recognize anybody who was on that recording, Mr. Coombes, as can I. One of the first things I did when I made planetfall was familiarize myself with all of the major players on this world. A category for which you qualify."

Coombes had difficulty accepting the role of a 'player.' "How do you come to this conclusion?"

"Easy," Roberts said. "You're the top attorney for the Charterless Zarathustra Company, and you have stood in for Gus Brannhard as Chief Colonial Prosecutor on at least two occasions. You are also friendly, if not exactly friends, with Governor Rainsford and Jack Holloway, not to mention your boss, Victor Grego. And they don't get any bigger on this planet than those three."

Coombes had to admit that Roberts had a point. "Very well, this little demonstration shows that you are up on local news and politics. Now, are you any good in your chosen vocation?"

Roberts laughed. "You decided that one before you left your office to come here, Mr. Coombes. You've already run a background check on me."

Coombes' eyes narrowed. "How did you know that?"

Roberts waved it off. "A man in your position wouldn't have come to me without doing his due diligence."

While he hated to admit it, Roberts had a very good point. He took a seat on the couch and looked Roberts in the eye. "I have a job for you."

Roberts took the seat across from Coombes. "What kind of job?"

"Oh? You can't guess?"

"This isn't a divorce case, as neither you nor your boss are currently married. If something was stolen from you, the CZC cops are more than able to handle the matter...discretely. You also have access to better equipment and information than I do, so I doubt you need an employee background check. So, you want me to shade somebody outside of the Company. I would guess it is somebody Mr. Grego is having dealings with that you do not trust. That means whoever is in your sights is either up to something, or you think he is, or he has resources beyond what he should have, or so you think."

Coombes nodded. "If you tell me the name of this person, you should take up palm reading, Mr. Roberts."

"Call me Jason," Roberts said. "No, deductive reasoning only goes so far. Your boss deals with dozens, if not hundreds of people. I couldn't begin to guess which one has your hackles up."

"Good," he replied. "I would be worried if you knew too much of the Company's inner workings. Have you ever heard of a man named Clancy Slade?"

Roberts' brow furrowed at the mention of the name. "Yes. Owns a bar as well as two restaurants, one downtown and one in Junktown, both called The Soup Kitchen. He is also the man who shot and killed Leo Thaxter, a former local gangster. All of that was on the *Mallorysport News* off the datastream. He is considered something of a local hero."

"Very good. Mr. Slade has been working with Mr. Grego to renovate and vitalize Junktown."

"I heard something about that," Roberts admitted. "Does that worry you?"

"As such, no," he said. "But there are other things going on right now that have me wondering."

"Like...?"

"Like how did a man who arrived from Gimli in hopes of finding employment suddenly come into enough money to begin such a venture?"

Roberts smirked. "He did get a 25,000 sol reward for bringing down Thaxter, or so I read."

"He did. There is also reason to believe he received a like amount from the people who forced him to take Thaxter's place in Prison House."

Roberts let out a low whistle. "It may not seem like it to you, Mr. Coombes, but that is a lot of scratch."

"Enough to open two restaurants and a bar?"

Roberts admitted he didn't know what the going rate for those businesses would be. Coombes suggested that Mr. Roberts find out.

"Okay, Mr. Coombes. Fill me in on what you already know. That will save me some legwork and you some expense money."

Coombes related what he knew about Clancy's finances and the fact that he still worked a regular job for the company while running three businesses. He also mentioned the bank account with a significant balance.

"That is a bit suspicious, but not necessarily criminal," Roberts said. "Mr. Coombes, you are an attorney for the Charterless Zarathustra Company. Mr. Slade is an employee of the same Company. If I do find out something, it could put you in an awkward position."

"How so?"

Roberts leaned forward and lowered his voice. "One of the perks of working for the Company as a security guard is that they have free representation if they find themselves in a legal jam, yes?"

"Within reason," Coombes affirmed. "As long as their criminal activity does not directly or indirectly affect the CZC. For example, stealing from the Company would negate our requirement to defend them in court. Herkard and Novaes, for example, tried to rob the Company gem vault, so my firm was not required to defend them."

"Yes, I read about that." Roberts stood up, went into his office, then returned with a bottle of scotch and two glasses. He poured two fingers in each glass and offered one to Coombes. "Now, if I discover anything and tell you about it, it could place you in an awkward position."

Coombes quickly downed half of his drink, then nodded. "I see what you mean. If what he is doing is not directly counter to the CZC's interests, I would be required to defend him. Yet, as an officer of the court, I cannot condone any illegal activities he may be part of."

"Exactly my point," Roberts said before he downed his drink.

Coombes thought about it for a second. "All right, this is what I want you to do; if Clancy is getting his funds by damaging the Company, or by harming any Fuzzies, I want to know about it. Of anything else I can remain blissfully ignorant."

"And if he is doing something especially unsavory that does not involve the CZC or any Fuzzies?"

Coombes finished off his drink and set down the glass. "I leave that to your own better judgment and conscience."

"Fair enough. As it happens, I have met Clancy Slade and his wife.

I have eaten at The Soup Kitchen in Mallorysport and bent an elbow in his bar."

"Oh? Will this affect your work?"

"I keep my personal feelings about a subject out of an investigation. If Slade is dirty, then I may have to take him down." Roberts paused for a moment. "You said *if* Slade was acting against Fuzzies. Do you have a reason to think he might be doing so?"

He considered whether to inform Roberts about what he knew of the Fuzzy slaving operation, then decided against it. For all he knew, Roberts could be in on it, though he doubted that. "I am not at liberty to comment on that, I'm afraid. Let's just say that there are certain things I simply cannot ignore or tolerate. Harming Fuzzies, children and small animals are among them."

Roberts nodded. "I can get behind that. Very well." He picked up a pad of paper and a pen and scribbled something on it, then handed a page to Coombes. "This is my fee, not counting expenses. I will start tonight. I will not pad the bill in any way, and once I start, I see it all the way through. I cannot be bought, bribed or threatened away."

Coombes smiled and pulled his wallet out of his jacket. "Good. Here is an advance on your fee and anticipated expenses. You will give me daily updates on your progress, and those to me directly, in person or by comscreen. I, of course, expect your discretion on this matter."

"All part of the service, Mr. Coombes. Shall I draw up an agreement paper or shall we just trust each other?"

"I would prefer to avoid a paper trail."

Both men stood and shook hands. "I will be in touch, Mr. Roberts. Good day."

XXIII

Gus Brannhard entered the Federation Bureau of Criminal Intelligence building just after his lunch hour. He would have preferred to attend to his business with Trask during lunch, but could not be certain to catch the man in his office at that time. Gus didn't want to make an appointment in hopes of ambushing the agent and putting him off balance.

In the main lobby he spotted a woman behind a desk and assumed she would be able to direct him to the source of his pique. As he approached her, the woman pressed a button on her desk console.

"Agent Trask? Mr. Brannhard is here to see you."

"Send him right up, C.K.," Trask's voice said from the intercom speaker.

"Yes, sir." C.K. tapped another button to sever the connection then, looked up at Gus. "Mr. Brannhard, you will find Agent Trask on the second floor, Suite 206. Just take the lift up and go straight down the hall."

Gus fought to hide his surprise and walked to the indicated lift. The ride up was just long enough to sort his thoughts. Trask had obviously anticipated Gus's reaction to the governor being veridicated and instructed his people to expect his visit. As for being recognized, well, he was probably the fourth best known person on the planet after the Fuzzy Trial and his frequent appearances in the datastream and on the news services. Chief Colonial Prosecutor was a fairly high profile position on a one-city world.

The lift stopped and the doors opened to reveal the hallway. White walls, gray carpeting, and doors with numbers on them. Straight down the hallway, as indicated, was Suite 206 with the door already open. Gus marched in expecting to find a desk and the other usual office furnishings.

What he found instead was a polyencephalographic veridicator with the control console and a man standing next to it.

"Mr. Brannhard," said the man, with an extended hand. Gus shook it while he processed the situation. "I am Agent Trask."

Gus cleared his throat before replying. "Agent Trask...."

"Call me Buck."

"Agent Trask, I want to discuss your actions with the Governor yesterday afternoon."

"And you want to make sure I don't go blabbing to the press that he was veridicated. Can you give me a hand for a second?" Trask sat down in the veridicator and pulled the head-piece down. "Could you attach the electrodes? I never seem to get that right."

Gus snorted as he made the attachments. "I suppose this is your way of putting me at ease before you try to put me in the hot seat."

Trask tried to nod, forgetting the skull cap would hinder the motion. "Is it working?"

"Too soon to tell," Gus said. "I suppose this is the part where I ask you questions and you give me the answers that will make you look good and make me more cooperative."

Trask smiled. "I have the feeling you have been through something like this before, Mr. Brannhard."

"No, but I have been told that I am a quick study. Now, drop the pleasant buffoon routine and let us get through this."

Trask jettisoned the smile he had been keeping and got serious. "Mister Brannhard...can I call you Gus?"

"Let us see how this conversation goes, first."

"Fair enough. Okay, you can ask me anything you like, but I will not compromise any ongoing investigations or reveal any sensitive material. Anything else is fair game, Mr. Brannhard. Shoot." The globe above Trask's head stayed an unwavering blue.

Gus found himself starting to like the agent despite himself. "Why did you question Governor Rainsford under veridication?"

"Fuzzies are being removed from their home planet and being shipped to Terra and who knows where else. It takes a lot of money and/

or clout to pull off something like that. You, the Governor, the CEO of the CZC and the Native Affairs Commissioner are the obvious suspects in this case. I decided to see if I could either rule each of you out or find anything incriminating. The Governor passed with flying colors, so he is no longer a suspect." Blue.

"But Jack, Victor and I still are?" He admitted to himself that Trask made sense. It took a great deal of money and resources to pull off something like this and Trask was correct on who had that kind of power.

"It is not inconceivable that any combination of you three could swing it while keeping the Governor in the dark," Trask said. "I know about your investments and savings, Mr. Brannhard. While you have nothing like the resources that Grego and Holloway have access to, you still have a pretty healthy bank account to work with." Blue.

"Do you plan on letting it be known that Ben was interrogated under veridication?"

"No." Blue.

"And if it ever leaks out," Trask said, his mouth drawn tight. "I will put every man and woman in this building in this chair until I find out who did it, then summarily dismiss them and file charges for interfering with an ongoing investigation." Blue.

Gus nodded. "Yes, that seems fair. I would have preferred that you went through me before questioning Ben, though."

"That was just luck," Trask said. "I know you would have blocked it had you been there, but it all worked out. Now, will you be willing to take the seat?"

Gus thought hard, then decided it was for the Fuzzies. "Fine. However, I have some stipulations as well. You will confine your questions to the case at hand. I will grudgingly answer questions about my activities since arriving on Zarathustra, but that is all. And you will not ask me why, either. I just think a man has a right to his privacy. Take it or leave it."

Trask lifted the head-piece up and pulled off the electrodes. "Actually, I knew a great deal about your activities before arriving here, but they aren't germane to this investigation, so far as I can tell. So I will accede to your restrictions."

"Thank you."

Gus took the seat and lowered the head-piece down. It was not lost on him that Trask knew exactly where to place the electrodes. A little white lie to set Gus at ease?

"Okay, Mr. Brannhard," Trask said conversationally. "Have you committed, or taken part after the fact, any crime since arriving on Zarathustra?"

"I have defended a number of alleged criminals. Does that count?"

"I sometimes wish it did," Trask admitted. "But no."

"Then no." Blue.

"Do you have any knowledge concerning the abduction, removal from this world and subsequent enslavement of the indigenous sapient beings, known as Fuzzies?"

"Only what I have learned since your arrival." The globe lightened to a violet hue. "Oh, and I prosecuted a bunch of slavers last year. I got the lot of them convicted and shot, too." The globe returned to blue.

"Hmm. Had me worried there for a moment. I thought this case would wrap up too quickly. Now, do you have any reason to suspect Victor Grego or John...excuse me, Jack Holloway, would be involved in enslaving or otherwise harming a Fuzzy?"

"Not currently." Blue. "Jack is pappy to one of the larger Fuzzy groups and dotes on them like a proud grandpa. Victor was slower to join the Friends of Little Fuzzy, but is now an ardent supporter." Blue.

Trask pounced on that last tidbit. "Victor Grego wasn't always a Fuzzy enthusiast?"

"No. He didn't want them proven sapient as it would cost him control of the planet. However, as Leslie Coombes once said, 'The Fuzzies had hurt him all they could. Now they could be friends.'" Blue.

"Interesting. Okay, do you believe that Holloway and Grego will allow themselves to be questioned under veridication?"

"As long as you stay on point, I doubt you will be able to chase them away. Jack would cheerfully shoot anybody hurting a Fuzzy. So would Victor." The blue of the globe supported Gus's belief in his statement, but Trask would not be able to trust it. He would have to get Grego and Holloway in the seat to verify.

"Any more questions?"

Trask said, "Lots, Mister Brannhard, but they fall outside of your restrictions."

Gus removed the electrodes and raised the head-piece. "In that case, you can call me Gus."

*   *   *

"How did it go?"

Trask looked up from his viewscreen to see Lt. Williams standing in the doorway. "Better than I expected. Brannhard didn't ask me nearly as many questions as I expected."

"I doubt he needed to. He probably ran a background check on you before he came over. Or maybe Marshal Fane did it for him."

"What?" Trask cried, then shook his head. "It would take a year for that information to come through from Terra."

Williams rolled his eyes. "Let me guess, this is your first time off Terra."

Trask leaned back in his chair. Clearly he had missed something. "Except for a visit to Mars Colony when I was twelve, yes. I was visiting my great-grandparents at the retirement facility there. Why?"

Williams took a seat. "I assume you ran background checks on people back on Terra."

"There were days when it seemed like I didn't do anything but."

"Then you no doubt came across records from off-world."

Trask nodded.

"Now, how do you think all of those records were so readily accessible?"

"I never really thought about it before," he admitted. "Now that you mention it, I should have wondered about it."

"That leads into my next question. Why do hyperspace ships stay in orbit around the planets they visit for a full week before spacing out to their next port of call?"

Trask shrugged. "Refueling, maintenance, passenger exchange, loading and unloading cargo, maybe even personnel change-over or just plain R&R."

"There is all of that, but most crew members want to get moving as quick as possible. The time dilation effect means they don't spend as much time in hyperspace as the calendar would suggest. A six-month journey is only three weeks subjective time to the crew members, but they are still paid six months' worth of wages. One tour of duty sets them up for a year or better when they get back home to their families. No, everything you suggested could be done in three days or less.

"The real reason is for information transfer. When a ship makes orbit, it automatically transmits and receives updates on bank transfers, the stock market, news, films and television shows, and, most importantly for us, criminal records, updates on ongoing investigations and background updates from every planet the ship made port. That makes for a Niflheim's worth of data and even the fastest transfer rates can't get it done in less than a week. If a glitch pops up, the departure of the ship will be delayed until the glitch is corrected. That doesn't happen often, fortunately."

"Isn't the information at risk of being tampered with?"

Williams shook his head. "The data is heavily encrypted with a password a light-year long. Only a special device attached to the transmitting and receiving computers can decrypt and open the data at either end, and the security on those devices is stupid heavy. They have been in use since Freya joined the Federation and none have ever gone missing or been tampered with, as far as I know."

"So, no matter what planet I am on, the same information will be available to me?"

"Give or take a month or two in transmission lag. Everything you could access on Terra before you left is available to you now. We are still six months behind, all in all, but it is the best we can do until somebody invents a communications transmitter capable of instantaneous data transmission from world to world."

Trask was impressed. "So I can access the same FBCI files here that

I could get back on Terra. Has Zarathustra always had this capability?"

"No. Zarathustra was owned outright by the CZC until three years ago, so only specific files were accessed, and those through the military installation on Xerxes. The Federation won't take chances that a private company will eventually find a way around the encryption and passwords. That was transferred to FBCI jurisdiction after the Pendarvis Decision... and after we got this office up and running. The receiver is on the roof, disguised, of course, and the computer is in the sub-basement.

"The sub-basement is completely encased in collapsium-laminated dura-steel and accessible only through one stairway guarded by robots and human guards. If you even try to enter without proper I.D. and access codes, you will be fired upon. No questions, no second chances. The guards are veridicated every week, so any attempts to bribe them will be discovered straight away."

He nodded. "No half measures. Good. So I can access my savings from the local bank?"

"The only bank. Yes, but not the interest it accrued in the last six months. I don't know why, but that is held back an additional year."

"I suspect it is because the bank can't track any purchases you made until the information makes the round trip. No point paying interest on an account that might not have any money left in it."

Lieutenant Williams mulled that over and agreed. "Anyway, Brannhard or Fane would have access to any information you do, save that which is barred by security restraints."

"Hmm...that might be all to the good."

"How so?"

"Transparency engenders trust. I expect to put a lot of people in the hot seat before this thing is through, and I will need Brannhard's help to do it. I am guessing the FBCI doesn't have a special prosecutor on this world."

"Zarathustra doesn't have a high enough population base to justify one. All our cases and requests for subpoenas and warrants go through Brannhard's office. So far we haven't had to butt heads with him. I hope we don't have to start now."

"I see no reason we should," Trask said. "We both want the same thing, namely to protect the Fuzzies, and he has veridicated proof that I am not the enemy here. We have cleared Brannhard and Rainsford. Now we need to have a chat with Grego and Holloway."

Williams let out a long breath. "Go easy with both. The CZC is still a major power on this planet and Grego could make life difficult for you. Holloway just might shoot you."

"I doubt that, Roger. I checked his file; Jack Holloway never killed anybody that wasn't either trying to kill him first, or was in the commission of a serious crime. However, that does not exclude the possibility that he might try to hand me a good beating if he feels the need."

Williams snorted. "I looked into Holloway and all the other politicos on this planet when I was assigned here, just in case we found another mess like we had on Yggdrasil and Baldur. Holloway has administered a number of beatings in his time, and none of them have ever been characterized as good. Remind me to show you photos of Leonard Kellogg after Holloway had a go at him. Kellogg was about thirty years younger than Holloway and never had a chance."

Trask nodded. "I saw those. One second Holloway is beating up Kellogg, the next he puts three rounds in the chest of a Kurt Borch. I checked Borch's record, too, and he had an impressive number of kills. Yes, I will be very tactful with Jack Holloway. Mostly because I think he will be a good friend to have in this investigation...if he doesn't become the focus of it."

XXIV

Darla Cross wrinkled her nose at the image on the 3-D display. The image was of a Fuzzy with his internal organs visible and functioning. Next to her stood a pair of Fuzzies who watched the display with morbid fascination. The male, Rhett Butler, reached up to touch the image only to find his hand went through the image. He jerked his hand back as though he had gotten a small shock.

"No, Rhett," Hoenveld said gently. "You mustn't touch."

Rhett Butler looked up and said, "Is not-so thing? Like on viewscreen?"

Hoenveld smiled warmly. He was getting better at smiling with all of the practice he had of late. "Very good, Rhett! Yes, is not-so thing like on the viewscreen. This is called a holographic image. Lars, restore the fur covering. Scarlett O'Hara seems to be distressed by the current image."

"Yes, Doctor." Lars tapped a few keys on the console and the holo-Fuzzy became hirsute again.

"Thank you, Lars. Is that better, Scarlett?"

She looked confused. "Why Fuzzee not have fur all over?"

"Unka Chris is trying to help Fuzzies, Scarlett," Darla Cross said. "Some Fuzzies can't have babies even when they eat the Wonderful Food. Unka Chris uses the not-so screen to see why."

Hoenveld was a little uncomfortable with the explanation but he let it pass. Even the brightest Fuzzy had difficulty grasping such concepts. This wasn't because the Fuzzies were not intelligent enough. It was simply a matter of their culture, which before the arrival of Terro-humans was that of a nomadic race that survived in the wild. Technology above low Paleolithic was new to them and had to be introduced slowly. Bows, arrows, and even firearms were easy enough for the Fuzzies to comprehend, but anything much higher than that would take time.

"Actually, Lars is working on the holographic aspect of our studies. I will concentrate on blood tests and other forms of bio-analysis. Miss Tresca is running tests looking for any commonalities in the sterile subjects—er—the Fuzzies who can't have babies. Ah, Darla, perhaps you could phrase it better."

Darla laughed. "Don't worry, Chris. They get that you are trying to help them, and that is what is important. Oh, that reminds me: is there anything I can do to help?"

Hoenveld, not normally known for his tactful manner, thought quickly for an answer. He couldn't think of any possible way an actress could help with research.

"Ah, what did you have in mind, dear?" he asked cautiously.

"Well, I have a Masters in biology. I was going for my Ph.D. when I got bit by the acting bug. So, I changed my major, but I still keep up on the scientific articles and read the Science Journal during my downtime. I realize everybody here is far more qualified to wade through the bio-chemistry and such, but maybe I could go through the Fuzzies' medical records and look for anything that might point us in the right direction."

Hoenveld was thunderstruck. "This is the first time I've heard about your science background!"

Darla waved that off. "What's to tell? You are the foremost scientific mind on the planet. I didn't think a Master's degree in one of your own fields would impress you. Most people are more interested in my acting career."

Hoenveld laughed. Not a polite chuckle, but a full throated belly laugh, possibly the first one he ever had. "Darla, darling, I hadn't even seen a movie since I graduated from college until I met you."

Darla's eyes went wide. "Really? Hey, when did you graduate?"

"When I was thirteen. What was your GPA?"

"Three-point-eight-nine. I didn't do so well on a couple of the required electives. You?"

"Four-point-oh. Yes, I think you could be of tremendous help by going through the records. If it won't interfere with your vocation."

Darla winked. "I have Lady Macbeth down cold. Let's download the Fuzzies' medical records onto my datapad so I can go through them between shows."

Hoenveld and Darla Cross walked away chatting on about their respective school days, while Lars shook his head in wonder. "Well," he said to himself, "it's a big universe and it takes all kinds to fill it."

*   *   *

"I spoke with Commodore Napier and he said he would increase planetary surveillance," Marshal Max Fane said. "He will also go over the logs and see if there are any discrepancies. He also said he would speak to the Native Affairs Commissioner about adding some more Marines to the protection detail planet-side."

Trask rubbed his chin and nodded. "That seems like a good start, Marshal. Tell me, is this Native Affairs Commissioner a good man? It would be pretty easy for him to secrete away a lot of Fuzzies without anybody getting suspicious." Actually, since Trask had gone over Jack's file thoroughly, he was more interested in the Marshal's opinion.

Marshal Max Fane laughed. "I would be careful what company you posited that theory in front of. It could land you in a fight, or even a duel. You are new here, so I will set you straight about Jack Holloway." The Marshal regaled Trask with the story of the Fuzzy Trial, the CZC gem heist and Little Fuzzy getting lost at Yellowsand. He underlined Jack's concern for Fuzzies. "And if that isn't enough reason to trust him, his son is one of the wealthiest men on the planet, if not *the* wealthiest. Before that, he was one of the most successful sunstone prospectors on Beta. So, he doesn't need the money."

Trask looked thoughtful, then asked, "Do you have records of his sunstone sales to the CZC?"

Max shook his head. "Never needed them. When Jack had to make bail before the trial, he just poured out his leather pouch and let the clerk select 25,000 sols worth of stones. You can't fake that. However, just to set your mind at ease and keep you from running down blind alleys, I'll request that information from the CZC…after I check with Jack to get his permission. Otherwise we'll need a warrant and we have precisely zero grounds to obtain one."

"I can see you like and respect this man, Marshal, and I understand the position I am putting you in." Trask took in a long breath and let it out. "Frankly, I like ruling people out. It doesn't make me any friends, but it helps keep my enemies' list manageable. I think you know as well as I that it isn't always about the money. Some people simply like doing bad things for the sheer thrill of it. I did a background check on Mr. Holloway before leaving Terra; he was a real hell-raiser before he settled down on Zarathustra. In a lot of ways his exploits are like something out of a Greek myth. I have a hard time accepting the idea that he would just leave all of that to settle down and dig for rocks on a backward planet."

Max wanted to dislike Trask for his line of reasoning. He couldn't, because he would have drawn the same conclusions had he never met Jack. "Jack was around sixty when he came to Zarathustra. A life like you described can take its toll on a man. However, it wasn't all lazy evenings in front of the viewscreen and drinks at the bar for Jack. His success drew attention, and that attention put him in a lot of crosshairs. Less successful prospectors tried to rob him on more than one occasion. In fact the undertaker on Beta started running a tab on his kills. Major George Lunt, back then still a captain, almost started writing up the attempted robberies as suicides after a while. So, he doesn't need money, and he gets all the action a man could want. I could go on and on, but I think I will just let you meet Jack and draw your own conclusions."

"Fair enough, Marshal."

"One other thing; Jack was making his mark on this world long before the Fuzzies were discovered. Now, just for giggles, do you have anybody else on your potential suspect list?"

Trask smiled. "Actually, I do. And this one would rule a lot of others out."

"Oh?" Max tried to think to whom Trask alluded. "Care to share, or is it me?"

Trask's eyes widened for a moment. "I already ruled you out on the veridicator. But, no, I was actually referring to somebody who left planet about two or three years ago. You probably know of him. He is an attorney by the name of Hugo Ingermann."

"Ah, yes, you requested that he be veridicated. His attorney, another prime example of legalistic slime, is blocking you in this. We don't have much leverage on him as he is currently facing capital charges for which, when he is found guilty, he will be executed. There is no discretion of the court in this, and policy has it that we cannot let him plea down to a lesser charge."

Trask nodded. "Plea bargaining is a tool to relieve pressure on the courts. Low-population planets don't have that kind of pressure, so they don't cut deals to save time and money. Changing that policy for Ingermann would set a bad precedent. What are the charges against him on Zarathustra?"

"Whoa! That's a pretty long list. What we can prove right now includes: receiving stolen goods, transporting stolen goods off-world, accessory after the fact in grand theft, conspiracy to murder Ivan Bowlby and Raul Laporte, racketeering, illegal mining on native lands, manslaughter of a native on those lands, engineering the escape of Leo Thaxter from Prison House...." Marshal Fane went on for a while before he ran out of charges he could pull from memory. "And that is just what we know about locally."

"That's an impressive list," Trask agreed. "Taking stolen goods off-world. That falls under FBCI jurisdiction. Maybe we can use that to get him into the chair."

Max gave it some thought, then smiled. "That's right. Federation law takes precedence over colony law. Chief Colonial Judge Pendarvis and Chief Colonial Prosecutor Brannhard will still have to be brought in, but they will be using a different set of rules of law to work with. I'll call Gus Brannhard." The Marshal reached for the comscreen, frowned deeply, then hesitated. "Agent Trask, all I have seen you do since you arrived is put people I know for a fact can't be involved in the hot seat. Ingermann is the first person I can believe might be implicated. Is this how you normally run an investigation?"

Trask could understand the Marshal's concern. "Actually, no. While

I have been ruling out people, Lieutenant Williams has been looking into other avenues of investigation."

"Such as?"

"Such as looking into large purchases of Extee Three. These slavers want living healthy Fuzzies. That means feeding them well. I don't see the poachers beating the bush for...what do they eat in the wild?"

"Land-prawns, goofers, roots, berries...anything they can find that can't eat them first."

"Right. That. So, they need large quantities of Extee Three to keep the stock alive and healthy."

Max had come to the same conclusions and had his own men looking into it. "I agree, but it is also possible that they brought the Extee Three with them, stole it from any of the Fuzzy villages, or even bought it from a speculator."

"Speculator?"

"Back when the Fuzzies were first discovered, speculators bought up as much Extee Three as they could get, hoping to hold out for high prices when the stock got low. Fortunately, Grego's boys at the CZC managed to obtain the formula and put it into production themselves. After that, the speculators couldn't give the stuff away. Now, they might have a new customer base and we have no way of knowing who most of the sellers are, or even if they still had any to sell, or who they sold it to."

Trask swore under his breath. He knew nothing about the speculators and hoped that Williams did. "I hate to admit it, but that one got past me."

Max shrugged. "No reason you would have known. It didn't even make it to the datastream. I'll have some men looking into it discreetly. We don't want to scare anybody off before we can catch them."

"Hmm...some of these speculators might be in on the slavery racket. We will need to do background checks on all of them, too."

Max agreed. "Already on that, too. In fact, Ingermann was one of those investors before he skipped planet. He dumped his stock at a loss after the CZC started turning out Extee Three. Now, what say we go speak with Gus about putting Ingermann in the chair?"

"The sooner the better," Trask said.

* * *

"Is Little Fuzzy bringing his girlfriend?" Pat Holloway asked.

Jack looked up quizzically. "What do you mean, girlfriend?"

Pat grinned. "Haven't you noticed how much time he's been spending with that cute golden-furred vixen?"

Jack's face reddened. "Sure, after I asked him to. Emily lost her Big One and I asked Little Fuzzy to look after her."

"Well, it looks like he's taken your advice to heart. They make a very cute little couple."

"Nonsense!" Jack sputtered. "Little Fuzzy's just being a gentleman. I'm sure he'd let me know if he was thinking of taking a mate."

"Oh, you do?" Pat said, raising her eyebrows. "Did you ask his permission when you decided to court Betty?"

He shook his head no.

"Jack, just what do you know about Fuzzy mating customs?"

Jack tugged at the ends of his mustache. "Not a lot. We do know Fuzzies pair-bond long enough to produce an offspring. Once the newborn is mobile and able to feed itself, the union typically comes to an end like Empire penguins. Only a few Fuzzies mate for life. That was in part responsible for the population drop before Extee Three came along when they suffered from titanium depletion in their diets. Most only have one child—"

"Wasn't that more a fertility issue, than custom? I mean, really, if the typical Fuzzy pair only has one child..." She shrugged her shoulders. "They would have gone extinct a long time ago."

"Damn good point, Pat. I'll have to have Juan check on the size of the northern Fuzzy families since they didn't have the population crash of their southern cousins."

"You might also do some research into mating rituals—"

"Now, Pat, you're just trying to get my goat!"

"Yes, and it looks like I've grabbed it by the horns!"

Jack chuckled. "But you do have a good point, Pat. Maybe it's time we put a team together to answer some of these questions. Fuzzies may have adapted to small families just a little too well for their own continued survival. And that could be a big problem down the line."

XXV

The moving men and technicians worked quickly and, for them, quietly setting up the equipment in Victor Grego's office. It was the second time that the polyencephalographic veridicator had been set up there. The first time was after Grego discovered a Fuzzy in his personal quarters and he had to be questioned to prove he hadn't abducted or harmed the Fuzzy.

"All set, Mr. Grego," Emmett Capac, the senior tech, said. "All we need to do is test it."

"Very good, Emmett. Now, who would care to volunteer to be the test subject?" Grego looked around and didn't see anyone jumping at the opportunity. "I promise not to ask anything embarrassing. And I'll add a fifty-sol inconvenience bonus. Make that one hundred."

Eric Strong wavered for a second, then agreed to take the seat. "Please keep my personal life out of this, sir."

"Fair enough, though now you have me curious. Emmett, would you do the honors?"

Strong took the seat while Capac attached the electrodes and lowered the head-piece. One of the techs powered up the console, then nodded.

"Eric, answer the next three questions truthfully. What is your full name?"

"Eric Dietrich Strong." The globe above his head remained blue.

"Age?"

"Twenty-seven." Blue.

"Have you ever killed anybody?"

"No." Blue.

Capac nodded. "Very good. Now answer the next three questions falsely. What planet were you born on?"

"Niflheim." The globe went from blue to red. Anybody could have spotted that lie even without the veridicator. Niflheim was as hostile to human life as a planet with an atmosphere could get.

"Do you have wings growing from your back?"

"Yes. Big blue harpy wings." Red.

Capac smiled. "No need to embellish, Eric. Last question, who do you think would win in a fist fight...Jack Holloway or Victor Grego?"

The globe turned deep violet indicating confusion. "I couldn't say for sure. I never met Mr. Holloway, though I've heard he can hand out a good beating. But he is much older than Mr. Grego, and Mr. Grego is in pretty good shape." The globe had returned to blue. Strong wasn't trying to butter up the boss; he just didn't have enough information to form a solid conclusion.

"Thank you for the honest assessment, Mr. Strong," Grego said. "However, Jack is a scrapper and I push paper. I wouldn't like my odds in a fight with him."

"I'll try another question. Eric, have you ever danced naked in the moonlight?"

"No." Red.

"Whaaaat?" Capac and Grego said it at the same time.

Strong sighed heavily. "I...was dating this woman who—"

"Stop!" Grego said. "What you do on your own time is no business of mine. Emmett!"

"The veridicator is in working order. And, I wouldn't mind meeting that woman," Capac said as he disconnected Strong from the chair.

"She lives on Freya," Strong said with a smirk. Capac groaned. It was well known that Freyan women were considered the most beautiful in Federation space. "I had to leave there to avoid certain entanglements with her family." It was also well known that Freyan fathers were fiercely protective of their daughters.

Capac turned his mind elsewhere. "Mr. Grego, if I am not overstepping myself, why do you need the veridicator?"

"You are not overstepping, Emmett," Grego said. "Blind obedience is the tool of tyrants, which I prefer not to consider myself. However, this is a sensitive matter and I cannot discuss it with you at this time."

Capac nodded and turned back to the techs who were gathering up the packing materials. They were just finishing when Jack, Betty, Patricia, Gus and Ben were escorted in by Major Lansky.

Grego put on his toothy smile and shook everybody's hands. "Where is this Agent Trask I have heard about? I thought he would come in with you?"

"Trask is bringing his own tech," Ben explained. "I guess he doesn't trust anybody he hasn't veridicated himself."

He shrugged. "Fair enough. My machine or his, the answers will be the same."

"Aren't you worried about setting a precedent?" Patricia asked. "I understand Gus was against Ben being questioned under veridication."

"Still am," Gus added.

Grego chuckled. "That precedent was already set three years ago when I insisted on being veridicated to prove I had nothing to do with Diamond appearing in Company House. I won't have it become the standard operating procedure, but I'll accept almost any indignity to protect the Fuzzies. I owe them at least that much."

Patricia shrugged. "Owe them? I thought it was you who started producing Extee Three and—"

"I'll explain later, Pat," Jack interrupted. He was about to say something else when Chief Steefer escorted Agent Trask and another man in. "Looks like the gang is all here. Time to get this party started."

Victor Grego walked over to Trask and extended his hand. "Captain Trask, welcome to Zarathustra."

Captain? He had me checked out! "Thank you, Mr. Grego, but I prefer to be referred to as Agent Trask, and people I work with can call me Buck. I hope to include you in the latter category."

Grego smiled wide. "I hope so, too. Shall we get this show on the road?"

Trask looked about. "I was hoping Mr. Morgan would be here as well."

"That is Mr. Holloway," Jack corrected. "John Morgan Holloway, Jr.

in Terran terms, John Morgan Holloway the Lesser in Freyan society. He got held up with something at H.I.N. and will be along after he sorts it out."

I'll have to update Morgan's dossier. Trask nodded. "Well, I understand he appeared on this planet about a year ago, so he is of low interest at this time. If nobody is opposed to the idea, let's get back to work."

"I have no objection if anybody else wants to get started," Grego said, "but I have to wait for my attorney, Leslie Coombes, to arrive. He would be somewhat put out if I took the chair before he got here."

"Hear, hear!" Gus said loudly. "See that, Ben? A man who waits for his counselor before allowing himself to be interrogated. You should take notes."

Governor Rainsford rolled his eyes in exasperation. "See the trouble you get me into?"

Trask laughed. "And where was Gus's lawyer when he took the seat?"

"Sitting in the seat with me," Gus shot back. "I *am* a lawyer, after all."

"You know what they say about a lawyer who represents himself." Everybody turned to see Leslie Coombes coming into the room. "You don't want me to finish that quote, do you?"

Gus chuckled. "Fool I may be, but at least I got to see Agent Trask here take the seat first. Say, do you use that tactic with all of your suspects?"

"No, this is a first," Trask admitted. "I knew I had to handle the most powerful men on the planet with finesse, and I absolutely had to know if any of you are involved in this case. So, who's our test subject?"

Grego glanced over at Strong who was looking everywhere else but in his boss's direction. Well, twice in one day was a bit much to ask of anybody. *We all have our secrets*, Grego thought.

"I'll go." Everybody turned to Patricia. "I've never been veridicated before. It'll give me something to talk about when I get home."

"I will ask the questions," Jack said. "No point letting any family secrets out."

Patricia laughed as she sat down. "As if we ever kept any secrets." Emmett Capac applied the electrodes and lowered the head-piece.

"Okay, Jack. Come and get me."

Jack thought for a moment before starting. "What did Pa mean by automatic transmissions?"

"That is what he called shiftless people." Blue.

"What is an automatic transmission?" Ben asked.

"It was part of the drive train in ground vehicles before contra-gravity was invented. Before that they had, um...stick shifts?...to put the vehicle in gear to go forward or backward," Gus explained.

"How many children do you have?" Jack asked.

"Five." Red.

"Very good, Pat. Now how many do you really have?"

"Four. Larry, Lori, Buddy and Dan." Blue.

"Has Jack always been fond of younger women?" Betty cut in. She smiled at Jack and winked.

"Back on Terra he always dated smart girls. They were always age appropriate, but that was forty years ago. I have no idea what shenanigans he has been up to since Adonitia passed away. Jack doesn't kiss and tell." Blue all the way through.

"I'll have to see what I can get away with when you are in the chair," Betty said to Jack.

"Just because I am in the chair, it doesn't mean I have to answer," Jack replied.

"Have you ever committed a felony?" Trask asked. Jack glanced over, though his expression was unreadable.

"Not that I am aware of, Agent Trask," Pat replied. Blue. "And I suggest you check with Jack before you try that again. He has a bit of a temper." Blue.

"My apologies."

"Okay, Pat. Lie about the next couple questions," Jack said. "What planet were you born on?"

"Mars." Red.

"What is your favorite alien species?"

"The Yggdrasil Khooghra." Red.

"How many times have you been married?"

"One hundred and twenty-seven." Red.

"Will that do, Agent Trask?" Jack asked.

Trask was satisfied and Grego took his turn in the veridicator, followed by Jack and even Leslie Coombes took a turn. The FBCI agent was both relieved and disappointed. It was all well and good that the most powerful men on the planet were not involved in criminal activity though it would have been nice to catch somebody at the outset. Now his avenues of investigation were more limited if less dangerous to his career. Trask was considering what he would do next when three more people joined the party.

"Morgan, Akira, this is Ca...Agent Trask of the FBCI," Victor Grego made the introductions. "He may want to ask you a few questions."

Morgan glanced over at the veridicator then back to Trask. "Do you have a warrant?"

"What is this about?" Akira demanded. Little John, startled awake, fussed for a moment, then settled down. "Morgan isn't sitting in that chair without a damned good reason."

Jack turned and whispered to Patricia, "I guess it is true what they say about men marrying women like their mothers."

"Not really," Patricia whispered back. "Ma was nothing like that."

"Morgan's mother was when she felt the need," Jack whispered back.

Trask explained about the Fuzzy slavery, horrifying both Akira and Morgan. Morgan took the chair without further comment while Akira fumed.

"Ask your questions, Agent Trask," Morgan said.

"Please state your name."

"John Morgan Holloway the Lesser." The globe briefly flickered to red when he said 'Holloway.' "I guess I haven't gotten completely comfortable with the new patronymic yet."

"Relax, Mr. Holloway," Trask said. "The same thing happens to recently married women. It takes a while for the mind to completely accept a new or modified identity. Now, prior to your arrival eleven months ago, had you even been to Zarathustra?"

"No." Blue.

"Have any of your employees, under your direction, been to Zarathustra before your arrival?"

Morgan had to think hard on that one. He had sent investigators throughout the Federation while searching for Jack. "Not that I can think of." Blue.

Now for the nitty-gritty, thought Trask. "Have you ever taken part in an action that could result in harm to a Fuzzy?"

Again, Morgan thought hard, then let out a long breath and said, "Yes."

"What?" Leslie Coombes looked around before realizing those words had come out of his mouth.

"Last year I used my yacht to ferry a couple hundred Fuzzies up to northern Beta to rescue Jack from the *Jin-f'ke*. George Lunt had me charged with a small list of crimes, and the Governor instructed Judge Javier to levy a fine on me. It was sizeable."

Trask was a little surprised. "Have there been any other such incidents?"

"Not that I am aware of...no." Blue.

"Is it possible one or more of your employees could be involved in such an action?"

"Possible? Maybe, but I doubt it. I pay and treat my people well, and they are thoroughly screened before I hire them on. I don't believe anybody like that is on my payroll." Blue.

"What about your friends on Zeta Continent?"

"Absolutely not!" Blue.

"Agent Trask, I think you are moving beyond the scope of the agreed-upon questions," Coombes warned.

Trask nodded. "I suppose I am. Thank you, Mr. Holloway, Commissioner. I think we have all we need."

Jack pulled Morgan off to the side after he had been freed from the chair. "Don't take it personally, Morgan. Agent Trask doesn't know Johann's people like we do."

"I know that, Father. Their isolationism could work against them. Don't worry, I won't strap on my pistol and call Trask out."

Jack laughed at the mental image that statement created. Agent Trask as Marshal Dillon and Morgan as the villain of the week. Jack made a mental note to show Morgan some of his old *Gunsmoke* recordings.

Morgan looked at him quizzically.

"I'll explain later, son."

Morgan noticed the look on Akira's face. "Please excuse me, while I talk my wife out of smacking me with a skillet when we get home. It is a good thing I left the bodyguards downstairs."

"Bodyguards?" Trask repeated.

"Thorans. They might have reacted badly to my being questioned in that thing."

Trask knew the reputation the Thorans enjoyed and had to agree. "Well, now that all of you have been ruled out as potential suspects, maybe we can get busy finding the real culprits. Mr. Brannhard, I understand you managed to arrange an interrogation session with Hugo Ingermann."

Gus chuckled. "Federation law, mostly, supersedes colonial law. Ingermann, by transferring stolen goods from planet to planet, placed himself squarely in FBCI jurisdiction. Colonial rules of evidence do not apply in that case, so Judge Pendarvis had no choice other than to allow you to interrogate him. Ingermann's lawyer can scream bloody murder from here to Terra and it won't make a difference. He's all yours. I would like to be present, of course."

"So would I," Ben added. "In fact, it could be a pretty crowded room."

"I am sorry, Governor, but I have to keep it to Mr. Brannhard and me," Trask said.

"He's right, Ben," Gus added. "There are still rules we have to follow, though Marshal Fane should also be present."

"He'll be quite welcome," Trask said. "Jack, as the Commissioner of Native Affairs this falls under your jurisdiction. Care to sit in?"

Jack smiled wolfishly. "You just try to chase me away. It's a shame we can't be there to see Ingermann get the news."

Gus chuckled. "Yes, he should be getting that piece of bad news right about now."

XXVI

"What!"

"I am sorry, Mr. Ingermann, but there was nothing I could do." Clarence Anetrou didn't bother shuffling papers for effect. The news he had just given his client provided enough drama. "There was simply no way to compromise the blood sample once it was collected from the crime scene, and I had no leverage on the med-tech that drew the sample from you. Not that it would have done any good since he signed a waiver agreeing to verify under veridication that the sample was yours and nobody else's. Same with the tech that ran the comparison sample."

Anetrou took a deep breath and let it out. "Now that they have legally established your identity, they have you for receiving and transporting stolen goods off-world, which clearly puts you under FBCI jurisdiction, and Federation rules of law. They can put you in the chair and ask anything they want now."

Ingermann sputtered and waved his arms frantically as if trying to find a way out of the interrogation cell. After a moment, he seemed to calm down and got a sly look on his face. "Wait, how did they get my DNA in the first place? From before I left planet?"

Anetrou shook his head sadly. "In the years you resided on this world prior to your abrupt departure, you visited three different dentists, had a couple emergency room visits, and several blood draws for various reasons at the hospital. Each of these kept samples. One dentist still has your wisdom teeth and the hospital kept your old X-rays and blood samples. Victor Grego was very concerned about xenopathogens and ordered the hospital to retain all such bio-waste for screening if any new diseases appeared. Leslie Coombes no doubt informed Gus Brannhard of this practice and the erstwhile colonial prosecutor secured warrants and seizure orders for the lot. There wasn't a thing I could do to prevent it. Had I known that these samples existed earlier, well...." Anetrou shrugged. "The time has come to make a deal, Hugo."

Ingermann slumped in his seat. "I have nothing to bargain with. Quigley spilled his guts to get a deal for his son, and Lundgren was squeezed dry of everything he knew by the Navy. In fact, I heard that he is working for them now, like an indentured servant."

"What about whatever it was this Trask is after? I doubt he came all the way from Terra just to go after you."

Ingermann's face brightened for a moment, then clouded again. "Anything he wants to know, he'll get while I am in the hot seat. If I refuse to answer, he will point out that he can speed up my execution date."

Anetrou looked surprised. "He can do that?"

Ingermann shook his head in disbelief. *The end of the universe must be at hand; my shyster lawyer admitted his ignorance!* "On almost any other planet, I would think not, but here on Zarathustra where the laws haven't evolved into anything too complicated, I bet he could. With Rainsford, Brannhard and Grego greasing the wheels the whole way."

Anetrou looked thoughtful for a moment. "Wait, they must be after a bigger fish than you, or this Trask wouldn't be here. Offer to help them with the net."

Ingermann thought it over. Almost any information that existed on the planet found its way into the prison grapevine. With a little effort, he would be able to find out almost anything. The information would be third and fourth hand at best, but he was ready to grasp at even the flimsiest straw. He would need a few things to bribe people with, as nobody liked him enough to give him anything for free, but he had assets even Brannhard hadn't found. He hoped.

"I think you are on to something there, Clarence. I'll need a few things to get started. First, some money placed into my commissary account...."

* * *

"I think I may have found a correlation, Chris."

Dr. Hoenveld put down the journal he was reading, *Scientific Federation*, and turned to Darla Cross who was sitting at the dining room table scrolling through her electronic tablet. Rhett Butler and Scarlett O'Hara were working on the construction kit that Hoenveld had bought for them.

"What is it, Darla?"

Darla tapped on the tablet and the viewscreen, one of the full wall models she used for reviewing her performances, came to life among a splash of color. The image resolved into three spreadsheets.

"Look here; the top spreadsheet contains all of the Fuzzies who ever had a medical workup here in Mallorysport or back on the Fuzzy Reservation. The second page lists all of the Fuzzies that are normal from the first list. The third shows all that have either compromised reproduction indications or are outright sterile at the time of the latest battery of tests."

Hoenveld looked over the screen. It was well laid out and showed all of the Fuzzies known medical history in short bullet points. He smiled, a rarity when away from Miss Cross, and nodded in approval. "It looks like you have something in mind."

"I do. All of the Fuzzies were given the usual inoculations to protect them from Terro-originated pathogens, so I eliminated the drugs, antibiotics and vaccines common to both groups. Then I went over the medical histories—"

"Wait. You did all of that in addition to your stage performances?"

"I read a page at a glance with total recall. It is how I can keep my lines straight and anticipate what everybody else does on stage before the first rehearsal. I studied the histories on my breaks. Sadly, I can't type anywhere near as fast as I can read so I was up early this morning putting this all together. Any-who, I noticed something odd while typing all this up; most of the Fuzzies who have become sterile have had a broken bone, or at least a serious strain somewhere on their body."

Hoenveld pulled a chair around and positioned himself where he could look back and forth between the viewscreen and Darla Cross without straining his neck. "It could be that something in the Fuzzy physiognomy shuts down the reproductive system if the Fuzzy is too injured to look after their young...but that doesn't explain Zorro or Leslie Coombes' Fuzzies. None of them, except Lame One—I forget what Mr. Coombes named her—suffered any severe physical traumas."

Darla scrolled through the records. "It was either Nelda Fleming, Kathy O'Grady or Gladys Fleming. The medical records only include the names of the adoptive parent and what they named them. All three had burns from the forest fire and minor breaks from their time out in the wild, so I can't be sure which one was Lame One. We should include what they were called by each other on the documents."

"According to Commissioner Holloway, their names in the wild are things like Old One, Young One, This One and That One. Mostly they call each other 'You.'"

Darla rolled her eyes. "I've heard names like Fruit Finder, Stone Breaker, Wise One, Makes-Things and Red Fur. Not very sophisticated, but a lot more diverse than just 'You.'"

"Agreed, but you will find those names in every third tribe, or family gathering, whatever they call those clans they travel in. Still, it might be a good idea to add that information." Hoenveld returned his attention to the screen. "Bring up a list of the drugs each of the affected Fuzzies have been given." The screen changed to show the common medications among Fuzzies records. "Hmm...they have all been given panacillain—"

"You mean penicillin?" Darla interrupted. "We still make that?"

"No, panacillain. It is a newer synthetic antibiotic that kills almost anything without the allergic reactions some people suffered from penicillin."

Darla nodded. She knew better than to compete with her paramour's knowledge in such matters. "Hmm...a lot of the non-affected Fuzzies were given panacillain, too. Maybe there is a drug interaction with something else?"

"Possibly, and we will have to look into that. Somehow, I think it is something much simpler, and obvious, but we may be too close to see it. I wish I was better at those hunches that Dr. Mallin is so fond of."

Darla thought for a moment then had an idea. "Hunches. We need a cop."

"What?" Hoenveld looked at Darla with widened eyes. "What is a policeman going to do here?"

"Cops are all about hunches. Let's find one with some higher education, like a forensic pathologist who works for the police and bring him in."

Hoenveld had his doubts but remembered how one of his lab techs had a hunch about land-prawns and their connection to Fuzzy fertility. "Yes, let us do that. It couldn't hurt."

"Great. Umm...who do we call?"

Hoenveld smiled; he was getting better at it. "We use what the police call the Chain of Command. I will speak with Dr. Jimenez, he will speak with Victor Grego, and from there things will happen very quickly."

* * *

Dmitri Watson straightened up and stretched. He had been bent over the microscope for hours looking at slide after slide and decided he needed a break. A walk around the camp would do him good. Outside of his tent he noticed that the extra personnel had arrived. Unlike the older, more developed planets, he had to settle for vagrant hires to fill the roles normally filled by pre-grad college students. Cinda did manage to find a couple of post grads like herself to fill in the more sensitive positions, but, for the most part, the workforce consisted of part-timers and out of work types culled from the Junktown ads posted at The Soup Kitchen.

Watson had to admit that they were active enough at their jobs, if not properly trained. Still, many hands made for light work, and some of those hands cheerfully accepted minimum pay and full stomachs for their efforts.

Across the camp Dmitri spotted Cinda sitting on the ground and typing into her datapad. Attached to the datapad was some strange gizmo he never saw before. Curious, he strolled over to get a closer look.

"Dmitri," Cinda said when she spotted him approaching. "I was just organizing the notes I took from today's work."

Dmitri sighed. "Sadly, there was nothing exciting to record. All we seem to have accomplished is retracing everybody else's steps."

"Ruling something out is still progress," Cinda said. "I think that is a police-ism, but it still applies to scientific discovery."

"Indeed it does." Dmitri took a seat next to the amber-haired intern and studied the apparatus. "Cinda, what is this device you have connected to your datapad? A remote for capturing the datastream out here in the boonies?"

"What? Oh, not at all. The CZC satellites cover the entire planet so remotes aren't needed. You can get the same signal at the North Pole as you can in Mallorysport. No, this is a solar energy converter. I use it to power my datapad when away from home."

Dmitri looked skeptical. "Why bother with something so archaic when a single atomic battery would charge your pad effectively forever?"

"Atomic batteries are pricey and I couldn't afford one at the time I bought the datapad. However, they were all but paying you to take the solar converters, and it works well enough for me. Maybe after I save up a bit I can switch over. For now this works fine."

"And if we have a cloudy day or two?"

"The internal battery is good for a week. I keep it fully charged just in case that happens."

Dmitri nodded. He expected Cinda would keep on top of any eventuality. He got up, told her to carry on and went to the mess tent for a sandwich. There he spotted Gregoire Rutherford.

"Hey, Greg, anything new?"

"Pretty much as you might expect. Nothing new, no surprises. I did send our resident giant, Dax, out for some new batteries. A couple lost their charge."

Dmitri chuckled. "That is what happens when you get secondhand equipment."

"Secondhand gear is all there is on this planet," Greg countered. "At least for the kind of work we are doing. Most of what we rented is leftovers from the initial planetary surveys done by the Federation shortly after Zarathustra was discovered, oh, about a hundred years ago. The rest was brought in at great expense by privately funded groups, then left behind since it was cost prohibitive to ship to wherever they went next. Even Rico drew the line at buying new equipment and shipping it here."

"Yes, I know," Dmitri agreed. "The cost of freight would have been almost as much as the equipment itself. We could have saved a lot of money on the atomic cartridges if he had gone solar."

Greg snorted derisively. "Solar! Ha! That is a K0 star up there, and we are twice as far from it as this planet should be. We wouldn't get enough juice to run so much as a comm link without a couple dozen collection panels the size of billboards."

"Oh, come on, you are exaggerating. Our Miss Cinda is out there right now running her datapad with a setup the size of a coffee maker."

Greg hesitated, then shook his head. "Not possible. She must be draining her batteries without realizing it."

Dmitri considered that. Cinda did say her batteries were good for a week. Still... "I would think after a year on this planet she would have noticed if the solar charger wasn't getting the job done. Have there been any new advances in solar conversion technology?"

Greg considered for a moment. "On Magni and Indra, where the primaries are mid-class F stars that spit out ridiculous amounts of light and radiation, solar energy is in popular use. Solar panels there reach as much as ninety-five percent efficiency, the best in the Federation, but the panels are expensive and only used on worlds with high output primaries. A K0 sun wouldn't charge a flashlight even with one of those panels. Not quickly, anyway."

"And yet we squint every time we look up at that sun," Dmitri said. "Why is that? I have been to Freya, which is half as far from its K0 primary, yet it is no brighter there, to the naked eye, than it is here. Why, I wonder?"

Greg thought hard for an explanation. "Atmospheric conditions, I would say. The ozone layer, for example, is half as thick on this world than on Freya, and about a quarter of that of pre-Atomic Terra." He thought some more. "That might account for the solar panels working better as more solar radiation sneaks in, but I still question their overall effectiveness."

"I think we need to take another look at Cinda's setup, Greg," Dmitri interrupted. "At least rule in or out whether her setup is working the way she claims."

"You think this is important?"

"At this point, Greg. I think every anomaly is important."

Greg shrugged. "Oh, Muhgawd, why not. I haven't had any luck on anything today. Maybe a break will recharge my own batteries. We'll stop by my tent first so I can grab my voltage meter. If we are going to do this, let's do it right."

*   *   *

Douglas cursed as he pulled the trigger. The harpy jerked in mid-flight, then plummeted to the ground.

"Good shot, Doug. The bastard never knew what hit him."

He muttered something under his breath. "Okay, we bagged our limit, now let's get the carcass, collect our trophies and get the Niflheim off this continent."

Andre snickered. "Still not a fan of hunting?"

He cleared his weapon and slung it over his shoulder before moving towards the kill. "I was raised to eat what you kill, and only kill what you intend to eat. I never learned to enjoy hunting as a sport. That's why I saved the meat from the damnthings. I'm not looking forward to trying these winged lizards, though."

Andre nodded. "They probably taste like chicken, like everything else. So why bother with the trophies?"

"It's part of our cover as sport hunters, though I do like my new walking stick. I still don't know what we can pull off a harpy, though."

"Leather. Boots, jacket, belt, wallet, stuff like that. I've seen a few shops in Mallorysport that claim to sell harpy leather goods. Might get a good price from a tanner for this guy's hide." Andre kicked the corpse to make sure it was dead. "So, what do we do now?"

"We skin this thing and take it back to Mallorysport and await further orders. Sooner or later we go back to catching Fuzzies and I want to be ready for it."

Andre nodded. "Still, a working vacation is better than no work at all."

He snorted. "Only if you like hunting. I don't. It loses a lot of the thrill when you have to hunt for food to survive. These days I would rather stalk the wild veldbeest steak properly prepared in a restaurant with potatoes, gravy and a snifter of brandy on the side."

Andre shook his head, then remembered that Douglas had come from the borderlands of North America where life was short, hard and unpleasant. If starvation didn't get you, a radioactive hotspot might. Only the people who couldn't find a way out lived there. Douglas had managed to get out.

"You never told me how you ended up doing this," Andre said. "Snatching Fuzzies, that is."

"Oh, the usual. After I finished my tour in the Marines I tried my hand at mercenary work, I picked the wrong job and ended up in prison, Terra-side. There I met some people who steered me to other people who eventually hooked me up with this organization down in South Africa. The pay is good, the risks reasonable and I get to travel."

"Reasonable? If we get caught...." Andre made a fist with two fingers extended and the thumb straight up pointed at the side of his head. "Bang! No discretion of the court, no plea bargains."

He shrugged. "Better that than life in a cage. Now let's get this stupid lizard skinned and get out of here."

As the two men returned to their aircar the comscreen beeped. Douglas flicked on the screen. "Rathbone here."

The image from the screen was that of a damnthing. "We have your assignment if you are done with your hunting vacation."

"More than done," he replied tersely.

"Excellent. You will be going to northern Beta."

XXVII

Throughout the Federation, few human beings have ever witnessed a hyperspace ship transpose back into normal space with their own eyes. Nor has there ever been a recording of such an event. The reason for this is not particularly strange; spaceship schedules are fairly loose when tracking the arrival of a ship from another planet. A schedule cannot be maintained too closely as there is no means of communicating potential delays from planet to planet. In addition, no matter how good the navigator and his calculations, it is fairly impossible to know exactly where the ship will reappear in normal space. Recording equipment is even less likely to capture the event as something disrupts the tape apparatus at the moment of transposition. So, unless one has tremendous free time and equally impressive patience and luck, one is highly unlikely to be looking at just the right spot when a ship appears.

Among the very few who have witnessed such an event, the story is uniformly the same; one second it was empty space, the next second there was a ship. No slow fade-in or even a flashy light display; just the sudden—jarring—appearance of the ship.

Within the hyperspace craft it is a slightly different story. On the viewscreen there is an unvarying gray nothingness until transposition, then there is a spectacular display of light and color until it vanishes to leave one staring at the darkness speckled with tiny dots of light.

Captain Conrad Greibenfeld observed this phenomenon for the umpteenth time as the *F.S.N. Hikaru Hatori* entered normal space. He felt the kind of excitement that normally comes from returning home after a long battle. Up until this moment he hadn't realized that he considered Zarathustra his home. Career soldiers learn early not to get too attached to places; there was always another battle to be fought and relocation was usually part of the package.

During his thirty plus years as a naval officer, Captain Greibenfeld had been to so many planets he could not recall them all without some hard thought. Still, every military man would remember his first posting, and his last, no matter what happened in between.

Geibenfeld's first posting, after his training on Terra, had been on Fenris. There, as a young ensign, he had met Jack Holloway. Jack had taught him a few things that the Navy manual never covered, and what he had learned saved his life on more than a few occasions. While the age difference between them was not that great, Jack had become a sort of father figure to him. With only one exception, Jack impressed him as being as solid as they come.

And even the exception was more than understandable: Jack had received a letter explaining his wife and son had died in childbirth, and Jack went on a bender that landed him in jail for a few days. When he got out, he paid his fine, said his farewells and moved on to a new planet.

Greibenfeld didn't see Jack again until his posting on Zarathustra, though stories about him popped up on many of the planets he was posted to along the way. Now, after two years on Terra dealing with a lot of bureaucratic foolishness, he was returning to Zarathustra. He hoped to find Jack and the rest of the bunch in good health. He knew he would be working closely with Jack concerning the latest catastrophe to affect the Fuzzies and looked forward to it. It would be a nice change of pace to deal with somebody with some good old-fashioned horse sense.

"All hands prepare for transposition to normal space. Repeat, all hands prepare for transposition to normal space," a voice issued from the comm ports.

Greibenfeld briefly wondered why such announcements were deemed necessary on military transports, then realized he answered his own question. While it had never come up during his tenure in the Navy, there was always the possibility that the ship could enter a battle zone in space. There was no way to know that until transposition was completed, and by then it could be too late to prepare for hostilities.

The men and women scurrying to battle positions confirmed that fact. Had he been a ship commander or some other regular ship's officer, he would have known that already, but not everybody in the Navy worked on a ship. The vast majority of his career had been spent on various planets on what he privately called baby-sitting duty, though he had seen some battles in his time.

Amid the wash of brilliant colors on all screens, the stars of normal space quickly came into view. There was a slight jarring sensation and he heard somebody swear.

"Is there a problem, Captain?"

Captain Ralph Osborne grunted. "Not really. We came out of hyperspace too close to Zarathustra's gravity well and got bounced back a bit. Nothing serious, but it will take a couple hours extra before we reach Xerxes."

Greibenfeld nodded. He had heard about gravity bounce before, though this was the first time he experienced it. It was mildly disappointing; he expected something more dramatic. "What determines the distance of the bounce? The size of the gravity well or the proximity of the planet when the ship transposes?"

Osborne shrugged. "Quantum physicists have been pondering that since the first bounce. There is a story that an exploration ship once transposed near a black hole and was bounced back several parsecs, but I can't say for sure if that is true or not. There is even some discussion of whether or not it really is the gravity well, or the atmosphere itself. One brain boy back on Terra, I don't recall the name, has a theory that it is the presence of matter that forces the ship back."

"Ah, the old 'two separate physical objects cannot exist in the same place at once' dogma. I can see that in the case of a solid, maybe even a liquid, but wouldn't gas simply be pushed aside?"

Osborne mulled it over for a second. "Normally, I would think so, but from the few outside observations of a ship transposing back to normal space, one second the space is empty, the next it isn't. That sudden happening of an object appearing out of seemingly nothing would make even a thin atmosphere seem very solid. A bit like diving into water: from a few feet up the water is easy to penetrate without harm to the body.

Take a belly flop from the high dive and it feels like landing on concrete."

Greibenfeld had to admit the theory had some merit to it, at least to his ignorant mind. "So the further into atmosphere the ship goes, the harder the bounce back effect. I can see how that might be the case. Have any ships ever suffered a bounce from an airless world with a significant gravity well?"

Captain Ralph Osborne snorted. "I don't know if such a body exists within a solar system. Any mass large enough to cause a bounce will also have captured or released gasses that are trapped by the gravity well. Not much exploring has been done outside of star systems; we tend to look for life and usable resources, not barren chunks of rock in the middle of nowhere."

Out of the corner of his eye, Greibenfeld spotted the viewscreen and noticed something odd. "What the Niflheim is going on?"

"What?" Osborne looked at the screen. "Is something wrong?"

"Wrong? Only about several hundred ships in orbit around Darius."

Osborne didn't understand the significance. On Terra, there were easily ten times as many ships in orbit every day. "Is this a lot?"

Greibenfeld walked over to the screen for a better look. "You better believe something is wrong. When I was last here, we had one ship in orbit per week. Just one. This mess makes no sense at all."

Osborne returned his attention to the viewscreen and rubbed his chin. "You have been away for, what, two years, now? A lot can change on a new planet open for colonization. These might all be hopefuls looking for some land to settle on."

"That land won't be available for another thousand years," Greibenfeld countered. He explained about the lease deal on the unseated lands with the Charterless Zarathustra Company. "News of that would have reached the farthest planets in the Federation by now. This is something else."

Osborne had an evil thought. "Invasion? Pirates?" he asked. His hand moved to the alarm switch and hovered there.

Greibenfeld adjusted the viewscreen for a closer look at the ships. "No, I don't think so. Look here; that one, that one and that one are yachts. Limited offensive capability, what they do have is mostly for moving cosmic debris out of their path. That one's a cargo hauler. They usually work moving back and forth between two close systems. They have insufficient armor to survive a pitched battle. That one looks like a refitted space liner for pleasure cruises."

"Pirates wouldn't be too picky about what kind of ships they pressed into service," Osborne argued.

"True, but then at least a few of them would be in orbit about Xerxes and the planet itself...."

"Xerxes!" Osborne quickly reset the screen to show Xerxes Naval Base. "Well, that settles that. The Navy base is undamaged and there is no sign of military transports hovering about. Invaders of any kind would have gone for the base first, then the planet. It should be safe to contact them and see what the Niflheim is going on."

* * *

Commodore Napier downed his scotch and debated having another when a Marine with gunnery sergeant stripes approached his table and came to attention while waiting to be noticed. An NCO in the Officers' Club stood out like a cactus in a rose garden, and could be just as prickly.

"Stand at ease, Gunny," Napier said. "What is it?"

"Sir! We have a request from the Commissioner of Native Affairs, by way of Lieutenant Sutherland to inspect the orbiting ships, sir!" The Gunny lowered his voice before continuing. "Sir, he has reason to believe that Fuzzy slavers may be using one or more ships to deport Fuzzies to other planets illegally."

Napier had heard about the reappearance of Fuzzy slavers from both Governor Ben Rainsford and Agent Trask and had considered inspecting the ships on his own authority. An official request saved him some head-aches. "Is that all, Gunny?"

"Sir, no sir! The *F.S.N. Hikaru Hatori* just entered normal space near Zarathustra and is requesting permission to dock here on Xerxes. They are also wondering, and I quote, "what the Niflheim are all those ships doing up there.' Sir!"

Napier motioned for the Gunny to take a seat, which he did. Nobody could sit at attention like a Marine Gunny, he reflected. "By any chance, did you personally hear the transmission?"

"Sir, yes, Sir."

"Who made the request?"

"Sir, he said he was Captain Greibenfeld returning from Terra, Sir."

"Captain Greibenfeld? About time he got back. This calls for a celebration. What will you have, Gunny? My treat, and consider it an order."

"Sir! A Three Planets, Sir."

The Commodore ordered the drink and wondered if new intestinal tracts were issued with the Marine uniforms. A Three Planets would put down a damnthing in short order.

*   *   *

Officer Clarke saved his duty report and shut off his datapad. He checked the wall clock and saw he still had twenty-five minutes until the end of his shift, so he decided to take a walk near the *Jin-f'ke* camp. At the edge of the ridgetop he stopped and pulled out his pseudo-pipe and leaned against a Samhain tree. The Samhain was not really a tree, but a very large plant. At the top was a pumpkin-shaped flower that opened only when both moons were full. Usually, it looked like a scarecrow construct one might set up for Halloween, hence the name.

From his vantage point, he could see the extreme edge of the Fuzzy village. At last count there were over three hundred Fuzzies living and working together under the leadership of Red Fur. It was an impressive feat for a normally nomadic species. Only the Fuzzies that had joined up with the Big Ones in the south had come close to matching that accomplishment, and they had a great deal of help.

Clarke finished his pseudo-pipe charge, a concoction that smelled and tasted like peppermint, and started back to the guard shack when a high-pitched whine assaulted his ears. Out of reflex, he covered his ears and ducked behind the Samhain tree. The barrel, or stem, was barely large enough around to hide the burly officer, and provided no protection from the noise at all. After several long agonizing seconds, the noise stopped and Clarke carefully peeked around the base of the plant. His ears were still ringing from the sonic assault though he managed to make out the sound of somebody talking. It was not Fuzzy speak. The officer could see two men with a large blunderbuss-like weapon on a tripod aimed at the guard shack about twenty meters from his current position.

*　*　*

"Do you think that got him, Doug?" a large man asked, as he removed his ear protectors.

"Huh?" The second man removed his ear guards and the first man repeated the question. "Anybody within fifty meters in the direction of the wave pattern will have brain matter coming out their ears. You want to go and take a look?"

The other man shook his head. "I saw what a sono-bazooka can do once. Once is enough."

The man identified as Doug nodded then packed up the weapon. "I just hope the Fuzzies didn't hear it. The wave form is supposed to be mono-directional, but there is always some spillage."

"Oh, hell, I didn't think of that. Fuzzies have, like, super-hearing compared to us. Like dogs."

Doug nodded. "Yeah, any Fuzzies in the direction we aimed or within twenty meters of the wave form are dead for sure. Any further out and they will be unconscious, possibly brain damaged, and stone deaf. Permanently. Fortunately, the village is behind us. Once we saturate the area with anesthezine gas, we can call in the ship to collect them all. Got the grenade launcher primed up?"

"Hell, no! I don't carry loaded launchers when moving over rough terrain. Don't worry, it only takes a second to load."

Clarke decided he had heard enough. Carefully, he pulled out his radio, set the audio button to mute replies, and called for back-up. It would take at least ten minutes for help to arrive. According to the manual, his best bet was to wait, watch, and record everything that happened, and to take no action unless there was no other choice. The manual was not going to work out in this instance.

Doug and the other man collected their gear and started towards the

Jin-f'ke village. That was all Clarke waited for. He stepped out from the copse of Samhain trees and leveled his pistol at the two men.

"Hold it. Put everything down on the ground and raise your hands in the air."

The larger man swore, then said, "He wasn't in the shack."

Doug grunted and dropped his equipment. The other man seemed to do the same, then swung the launcher and discharged a grenade. The charge missed Clarke but burst in the air near him releasing the anesthezine gas. Clarke fired once as he held his breath. The larger man went down while Doug bolted for cover.

*   *   *

Damn. The bastard knows I can't hold my breath forever. Once I inhale the gas he can kill me at his leisure. Officer Clarke tried to run out of the expanding cloud of gas. He almost made it before his lungs gave out. Even with the gas working on him, he still managed another ten meters before he started losing consciousness. As he fell to the ground he could see Doug coming out of the brush with a hunter's knife. He tried to raise his gun and failed. Clarke's last thought was that he would never wake up.

Clarke came to consciousness with an oxy-mask covering his nose and mouth. Above him were Officers Mark Schmidt and Jamal Jones. He tried to sit up and became dizzy.

"Give it a moment, Mike," Jamal said. "You must have inhaled a hell of a lot of gas." The officer held up the expended cartridge. "This is nasty stuff. I don't know how you got as far as you did."

"I think you owe somebody a big thank you when you get back on your feet," Mark added.

Clarke turned his head and saw a furry of Fuzzies standing near a body. The body was the one called Doug, and it was in very bad shape. Even disoriented from the gas Clarke could tell that the Fuzzies had taken care of the slaver before Doug took care of him. One of the Fuzzies broke away from the gathering and approached the trio of ZNPF officers. It was Red Fur.

"Clarke not make-dead." Red Fur said. It was more a statement than a question.

"I not...make-dead," Clarke replied. "Thank you."

Red Fur nodded and walked away. Mark watched, then commented: "Not much of a talker, is he?"

"Actions...speak louder...than words," Clarke said. "He...saved a Big One. That says...a lot...for a *Jin-f'ke*." Clarke again struggled to sit up. Mark and Jamal helped him. "The poachers said...something about calling...for a transport to collect...the Fuzzies."

Jamal nodded. "So this mutt is part of the slavery ring. I had a feeling." He pulled out his radio and relayed the information. "Yeah, they would have to be fairly close. See if we can get some eyes in the sky and spot them."

"Where's the...other one?"

Jamal looked around. "Other one? That must be Andre Sabahatu, Douglas Rathbone's partner. That's who this mutt is, if you were wondering."

"I...shot one."

Mark spotted Clarke's gun on the ground and collected it. "With this cannon? Not a lot of people survive getting hit with a .44. We'll look around just in case. It would be nice to get some information from a live slaver."

Andre Sabahatu was found twenty meters away from where Clarke had shot him. He crawled as far as he could before succumbing to his injuries. He still might have survived if Red Fur and his gang hadn't found him first.

"Does anybody know how to explain to a Fuzzy that a live bad Big One is more useful to us than a dead bad Big One?" Mark said rhetorically.

"We have the bodies and their equipment," Jamal said. "We might still get something useful out of that. Mike, feeling up to the trip home?"

"I am, but I am not sure the Fuzzies will let me," Clarke replied. Jamal and Mark noticed that Clarke was surrounded by Fuzzies, all with their *shoppo-diggos* at port arms. "I think they are guarding me."

"I think you've been inducted," Jamal observed.

"You got hurt, as best as they see it, protecting the village, Mike," Mark said. "You are one of them now."

XXVIII

"We were ordered to stand down, T-Rex."

The masked man whose name was not actually T-Rex turned in his seat at the aircar's control console. "Look, there isn't a ZNPF patrol car within fifty miles from here, and there are at least thirty wild Fuzzies gathered together down there. Do you have any idea how rare that is? Fuzzies run in groups of two to eight and rarely gather en masse like that. Christ on a crutch, this might even be a totally unique occurrence. Ironically, it would be downright criminal of us not to avail ourselves of this opportunity, Steg."

Steg, which was also not his real name, looked at his partner in annoyance. "How do you know these Fuzzies don't have radios to call for help? I heard that the ZNPF issued out a couple hundred to the natives when Branner got abducted last year."

"Brannhard, not Branner. Look at the screen; do you see any dogs with this bunch? Metal weapons or even a backpack? No. That means these are wild Fuzzies who probably never even heard of Big Ones. No radios."

"It won't matter anyway, T-Rex. Even with the sound baffles on the engine, those Fuzzies will hear us coming and scatter. The only thing more sensitive than their hearing is their taste buds. And they can taste the tiniest trace of titanium in a land-prawn or a tin of Extee Three."

T-Rex snorted. "None of that will do them the least bit of good once I drop this charge of anesthezine gas. I'll drop it from high enough up they won't see us, even if they do hear us. Set the charge to go off at sixty feet above the ground. That should allow sufficient dispersion to catch them all without concussing any of them."

Steg rolled his eyes in frustration, then set the charge. Previous experience had taught him it was a waste of time to argue. Besides, it was a pretty good catch if they could get away with it.

* * *

Little Foot, the youngest of his clan, chased down the land-prawn and expertly severed the head before flipping it over and cracking open the carapace. He took pride in being able to do this without help from the older members of the clan.

When he was younger, still too small to hunt alone, he stepped in one of the footprints made by the Wise One and remarked how big the elder's foot was. The elder Fuzzy laughed and said that it was not that his feet were big, since most adults had feet that size. He pointed out that he had a little foot. The Wise One had made-dead some time ago and a new Wise One took his place, but the name, Little Foot, had stuck.

As Little Foot scooped out the gooey insides of the dead land-prawn and stuffed it into his mouth, he heard a strange sound from above. Two strange sounds. The first was like thunder during a storm, though not as loud. Looking up, he saw a giant round-thing that was darker than a night without moons with thorns sticking out of it everywhere. It hummed as it came closer.

Frightened, Little Foot dove to the ground behind a rock and cautiously peered around it. Back at the meeting place where a hand of tribes had come together he could see everybody was lying down as though asleep. This was a never do thing! Then Little Foot became even more frightened; what if the people had all made-dead?

The big round-thing came closer to the ground then stopped. A hole opened in the side and a hand of melon-seed shaped things flew out and landed on the ground next to the sleeping, or dead, Fuzzies. Little Foot watched in horror as people, not like his people, came out of the flying things and collected the tribes. Little Foot wanted to stop the strange new people, but there were so many of them, and they were all big-big, like three of his people standing on top of one another.

Little Foot slumped down behind his rock hoping the Big Ones did not see him.

* * *

Anthony Rocco "Frodo" Tumino jerked his head in the direction of the blast. It came from somewhere over the crest of the hill. He cursed luridly and with great imagination.

"Abe? Did you hear that?"

The Fuzzy turned to Frodo and nodded. "Come from that way, Pappy Frodo."

"Damned claim jumpers! Let's go, Abe." Frodo powered up his air-jeep and the two raced towards the source of the noise.

After cresting the hill, Frodo was confused. There was no sign of an explosion; no dust in the air or crater in the ground. Also, there was no mining equipment in evidence. Abe looked up into the air and pointed at something that Frodo couldn't see.

"Sorry, Abe. My eyes just ain't as good as yours." Frodo made a mental note to replace the broken field glasses next time he was at the trading post. "Let's check the ground a bit. Maybe we can see something there. That explosion wasn't just for show."

Frodo moved the jeep back and forth through the air while Abe watched the ground. After a few minutes the Fuzzy yeeked excitedly. "On ground! Fuzzy behind big rock. We go help?"

"You bet we do," Frodo replied. "Show me which big rock."

* * *

Back at the Fuzzy northern outpost, Major George Lunt of the ZNPF listened carefully, for the third time, as Little Foot told his story. He was aided by Ahmed Khadra who spoke the Fuzzy language better than he did. Part of the problem was that the young Fuzzy had never seen a Big One before, other than those that captured his family, and was still scared near witless. Even the Extee Three did little to calm him. George decided to have Little Foot escorted out by other Fuzzies who would show him around the station and assure him he was safe.

"Thank you, Little Foot," George said. "Here is an *idee-disco* for you to wear. Dr. Crippen and Lizzie Bordon will take you to get a new *shoppo-diggo* and shoulder bag."

The Fuzzies scampered out and George pulled the ultrasonic hearing-aid that allowed him to hear Little Foot's hypersonic testimony out of his ear with relief.

"What do you make of all of that, Ahmed?"

Ahmed considered the question. "Big, round, black, and carried aircars in it. Has to be a hyperspace ship, George. But a relatively small one to avoid detection."

"I can buy that. I wish ol' Frodo had seen it before it got away. Dark and thorny is an odd description. Black paint for camouflage, certainly, but the thorns?"

"It could be detection equipment," Ahmed suggested. "To keep an eye out for us."

George nodded. It made sense, up to a point. "Why didn't it detect Frodo's jeep?"

"He said he was powered down until he heard the explosion. That and his position on the other side of a hill might have hidden him from the ship's signal and detection equipment."

That was what George had thought and was glad Ahmed confirmed it. "Now for the biggie: how is this ship avoiding being detected by us and the military? Black paint and an early warning system wouldn't get the job done, at least not now that we are actively looking out for them."

"You have me on that one, boss. Maybe some new tech from Terra that hasn't made it out here, yet?"

"Humph. Maybe. No way to know until...unless we catch one of these Khooghras." George let out a long breath. "Time to call the chief and report this. He'll have to relay it to Jack."

"Then let the Fuzzies go along," Piet barked over the radio. "I want Clarke, the bodies and any equipment you find down here ten minutes ago!"

"Yes, sir, Chief!" Jamal's voice said from the radio.

"Be sure to take pictures and do a forensic sweep first, though. This is the first real break in the case we've had so far." Piet cut the connection and looked over at his visitor. "Oh, did you want me to get anything else, Agent Trask?"

Trask shook his head in negation. "It sounds like your men are on top of things, but I will want a look at the bodies and equipment when they get here. And to speak with Officer Clarke if he is sufficiently recovered from the gas."

"Absolutely. These bastards are getting bolder to pull something like this. It was just dumb luck they didn't see Clarke leave the shack. Jack will go ballistic when he hears this."

"Hears what?" Piet and Trask turned to see Jack enter the office with Morgan and Ben in tow. "I just got in. What have I missed?"

Piet jumped up at attention. "Governor Rainsford. I was not informed you would be visiting...."

"Please, sit down and relax, Deputy Dumont," Ben motioned for Piet to take his seat. "I'm on vacation so just consider me one of the guys."

"Yes, sir." Piet remained standing and addressed Jack. "We picked up two slavers near Red Fur's village." He went on to give the particulars as he understood them.

"Damn," Jack swore as he pulled out his pipe. "I wanted a live one to interrogate. We'll have to try and impress that on Red Fur...and our own people. Put Officer Clarke in for a commendation."

"Already done." Piet looked out the window then back to Jack. "Ah, where is your rather formidable sister?"

"Back at the CZC with Betty. Victor Grego is giving her the five-sol tour."

Morgan spoke up, "I left Akira at the castle, before you ask. Thor Folkvar and my Thoran security team are out near the yacht waiting to pitch in."

"I'm afraid there is nothing for them to do yet," Trask said. "We still have no line on these slavers, just corpses. However, we do know they are using a transport of some kind large enough to hold Red Fur's village."

"Something that big should stand out on satellite surveillance," Jack said, taking a seat. Ben and Morgan sat on the davenport. "How has it gone unnoticed?"

"Camouflage," Ben said. "I used a lot of it back in my field days. If you have the money you can get some pretty sophisticated stealth gear.

I saw a canopy that mimicked the local landscape so perfectly it was as good as invisible to the naked eye. And it changed to suit whatever area you set it up in."

"I think this transport might be a hyperspace yacht," Morgan cut in. "A canopy like Ben just described would cover the top half of the yacht without difficulty, and three hundred Fuzzies could easily fit inside. I carried two hundred Fuzzies plus their dog mounts to Northern Beta last year, and we weren't the least bit cramped for space."

"George and Ahmed think the same thing," Piet added.

Trask considered it and it made sense. He said as much. "This also explains how they got the Fuzzies off Zarathustra in the first place without going through the Mallorysport terminal. But how would they avoid detection as they left orbit? The signals and detection grid on Xerxes wouldn't be hampered by this camouflage."

Nobody had a quick answer for that one until Piet spoke up. "The traffic up there has been pretty heavy for the last few months. A few ships coming and going could easily get lost in the mix."

"Maybe recently," Trask said, "but the slaving operation has been active at least a year or more. How did they sneak in and out before the sky filled up with tourists?"

Everybody sat silently as they considered possibilities. Ben spoke up first, "Somebody in signals and detection is being paid off."

Jack agreed. "That makes the most sense."

"I don't think so," Trask argued. "People in sensitive military positions are veridicated regularly. I don't imagine Commodore Napier would be lax on this, unless...?"

"You can forget about that," Ben interrupted. "Napier is as solid as they come. If he wanted to sell Fuzzies, he would have helped Grego prove that they were just clever animals."

Trask had to agree. Smart criminals didn't make their jobs harder by increasing the risk involved in an operation. As animals, the Fuzzies could have been trapped and exported legally. As sapient beings, they had to be smuggled and hidden, with a much greater risk for all involved. Why risk a bullet in the head when you could get off with a fine for illegal importation of exotic animals?

"If we are agreed that Napier can't be involved, why not ask him how a ship could get away undetected?"

"Morgan is right," Jack said. "Ben, would you care to do the honors? Nobody could refuse to patch you through."

Ben thought about it for a second. "Shouldn't we go through Juan Takagashi?"

"Can we be sure he isn't involved?" Trask asked. "I never got to veridicate him."

That brought on another silent pause. "I'm the only one here who really knows him, and I think he is okay," Ben said. "I would have never taken him on as my deputy governor otherwise."

"Ben, until he is checked out, it's better to keep him out of the loop," Jack said. "I hate to say it, but we can't take any chances. You just get your foot in the door and I'll make the request."

*　*　*

"The goal here is to make an Abbott Lift and Drive small enough to install in a standard aircar."

"Why?" Patricia peered at the prototype engine. To her it looked like somebody crossed a microwave oven with a sonic jack-hammer. "Contragravity works just fine."

"Contragravity only eliminates weight, it doesn't provide propulsion," Juan Jimenez explained. "Aircar propulsion still requires fossil fuels which are becoming harder to find and more costly to transport to planets that have no oil. An Abbot runs on an atomic battery and fissionables are among the most common usable energy sources in the known galaxy."

Patricia still wasn't convinced. "We can make fuel out of organic trash, though."

"At three times the cost of drilling and processing crude oil," Juan countered.

"Oh...I didn't realize it was so costly. Okay, what is in this next area?"

"Hmm...this is the EMP cannon prototype. The idea is to disable enemy vehicles and equipment without harming living organisms."

"Oh, are we at war?" Patricia asked. "I may have missed the announcement while in hyperspace."

Juan chuckled. "No, nothing like that...as far as I know. This is just pre-emptive research. A planet might decide to secede from the Federation, or we might find an advanced alien civilization that is hostile to us; we need to be prepared for anything."

Patricia looked over the cannon critically. "Does it work?"

"Yes and no. The lab models work well enough on small devices, but we have yet to field test with this full-sized model."

Patricia peered at the cannon more closely. "How would it be deployed?"

Juan walked over to a viewscreen and tapped in a command. A vidfeed came up showing the cannon in action. "This digital mock-up shows the EMP cannon being mounted onto a contragravity platform for mobility. The platform can be set to any height or angle. As a ground-based weapon it would be almost invincible."

"Until somebody threw a stick of dynamite at it," Patricia noted.

"Even then," Juan corrected. "Collapsium-laminated casing. It wouldn't be much good in a space battle, though."

"Why is that?" she asked.

"Well, while it could disable any spacecraft, despite its collapsium hull—due to the weak spots where communication gear is set up—it leaves the ship carrying it vulnerable to reprisal while the EMP cannon is being deployed. The collapsium plating, where the cannon is mounted, would have to be retracted in order to allow the cannon to function. Any signals and detection officer worth his commission would spot it and target that spot while the EMP was building up to discharge. It would be too dangerous to charge it before deploying, as it might affect the ship's systems—even with the shielding."

"Why not just mount it on the hull?"

"Same problem, a permanent weak spot for the enemy to take advantage of."

She nodded knowingly. "So this would be purely ground-based planetary defense. Still useful, I should think."

"Until our tech is rendered immune to the effects of electromagnetic pulses, you're right. Actually, we are working on that technology as well. Now let me show you the next thing. This is my personal-favorite; human-form robots."

"For what? Will they make better bartenders or something?"

Juan chuckled. "Maybe. But we were thinking of body doubles for high risk targets, like the governor."

"Or your CEO?"

He nodded. "There is that, too. The problem is the legs. You have no idea how many corrections the human body makes just to stand still. We've designed an elaborate magnetic pulley system to mimic leg muscles, but they can't always react fast enough to keep the robot on his feet. Part of the problem is the overall weight. Robots tend to be pretty top heavy when designed to look like people."

Patricia looked over the model. "Why not install a contragravity unit in his chest?"

He shook his head. "A unit big enough to work on that much weight would increase the size of the torso about fifty percent. That might work if they were designed to look like Thor Folkvar or Johann Torsseus, but not normal-sized people."

"I don't mean something to make it fly, just something to offset the weight so it could keep its balance. Like those hover boards I saw some Fuzzies playing on."

Juan opened his mouth then shut it. Then he made a note on his datapad to check the idea out with the engineering team.

"Say, do you have any Fuzzy robots?"

Juan shook his head. "We have some smaller model robots about the size of a Fuzzy. Those actually keep their balance pretty well since they have a much lower center of gravity—"

Patricia interrupted, "I have an idea I would like to run past your boss."

XXIX

"Thank you, Major Lunt," Piet said as he cut the connection. "You all heard it. We have an eyewitness to a Fuzzy abduction. A black... vessel, probably a hyperspace yacht, like Morgan's, scooped up a bunch of Fuzzies. Not exactly the camouflage we expected."

"They might have a canopy set up to hide under when powered down," Morgan suggested. "I don't get the value of the black paint, though. At night it would be effective against the naked eye, but in the day it stands out like a damnthing at a Bar Mitzvah."

"Nazi at a Bar Mitzvah," Jack corrected.

"Oh? What's a Nazi?"

"I'll explain later, son, when I ask you what you learned in history while in college."

There was a ding and the comscreen came on, with Commodore Napier staring out from it.

"Commodore, I am glad you could get back to us so quickly," Jack said.

"My apologies for not taking your call right away. I was in a staff meeting. Jack, I would have taken your call without the Governor fronting for you."

"We just wanted to be sure your assistant wouldn't hold us up, Commodore," Jack said. "Have you started the inspections yet?"

"We have. So far nothing has turned up. The ships are empty of everything but cargo, non-living, and a skeleton crew. The tourists are down on the surface making the local businesses fat, and the rest of the crews are whooping it up in the bars and brothels. We did stick a few volunteers into a veridicator, and while we did learn some interesting things, none of them are connected to the Fuzzy slavers."

"We have something new," Jack explained about the eyewitness and the black ship.

The Commodore didn't actually swear, although he looked like he wanted to. He tapped out a series of commands on his console before speaking again. "I have just activated security precautions for this transmission. Gentlemen, I will have to bring you in on a military secret. That black paint has to be military-grade stealth technology. It will block almost anything signals and detection can throw at it. How these Khooghras got ahold of it, I don't want to guess at, but enough heads back on Terra will be rolling to start a macabre bowling league."

Everybody started talking at once, then Jack spoke up, "We can't track them from space from here and we don't know where they will be going next. Everybody involved on this planet that we know of is dead—thanks to Red Fur and his posse. So how are we going to catch these Khooghras?"

"Where do they get their supplies?" Morgan asked.

"Wouldn't they carry food and what-have-you from wherever they came from?" Trask asked back.

"Up to a point. Look, I actually own a spacefaring yacht and it takes a good sized crew to run it. A good twenty percent of the ship's usable storage area is just for food, hygienic supplies and the carniculture lab. Another twenty percent is used for sleeping space, showers, etc. Our slavers wouldn't be able to carry enough supplies for the voyage here, then several months in hiding while poaching Fuzzies. Moreover, they would need lots and lots of Extee Three to feed the Fuzzies, plus space to keep them locked up. And then there are the maintenance issues: replacement fuel elements, worn parts that need to be replaced or serviced. There aren't many moving parts in a hyperdrive engine, but there are some and they take a beating with every transposition. Unless these are brand new ships, something is going to need to be fixed sooner or later. So, where are they getting their supplies?"

"Like you said, carniculture for the meat, maybe some hunting, and foraging for the rest—" Piet started then stopped. He knew nothing about space yachts but he had done some wilderness living in his youth.

It would be difficult to keep that many people fed out in the wild without somebody noticing something. Even on a planet with as low a population as Zarathustra.

"They must have people in Mallorysport," Trask and Ben said together. Trask continued. "I'll put my people on this right away. The Extee Three may be coming from those speculators who got stuck with loads of Extee Three when the CZC started making it, hence nearly impossible to track, but human-type food in quantity should be traceable."

"I think Victor Grego could be of help here," Ben added. "Ninety percent of everything on this planet goes through the CZC, and he'll be able to tell us where. And carniculture doesn't make meat out of nothing. They will need nutrient salts, proteins, stuff like that. How many people will need that on a planet like Zarathustra?"

"My people on Xerxes and that mob in orbit," Commodore Napier cut in. "There might be a few on the planet that prefer carniculture to the real thing, though I can't imagine there would be many."

"Now we are getting somewhere," Trask said.

*   *   *

Jason Roberts and Mike Hammer decided to head over to The Soup Kitchen, then Clancy's Bar, both owned and operated by Clancy Slade and his wife. Roberts needed to look into Clancy's businesses; dinner at The Soup Kitchen would give him that chance. Clancy's Bar was styled in the fashion of old Terran Irish pubs. It was decorated in early 20th century, or 1st Century Pre-atomic, European style. The appointments were all handmade and the help was all human; not a robot or auto-dispenser in sight.

Next to Clancy's Bar was The Soup Kitchen, another history-themed restaurant based on the soup kitchens common to the same era as the pub. While both were designed to be money-making operations, The Soup Kitchen had the policy of not turning away anybody who was hungry—even if they couldn't pay. People down on their luck could get a meal, and even some work. Many chose to earn their dinner by washing dishes—there were no robots to do this job—sweeping the walk in front of the two businesses, or even running errands. The Slades had even set up a second Soup Kitchen as a completely non-profit operation in Junktown.

Jason Roberts, while far from a teetotaler, never drank on an empty stomach. The scotch in his desk was purely for show and hadn't been opened in all the time it sat in the desk drawer, save for when a client seemed to need a belt. He and his Fuzzy operative stepped into the restaurant and took their usual seats.

"Jason, Mike, welcome back."

"Nikki, how's tricks?" Roberts asked.

The waitress feigned anger. "You know I don't do that anymore."

"Well, if you change your mind, I'll be happy to give you all my business."

Both laughed.

"If anybody but you made that offer, I would have to shoot them."

Roberts put on a surprised face. "You mean you don't get offers like that a dozen times a day? Are these people blind?"

"Maybe. Or maybe they know better than to mess with anybody who works for Clancy Slade," Nikki said. In a lower voice she added, "I suspect most people think that Clancy is really Leo Thaxter and that he faked his death in order to go straight."

Roberts had never met Thaxter as the gangster had been imprisoned before he made planetfall on Zarathustra. He did know the man's face and background, though. Clancy looked a hell of a lot like the mobster.

"I can see that, except Clancy has kinder eyes than anything I saw in Thaxter's pictures. The eyes are the windows to the soul, the saying goes, and Clancy seems to have a good one." Roberts felt his stomach growl. "So, what do we have on special today?"

"Fresh-killed wild veldbeest ground up into a meatloaf with secret spices. Clancy shot this one personally, yesterday." Nikki turned to Mike. "We also have Zarapizza made by Julia Childs with land-prawn and Extee Three toppings."

Julia Childs? Well, as Fuzzy names went, this one was appropriate for a Fuzzy chef, Roberts thought.

"Nikki, does everything on this planet have to have 'zara' in front of it?"

The waitress giggled. "We were going to call it Fuzzy Pizza, but Julia thought that Fuzzies would be the topping. It took a while to calm her down after that."

Roberts nodded. He could see Mike Hammer being similarly distressed. Anything even vaguely resembling cannibalism was anathema to a Fuzzy. "Okay, I'll have the meatloaf with fried pool-ball fruit and a beer. Mike?"

"Zarapizza sound good, Pappy Jay. With extra *estee-fee*, plis. An' juice."

Nikki wrote down the order on a paper pad instead of the computer variety. The Slades strove for authenticity. She winked at Mike then moved on to place the order.

Roberts and Mike chatted while they waited for their orders. Roberts made a point of speaking to Mike like a full-grown Terran human, and not like a child as he had seen so many others do. It seemed to him that Khooghras were treated more like adults than Fuzzies were and it annoyed the Niflheim out of him.

Roberts accepted being called "Pappy" because it held a different meaning to Fuzzies than it did to humans. A Pappy was a man who lived with and cared for a Fuzzy. Not a lot of difference from the technical term, except that in Fuzzy society, there was always a Wise One to do the heavy thinking for the group. Pappy was just another word for Wise One to them.

Roberts considered how he would dig into Clancy's finances while he waited for his dinner. Mr. Coombes had done a first rate job of digging into Slade's bank accounts, but the counselor had no idea what Clancy kept in his mattress. One discrepancy stood out, though; the house where Clancy currently lived had been bought in his name by Leo Thaxter, while he was sitting in the cell meant for Thaxter.

Roberts spent a great deal of time learning the lay of the land after arriving on Zarathustra. As a former policeman himself, he knew that people could talk freely while intoxicated and forget what they said the next day; even a veridicator couldn't catch them in a lie if they couldn't remember what they'd said. By plying a number of cops with enough hooch he learned that Thaxter had been sprung from jail and Clancy put in his place. The governor had ordered that information kept quiet.

From there, Roberts surmised that Thaxter had used Clancy's good name and bought the house with money from previous ventures, legal and not. The next leap would be that Thaxter had kept a stash of ill-gotten gains either in the house, someplace else, or both. When Thaxter ended up dead—conveniently so for a number of people—Clancy simply took ownership of the domicile. Why not? On the books it was his anyway.

So, Clancy and his family moved into the new house and discovered Thaxter's secret stash. Now he found himself with more money than he knew what to do with. *So what does he do?* Roberts asked himself. *He opens a bar and two restaurants, while people assume he used his reward money from shooting Thaxter to pay for it.* He snorted. It was a nice story, but if it was true: how was he going to prove it?

"Mr. Roberts?"

Roberts turned from his ruminations and saw Parsec Paul addressing him. Parsec Paul was a former space freighter captain who had fallen on hard times. He had been to nearly every planet in the Federation and even a few more nobody ever heard of, hence his name. Nobody knew what Paul's real age was, either. Even he didn't know. The time dilation effect of hyperspace left him a lot younger than his birth certificate would suggest, if he knew where it was; yet he still had thinning white hair and deep lines on his face and hands. Local legend had it that Paul was part of the original scouting team that discovered Zarathustra the better part of a century ago. Paul couldn't confirm or deny it since he had been to so many new planets he couldn't keep them straight anymore. In fact, he couldn't even remember his own last name since injuring his head while on Shesha.

"Hey, Paul. Pull up a seat and pop a squat." Roberts indicated the chair to his left.

The old space captain readily complied. "Mr. Roberts, I have some information for you. Important stuff."

Paul usually did. "What do you think it's worth?"

"Gratis. I owe ya for coverin' my tab at Clancy's last week. Besides, this involves Mike, too."

Involved Mike? "Okay. But dinner is on me. You look like you could use a good meal."

Paul shook his head up and down. "Look, I overheard a couple guys talkin' 'bout some bad doin's over on Beta. Real bad doin's."

Roberts noticed that Paul's hands were shaking. Parsec Paul wasn't a drunk by anybody's definition, which ruled out the DTs or withdrawal. He was scared. Roberts signaled to Nikki for another beer and handed it to Paul.

"Thanks. I guess I need this." Paul downed half the drink in one pull. "Look, there's some guys lookin' for Extee Three and other supplies on the down-low. I heard that it was being taken to Beta Continent."

Roberts felt disappointed. While most of Beta was Terran *verboten*, there was enough open area for legitimate work there. He said so, although he agreed that the Extee Three part was hinky.

"You don't understand. They was looking for ex-cons, dishonorably discharged Marines and former gangsters to carry the supplies, and maybe stay on for other work. And why are they going through Spike Heenan to get them? Now what do you do with that kind of crowd and a crap ton of Extee Three?"

Now this was a damnthing of a different color. "How did you get wind of this?"

"I was sleeping in an alley behind a dumpster over in Junktown. I heard what sounded like a couple guys being recruited."

It took Roberts a moment to process the word 'dumpster.' He had to remind himself that most buildings in Junktown didn't have mass-energy converters to get rid of their refuse and depended on collection companies to haul it away. The trash was separated by robots and either recycled or converted to energy. The CZC recognized that recycling was more cost effective than mining or importing raw materials. He had explained the concept to Mike, who thought burying it would be more efficient.

"They're going to Beta Continent to grab something up on the Rez,"

Parsec Paul continued. "They want people with hunting and trapping experience to live capture some game, is my thinking."

"Game hunting is certainly legal enough off the Rez," Roberts thought aloud. But why the Extee Three, then? "Mike, is there any animal on the Reservation that can't be found off of it?"

Mike Hammer made a show of thinking about it. "No, just Fuzzee."

Paul looked meaningfully at Roberts and nodded. Roberts swore up a blue streak. "Can you identify any of these men?"

He said no, because of the darkness. Junktown didn't enjoy the same level of services the metropolitan area did.

"Damn. I'll have to take this straight to Chief Carr. He will have to contact the native affairs commissioner, and Marshal Fane. Paul, you just found one galaxy class can of worms that somebody else already kicked open."

"Here's your grub, boys."

"What? Oh, right. Nikki, Mike and I will need to take that to go. Get Parsec Paul anything he wants and put it on my tab. No arguments, Paul. Get some meat on your bones on my sol. You've more than earned it."

The Coombes case would have to be put on hold. Roberts made a note not to charge for the time off the case. This was something potentially big and couldn't wait. Then Roberts had another thought. What if Coombes knew about this and wanted to know if Clancy Slade was involved in it? The client was very tight lipped about why he wanted Clancy checked out, and the pro-Fuzzy position of the CZC was well-known, if a bit suspect. Roberts shook that off. Not everything was connected until he found evidence to the contrary.

XXX

Night in Mallorysport could be interesting, exciting or dangerous, depending on what part of the city one wandered through. Longtime residents knew enough to avoid areas like the sports arena after a game or Junktown in general.

The inner city, mostly still owned by the CZC, boasted significant security thanks to the Company police as well as the regular police force. Here the better restaurants and eateries could be found, as well as the nicer boutiques, arcades and shopping malls.

Jack, busy with the current crisis, asked Betty to show Patricia around Mallorysport after her tour of the Company. Betty jumped at the opportunity to show Patricia the sights while pumping her for information.

After Jack's interruption, Pat continued her story, "...well, even though Pa couldn't get the bone regenerated until the next day, he still finished his shift at the construction site. Pa liked to hit the bar on the way home after a hard day, and this time was no different. One arm in a cast wasn't enough to keep him off the barstool. Now, Ol' Vern Brown had a grudge against Pa for years but never had the stones to do anything about it until he saw Pa with his arm in a cast."

"What?" Betty was shocked. "He would attack a handicapped man?"

"Oh, yes. He invited Pa outside to settle things, and Pa wasted no time accepting the invitation. Well, Pa never said anything about it, but damn near everybody else did! He beat on Ol' Vern like he committed a crime, all one-handed. Vern barely laid a finger on Pa, but he looked like he'd been hit by an airfreighter."

Betty laughed. "So it runs in the family. Jack doesn't talk about any of you, or, well, anything from his past, really."

Patricia nodded. "Well, that's just Jack being Jack. He doesn't brag about himself or anybody else. My fault, really. When he was younger every time he wanted to boast about something, I would say 'Brag was a good ol' dog,' and he'd shut up quick."

"Hmm. My mother always said a man needs to talk about his accomplishments to make them real. So, what did you think of Mallory Mall?

Patricia smiled. "Usually, if you've seen one, you've seen them all: The indoor gardens, the Fuzzies working in the shops, and that indoor firing range...it was a lovely place. On Terra things are so utilitarian these days. And nobody carries a gun around like on these colony worlds. You need permits to carry concealed, in fact. When Jack and I were kids, things were a lot looser."

Betty thought for a second. "Oh, yeah. That politician on Terra, whazzis name, was killed at a rally or something and the anti-gun crowd pushed through a bunch of anti-gun laws."

Patricia nodded. "Exactly. Then crime went up and they passed more anti-gun laws. I think politicians are immune to intelligent consideration of cause and effect. Even they should know that an armed society is a polite society."

Betty laughed. "They should take a good hard look at life in the colonies. Almost all of the newer ones have permissive gun laws and we enjoy the lowest crime rates in the Federation."

"Exactly! And speedy justice doesn't hurt, either. I understand the death penalty is carried out very quickly here."

A beeping sound issued from Patricia's wristwatch. "Oh, I have to stop and take a pill."

"We can stop at this café." Betty pointed at the Darius Café. "I come here on my way to work, sometimes. They serve beer and spirits, here, too."

"A café selling alcohol?" Patricia shook her head. "On Terra they are all against that sort of thing, except the German-owned places. Gast houses do a brisk business on the whole, though."

"Well, we might get that way, eventually. Governor Rainsford vetoes about a dozen silly bills a day that put alcohol strictly into licensed establishments. Back when Victor Grego, or the CZC, owned the planet outright he saw no need for those kinds of restrictions. I think it is the association of bars and taverns pushing for the more restrictive rules. That way they push a lot of competition out. If that ever passes they'll go after private stills, next, I suppose."

Patricia noticed a few people outside the café with video headsets looking at them through the window. "Betty, what is that all about?"

Betty looked and spotted what Patricia pointed at. "Oh, them," she said with some disgust. "Those are Streamers."

"Streamers?"

"You know, people with no real lives who walk around looking for somebody famous or interesting to record or stream directly to the datastream. They have different names on other planets: Vidhawks, paparazzi, datafreaks, starstalkers...they hope to catch important people in compromising situations and sell the rights to their vid feeds."

"Gotcha. But why are they watching us?"

"Oh, well, Jack is pretty well-known on Zarathustra. He is probably the biggest celebrity we have and he rarely goes out in public where these buzzards can follow him around. A few tried to sneak onto the Rez. That did not go well for them at all. So, instead, they follow me around ever since it got out that Jack and I were in a relationship. They make a big deal about my being half his age."

"You know, you haven't said anything about Jack until now."

Betty wrinkled her nose. "I don't like to talk about things like that. Well, no, that isn't true. I have spoken with Akira about it. I just didn't think it appropriate subject matter for his sister, Pat."

Patricia chuckled. "Worried that I don't approve?"

"Um...maybe a little. The gossip columns have been taking pot shots at our relationship for months now. Fortunately, all Jack reads in the datastream are politics and current events. He doesn't like gossip in general and news articles like that in particular."

"Why would Jack even be of interest in the gossip columns?"

"Well, like I said before, Jack is one of the most famous people on the planet, Pat," Betty said. "Between the Fuzzy Trial, Little Fuzzy being lost and rescued from the forest fire, and the duel between him and Morgan, there isn't a person on Zarathustra who doesn't know about Jack Holloway."

"Huh. Well, Jack just doesn't care what people think, Betty. And you shouldn't either. Whether I approve or not is not your problem, or Jack's. Jack does what is right for Jack, mostly, and those he cares about. But nobody, and I mean nobody, tells him who he can be involved with. Not even me. And for the record, I approve. Oh, and there's an empty table in the corner."

Patricia took a seat at the table and set her purse on it. The purse fell on its side and several items rolled out onto the floor. Betty scrambled to help Patricia recover her errant property.

Betty couldn't help noticing the label on one of the bottles. "Here you go, Pat. Um...these are accommodation pills like Jack used after his heart transplant. Oh, I don't mean to pry...."

Patricia nodded. "They are and it's okay. Yes, I am still taking them for my last transplant."

Confusion clouded Betty's face. "Jack only needed his for a month. Is there something going on...I don't know...about?"

Patricia ordered some decaffeinated chamomile-tea from the robot waiter before answering. "Second surgeries can take longer for the new organ to acclimate."

Betty ordered a Darjeeling tea, then asked, "Why do people even need accommodation meds? The organs are grown from your own DNA, aren't they?"

"I asked the same thing of my doctor. What he explained is that the human body is an incredibly hostile environment. The food we eat, the alcohol we drink, the things we smoke, the parasites that get into us... it all goes to make us very toxic to new body parts grown in a sterile lab. The drugs don't keep the body from rejecting the organs; they keep the organs from rejecting the body until they acclimate to their new home. Without the drugs, it would be a bit like dropping a newborn babe on Niflheim without protective gear."

Betty thought it over. "But once the organs adapt, you're in the clear, right?"

"Yes. Don't worry, Jack will outlive a lot more people before he goes to that big rifle range in the sky."

"I wasn't worried about Jack, Pat. He has been off the meds for the better part of a year, now. I am worried about you."

"Me?" Patricia was surprised. "Why me? In a month I will be gone."

"Look, I like you. In a way you remind me of my mother back on Terra. She wasn't much good with a gun, mind you, but she is a plain talker and plays it straight with people. I think you two would get along. Maybe you can look her up when you get back home. But Jack loves and respects you, and he is very selective about whom he respects. I really don't believe you being his sister enters into that equation. And I think there is something going on that you are hiding from him."

Patricia looked Betty in the eyes for a moment then drew a heavy sigh. "Well, I can see Jack is going to have his hands full with you. Good. It will keep him interested."

"You're dodging."

"You bet I am. Okay, dear heart, I am going to tell you something and if you breathe a word of it to anybody, I'll have to shoot you...."

* * *

"Robot Fuzzies!?" Jack exclaimed.

From the comscreen Victor Grego nodded. "Yes. We have a number of humanoid prototypes already constructed and it would only take a day or so to dress them up to look like Fuzzies. We can send them out into the bush and wait for them to get snatched up by the poachers."

"Pat's idea, eh? Sounds like her. How...Fuzzy-ish would they act?"

Grego spoke to somebody off-screen before answering. "According to Joe Verganno, they can walk, make yeeking noises, and gather things up. They can't eat anything without some redesign to the heads and torsos, and they won't make good runners. But they can be programmed to play dead if somebody uses gas on them."

Ben shook his head. "It won't fool anybody who has spent any amount of time with the real thing."

"I don't know about that," Jack said. "These slavers aren't looking to make friends. Just bag, tag and stuff in a cage. We'll discuss it more later. Something's happening outside."

"Sure thing, Jack. I'll get Joe started on the programming." The screen went dark and Jack turned to see what all the noise was about.

From outside the sounds of Fuzzies yeeking and the whine of an aircar landing could be heard. Piet went out to check it and returned with Clarke and what appeared to be an honor guard of Fuzzies.

"Officer Clarke, how are you feeling?" Jack asked. "And what's that around your neck?"

"I'm feeling much better, sir," Clarke replied in his deep bass voice. "The side effects of the gas seem to have worn off completely. As for this," Clarke touched the furry collar around his neck, "the Fuzzies gave it to me. They cut locks of fur from their chests and wove it together. I think I have been inducted into the *Jin-f'ke* and this makes up for my otherwise hairless body." He ran a hand over his bald head for emphasis. "I'll take it off if—"

"No, better to leave it on," Ben said. "It might offend your Fuzzy friends if you remove it."

Jack agreed. "And who have we here?" He nodded to the Fuzzies.

"They insisted on coming along to protect me from any more bad Big Ones. Knowing how strained relations are with the *Jin-f'ke*, we thought it best to let them come."

"Good thinking, Officer Clarke," Jack said. 'Let's just hope they don't think guarding you is a permanent job."

"We stay until bad Big Ones make dead," said the largest of the Fuzzies. It was easy to forget that some of the *Jin-f'ke* had been learning Lingua Terra. "Want help fight bad Big Ones."

Piet smiled. "So far the *Jin-f'ke* have had more success dealing with these Khooghras than we have. Say, maybe these are the Fuzzies we need to work with the robot plan."

Jack looked dubious. "I already have the CZC and ZNPF Fuzzies, along with my own gang—"

"The Fuzzies are already in danger," Piet interrupted. "But the slavers want them all alive and unharmed. That's more than could be said of any humans they might come across. Like Clarke."

"Jack, I'm still against this on general principles, but Piet has a point," Ben said. "If they want to help in their own defense, who are we to stop them?"

Jack knew better than anybody, except for maybe Ruth van Riebeek and Ernst Mallin, that Fuzzies were not the children they appeared to be. And Ben was right; the Fuzzies were the ones in danger and if they wanted to do something about it, it was their right.

"Fine. First I want Little Fuzzy to do the translating. He understands the *Jin-f'ke* and Terran languages better than anybody. I want these Fuzzies to know exactly what they are getting into."

XXXI

Darius rose, full and bright, illuminating the landscape with a soft light. Off to the side was Xerxes, also full, though far less luminescent. Dmitri Watson looked up at the orbiting spheres and noticed that they looked brighter than they should. He shook that off and decided the thinner ozone layer might have something to do with it.

Dmitri felt a rumbling in his stomach and decided that a sandwich in the mess tent was in order. There he found Gregoire Rutherford scribbling furiously on his datapad, shaking his head every few seconds.

"Something interesting?"

"Infuriating is more like it," Greg growled.

"Oh? What is the problem?"

Greg put his datapad down and swore something in a language Dmitri didn't understand. "This damned solar receptor unit works exactly the way it should, only it shouldn't."

"Can we try that again in Lingua Terra?"

Greg tapped on Cinda's solar converter. "This unit collects and processes enough energy to power three datapads effectively. Only there is no way in Niflheim it should be able to on this planet under a K0 star. I have been doing the math and it simply doesn't add up."

"So, the solar unit works as advertised?"

"As advertised on Odin under a G0 subgiant star," Greg said with annoyance. "Where is all this extra energy coming from?"

"Maybe there is something different about Zarathustra's sun? A shift towards the infrared."

"No, a K0 star is a K0 star," Greg said emphatically. "They are classed as such for the degree of energy output. I could print out reams of research done on this world's primary and all of it would be unexceptional.

Hell, this is your area of expertise. You know all this better than I do."

"I'm spit-balling. It's part of my process." Dmitri thought for a second. "I noticed that the moons were brighter than they should be. Maybe they—"

Greg cut him off. "No, those satellites have also been studied to death and resurrection. No unusual energy output. Even the planet itself has lower than normal, for us, background radiation. Even lower than Freya or Heimdall. Wherever this energy is coming from, it is not the sun, the moons or the planet itself."

"Then what is left?"

"Damned if I know."

Both men sat silently for a moment until Dmitri's stomach made a noise. "I'll have a sandwich, and then we can think some more. Food for thought and all that." Dmitri made a veldbeest and zaragoat cheese sandwich, poured a cup of black coffee, then returned to the table.

"You know...there might be something...unusual about the make-up of the power unit," Dmitri said between bites.

Greg was skeptical. "Such as?"

"How would I know? Maybe...an impurity in the...construction that had...a beneficial side effect." Dmitri swallowed a bite of sandwich, and chased it with some coffee. "We may have found a super power accumulation device created by accident."

"That is ridiculous." Greg thought for a second. "Damn. I doubt this is some sort of industrial accident, but we have to check it out before moving on to other possibilities. Most of which are even more preposterous...."

"Like what?"

"I haven't a clue. We'll have to ask Miss Dawn where she bought this unit—"

"The Chartered Odin Company," Dmitri said. "Says so on the bottom. See?"

"Humph. But what planet did she buy it on? Did she get it second-hand after somebody else tampered with it? Was it a display model, or new in the box? Hell, did a Khooghra look at it cross-eyed? There are a lot of factors that need to be taken into account."

Dmitri finished his sandwich and downed the rest of his coffee. "I will go find Cinda and see what she knows. She mentioned that she couldn't afford an atomic battery, so the unit may well be secondhand."

"Damn! That will make it a lot harder to figure out what the deal is on this thing."

"The joys of research, Greg."

Dmitri left the tent and spotted Tres. "Mr. Poe, could you tell me where Miss Dawn got off to?"

"I think she went down to the lake. You should take a camera with you. Two full moons together is an infrequent occurrence here and the reflection off the surface will be spectacular."

"Thank you. Maybe I will."

"Oh, and watch out for the proto-snakes."

Dmitri stopped and turned back to Tres. "Proto-snakes?"

"Yeah. It is a species indigenous to this area," Tres explained. "About thirty inches long with tiny legs in the front and back. They don't attack humans as a rule and are non-venomous. However, if you accidently step on one, it will curl around your leg and give you a nasty bite."

Dmitri made a mental note to read up on the local wildlife. "Thank you. I will be careful. Are there any other unique lifeforms I should be wary of?" Tres said no and the scientist thanked him again, then started toward the lake.

Dmitri worked his way through the brush. Even away from the camp lights he could see adequately by the light of the moons. Once down to the shore he found that Tres had not misled him about the spectacular vista before him; the reflection of the moons on the water was truly breathtaking.

He looked around and finally saw Cinda. As she stepped out of the water onto the shore, the light from the two full moons bathed her nude body in an almost incandescent glow, giving her skin the appearance of the purest opal and her red hair a flame-like quality. The mist coming off the waterfall in the distance added to the surrealistic quality of the tableau. Cinda shook her head sending droplets of water all around. The light caught the drops as they flew through the air making them look like sparks. She looked like Venus minus the half-shell to the scientist. The young woman picked up a towel and slowly rubbed her body free of moisture with the super-absorbent cloth.

Dmitri, almost hypnotized by the activity, quickly stepped back into the brush. He had not considered that she would be bathing outdoors since the inn they were using had working water and electricity. He considered alerting Cinda to his presence, then decided against it; despite appearances to the contrary, she might actually be quite shy about her body. He took one last look as she dried herself off then retreated back to the camp. It wasn't until he was back in the mess tent that he realized he'd had his camera with him the whole time. Just as well, he thought, there are some lines a man shouldn't cross.

*   *   *

Deputy Governor Juan Takagashi leaned back and smiled at his guest. On the other side of the governor's desk sat Morgan Holloway.

"Mr. Holloway, you do understand that my position is temporary? Governor Rainsford will resume the reins of power in about a week or so, then it will be up to him to determine whether or not to grant your request."

Morgan shuffled some papers, real paper from a Freyan paper mill. "I do. I just want to get the ball rolling. I have done a little research on the matter and found a few precedents to support my position. And I have spoken with Ben Rainsford. He said he would support whatever you decide in the matter."

Takagashi sat up straight in his chair. "He did?" *Ben must have more faith in my ability than I realized*, he thought. "Very well, let us go over the precedents. I will have to have these verified, of course."

"Good." Morgan pulled out his datapad and opened a tagged file. "Let's start with the most recent. Here we have an Ullerite colony being established on Fenris. It is primarily a mining colony, but the Ullerans have their own ruling body, police force and laws. The Federation has granted them autonomy in settling their own affairs as long as Terrans are not involved."

Takagashi drummed out a rhythm on his console and brought up his own information from the datastream. "I see what you are saying here, but they are not considered a permanent colony at this time. Their contract states that if the ore they are mining runs out, they can be returned to Uller."

Morgan sighed. It was time for his trump card. "Then there is the Thoran colony on Imhotep. Over three hundred Thorans established a colony there. They also have their own ruling body, laws, and Federation charter separate from the local government. They do have treaties with the Terro-human colony there and even work in some of the Terran companies as day laborers and security. Most work for the...I'll say 'Lord' since I can't pronounce their word for this."

Takagashi looked up from his viewscreen. "I thought you could speak Thoran."

"After a fashion. My security team has been coaching me but I think the human speaking apparatus is just not designed to handle that language. Even Ulleran is easier."

"Ah, yes. I believe there are a number of vocalizations in that language that would be difficult to master. 'Lord' will do for this conversation. Hmm...I think you may be onto something here. This is expected to be a permanent colony, more or less, and they do have their own charter with the Federation. The Chartered Imhotep Company didn't protest because the Thorans won't compete with them in any meaningful way. All right, I think this is an acceptable precedent, but what are you going for, here? Setting yourself up as a king on Zeta continent? I don't think I could sell that either to the governor or the Federation."

Morgan shook his head. "No, and I wouldn't accept that position. That would work against what we are trying to accomplish. The Freyans of Zeta continent feel that they need their own government, but do not want to completely cut all ties with the homeworld."

"Huh? From what I understand of their position I am surprised they want anything to do with Freya or Freyans, for that matter!"

Morgan smiled ruefully. "These are a very pragmatic people. While they do not wish to return to Freya at this time, they realize that their offspring may decide to at some distant point in the future. So, they wish to pattern their colony on the Freyan civilization model. That means having their own noble class, government, the works."

"Well, if not their king, then what?"

"I would be a prince regent or something along those lines. That is the closest I can translate the term."

"And why you? You are half-Terran. Doesn't that make you something of a second-class citizen on Freya?"

"On Freya it would, except that I am still of a noble house. Rank has its privileges and all that. I don't get invited to all the parties, but nobody can snub me in public. However, I am on the outs with the royal court for my part in rescuing the Freyans and embarrassing the noble families that took part in their enslavement those many years ago. As for why I got tapped for this position, well, they need a public face. They are still very shy about their physical mutations and believe they would not be accepted should they send an envoy to Freya. I, however, am already of a noble house, obscenely wealthy and un-mutated. My own mixed heritage is considered a plus with the Zeta colony. It gives me something in common with them."

"And it doesn't hurt that you were the one who rescued them in the first place."

"There is that."

Takagashi stood up and put out his hand. "I'll have to get Gus to go over this and make sure there are no traps in it, and then check with the governor and Victor Grego."

"Why Grego?"

"Just covering my bets. He had to sign-off on the buyback of Zeta, and there may be some legal entanglements that need to be addressed. Otherwise, I think we can make this work."

Morgan grasped Takagashi's forearm Freyan style. "Thank you, Deputy Governor."

"If there is a coronation or something, I'd like to attend."

"Front row seat. I promise."

XXXII

Cinda returned to the campsite and headed for the mess tent. On the way, she passed Tres Poe as he fiddled with some apparatus she didn't recognize. Tres turned, spotted her, and waved her over.

"Cinda, did Dr. Watson find you?"

"I didn't know he was looking for me. Did he say what he wanted?"

"No, but I told him you were down by the lake. I thought maybe he saw you there."

"How long ago?"

"Oh, twenty minutes or so ago."

She reddened a bit. "If he did, I didn't see him. Maybe he and I need to have a little talk."

Tres noticed the blush. "Should I tell him you are looking for him if he comes back?"

"Oh no, I will want that pleasure for myself. Later, Tres."

As Cinda walked off Tres wondered if he had said something wrong. Cinda did not look particularly pleased at the moment.

The mess tent was empty, as was Dmitri's tent. Unlike his fellow scientists, Dmitri preferred to sleep out of doors instead of inside the Bed and Breakfast building. *It would have served him right if I caught him undressing for bed*, Cinda thought. She was about to give up when she spotted somebody walking off into the brush. Cinda couldn't be sure at that distance but thought it might be Dmitri.

After several minutes of following the man through the brush at a discreet distance, Cinda considered going back, then realized she had gotten lost. She would have to keep the man in sight, then follow him back out again.

*   *   *

"How many Fuzzies?" Dr. Hoenveld looked out across the sea of furry faces. With him were Darla Cross, Juan Jimenez and Captain Greibenfeld.

"Lynne Andrews is on her way along with some people from the hospital to help with the blood draws and workups," Juan said. "We also sent for Ahmed Khadra since you asked for a cop. Umm...why do you need a cop?"

"It is an idea I had," Darla Cross said. "We need a layman familiar with deductive reasoning in the hopes of getting to the bottom of the Fuzzy infertility problem."

"Dr. Hoenveld? You agree with this idea?"

Dr. Hoenveld looked distinctly uncomfortable. "It has been brought to my attention that while I am brilliant in my fields, I have a linear thought process. While I will certainly get to the answer eventually using my own methods, it would be more beneficial for the Fuzzies if we could get to the solution faster. I have no faith in hunches, yet I can't deny that Victor Grego discovered how to synthesize the titanium based long chain molecule in his kitchen, when it would have taken me over a year to do with proper scientific methodology. The Fuzzies may not have that long if this is something that can be spread throughout the populace. My ego is not so great that I would allow them to suffer genocide if we can prevent it."

"If it helps, I brought along everything we could recover from the sla-vers' computers about their own breeding program," Captain Greibenfeld said. "Or, more to the point, their lack of success in running one. Every last one of these Fuzzies was given a full medical workup before we sent them here. And every last one of them appears to be sterile!"

"All of them?" Darla cried out. "Great Ghu, how horrible!"

"Wait, all of them?" Hoenveld looked at all of the Fuzzies. He could tell that they already knew as they simply stood there and looked back in silence. "That would have to mean something in Terra's atmosphere, or possibly even in hyperspace, must have caused it. I want those medical files uploaded to my private computer immediately. And get me this Ahmed Khadra person. We have no time to waste!"

* * *

Cinda followed the man a while longer. It was difficult keeping up, even with the light of the two moons overhead illuminating the forest. There were many points where she passed through complete darkness due to the canopy of foliage above. Only his flashlight ahead allowed her to stay on his trail.

Cinda decided she had enough. She started to close the gap between herself and her quarry when he stopped suddenly in front of something made of glass and metal. Curious and wary Cinda stopped and ducked behind a tree.

The man checked his watch and nodded, then slipped on a dark hood and typed out something on the console. The screen lit up in a splash of color to reveal the face of a damnthing!

"Report," the hooded man said.

"We made a significant capture, though team three was supposed to have stood down at that time. Over thirty adult Fuzzies and a few immature ones," the man in the damnthing mask said. "I decided against chastising them since they have made the largest single capture to date."

"Agreed, but warn them against further such missteps," the hooded man said. "We have survived this long by not taking any unnecessary chances. One team gets caught and we are all in danger."

"The cell structure is unchanged. One team being captured would still leave the rest of us undiscovered."

"Assume nothing of the sort," the hooded man said. "We were lucky last year when the Holloways discovered one of our Beta teams. The one that killed the team leader did us a favor."

"I believe that was the younger Holloway," the one wearing a damnthing mask replied.

"Whatever. I think it is time for us to take our leave of this planet," the hooded man said. "It is time to pull a major raid on Hok—"

"Is that somebody behind you? Look!"

Cinda ducked back behind the tree. She could hear the hooded man approach and fought down her panic. Ducking down close to the ground her hand fell upon a stick. Cinda picked it up and threw it through the brush hoping he would follow it.

"Nice try, whoever you are," the hooded man said. "I've seen all the old movies, too. Now come out or I will find you."

Cinda ran blindly into the trees. She heard a shot and felt something buzz past her ear. She didn't realize the bullet had grazed her temple until the blood dripped into her eye. She remembered an old war film where soldiers running into enemy fire zig-zagged to make themselves harder targets. She hoped it worked when running away from enemy fire, too.

Cinda slowed briefly as she fumbled out her pistol. Nobody with any sense went out in an unfamiliar area unarmed. A second bullet creased her head, knocking her down. As luck would have it, she rolled down a steep embankment and fell into a stream. Barely conscious, she flailed about until she chanced on a floating piece of wood. More out of instinct than conscious thought, she grabbed the half-submerged log and held on as the stream floated her gently away.

Cinda lost all sense of time as she drifted. When a bend in the stream pushed her to the bank, she had enough presence of mind to crawl up onto the land. Not even looking where she was crawling, her hand fell onto something warm and leathery. As she looked forward she could see a boot in the dim light of the moons. Looking up, she followed the legs, very thick legs at that, up to an even thicker torso. Atop the torso was an incredibly thick neck topped with a human head. Or so she thought until her eyes adjusted to the moonlight.

The face she saw was like nothing she had ever seen. More simian than human, she thought. The face came down to better inspect the water-logged young woman. It said something in a language she did not recognize. At this point Cinda did the logical thing for a person in her circumstances.

She fainted.

XXXIII

It took some time to find the recruiters Parsec Paul had told Roberts about. When Roberts did find them it was in a warehouse on the edge of Junktown. That much was no less than the private investigator had expected. What disconcerted him was that the warehouse was owned by one Clancy Slade. It seemed his personal business dovetailed with his current client's case. Roberts made a mental note to adjust his client's fee accordingly.

"Ah, Clancy, what have you gotten yourself into?" Roberts said to himself. He glanced in a darkened window to make sure his pseudo-flesh mask was on straight and staying in place, then walked over to the warehouse entrance. There he was given the once-over by a burly man with a repeating pistol holstered with the strap off.

"Name?" the man demanded.

"Bob Sherman," Roberts answered. He hoped they didn't have a portable veridicator trained on him.

"Where did you hear about us?"

Roberts wasn't ready for that question and quickly improvised. "Fast Eddie." Every planet had at least one Fast Eddie.

"Which one?"

"What do you mean which one? I only know of one. The one with the scar." It was even odds that anybody named Fast Eddie would have a scar somewhere on his body. Criminals tended to get into scrapes that they couldn't explain to a medical professional for fear of it being reported.

"What? How did he hear about us?"

"I didn't ask. Do I get in or go look for other employment opportunities?"

Before the man could answer, another man, larger and burlier, came up to the door edging Roberts out of the way. "What's going on here?"

Roberts glanced at the man then quickly looked away for fear of being recognized. It took a moment to remember he was still wearing the mask.

"And who are you?" demanded the doorman.

"Clancy Slade and I own this building. What the Niflheim is all this about?"

The doorman took a step back blocking any view into the building. "My employer rented this building from you, yes? Well, what we do is our business."

"Not if what I heard is true. I hear you guys are hiring people to go to Beta Continent and do some hunting. Just what are you after and why do you need my building to do your hiring?"

Damn! Parsec Paul must have spoken with Clancy after I left. Well, at least I know Clancy isn't involved in whatever this is.

"Mr. Slade, my employer will contact you in the morning and answer any questions you may have...." As the man spoke, his right hand moved slowly to his repeating pistol.

Roberts couldn't wait. His left hand shot out and connected with the doorman's jaw. Clancy watched in surprise as the man went down.

"Clancy, move!" Roberts reached out with his left and grabbed Clancy's arm as his right hand drew his gun. With some difficulty, he pulled Clancy away from the door and started running, dragging the larger man with him.

"What the hell was that about?" Clancy cried out as he struggled to keep up with Roberts. "And who the hell are you?"

"Jason Roberts. Ghu, I should have left this damned mask at home for all the good it did me tonight. This way!"

Roberts pulled Clancy around a corner, then around a second one and stopped running. He let go of Clancy's arm and pulled off the pseudo-flesh mask. "Take off your jacket and throw it away. Good, now put this on."

"Your mask? Won't they recognize it even on me?"

"It re-contours itself to match your bone structure. That way it looks more natural when you speak. Your face is wider and with that lantern jaw of yours, the mask will make it look a lot different from how it looked on me."

"What about you?"

"What about me? Those mugs never saw my real face. Now let's just walk natural-like until our ride gets here." Roberts tapped his left wrist then put away his pistol.

"That man you hit...you dropped him with one punch. Don't take this wrong, but you don't look that strong."

Roberts smiled. "You're correct, I am not. This arm, however," he held up his left hand, "is artificial. A souvenir from my days on the force."

"Robot arm?" Clancy let out a low whistle. "Why not get a new arm grown?"

Roberts shook his head. "Radiation poisoning. Not enough to make me sick...well, not long with treatment, anyway...but bad enough that any attempt at regrowth treatments would likely grow a mutated appendage. If that happened, chances were that I couldn't get the artificial afterwards. Nerve mutation. I had maybe a one out of twenty chance of growing a usable arm. I didn't care for the odds, so I took the mechanical option. I have touch sensors in the fingers; they're almost as good as the real thing. Most days I forget it isn't real."

"Huh." Clancy realized he was staring and averted his gaze. "I didn't know they were that strong."

"Well, I had to have some reinforcements installed on my ribcage and spinal column to handle the load. I also had a few after-market extras installed. Took half my savings. Worth it, though." Roberts looked around. "Hmm...looks like we either lost them, or they didn't bother chasing us."

"I had no idea what those punks were up to," Clancy said. "Still don't, really. I just know they're up to nothing good."

"I didn't know you owned that warehouse, Clancy. Where did you get the scratch for that, plus your other businesses?"

Clancy thought it over, then shrugged. "Ah, hell, you probably just saved my life, so I guess I can trust you as much as anybody. You know about Leo Thaxter, right?"

Roberts nodded. "The man you shot and received a hefty reward for. You were also blackmailed into taking his place in Prison House for a while."

"Hey! That part wasn't in the news...was it? No matter, it's true. Well, I was paid to take Thaxter's place—25,000 sols. Not that I had a choice with my daughter in danger...."

"Yeah, that's enough to pay for the bar and the liquor license," Roberts said, "but well short of covering two restaurants and that warehouse."

"Yeah...about that. While Thaxter was out of Prison House, he used my name. We look like twins so he had no trouble passing himself off as me. Well, Thaxter rented a spaceport locker and bought a house in my name. The locker turned out to be loaded with cash and sunstones. According to Gus Brannhard, since it was all in my name, it is legally mine."

"Hmm...," Roberts replied. "It wouldn't have taken much to prove who the real owner was, then the police could have confiscated everything: house, locker contents, the works."

"Ah...well, they could have," Clancy said, "but then they would have to admit to some legal dancing on their part. To enter the house Thaxter bought in my name they had to get permission from the owner...."

"And you were the owner of record and gave that permission," Roberts said. "If they admitted to that, it would have created a big mess in the courts when they caught up with Thaxter. You saved everybody a lot of trouble when you shot him."

"Yeah, Brannhard said the same thing. And they couldn't say that the house was mine and not the locker contents. It was all or nothing. I made out pretty well, though if I had it to do over again I would have left planet before letting my daughter be put at risk. Um...if you can keep a secret, there was one more thing."

Roberts admitted he could keep a secret unless Clancy committed a serious crime.

"Fair enough. Thaxter had a huge stash of cash and stuff hidden in that house. Way more than what was in the locker."

Roberts started laughing. It was perfect. Clancy didn't even have to pay taxes on any of it since Zarathustra didn't have any. No need to declare the money. And Roberts had already suspected that Thaxter stashed more loot in the house that Clancy probably found. No matter, it wasn't Roberts' concern. Leslie Coombes would be relieved that Clancy was on the up and up though he couldn't be read in on the details. Another successful conclusion to a case.

From above Roberts could hear an aircar descending. "Our ride is here. We'll call the police after we get airborne."

Clancy squinted up at the aircar. "Who's flying it?"

The aircar landed and the hatch opened to reveal Mike Hammer at the controls. He needed a booster seat and a scaled down console that plugged into the master unit. "You call, Pappy Jay?"

"You bet, Mike. Let's get out of here."

"A Fuzzy pilot!" Clancy exclaimed. "Just when I thought this night couldn't get any stranger."

* * *

Cinda awoke in a dark room. The first thing she noted was that she was in a bed with clean sheets of an unidentifiable nature. Second, she noticed the headache caused by the small wounds near her temple. The hooded man clearly had tried to blow her head off. The next thing she noticed was that she was completely naked.

Throwing off the sheets, Cinda got out of the bed and found a light switch. The room wasn't like any she saw in the Bed and Breakfast. She went to the mirror over the bureau and looked herself over. She was clean and her injuries had been tended to. Then she remembered being found by something humanoid that couldn't possibly be human.

There was a polite knock at the door. "Wait! I'm not decent!" she cried, looking around and realizing there were no clothes anywhere in the room. Having no other option, she pulled the sheet off the bed and fashioned a toga. "Okay, you can come in, now."

The door opened to reveal a short, extremely muscular man. Cinda hesitated to look at the face as the memory of what she saw the night before was still fresh and frightening. When she finally looked up, the face she saw was not only normal, but exceptionally handsome.

"*Guten Morgan, Fräulein*. I am Rheiner Sostreus. I hope dat you are vell dis morning."

Cinda had some trouble with the accent though she caught the meaning. "I'm...fine. Where am I?"

"Ach! Ja, Heinrich find you at der river und bring you here. Dis ist Neu Freya, a neu settlement on Zeta Continent."

"Oh. Okay. Now...where are my clothes and who took them?"

Rheiner stepped back a pace. "Hilda und Siegrid attended to you last night. No man vould dare come near you vit' dem dere."

Cinda settled down a bit. "Then where are my clothes?"

"Ach, dey vere vet, torn und dirty. Ve are trying to find somet'ing dat vill fit you."

Cinda sat down on the edge of the bed. "Heinrich, the one who found me...."

Rheiner nodded. He knew what was coming. "Ja, you saw vhat you saw. I vas asked to meet vit' you so you vould not be frightened." He grabbed a chair and spun it around before sitting down with his massive arms crossed over the back. "Mein people are Freyan t'ough most of us vould look like monsters to you."

Cinda thought about the face she saw before passing out. "Well, I wouldn't say monsters. Just different. Ullerans look more monstrous to me than almost anything, like a walking crocodile. To each other I imagine they look just fine. Oh, that sounds awful, doesn't it. And I would like to thank Heinrich personally for helping me."

"*Sehr gut!*" Rheiner nodded. His brow furrowed. *Fräulein...* Um, vhat ist your name? You haff no I.D. vit' you."

She blushed before replying, "Cinda Dawn."

"*Sehr gut,*" Rheiner nodded. "Now, *Fräulein* Cinda, vhy vere you in der river?"

It came back to Cinda in a rush. "The hooded man! He was up to something out in the woods. He was talking to a damnthing on a viewscreen in the forest...."

Cinda ran on for a few minutes while Rheiner tried to keep up with his limited knowledge of Lingua Terra. A damnthing on a viewscreen in the forest? It sounded to him like the young woman's head injury might be more serious than originally thought.

"Ist der somevun you need to call?"

Cinda thought about it. She didn't think it wise to contact the camp; the hood would be after her now, since she had no idea who he was. "I...I don't know. Is there somebody in charge that I could speak to?"

"Ja. Johann Torseus. He vill know vhat to do." Rheiner glanced over Cinda's makeshift toga. "First, let us find you some clozing."

*   *   *

Morgan was going over some documents when Johann politely knocked at the open door. He looked up with a smile that quickly melted away. "Johann? What's wrong?"

"Der ist a *jung Fräulein* in Neu Freya dat has a very strange story to tell. I t'ought she should speak vit' you."

"Freyan woman?"

"Terran."

"In Neu Freya?" Morgan thought a moment, then remembered being told about the scientific expedition. "Ah, one of the scientists. Is she online?"

"Ja. Shall I haff der call transferred here?"

"Certainly." Morgan cleared his desk and glanced at the small mirror above his private comscreen to make sure he was presentable. The screen exploded in an array of colors before resolving into the image of a young woman, with red hair and a bandage on her forehead, and Rheiner. "Good morning. I am Morgan Holloway. How may I be of assistance?"

"Herr Hollovay, dis ist Cinda Dawn," Rheiner said.

"Mr. Holloway, I think something bad is going to happen." Cinda quickly related everything she could remember from what she saw the night before. "Are you the...uh...younger Holloway they mentioned?"

Morgan nodded. "I must be. I shot a Fuzzy slaver last year when he tried to kill my father. You say this Dmitri Watson is involved?"

"Well, I don't know for sure if it was Dmitri, sir. I only saw a single man from behind at a distance in dim light. It could have been anybody, really."

"Do you have any idea who the damnthing...it must be a mask or digital overlay...might be?"

"I'm afraid not. They didn't use names." Cinda felt relief wash over her along with some weakness. It was good that somebody accepted her story without thinking she was delusional. "I don't think it would be anybody else in the expedition."

"Well, this hooded man wouldn't need a hidden comscreen for that, but it isn't safe to assume that nobody else in the party is involved. I advise that you stay with Rheiner for the time being. Don't even contact your camp to let them know you are alive. That will be the safest course while I bring the authorities in. Rheiner, does Miss Dawn understand the situation there?"

"*Jawohl,* Herr Hollovay. Heinrich gave her a bit of a start, but I believe she vas already pretty shaken at die time."

"I understand and won't be distressed by Rheiner's people," Cinda cut in. "They've been very kind to me and I feel very safe here. I doubt even the Space Marines would want to pick a fight with these guys."

Morgan's smile returned. "I think you are right about that. Rheiner, see to it that nobody from the expedition leaves Neu Freya. Invent a reason. I'll be in touch. Morgan out."

After cutting the connection, he called for Johann. "Call Marshal Fane and bring him up to speed. Play the recording of the last call if you have to. I'll call my Father."

XXXIV

"...so unless you want more information on Clancy, you will just have to accept that he isn't doing anything illegal."

Leslie Coombes leaned back in his chair and thought for a moment. It was possible that Roberts spent his time in the bar, then fabricated a story to get paid. If that were the situation, though, he would have drawn the case out to get more money. Besides, his credentials were impeccable.

"Hmm...I know I said I didn't want to know anything beyond whether or not he was doing something that would harm the Company or Mr. Grego, but...?"

"I'll tell you this much if it will ease your mind," Roberts said from the comscreen, "Clancy...ah...inherited a substantial sum shortly after Thaxter was taken down. More than enough to float several businesses. If you want more information on that, I suggest you speak with Chief Colonial Prosecutor Brannhard. He knows all about it, but I can't say whether or not he'll want to read you in on it."

"Oh, well, if Gus is in the know then it must be on the up and up," Coombes said, with some relief. "Our Colonial Prosecutor doesn't play fast and loose with the law...as a rule. Very good, Mr. Roberts. Please send me your bill."

"Mike already handled that. By the way, you should come have dinner at The Soup Kitchen tomorrow. The special is their roast banjo bird, which is something not to be missed. Mrs. Slade must have sold her soul to learn how to cook like that."

Coombes smiled. "I'll check my schedule. Thank you, again, Mr. Roberts."

Just as Coombes was about to break the connection, Roberts spoke up again. "Say, Mr. Coombes, how would you like to earn some of your money back?"

Coombes was amused at the thought. "Doing what?"

"Well, we have this guy in Junktown that used to be a freighter captain, maybe more, but his memory is scrambled. Nobody knows what his real name is and I think he needs a leg up. If you can track down any information…."

"I should think you would be better at this than I," Coombes said, with some suspicion.

"Ordinarily, yes, but I think that info is in the CZC computers and I don't want to break any laws gaining access to them. You, on the other hand, could very easily get what I am after without any fuss."

"I could. Very well, give me whatever information you have on this man, maybe some fingerprints, and I will look into it."

Roberts smiled wide. "Great. I will messenger over a packet with everything I have."

After breaking the connection Coombes sat in thought. Gus Brannhard was in on whatever supplied Clancy Slade with a great deal of money. It was even possible Gus gave Clancy the money himself, although that seemed unlikely. Coombes shook it off. No need to look for problems; there were enough of them knocking on the door. He turned his attention to other matters.

*   *   *

Juan Jimenez had just finished going over the financials when Ahmed Khadra knocked on the door. "Officer Khadra, come on in and have a seat."

"Thank you." Ahmed took the chair in front of the desk. "I just finished my…ah…analysis?" He shrugged. "…of the Fuzzy procreation problem. I really don't know if I was of any help since I know very little about biology beyond a lab requirement in college…."

Juan waved that off. "That isn't why Dr. Hoenveld asked for you. Lately he has come to respect hunches and deductive reasoning. He is very set in his ways and it takes him time to adapt, but Darla Cross has been steering him in new directions. Frankly, I think asking for you was a stroke of genius."

"I'm not so sure," Ahmed said. "I looked over all of the data...a lot of which I didn't even understand...and only found one possibility that makes sense to me."

"If you've narrowed it down to one, that is great. What did you come up with?"

Ahmed took a breath. "I read over everything Ms. Cross laid out for me—she narrowed things down quite a bit, I understand—and looked for commonalities. I noticed that every Fuzzy who had been X-rayed was sterile. However, not all of the sterile Fuzzies had been X-rayed. Then I noticed that all of the non-X-rayed Fuzzies had been to Terra."

"Terra? That would be Leslie Coombes' Fuzzies."

"Yes, initially. We also have a few dozen more that just came in."

Juan nodded. "The Fuzzies captured by slavers."

"Oh, you know about that?"

"I had to be briefed since Science Center is doing the workups on the repatriated Fuzzies," Juan explained.

"Good, saves time and equivocation," Ahmed nodded. "Anyway, I started thinking about Terra. What was so different between Terra and Zarathustra? The answer was pretty obvious, really; radiation. Terra has been nuked to within an inch of its ability to sustain life. The background radiation in even the least affected areas is more than double what it was in pre-atomic times. Almost five times that of Zarathustra."

Khadra waited while Juan made the mental connections. It didn't take long. Every middle school student knew about radiation and the changes wrought by the wars on Terra. The northern hemisphere was virtually un-inhabitable even after four centuries of terraforming. Contaminated soil was slowly being stripped away and stuffed into mass-energy converters, the simplest and fastest way to dispose of the material, and replaced with bio-matter imported from other worlds like Yggdrasil and Heimdall. It was a slow and expensive undertaking.

"Zarathustra has the lowest background radiation of any Terra-like world," Juan said. "Only Freya even comes close to these low levels. Good

God! That has to be it."

Ahmed nodded. "Dr. Hoenveld said much the same thing. He seemed very upset by it, in fact."

"Really? Normally he takes great satisfaction in the resolution of a problem." Juan stood up and came around the desk. "I think I'll go speak with him. Thank you for your help, Officer Khadra."

"I might be wrong, you know. It could be something completely different that I am too ignorant to recognize."

"It is possible, and I almost hope you are wrong. Unfortunately, it makes perfect sense." Juan extended his hand and Ahmed shook it. "I'll go see what Dr. Hoenveld has found."

"You might have to wait a while. He left the facility with Ms. Cross right after I gave him my findings."

"Left?" *That isn't at all like Chris.* "Did he say where he was going?"

"No, but I think Ms. Cross took him out for a drink. I have to say I think he needed one."

XXXV

The Marshal's office was almost as spacious as the Governor's. This was less a nod to Max Fane's high standing than the fact that quite often the ranking members of the Zarathustran police force gathered in his office for strategy and policy meetings. Max kept a wet bar, paid for out of his own salary, for when meetings ran long. While he personally never drank on duty, a shot or two could relieve the tension of a difficult and dangerous job among his subordinates.

Trask stood at the bar while nursing a Three Planets. The drink consisted of 151 proof Terran rum, Thoran *nildan*, a distant cousin to absinthe, and a splash of Lokian *looehlaf*, a fruit extract that had no debilitating effects on the Lokian natives, but hit human metabolisms like a fifth of 100 proof whisky. Max felt his stomach twist just watching Trask sip the concoction. He didn't go for the really hard drinks; instead he preferred simple Terran bourbon. Next to Trask were Jason Roberts and Clancy Slade. Roberts nursed a scotch and water while Clancy worked on his second Freyan ale.

The Marshal was about to say something when the communication screen beeped. "Ah, that should be them." Max pressed a button on the console and instructed his assistant to send the visitors in. He was more than a little surprised when officers Gilbert and Sullivan appeared.

"Marshal Fane? We were ordered by Chief Carr to report to you about a special assignment," Gilbert said.

Frank didn't waste any time on this, Max thought. "He did. If you can hold your hooch, just belly up to the bar and help yourselves. Be forewarned, the Governor, the Native Affairs Commissioner and the CZC CEO will be joining us shortly, so don't overdo it."

The two men gave a "yessir" before going over to the bar where they both ordered a club soda on ice, then struck up a conversation with the others. Max watched with approval, then rushed to the communications console.

"Rasmussen, when Rainsford, Holloway and Grego get here, just send them right in. No point in standing on protocol right now." Officer Rasmussen acknowledged the order and signed off just as the door opened.

Max turned and saw Ben, Jack, Grego and an older woman he didn't know along with several Fuzzies. "Let me guess; you were standing out there and heard my order to Ras." They did. Max let out a sigh. "Well, welcome to the party. Ma'am, I don't believe we have had the pleasure—"

"Call me Pat, Marshal. I'm Jack's sister visiting from Terra. If this is a sensitive meeting I can take the Fuzzies and tour the city."

"If Jack has no issue with your being here, Pat, I certainly don't. Has everybody eaten? Why don't you all take seats while I send out for some pizzas and Extee Three."

"No time for that, now, Marshal," Jack said. "I just got word from Morgan—"

"He called me, too. About that science expedition. Some mutt wearing a hood may be ram-rodding these Fuzzy slavers. I sent out three units to Zeta as soon as I heard. First I had to clear it with Johann Torseus since we have no official presence there, per the Governor's treaty with the Freyans. We also have new information that these slavers are also working out of Junktown recruiting lowlifes."

Max nodded toward Roberts and Clancy. "Mr. Slade owns a warehouse on the edge of Junktown where he and Mr. Roberts here discovered some sort of recruitment operation. Based on additional testimony by...ah...Parsec Paul?...we believe this was connected to the Fuzzy slaving operation. Unfortunately, by the time my men got there the mutts had all cleared out. Forensics is tearing the place apart looking for anything that might help us track these people down. Mr. Slade, the MPD will compensate you for the repairs to your building."

Clancy waved that off. "Take the place apart brick by brick if you have to. Catch these sons-of-Khooghras and we'll call it a wash. Mr.

Grego, shouldn't Chief Steefer and maybe Major Lansky be here?"

"I'll brief them later, Clancy," Grego replied. "Marshal, the Company police will be at your disposal."

Gus Brannhard entered through the door, nodded at the others, then went to the bar to pour a sizeable drink before sitting down at the table. He noticed that several Fuzzies were there, including Little Fuzzy and a friend—female?—he hadn't seen before. He wouldn't have forgotten that spectacular golden fur.

"Good. But what are we waiting around here for, then?" Ben asked.

"That was my idea, Ben," Gus said. "We don't know the identity of the hooded man; so corralling the expedition people would be a waste of time. We can't veridicate everybody there without warrants, which Judge Pendarvis won't issue without something more solid than: 'we think the slaver boss is one of them.' Bad guys, even most good guys, don't volunteer to take a seat in the veridicator just because we ask, pretty please."

Ben rolled his eyes. "I get it, Gus. Now let's consider what we can do."

Grego said. "Pat, here, made a suggestion about using Fuzzy robots, if you will recall, as decoys. Well, I have a hundred ready to go as soon as we know the best places to put them."

"We'll still have to mix in some real Fuzzies," Jack said. It was clear from the tone of his voice that he did not like the idea.

Max nodded. "It is a risk, I grant, but these dirtbags want live Fuzzies, not dead ones, so they aren't in too much danger."

"And with robots along, we can track where they're taken," Victor Grego added.

"Homing devices in the robots that will activate after they are on whatever conveyance the slavers are using, right?" Ben asked.

Grego nodded.

"The main problem is that we think the slavers are using hyperspace yachts about the size of that one your son has, Jack," Max added. "They send out teams to collect small groups of Fuzzies, then gather them up into the ships and send them to Terra or Baldur or wherever the Niflheim they go. We need a way to disable their crafts before they exit the atmosphere. Once they are away from the gravity well, they'll transition into hyperspace and nothing will be able to get them."

"For that I have a plan," Grego said with his toothy grin. "We let them snatch up a few small parties of robots with some real Fuzzies. Once on board the ships, the robots will release a colorless, odorless gas that will render everybody unconscious—"

"Including the Fuzzies?" Jack demanded.

Grego shook his head in negation. "We can inoculate the Fuzzies."

"All fine and well, but who controls the ship, then?" Jack asked. "It takes months of training to operate a ship like that, and robots have never been successfully used as pilots."

Grego smiled wider. "True. But these robots have remote capability. Damien Panaioli, my best drone pilot, will be hooked into a virtual reality helmet and control gloves that will remotely operate a robot from the CZC. He won't be able to do anything really fancy, but he can bring the ship down for a soft landing where, hopefully, we will be waiting."

"The robot can receive a signal through a collapsium hull?" Ben wondered aloud.

"Not through the collapsium directly," Grego explained. "Nothing we know of can do that except gravity. However, there are weak spots on every ship where signals and detection equipment are hardwired in. Otherwise every ship would be flying blind."

Jack thought it over. "So, if we can get some robots taken, if they aren't discovered, if the gas works as advertised and if the ship comes down without killing everybody on board, we will have at least some of our slavers. There are a whole lot of ifs in there."

"Jack, the Fuzzies are the only ones taking a real risk, yes," Patricia asked.

"Well, yes, Pat. That is my point."

"Then why don't you ask one of them what they think of the plan?" Patricia looked meaningfully in Little Fuzzy's direction. "Little Fuzzy, what do you think?"

Max thought Patricia was joking. "Ma'am, this is hardly the time to be making light of this situation."

"You don't have any Fuzzies of your own, do you, Marshal?" Grego asked. "If you recall, I underestimated them once, and look what happened to me?"

Max was still skeptical. "Jack, what do you think?"

"I think we should hear what Little Fuzzy has to say."

Since Jack wasn't known to joke about anything serious, Max shrugged and turned his attention to Little Fuzzy. "Little Fuzzy, do you understand what we are talking about?"

Little Fuzzy thought for a second, then nodded. "Bad Big Ones take Fuzzee away for bad things. Good Big Ones want to stop bad Big Ones. Need Fuzzee to help. Hokay. Fuzzee help."

"Little Fuzzy, do you know how we need you to help?" Ben asked.

"Fuzzee go with made-things...ro-bot...robot that look like Fuzzee?... an' let bad Big Ones catch us. Then robot call Pappy Vic an' Pappy Jack come get us an' catch bad Big Ones," Little Fuzzy finished with: "Is so?"

"Is so, Little Fuzzy," Jack nodded.

"Sir, I realize I am not included in this," Detective Sullivan said, "but isn't there a way for a couple of men to escort the Fuzzies? I mean, stay close and report on their progress? Something?"

"I like the way you think, son," Max replied. "Now, how do we do that without getting spotted ourselves? We would have to know exactly when and where these varmints are going to hit. If we knew that, we would just come in and take them."

"Could we equip a couple of Fuzzies with radios?" Roberts asked. "Something that wouldn't be detected by the slavers?"

"We have to assume that the slavers are scanning all frequencies before they move in," Max said. "Otherwise we might have caught one by now."

Roberts nodded, then spoke again. "Okay, give them radios that send a signal that would sound like static. One set to be used if slavers are nearby, another to report all clear."

"Hey, that sounds pretty good, Marshal," Ben said.

Max turned to Grego. "Do you have anything like that handy?"

"No, but we can reconfigure a few radio sets in a couple hours. I'll get my people on it straight away."

"Do we have any Fuzzies trained in police work, Commissioner?" Officer Gilbert asked.

"Not really," Jack said. "We train Fuzzies for survival, not...Oh Niflheim! Maybe we do. George Lunt's crowd: Dr. Crippen, Dillinger, Ned Kelly, Lizzie Borden and Calamity Jane."

Patricia laughed. "I just love the names you all give the Fuzzies."

"There are also the Company Police Fuzzies: Allan Pinkerton, Arsène Lupin, Sherlock Holmes. Irene Adler and Mata Hari," Grego added.

"A Fuzzy learns as much from watching Big Ones as anything else," Jack said. "We'll ask the cops who have their own Fuzzies, if they are willing to let their Fuzzies in on this."

"An' me." Everybody turned their attention to Little Fuzzy. "I go, too."

Jack wanted to say no, and barely stopped himself. He couldn't ask the others to send their Fuzzies on a dangerous mission, then refuse to send one of his own. Still...? "Little Fuzzy, are you sure?"

"Bad Big Ones hurt Fuzzee. I go," Little Fuzzy said with finality. "Koko, Mike, Mitzy, Cinderella, Mamma Fuzzy an' Baby Fuzzy come, too." Then he paused, looked over at the new Fuzzy standing beside him. "Emily, too."

Off to the side of the room Jack could see his Fuzzies all nodding in agreement. So were Flora, Fauna, Diamond and Sunstone. Jack was both proud and worried.

"Jack, I'm sorry," Patricia said. "I didn't mean to open a can of worms. You can stop them, or at least some of them, from going. Right?"

"Colonial law is a bit picky," Gus said. "We can't stop a Fuzzy from going out into the wilderness if he wants to go, for example. Legally, Fuzzies are incompetent aborigines with the same rights as a ten-year-old child, but they have survived on this world for hundreds of thousands of years without us. No adopted Fuzzy can be legally prevented from leaving if they want to go. I would say the same applies to this situation."

"I admit, I don't like putting any Fuzzies at risk, especially not my own family," Jack said. "But, if I were in their shoes, I would do the exact same thing."

"Fuzzee not wear shoes," Little Fuzzy said confused.

"Is not-so thing Big Ones say," Ben explained. "It means Pappy Jack would do what you are doing, if he was in your place." Ben feared he would have to elaborate further, but Little Fuzzy nodded.

"Then it is settled," Max said. "We have to take a stab at the most likely locations the slavers will attack next and have our Fuzzies waiting there."

"What do we know about it?" Jack asked.

"Cinda Dawn had her memory scrambled a bit from her unpleasant incident," Max reported." After a bullet creased her skull, she spent some time in the river. She did recall that the man in the hood was planning one last big snatch. Maybe we can narrow down where this would be."

Officer Gilbert stepped up to the conference table. "The Northern Fuzzies would be the most vulnerable. We have the smallest ZNPF presence there due to the agreement between their leader and Commissioner Holloway."

Max turned to Jack. "What do you think?"

Jack thought it over. "It's a good possibility. Outside of my bunch down at the Reservation school, there is the greatest concentration of Fuzzies on the planet. Larger than any of the villages, even."

"Ah, there may be another sizeable target," Grego said. "Science Center Beta on the western edge of the Reservation. Gerd has been doing studies on the Fuzzies to help out Juan's crew back in Mallorysport."

"And, of course, there is the school itself," Jack finished. "Okay, we have three possible targets. Maybe even all three at once with all the people they have been recruiting. If only we knew how many ships they have."

"That brings us to the other problem," Ben said. "How do we stop a collapsium-plated yacht with stealth technology from leaving the planet? I don't think even Commodore Napier has that kind of firepower."

That brought everybody up short until Clancy reminded everybody about the knockout gas in the robo-Fuzzies.

"That assumes that the gas works, the robots aren't detected and ejected, or that they even get picked up in the first place," Jack noted. "We need to come up with a way to blockade the sky, and we simply don't have those kinds of resources."

Grego thought for a moment before speaking. "I have a few interplanetary craft. They can't enter hyperspace, but then we don't want them to."

"Morgan has his yacht, and I am sure he'll let Captain Zeudin join the party," Jack said.

"Napier has at least three interplanetary craft as well," Ben added. "That's seven ships in all."

"Eight." Trask, who had remained silent up until this point, decided it was time to chime in. "There is the armed military hyperspace transport that hauled all of the Fuzzies we rescued back from Terra."

Jack slammed the table with his fist. "We have eight ships to cover a sizeable chunk of the planet. Damn-it! Even if we assume that the slavers will try to escape from Beta Continent, that's a helluva lot of real estate to cover."

Patricia laughed. "Jack, I think I know where you can find a whole passel of ships."

Everybody stared at her.

"You do know that there are about a zillion ships up in orbit, right?"

"The Fuzzy Adoption League," Gus said as he slapped his forehead. "That's what I have been calling that mob of tourists up there. Max, could you call Commodore Napier and see if he can press those ships into service?"

Marshal Fane smiled wolfishly. "Now, things are starting to come together."

Jack sighed. "Don't forget my list of ifs."

XXXVI

On a larger world, with a population in the tens of millions or more, a Charterless Zarathustra Company operation like the Science Division would operate at peak capacity around the clock. Colonial worlds, still in their infancy, lacked the qualified personnel to properly run such a large business for hours on end. So, like most businesses, the CZC Science Division operated on a nine to five basis, save for the occasional experiment or detail that could not be run on such a schedule.

It was the end of the business day and Juan Jimenez was ready to go home. As Division Head, he tended to be the last to leave at the end of the day. It wasn't a sense of duty or overdeveloped propensity for diligence that kept Juan late, although he did possess those qualities to a sensible degree. It was the paperwork. Mountains and mountains of paperwork that accumulated every day. Every document, every requisition had to be read, signed and deposited in the correct slot.

Juan knew he could shorten his workday by spending less time in the laboratories and more time in his office; the previous Division Head had rarely spent any time out of his office. The scientist in Juan just would not stand for that. With the last document signed and disposed of, Jimenez stood up, stretched the kinks out of his back, shut down the computer and closed up his office. Unlike Mallin, Juan preferred his office to be adjoining the labs and not on the top floor of Science House. He took that idea from Dr. Hoenveld, who practically lived in the laboratory.

Walking through the main area he wondered where they all went at the end of the day. The interns were likely headed out to shower and change before going out on the town. Those with families were off to spend time with them, presumably.

That thought reminded Juan that he hadn't even had a date in months. It was difficult to find a woman that didn't work for the CZC in some capacity or other and, as a Division Head, dating a lower employee was frowned upon. Even Victor Grego suffered from that particular unwritten rule.

Juan shook the thought away. The women were out there, he just needed to spend a little time looking for one. Even Dr. Hoenveld had managed to wrangle a woman. And what a woman! Darla Cross might have been a little past her prime, as actresses went, but she was still quite the looker. How Hoenveld managed to land her defied the imagination.

He glanced at Hoenveld's office and noticed the door was open. After a moment's hesitation, he decided to go and say goodnight to the good doctor. As he approached the door he could hear voices: one Hoenveld's, the other a woman's—no doubt Darla Cross. He was about to turn away and leave them to their private conversation when he heard a sob.

"I should have known better."

Juan did not like to eavesdrop, but hearing Hoenveld in such distress rooted him to the spot.

"Chris, it isn't your fault. You were just trying to help. How could you possibly have known?"

Hoenveld sniffed and fought to control his voice. "Darla, it is a well-documented fact that the planet Zarathustra possesses the lowest background radiation levels of any known Terra-like world. I should have taken that into account before...before...."

Hoenveld sobbed again.

"Oh, Chris. Maybe you can find a treatment, or even a cure for the condition."

Though Juan couldn't see it, he could imagine Hoenveld throwing up his hands in despair. *What the hell did he do?*

"On Terra cases like this still cannot be reversed," Hoenveld said haltingly. "Radiation sickness is easily treatable, but much of the damage it causes is irreversible. Zorro does not show any of the classic symptoms, other than...."

More sobbing. Juan had never heard of Hoenveld getting upset like this. Anger? Certainly. His temper was well-known and feared by the interns, and even some of the younger doctors. But weeping? Gods and monsters, *what did he do?*

"Maybe he will recover on his own? I remember this producer on Thor who caught this bug that was going around—"

"I appreciate your concern, darling, but this is completely different. When I took that X-ray of Zorro I sterilized him, quite likely, permanently."

"Maybe not, Chris. You're a smart guy. Didn't you discover the stuff that fixes the Fuzzies' hormone problem?"

"The titanium-based long chain molecule that suppresses the NFMp hormone? Yes. That bit of irony is not lost on me. I find a way to allow Fuzzies to reproduce, only to sterilize one!"

Hoenveld started another round of sobs while Darla made soothing noises trying to calm him. Juan decided he had heard enough. He quickly and quietly backed away from Hoenveld's office and headed to the elevator. His mind replayed what he heard over and over. Juan was still thinking about it when he got home.

*　*　*

Dmitri awoke in a room at the Bed and Breakfast from the noise outside. After seeing Cinda at the lake, he had decided to take a room instead of his tent in case she found out about him seeing her. If she were to brace him on it, he preferred it be during the day, not at night and certainly not in his private tent.

There was a great deal of shouting and the sounds of contragravity vehicles moving about. He checked the time and saw it was just past 0700 local time.

"What the hell?" He threw off his blanket and went to the window. People were running all over and vehicles were moving in and out of the campsite. "We weren't supposed to be doing anything until after the morning meeting, damn-it."

Throwing on his pants and jumper, Dmitri grabbed his boots and hat and ran out to see what was going on. Outside he could see several people in a group around Tres Poe. Tres was doing all the talking and pointing at a large paper map. The men appeared to be paying very close attention, then nodded and scattered. Dax came over, said something, then lumbered off.

"Mr. Poe," Dmitri called out as he hopped into his boots. "What is going on?"

"Miss Dawn has gone missing, Dr. Watson," Tres said. "Nobody has seen her since last night."

"While she was down at the lake?" Dmitri feared something happened that he could have prevented had he remained there last night.

"No, I saw her afterwards. I asked her if she saw you there and she said something about talking with you about it."

Dmitri's stomach did a slow roll. He could well imagine what the subject of that conversation would be. "She never caught up with me last night. I turned in early. Is it possible she went back to Mallorysport?"

"Not on foot," Tres said. "Every vehicle is accounted for and nobody saw an airtaxi come near the camp. I can't think of any reason why she would leave suddenly like that anyway."

"No...neither can I."

"Anyway, I have organized the workers into search parties. Dax is especially upset. He won't admit it, but I believe he's sweet on her."

Dmitri recalled seeing Cinda in the moonlight the night before. "Yes, I can imagine. Say, have you contacted the locals? They might be able to help with the search."

"Yeah, they said they would patrol the outer perimeter. I get the strong feeling they don't like outsiders. Probably for reasons like this."

"Possibly. They didn't allow any visuals on the comscreen when we first came out...or since, now that I think about it." Dmitri thought it over. "Do you think one of the locals might have abducted her?"

Tres thought is over. "It's possible, since the only people on this continent are us and them, and nobody has a monopoly on virtue. Still, no one has seen a stranger in camp and Cinda wouldn't just walk away with somebody she didn't know." Tres removed a cigarette from his coat pocket and lit it. "We should check her room at the inn and see if she took her gun with her."

"Cinda has a gun!"

"Everybody on this planet has a gun, Dr. Watson. Colonial planets are dangerous and people don't wander around unprotected waiting to be eaten. Zeta Continent was recently cleared of all known inimical life forms, which were relocated to a preserve on Gamma."

"Then Miss Dawn wouldn't need her gun—"

"I said all *known* life forms, Doctor," Tres corrected Dmitri. "There is a lot about this world we still don't know. Plus, there are two-legged predators. Cinda should have known better than to walk around unarmed, but sometimes it happens. She hasn't been on Zarathustra as long as I have and may forget to carry now and then."

A man Dmitri didn't recall the name of ran up to them. "Tres, we found Cinda's pistol in the woods. It was on the ground near the drop off by the river. Franz thinks she may have tumbled down the rise and gone into the water."

Tres looked worried. "Was the pistol fired?"

"Full clip, no smell of cordite."

Tres swore. "I wish I knew if that was good or bad news."

"Surely if she ran into trouble out there, she would have fired her weapon, wouldn't she have?" Dmitri asked.

Tres shook his head. "If she had the chance, or wasn't attacked from behind—or someone didn't shoot her first."

"Wouldn't we have heard the shot?"

"Not through all that timber," said the other man. "For that matter, an assailant could have used a noise suppressor, a tranq-gun or something else that would work silently. Tres, we need some Fuzzies out here."

"Fuzzies?" Dmitri was confused. "Why?"

Tres nodded. "That is a damned good idea, Brent." He turned to Dmitri. "Fuzzies are the best trackers you'll ever hope to meet. Beat a Khooghra ten ways from Sunday. They can't track scent as well as a bloodhound, but they can read signs that would be invisible to anyone else. Brent, send the bus back to the Rez on Beta and explain what is going on. I'll bet Commissioner Holloway will send his best trackers to help out."

Dmitri liked the idea and said so. "Pick up some of that...what do they eat?"

"Extee Three." Tres and Brent said in unison.

"Really? Oh, well, different tastes." Dmitri took out his wallet and pulled out several bills without even looking at the denominations. "Pick up as much as you think we will need and tell Mi...Commissioner Holloway we will pay the Fuzzies whatever he thinks is fair for their services."

Brent simply nodded and ran off. Had the situation been less dire, Tres would have laughed at the idea of giving a Fuzzy money. The Fuzzy would likely try to eat it and spit it out.

*   *   *

In the sub-basement of the bed and breakfast, the hooded man set up his portable comscreen on a dusty table and inserted the activation key. The screen lit up in a kaleidoscope of color that resolved itself into the face of a damnthing.

"Where in tarnation have you been?" demanded the damnthing. "You've missed three check-ins!"

"Need I remind you who is in charge here?" the hooded man said sharply. The damnthing remained silent. "I thought not. I had to wait and see if our observer last night saw or heard anything damaging to our operation. It was also necessary to find a new place from which I could contact you. This was the first opportunity I have had to call."

"Then you know who saw you?"

"Maybe. I didn't get a good look in the darkness. Only that it was somebody small in stature. However, one of the locals who is working with the team has come up missing. At present, the common belief is that she tumbled down the side of a hill and was washed away by the river. Even if she does turn up alive, she could hardly identify me with the hood on. I am confident we are safe for the moment, though we should accelerate our plans."

"I do not share your optimism," the man with the damnthing mask said. "I think we should take precautions in case your missing teammate is alive and talkative."

The hooded man considered it and agreed. "What do you suggest?"

"I learned something while reading the news that may be put to our advantage. I have some men on standby should you agree."

"What is your plan?"

XXXVII

Jason Roberts and Mike Hammer took a seat at their usual booth with Parsec Paul. It was 1700 and the after work crowd was just starting to filter in. Roberts was considering what to order when he spotted Patricia coming in with Betty Kanazawa. Patricia he had met in person, briefly, while Betty he only knew by the articles about her in the datastream.

"Mrs. McLeod, over here."

Patricia and Betty followed the voice to its source and Patricia took the lead heading over to the table. "Jason Roberts, right?"

"Correct, ma'am. Why not join us?"

"I would be pleased to do so. Betty, have you met Mr. Roberts? He led Jack and them to the slavers' recruiting place in Junktown."

"Call me Jason," Roberts said as he stood to allow Patricia to slide into the booth. Everyone took their seat and Roberts made the introductions all around. "Paul here actually gets the credit for the warehouse."

Parsec Paul nodded. "Ma'am."

"Call me Pat. Parsec Paul is an interesting name."

"Huh. I got it by travelling to da— ...Uh, nearly every planet in the Federation and a few more besides. In fact, I think I was on the crew of the ship that discovered Zarathustra...at least I seem to recall serving under a Captain Mallory around that time."

Betty looked dubious. "That was something like a hundred years ago. You don't look quite that old."

Parsec laughed. "All that and more, little missy. The time dilation effect of hyperspace travel can really keep the years off of you. In my time I spent more years in hyperspace than I did on the ground for a very long while. It would take a whole whale of computer time just to add up my natural age with all the hyperspace adjustments involved."

"Well, can't you remember stepping foot on Zarathustra and seeing, I don't know, a damnthing or something?" Patricia asked.

Paul shook his head. "My memory is more than a little scrambled. I took a bullet to the head on...um...I think it was Shesha. At least I think it was a bullet.... I have a pretty impressive scar to show for it...or did I get that fixed? I can't remember everything in order so good.... I don't even remember my proper name anymore."

"Oh, that's terrible!" Patricia exclaimed. "Have you seen a doctor?"

"I think so. I seem to recall something about how they can't regenerate that part of the brain without my losing what memories I still have," Paul said thoughtfully. "A man is the sum of his experiences, so I decided to just live with my current condition."

The waitress came up and took every one's orders. While they waited, just to keep conversation going, Roberts asked if there was any progress on the Fuzzy issue. He was careful to keep it vague.

"We can't talk about that, Jason," Betty said. "Especially in public. We don't want the wrong ears picking up anything." For emphasis she threw a meaningful stare in the direction of the window. Roberts surreptitiously glanced in that direction and spotted a young man with a vidset on his head. A Streamer.

"By Ghu's guts, I hate those guys even though I sometimes use them myself," Roberts said.

"Why would you use them?" Patricia asked.

"Divorce cases, mostly," Roberts admitted. "These vidsets are everywhere, to the point that nobody even notices them anymore. They can track an unfaithful spouse almost anywhere and record it along the way. Saves lots of wear and tear on the footgear."

Their orders arrived and everybody started eating. Roberts kept looking out the window as if he were watching for something. Patricia became curious and asked him about it.

"I was expecting Agent Trask to join us. We spoke a bit back in the Marshal's office and hit it off. At least I thought we did. I invited him to come over here for dinner but he hasn't arrived yet."

"You specified which Soup Kitchen, didn't you?" Betty asked. "He might be sitting at the one in Junktown wondering where you are."

Roberts winced and admitted he hadn't thought of that. "And me a private eye who should be all about the details. Hey, Dora, could you call the other place and see if a Buck Trask is there?"

"Sure thing, stud." A moment later the waitress informed Roberts that Trask left there over five minutes ago and was headed here.

"Well, I guess his dinner will be on me," Roberts said wryly.

Mike Hammer looked confused? "Why you put dinner on you? Make mess."

Everybody laughed while Roberts explained the not-so thing. "Mike still has trouble with Big One expressions."

Dinner was finished when Roberts noticed an airtaxi settle outside. Something was wrong about that but he couldn't put his finger on it. "That might be Buck now."

"Well, let's all go outside and say hi. Betty and I are headed out to... what was that place...?"

"The Phantasmagorical," Betty supplied. "It's a shop near Mortgageville."

Patricia's face twisted with displeasure. "Gawd, I would rather use a certain obscenity in public than say that word."

"What? Phantasmagorical? It means—"

"I know what it means. It just sets me on edge for some reason."

Everybody paid their bill and went outside. Betty suggested that they take the taxi to the shop she would not name. Down the walk Roberts spotted Trask coming up.

"Hey, Buck. Sorry about the confusion."

"My fault. I knew there were two Soup Kitchens and should have realized you meant the one in Mallorysport proper."

"Hi, Buck. I'm sorry, we can't stay. Pat and I have plans." Betty turned to the taxi and held up a hand. The side hatch opened and she started to get inside. That was when Roberts realized what was wrong with it.

"Betty, get out of there!"

Betty turned and started back out when two burly men grabbed her and started to haul her back in. Patricia, Roberts and Trask all pulled their guns. Patricia, being closest, had the best shot and she took it. One man went backwards with a bloody hole in his head; the second man swore as the next shot caught him in the shoulder.

Patricia ran up and grabbed Betty's arm. She lacked the strength to wrest Betty away from the wounded man, so she raised her gun for another shot. An arm belonging to a third man, the pilot, seized her hand and yanked her inside the taxi.

The wounded man saw Trask and Roberts running forward. "Forget about her! We have to go."

The pilot twisted Patricia's gun out of her hand and shoved her back inside, then quickly took his seat. A few button taps later the hatch was dogged and the airtaxi started up. Trask fired at the cab hoping to disable it until Roberts stopped him.

"You're wasting bullets, Buck. All aircars on this world are made of polysteel alloy. Not as tough as collapsium, but bulletproof. You could hurt a bystander with a ricochet."

Without thinking, Buck kicked the dead man lying on the pavement. "Damn-it! Holloway is going to go nuclear."

Roberts nodded. "No doubt. This kidnapping is to make him back off. Clearly they were after Betty, and got Pat as a bonus. I should have realized what was off about that airtaxi sooner."

"Off?"

"The medallion on the hatch. It started with a 'Z.' All taxis in Mallorysport start with an 'M'. Now Betty and Pat—"

Trask shook his head. "C'mon, we've got to call this in."

Roberts rushed to follow. "Actually, I hope they do know who Pat is. Otherwise, she will be dead weight. Emphasis on dead."

*　*　*

Jack sat silently as he listened to the news. Roberts and Trask were very careful and exact in how they described the situation. Ben, Gus and Max Fane all stood ready to intercede if Jack couldn't control his temper.

Trask finished speaking and everybody waited.

"It wasn't your fault, and I appreciate you not shooting in my sister's direction," Jack said, as he unthinkingly twisted the ends of his mustache. "We'll get her and Betty back—in one piece. Meanwhile, you can pity Pat's abductors. They have no idea what they are in for."

Ben was surprised while Gus nodded knowingly. "From what you told me, she'll keep those mutts on their toes…assuming she doesn't step on them first."

"What about the dead one?" Jack asked.

Marshal Fane replied, "Just some low-level muscle from Junktown. He must have been part of that group we almost busted."

"Max, I say we go grab up this expedition team and sweat the information we need out of them," Ben said.

Max shook his head. "Our greatest advantage is that they don't know what we know. Snatching Pat and Betty has to be their idea of insurance."

"Our best bet is to pretend we don't know that the hooded man is one of them, and track their movements," Gus said. "Max, you sent those two men in undercover, right?"

"Gilbert and Sullivan are going in with the next bunch of day laborers. We can't send them in any other way without rousing suspicion. Once in, they will put spy-eyes and trackers on everything that moves and some that don't."

"The Fuzzy trackers I sent out will also be following the scientists around," Jack added. "Fuzzies are almost invisible in the woods. They'll keep them in sight without getting into trouble. That cabbie who brought Helmut over volunteered to take the Fuzzies and the dogs in his cab, at no charge, even. He had to go a long ways to not get a paying fare."

"Al is a friend of Pat's and he wants in on the search," Max explained. "I feel bad about having to keep him in the dark."

"We'll reimburse his fare with a good tip," Jack said absently.

"Napier is organizing the Fuzzy Adoption League ships into a planetary barricade," Gus said. "We should be able to keep the slavers' ships from escaping the atmosphere if we can't pin them down on the ground. Now we just need them to take the bait."

"The robot Fuzzies." Ben thought for a moment. "If we are sending in the real thing, are the 'bots really necessary?"

"The robots won't be affected by gas or sonics," Jack said. "And the tracking devices we can install internally without harm. Can't say that about the real deal. That's it. I am headed back to the Rez. Nothing I can do here."

Gus stood up. "I'll walk you out, Jack."

Outside of Marshal Fane's office Gus stopped Jack. "That was a nice little show you put on in there."

Jack exhaled loudly, then fumbled for his pipe. "Thank you. Pat really can take care of herself, usually, but she's never been kidnapped before. Don't forget she wounded one man and killed another one, and they weren't after her in the first place. They may have killed her as soon as they drove away. If so, you won't need a drawing for the firing squad this time."

"Jack, if your sister is half as clever as you've made her out to be, and I think that is a very low estimate, she will announce who she is and her relationship to you the second they try anything."

Jack nodded, then stopped short. "They may decide they can kill one just to prove they are serious and threaten the other if we corner them."

Gus had to admit Jack had a point. "I don't think they'll do that, though. Your reputation will make them cautious."

"I never cared about having a reputation before. Let's hope you're right."

*   *   *

The man in the damnthing mask stared at the two women before him with annoyance. The women were locked in a small room with a two-way mirror between them and their captors. They only needed the young one, so why did his men bring both? He said as much.

"It was bring her or get caught," said the man with a bandage on his arm.

"And she is still alive, why?"

"Our orders were to grab up the hot one, not kill anybody, though we were prepared to do so after the old broad killed LeBron and gave me this." He indicated the wound on his shoulder. "I think you will agree that sparing her was the right thing to do when you hear what she told us."

The damnthing snorted with impatience. "And that is?"

"The old bag is Jack Holloway's sister."

The man in the damnthing mask turned to look at the elderly woman through the glass. "Reeeeally? That is a bonus. Well done. If Holloway did get anything on us from that fiasco on Zeta, we now have two very important people he will want back in one piece."

The wounded man tried not to show his relief with little success. "What do we do with them if we get away clean?"

The damnthing thought for a moment. "I would like to just kill them and eliminate them as witnesses. Then again, having somebody with Holloway's reputation after us is bad for business."

"Why not have Holloway killed, too?"

"Bad idea," said the man who'd driven the ersatz taxi. "I read that his son is Freyan. Mess with his papa and he will scour the galaxy looking for us. And he is rich enough to do it, too."

"Freyan? Is that important?" The damnthing asked.

"You would rather have a bunch of Sheshans and Thorans after you than a Freyan," the driver explained. "They raise the concept of a vendetta to a whole new level. This one spent over half his life looking for his father just to satisfy family honor."

"Only to shoot Holloway in that duel," the damnthing countered. "I saw it on the datastream…he didn't hesitate. He didn't go for a flesh wound, either. He put his father in the hospital for a month."

"And made nice afterward. I read all about it in the *Mallorysport News*. Yes, I read the paper…and the two of them are tighter than a Thoran treaty, now. In fact, if we kill any of them, he will never stop looking for us."

The wounded man nodded. "Yeah, I read about this Morgan Holloway. He even employs Thoran guards. His personal bodyguard is from Magni. Those guys hunt damnthings with a stick. You want these broads dead, you'll have to pull the trigger yourself."

"Ghu, I wish I knew about this before grabbing them up," the driver added.

The damnthing threw up his hands in disgust. "Fine! We only kill them if we have to. We'll keep them isolated so they don't learn anything. Everybody wears masks around them, too."

The others agreed. Mostly.

"If we do have to kill one of them, I call dibs on shooting the old broad," the wounded man said. "She did this to me and killed Jeremy."

The driver snorted. "If the old lady could do that, imagine what her brother is capable of."

XXXVIII

The Fuzzies were gathered and waiting. Gone were the shoulder bags, metal chopper-diggers and any other evidence that they were anything other than wild Fuzzies. Instead, they were armed with wood and bone as they were before Jack Holloway discovered Little Fuzzy in his shower stall.

Also missing were the dogs they normally rode about on. This was an especially difficult part of the deception for the Fuzzies. Fuzzies saw their dogs as more than simple mounts; they were like family to them. Fuzzies often slept with their dogs, fed them, hunted with them, cleaned up after them, bathed them and tended their hurts. In turn, the dogs carried the Fuzzies, protected them from dangerous wildlife, and guarded their Fuzzy masters with a loyalty only a Thoran could match.

The separation was equally hard for the dogs. They whined piteously as their masters left them in the fenced in corral. Some barked and a few tried to climb over or dig under the fencing. Fuzzies who were staying behind promised to tend to the heart-broken canines.

"Damn, listen to that noise," Jack said as he looked out at the dogs. "The one thing a Curtys cannot stand is being separated from his master."

Morgan nodded. "I understand that there are many breeds of dogs that dislike being left at home while their owner goes to work or other activity."

"True. I had a husky shepherd mix that was like that as a child. I called him Wolf because he looked like one. He followed me every day to school, waited outside, then escorted me home. It broke my heart when he died. We couldn't afford longevity treatments in those days."

"I had a dog...or rather the Freyan equivalent," Morgan said. "I named him Vengeance. Ah, I had a bit of a one-track mind in those days."

Jack searched his memory and recalled that a Freyan version of a dog was about four feet at the shoulder and weighed about eighty kilos. It looked like a dire wolf with legs like a Great Dane. They were hard to train and known to turn on abusive masters. Treat them well and you couldn't ask for a better pet. Jack smiled. Vengeance would be a good name for an animal like that.

Jack watched as Little Fuzzy gave each group their marching orders. He was too far away to hear what was being said though he had an idea. Little Fuzzy had a position of high status among Fuzzies. He was the first, the one who brought them out of the wilderness to the Big Ones who did so many wonderful things for them. Jack hated to think that position might be abused in going after the slavers.

For Christ's sake! Jack thought, *the slavers shouldn't even be the Fuzzies problem. It's a Big One's problem, one we brought with us. And we should be the ones to fix it without endangering the Fuzzies. If only we had more time to properly program the Fuzzy-bots....*

"Father?"

Jack broke out his reverie and turned to Morgan. "Are you worried about Aunt Pat?"

"Actually, I am trying not to be. Worry can make you do stupid things and we don't have time for any foolishness. I keep reminding myself how tough she is, even at her age, and that the people who took her have a damnthing by the tail. However, she has never, ever been kidnapped before and she is more likely than not outnumbered by a lot of men half her age. If they aren't careful she is going to damage at least a few of them. And that could end up getting her killed.

"I know you will take no comfort in this," he added, "but it would be an honorable death worthy of even the greatest of warriors on Freya. She should have been born a Freyan."

Jack smiled and shook his head. Yes, Morgan would think that way. "Well, maybe we can save a few slavers for the firing squad if we get to them before Pat makes her move."

"Agreed...oh, the Fuzzies are moving out."

Jack watched as the Fuzzies broke off into three directions. Some had already been taken to Science Center Beta and the *Jin-f'ke* village. These Fuzzies had to go out into the wild and wander around hoping to draw attention and get picked up. There was nothing the Big Ones could do until the Fuzzies were picked up and one of the Fuzz-bots sent the signal.

He noticed that Emily, standing forlornly by herself, had been left behind. He went over to her and asked, "Aren't you going with them?"

She turned her big eyes on him and said, "Little Fuzzy told me to stay here on the Reservation. He's afraid that if I get hit in the head again, I might lose more than the ability to speak."

"Little Fuzzy's only watching out for your safety, Emily. And he's right; another knock on the head might do real damage. They'll all come back safely, I swear it." Jack promised, even though he knew that there was little substance to his promise. Still, it gladdened his heart to see her perk up.

"Thank you, Pappy Jack."

"And keep up the good work at the Rez school. I've heard great things about your work with the little ones. They're learning better language skills from you, than their Big—I mean human teachers."

If she hadn't been covered in golden fur, Jack would have sworn Emily blushed.

* * *

The airtaxi and personnel transport both set down in the clearing near the campsite. The taxi hatch barely had a chance to open when several Fuzzies and dogs bounded out. Al stepped out close behind them and looked around. He spotted Greg Rutherford and sprinted over to him.

"Hey, you, where can I find Dmitri Watson?"

Greg took in the cabbie and decided he wasn't dangerous. "You must be Al, the man we rented the transport from."

"Yeah. You must be one of the scientists doin' research here. I was told Watson was ramrodding the search for Cinda. I wanna talk with him. I brought in the Fuzzies to help with the search like he asked."

Greg was taken aback. Dmitri hadn't mentioned to him that he had made any such arrangements. It was just like him, though. Saving a damsel in distress would appeal to his self-image.

"Dmitri is over in the mess tent organizing the search parties. He will be glad to see another volunteer. What are the Fuzzies and dogs for, anyway?"

"Fuzzies are the best trackers on the planet. They have better hearing, vision and sense of smell than any human, and they are a lot closer to the ground where they can read signs. The dogs have better noses than even the Fuzzies and can move faster in the brush. Dr. Watson was smart to call them in, though I don't know how he knew Fuzzies would be good at this. I don't mean to be short with you, Mister...?"

"Rutherford. Greg will do."

"Greg it is. I need to speak with Dr. Watson straight away. Thanks." Al ran off without waiting for a reply. The Fuzzies, who had been standing quietly with their dogs, rushed to follow.

Greg watched as the party moved off. *What was that all about?*

In the tent Al spotted several people poring over a map. Al recognized Dmitri Watson from their brief encounter at The Bitter End. "Dr. Watson, where are we at with the search?"

Several heads looked up to see who the newcomer was. Among them were Enrico Garza, Johannes Chang, Melvin Kepler and William Sokoloski. Dmitri continued to study the map.

"We have found her pistol and evidence that she moved off into the direction of the river. We have a team moving along the riverbank looking for any sign that she may have fallen in and crawled back out."

"Okay," Al nodded. "I brought the Fuzzies you asked for to help with the search, along with their dogs. Do you have any of her clothing that hasn't been washed?"

Dmitri turned to one of the female interns. "Debbie, could you check Cinda's tent, please? Missing or not, we shouldn't have any of the men going in there."

"On my way, Doctor." The young woman quickly ran out of the tent.

"These dogs with the Fuzzies...what breed are they?" Enrico asked.

"Curtys."

"Hmm...bloodhounds would have been better," Enrico observed. "I don't imagine there are too many of those running around on this planet. A Curtys is a competent tracker, though."

"They should start where we found the pistol," William said. "Mr. Poe, can you escort the Fuzzies there? After Debbie gets back, of course."

"Yes, sir. I will be happy to."

Al was relieved. He feared that the eggheads wouldn't be giving the search all the attention it needed. "What about the locals? Are they helping?"

"Yes, they have two contragravity vehicles going over the area with sensors. If Cinda is still alive, and we all pray to the Grandfather God that she is, they might spot her with infra-red imaging."

"Only two?"

"The forest canopy interferes with too many aircars searching from the sky and we have been informed that they only have two vehicles equipped to be useful for the search. As it is, the search teams have to wear infra-red ablating gear to keep from confusing their sensors."

Al recalled reading in the datastream that Little Fuzzy was too small to distinguish from the other wildlife when they were searching for him right before the big forest fire on Beta. However, something man-sized, or woman-sized for that matter, would show up pretty quickly as long as there weren't a lot of other heat sources around to confuse the sensors. Even without fancy equipment, the more eyes looking down to the ground from the sky the better.

"I want to talk with whomever is in charge of the locals. We need more help with this," Al said.

"The only local we have seen face-to-face is a Rheiner someone...?"

"Sostreus," Melvin said.

"Really," Enrico asked. "Sostreus is a Freyan patronymic."

"I don't care if he is a Sheshan cannibal," Al said irritably. *Eggheads are distracted so easily.* "How do I get in touch with him?"

Dmitri took out a piece of paper and scribbled something on it.

"This is his comscreen code. If you can get us more assistance, all the better."

* * *

"Miss Dawn, dere is a chentleman demending entrance to der settlement. He claims to be a friend of yours und vants more assistance from us in finding you."

Cinda put down her datapad and looked at Rheiner quizzically. "Is it Tres?"

"Der chentleman failed to provide us vit' his name. However, he called me 'Bubba.'"

Cinda jumped up from her chair. "That's Al! Oh...I hate for him to think I am lost or dead. Well, I hate for anybody to think that, but Al is a good friend and won't give anything away. Can we allow him in? Oh, did he see anybody?"

"Only me," Rheiner said. "Die rest are vearing helmets und face coverings. Herr Al did t'row a few punches at me vhen I refused to allow him in. Not'ing connected, fortunately for him. He might haff hurt himself."

"He landed outside the perimeter and walked in?" The settlement had a field over it that interfered with air transport navigation systems unless they were equipped with a compensating unit. This had originally been set up to discourage newsies and Streamers.

"He did."

"Did he hurt you?"

Rheiner's eyes twinkled. "Nein. My people vere provided vit' exceptionally dense bone und muscle structure to deal vit' Magni's heavy gravity und der stresses of vorking a mine dere. I fear Herr Al may haff injured his wrist, dough; he struck Heinrich very solidly on die jaw."

"Oh, I am sorry to be so much trouble...."

"*Es macht nichts, Fräulein*. It speaks vell of you dat you haff such devoted und protective friends. It vas an honor to be so braced by Herr Al."

It must be a Freyan thing, Cinda thought. "If it is allowed, I think Al can be brought in. He won't be shocked by your people...at least I don't believe he will be."

"*Sehr gut!* I shall send for him. I vill allow you to explain die situation as I t'ink he vill accept your account better den ours."

Al was escorted in by two men wearing helmets with darkened faceplates. When he saw Cinda, surprise, relief and confusion fought for dominance on his face. "Cinda, you're alive! What are you doing here? Why haven't you told anyone at the camp where you are?"

Cinda rushed over and gave Al a hug then, quickly explained her situation. Al nodded. "So, one of the eggheads might be up to something bad. It's the Sinister Six all over again."

"Der vas?"

Al explained about Hugo Ingermann's team who attempted to take over the planet. "The story is still being run on the news feeds. Don't you guys get the paper, Zarathustra News or the datastream out here?"

"Al, there is something else you should see. Heinrich, please come in."

The door opened and Heinrich entered without his helmet. Al's reaction was sudden and violent. He launched a vicious punch into Heinrich's jaw. Heinrich didn't even flinch, as Al held his injured hand up against his body.

Al swore luridly. "Ghu, your jaw is even harder than that helmet."

"Are you all right, Herr Al?" Rheiner asked. "Striking Heinrich tvice like dat may haff damaged your hand."

Al grunted then said he was fine. Cinda chastised him for his reaction. "Heinrich is the one that found me by the river and brought me here. Now apologize."

He looked back at Heinrich, who didn't seem the least bit put out by the attack on his person. "Um, sorry Mr. Heinrich...that is...."

Heinrich laughed. "*Est macht nichts.* I expected somet'ing like dis. Und I t'ink you got die vorst of it."

"Thank you, Mr. Heinrich," Al said, cradling his hand. "Jeeze...you got collapsium plating in that jaw?"

"On Magni ve develop very solid bones to survive die gravity dere. I hope dein hand ist not broken."

"I'll live. At least long enough to buy you a beer and thank you for helping Cinda." Al turned back to the young woman. "Why don't you want me to alert the search teams outside? There are a lot of people and Fuzzies worried about you out there."

Cinda shook her head. "Because I only saw the hooded man from the back, and it was pretty dark out. I thought it might be Dmitri Watson, because he was following me earlier. But I can't say for sure. Truthfully, it could be any one of them—or even all of them."

"That is a problem," Al said. "How long are you going to stay undercover?"

She shrugged.

"Cinda, as long as everybody thinks you are missing, is there anything you need? Should I contact anybody, like your parents, before the news services get ahold of this?"

"Oh, Ghu, I didn't even think about that. Has my disappearance gone on the news feeds?" Al admitted that it had. "Oh, we can't tell them. Not yet. Too many people keeping a secret is no secret at all."

"Yeah. If your parents knew something and this hooded guy found out somehow, it could go badly for them."

"Better dat ve keep qviet until ve know for sure," Rheiner said. "Ve can protect Fraulein Cinda here."

Al glanced over at Heinrich and nodded. "Brother, I can believe that."

XXXIX

A gambol of goofers chewed away at the base of the ironwood tree. One stopped and looked around, then another and another. Goofers were as close to the bottom of the food chain on Zarathustra as a mammal could get and they were very wary of predators. Seeing and hearing nothing, they went back to destroying the protective bark of the tree trunk. It was a meal they would never finish.

In the tall grass, a furry of Fuzzies studied the goofers. Little Fuzzy watched the goofers, then looked at the sky and all around. He didn't see any predators, or more importantly, a big black ball in the sky. Little Fuzzy was disappointed. He hoped the bad Big Ones would be close by. Fuzzies didn't like waiting around for something to happen any more than the Big Ones did.

"Hungry," complained Baby Fuzzy. "We eat goofer?"

Little Fuzzy nodded. "Doctor Crippen, you go that way. Mata Hari, you go round to other side." He looked at the robot Fuzzies. He didn't understand what 'programmed' meant, he only knew that the robots would be no good in a hunt because of the way they were made. They could only follow simple commands. He pointed to the robots. "You stay. Watch for black ball in sky."

* * *

"We got a sighting," Steg said.

T-Rex looked at the viewscreen. "Which camera location?"

"Gamma. About twenty miles out from—"

"I know where it is," T-Rex said irritably. "We are supposed to be gearing up for the raid at the school. Hmm...still, this bunch looks like an easy snatch. Send out a team to grab them up. Tell them to wait until the Fuzzies have eaten; that will make them slow and lethargic."

Steg smiled. "The transport should handle that crowd well enough. A little gas on the Fuzzies and away we go. We won't even blow our time-table for the school raid." Steg had a thought. "Umm, the boss might get mad, though. Word came down not to do any more unplanned snatches."

"So we don't tell him. We just grab up some extra bonus money for getting a larger catch. I'm already spending the bonuses we'll get in my head."

* * *

The whine of the contragravity engine drew everybody's attention. Everybody except the robots. Little Fuzzy noticed that they were not looking the right way and ordered them to correct it. The Big Ones might notice something was wrong if they saw some of the Fuzzies acting differently from the rest.

"We wait for bad Big Ones to take us into big ball?" Allan Pinkerton asked.

"No," Sherlock Holmes countered. "Not make it look easy. Make run fast, fight when they come."

"Oh. Robot not make run fast," Little Fuzzy remembered. "Throw rocks at big ball. Will look like we fight."

The Fuzzies watched and waited. When no black ball appeared they became confused. "What make noise?" Mama Fuzzy demanded.

The Fuzzies looked around in the high grass; if the noise wasn't in the sky, it had to be on the ground. After a while, Arsène Lupin discovered a shiny ball that emitted the sound. She called the others over to see what it was.

The Fuzzies investigated the strange ball until Little Fuzzy decided it was a trap. "Big Ones sometimes use something called bait to set trap or lure fish."

"This bait for what?" Mata Hari demanded.

"Us."

"What are the Fuzzies saying?"

"Beats the Niflheim out of me," Steg replied. "I turned on the hypersonic filter but they're speaking Fuzzy, not Lingua Terra."

T-Rex shrugged. "No matter. They are all in the trap so let's spring it."

Steg nodded and tapped a few buttons on the console. On the viewscreen they could see the gas nozzles open on the ball and shoot out a yellowish vapor. Most of the Fuzzies collapsed immediately. Three stood still for a moment, then fell over.

"Did you see that," Steg asked. "Three Fuzzies seemed to be unaffected, then just dropped."

T-Rex nodded. "They might have a higher tolerance for the gas. No matter. We got 'em. Send out a robot to collect our prizes."

"Why a bot? It would be faster to send a couple of men—"

"What happened to Ray?"

"Huh?" Steg was thrown a moment by the non-sequitur. "Killed by a damnthing in Upper Beta."

"And Ted?"

"Fuzzy got him with poisoned arrows."

"And Doug and Andre?"

"ZNPF officer and more Fuzzies."

"That's why we are sending out robots."

*   *   *

Jack watched the viewscreen intently as Morgan came into the room. On the screen both men could see robots collecting the unconscious Fuzzies and placing them into cages.

"The spy-eye is a good idea, son," Jack said through gritted teeth. The robots weren't being as gentle in collecting the Fuzzies as he would have liked.

"They might not have worked if Commodore Napier hadn't given us enough of that cloaking goo, as he called it, to block any sensors that might spot the surveillance units. I still don't see the ship...."

"These louts sent out a shuttle with robots to collect the Fuzzies. Will the spy-eye be able to follow the shuttle back to the ship?"

Morgan wasn't sure. "The spy-eyes are too small to house a powerful propulsion unit. It will depend on how fast the shuttle goes."

Jack thought it over. "Can we have it attach itself to the shuttle before it takes off?"

"Maybe." Morgan pulled out a radio-communicator and called Captain Zeudin. He quickly explained the situation."

"I am on it, sir."

The Holloways watched as the picture shifted from the Fuzzies being collected to an image of the shuttle. Morgan noted the shuttle was of the type commonly used in space yachts.

"I have three like that, in fact," Morgan added. "If we can get the spy-eye to focus on the registry, we will be able to track the ownership of the yacht it came from." The spy-eye scanned the starboard side of the shuttle. "No good. They painted the hull."

"Well, it isn't really important," Jack said, "if the Fuzz-bots do their job the way Grego said they would."

Morgan watched as the last of the Fuzzies were loaded onto the shuttle. "It's a good thing they used robots to collect the Fuzzies; a human might have noticed something off about the...Fuzz-bots?"

"Pat's idea. Grego is going with it for the brand." Jack looked pained when he said Patricia's name. "The shuttle is lifting off. The spy-eye seems to be holding on...Ghu on a goat!"

The image on the screen showed a black ball in the distance. It slowly grew in size as the shuttle approached. The last image the spy-eye could generate showed the shuttle bay as the craft entered, adjusted its orientation in relation to the yachts internal gravity field, and settled down. The image went black.

"What happened?"

"The shuttle bay hatch closed," Morgan explained. "The signal can't get through the collapsium-plated hull even without the cloaked outer layer."

"What? Why not? Grego said his drone pilot would be able to control a Fuzz-bot inside the ship."

"The spy-eye is about the size of your thumb, Father, and designed strictly to monitor open areas. To fit in the extra equipment needed to take advantage of the ship's internal telemetry it would have to be about ten times larger. A ball that size could not be confused with something else, like a bird or insect, to the naked eye. Had we known they would use robots to collect the Fuzzies, we could have arranged for such a device as the robots would be unable to sense it with the, ah, goo on it."

Jack admitted that what Morgan said made sense. "How did you get so smart about this kind of stuff?"

"As the owner of a yacht, I made it my business to know its strengths and weaknesses," Morgan said. "That includes the equipment and personnel within it."

Jack typed out the combination to Gerd's place. "I guess we'd better let the rest in on what just happened so they can prepare."

Morgan thought for a moment. "The slavers might use different tactics. In fact, they may still be coming to the school."

Jack's face took on a grim mien. "Then we had better be ready, too."

* * *

Gerd shut off the comscreen and left his office. Like the Company Science Center in Mallorysport, the Beta Division had the same floorplan and overall design, even though it was a brand-new building, Gerd knew his way around as if it had stood for years.

Many parts of the building were still under construction. Most of the upper level was open to the sky with only a transparent duraplast tarp covering it. Gerd elected to use this level as the platform for the defense of the facility.

All around Marines in mufti moved about. They tried to look like construction workers. Unfortunately, the heavy weapons they carried ruined any possibility of pulling that particular deception off. Yet, they couldn't leave their weapons hidden; if an attack came suddenly, they had to be ready.

In the center of that level was their secret weapon. Gerd went right up to it and spoke to the man working on it. "Will it be ready?"

Joe Verganno turned to Gerd and shrugged. "Depends on when, and if, the unwelcome visitors arrive. The programming is in and solid, but since we never tested this thing, we have no idea what will happen when we use it. There is also the question of damage to the ship's cargo."

"Cargo?"

"Oh! The captured Fuzzies! Damn. If this thing knocks the ship out of the sky, it could end up killing a lot of Fuzzies."

"If it doesn't knock that ship out of the sky, a lot more Fuzzies could be carted away into slavery," Joe pointed out. "This is one of those tough decisions officers make all the time. However, I don't think this weapon will affect the artificial gravity on the ship. You see, the equipment that generates—"

"Sir, if I may interrupt."

Gerd turned to see one of the Marines in mufti. "Yes, Gunny... Fitzpatrick, isn't it?"

"Gunny will do, sir. If the ship itself comes down, and not a bunch of shuttles, we should attempt to bring it down over the Rainbow Lake. It isn't very deep but it would cushion the craft's fall, maybe enough so that the Fuzzies only get bruised instead of broken. This depends on how high the craft is, of course."

Gerd thought it over. The lake was less than a mile from the Science Center. "I think you are on to something, Gunny. The problem is in getting the ship to go that way."

"Oh, that will be easy," Joe said. Gerd and the Gunny looked mutely at him.

"Gentlemen, these sons-of-Khooghras are coming for one thing; Fuzzies. We just have the Fuzzies, real and robot, play on the edge of the water. The ship will make a beeline for them."

Gerd shuddered for a moment. The idea was to protect the Fuzzies, not put them in danger. Still, didn't Jack send some out to be captured?" All right, I'll go find some volunteers."

"I'll set up some spotters on the trees around the lake," the Gunny said. "If anything happens, we will know it instantly."

"And I'll get this thing positioned to the best vantage point," Joe said as he slapped the casing on the device.

"Wait, won't they be able to spot you with their sensors?" Gerd asked.

The Gunny shook his head. "We'll be wearing this new adaptive camouflage. Anything further away than ten feet won't even see us, let alone spot us with sensors. It's classified tech and I can only tell you two about it. Of course, if you talk about it to third parties, I will have to shoot you both."

Gerd decided that the Gunny was joking though he had no intention of testing that theory.

*   *   *

Officer Clarke sat down on the log next to Red Fur. His mission had been to explain to the Fuzzy chief about the plan to capture the bad Big Ones. Red Fur had been surprisingly easy to convince; he wanted the slavers in a bad way and was prepared to risk his own life to get them. The rest of the Fuzzies agreed with him.

"This could be very dangerous," Clarke warned.

"Yes," Red Fur nodded in imitation of Big Ones he had seen. "For bad Big Ones."

"I mean for your people," Clarke persisted. "Some might die if things go badly."

Red Fur looked straight into Officer Clarke's eyes. "*Jin-f'ke* die all the time. Screamers...um...bush goblins come and attack. The...dammt'ing kill us for food. Ha'py take us away, though not for many moons, now. We hunt, and are hunted. We live and we make-dead. Bad Big Ones just another thing we must fight to live."

Clarke was taken aback by the eloquence of the Fuzzy chief. It was too easy to underestimate the intelligence of the diminutive natives with their small size and limited vocabulary. Clarke knew better.

He shivered for a second then adjusted his cold suit. The suit, a military one on loan from the Space Navy, was designed to make his outer temperature match that of the surrounding air. This effectively rendered him invisible to infrared sensors. The chameleon outer weave allowed him to blend in with the surrounding terrain. It would adjust itself automatically to match any area he might march through. The big man suspected there were other surprises in the suit, but the Marines were mum on the subject.

While he spoke with Red Fur he had the hood drawn back leaving his head visible and exposed. He was counting on the Fuzzies' superior hearing to tell him when trouble approached. There was a contingent of Marines and ZNPF officers hidden in the bush in similar gear.

The plan was to try and capture as many of the slavers as possible if they came out of the ship. If not, then some Fuzzies, including the Fuzz-bots, would allow themselves to be taken prisoner, though not without a fight. Once inside the ship, the Fuzz-bots would release anesthezine gas taking down the crew. If this didn't work, their best bet was to track the ship from space via a homing device installed in one of the robots.

Commodore Napier had a fleet, of sorts, waiting to welcome the ship if it tried to leave the atmosphere. However, without the homing device he would be unable to track the ship with anything other than human eyes, which would be nearly impossible in the expanse of the orange sky. A hyperspace ship was a very small thing indeed compared to the immenseness of the outer atmosphere, made all the more difficult by the blackened hull.

"When do bad Big Ones come?" asked the Fuzzy that Clarke thought was called Makes-Things.

"Don't know," Clarke admitted. Makes-Things looked dubious. "When does damnthing come? When does bush goblin? They come when they come."

That seemed to satisfy the Fuzzy.

"Hope they come soon," Red Fur said. "Want to make bad Big Ones dead. Go back to life before bad Big Ones come."

Clarke could understand the Fuzzy's position. "Be careful what you wish for, Red Fur. You might get it." Clarke spent the better part of an hour trying to explain what a wish was to the Fuzzies.

XL

Rheiner leveled off the shuttle and set the automatic pilot. Behind him Cinda fiddled with some dials and buttons on a machine that normally had no business being in a shuttle.

"I do not know how you talked me into dis," Rheiner said as he swiveled the plot chair around.

"You gave me the idea when you wondered how a K0 star could be so bright from so far away," Cinda said as she made another adjustment. "It got me thinking about it and I realized that even though it is a sub-giant, a K0 star is still a K0 star. It looks bigger from the surface of the planet, and it is, but it doesn't put out any more light and heat than a standard-sized K0 star. Well, that got me thinking that maybe there was something in the upper atmosphere that somehow magnified the light... and maybe even the heat. Besides, I have to do something while I'm in hiding. I am glad Mr. Holloway allowed us the loan of this shuttle."

Rheiner shook his head. "Herr Morgan ist a kind und generous man. I am not so vell educated as you are, *Fräulein*, but even I know dat magnifying der sun's rays vould only concentrate die energy in specific locations vhile leaving ot'ers colder. Energy cannot be created or destroyed, only altered in form."

Cinda hesitated a moment, then continued with her work. "There are lots of ways energy can be altered, and more than just the sun's rays available this high up."

"Like vhat?"

"Um...cosmic rays, for instance. Uh...that is all I can say since this isn't my field. Actually, I am looking for something else."

"Again, vhat?"

"I can't be sure," Cinda admitted.

"Den vhat made you t'ink dere ist somet'ing to find?"

Cinda stopped what she was doing and turned in her chair. "I read back in college that there was a bacterium that consumed rock and produced energy. On Terra there was an example of this in a place called Yellowstone. One of the scientists from the expedition reminded me of this a while back. Well, maybe there is something like that in Zarathustra's ionosphere that works like that?"

"Vhat? In almost airless space vit' not'ing to consume?" Rheiner was dubious.

"There are many anaerobic bacteria that can survive in space. We discovered a variety of them on Luna hundreds of years ago. As for what they might consume, well, they could be photovors, surviving on light rays, not just from the sun, but the stars as well."

"Hmm...I am not so certain. Still, ve are here, so I vill keep my opinions to myself und allow you to verk."

"Thank you. Um, *danke*?"

"*Ja, bitte, Fräulein.*"

Cinda turned back to her console to notice a flashing light. "Rheiner, we found something!"

"Vhat?"

"I don't know, yet. The readings are confusing, but it might be the bacteria I was looking for."

Rheiner turned back to the helm. "I vill deploy a probe to collect a sample."

"Use the quarantine protocol," Cinda warned. "We don't know what effect it would have on us and I don't want to find out the hard way."

"*Natürlich.*" Rheiner launched the probe. "Ve vill have to vait until ve get beck to Neu Freya to analyze der sample. Dis shuttle has not die facilities."

"I expected that. We will need more than one sample, too. Can you move us over the North Pole for another try?"

Rheiner smiled wide. "Ja. Perhaps ve vill see Santa Claus, too."

Cinda laughed. Children were no longer told about Santa and Christmas wasn't observed as religiously as it was in pre-atomic times.

Rheiner had been studying Terran history, she surmised.

"You heard about Santa?"

"Ja. Der pictures I saw on der datastream looks much like Woteus, vun of der Freyan gods. Woteus is a high god who chooses die vort'y dead to reside in his realm. He also grants victory to great varriors in battle."

"Huh. He sounds a lot like Odin. In the...what is that!"

Rheiner turned back to the helm and looked out through the viewscreen. The sky was filled with ships of every type. He recognized the design of many of them as spacefaring yachts of the type the über-rich would use.

"Is Zarathustra being invaded?" Cinda asked, as if Rheiner had some special knowledge of such an event.

"I t'ink not. Most of doze ships are private pleasure cruisers und too small to carry an invasion force. Vait...I heard somet'ing on der news service about vealt'y people coming to adopt Fuzzies. Dis must be dem."

Cinda was appalled. "They would take Fuzzies away to strange worlds and after the novelty wore off just ignore them, I bet. I hope the governor puts a stop to this right away."

"Der governor has to be careful about annoying such people. Dey can cause trouble for him und der CZC." Rheiner adjusted his course. "Even der king on Freya is careful how he deals vit' such citizens."

"Humph! Well, let's just get our samples and get away from here. The air is getting bad."

Rheiner wondered what Cinda meant about the air as it was a conditioned environment. He also wondered if she had had a bad experience with a wealthy person. He made the appropriate course correction then changed the subject.

"Vhat about Al? He vas very upset when he t'aught you vere dead. Vill he stay silent?"

"Don't vorry...by Ghu, you got me starting to use your accent...don't worry about Al. Now that he knows that I am alive and hiding, he will keep mum. And if something really happens to me, I would hate to see what happens to the guy he thinks did it."

* * *

"What do you think they are going to do with us, Pat?"

Patricia thought it over and decided to be straightforward with Betty. "They intend to hold us as human shields to get the government to back off. They want to take as many Fuzzies as they can get, then leave planet. Keeping us is insurance against getting blown out of the sky."

"So, once they get to hyperspace they won't need us anymore," Betty said flatly. "In other words, we're dead."

"That would be the gist of it, I'm afraid. Only they don't know my brother very well. Jack will do everything he can to make sure this ship doesn't leave orbit, and on this world he has the friends and clout to do it." Patricia pulled out her knitting. "The problem is that these idiots will likely end up killing us the second Jack has them cornered."

"What? Why? All that would do is buy them a bullet in the head."

"You can only execute a man once, assuming the job is done right the first time. Every human on this ship is as good as dead, if captured—and they know it. I read up on those ferocious laws your governor enacted to protect the Fuzzies. Killing us would just be a pre-emptive revenge."

Betty sighed in resignation. "Well, that settles it, then."

"Oh, no it doesn't," Patricia said. "When you know you are going to die, you have nothing to lose. I plan on going down fighting."

Betty perked up a bit. "Fighting how?"

Patricia held up a knitting needle. "These Khooghras didn't bother taking my needles. By sitting here knitting away they forgot that I killed one of them and wounded the other. They see me as a harmless old woman, now."

"Not the wounded man, I bet."

Patricia chuckled. "No, I don't imagine so. However, they do not see me as a threat without my gun. That is their mistake. If the chance comes, here is what I want you to do…"

* * *

Akira was lost in thought as she rocked Little John while nursing him. Betty was her oldest friend on Zarathustra. She didn't know what she would do if Betty didn't make it back.

She also worried about Patricia: more for Morgan's sake, than her own. Morgan had spent many years as an outcast on his own planet and had only recently found his father. Now he was learning about having more family than he believed was possible. Patricia was the kind of aunt who would paddle your backside for breaking the neighbor's window one moment, then defend you to the neighbor the next. Just the kind of family member Morgan could appreciate and respect.

Akira worried about what Morgan would do if anything happened to Patricia. What Jack would do when he caught up with the abductors wasn't in doubt; he would shoot the lot of them himself. Even without the Governor's protection there would be very little the law could do if Jack did execute the Fuzzy slavers—no action could be taken against anybody acting to prevent a criminal act.

The real problem was what would happen afterwards. Akira had heard how Jack had behaved after Little Fuzzy came up missing from Yellowsand a few years back; heavy drinking, a couple of brawls, maybe even something that didn't get reported. The point was that Jack didn't take the loss of a loved one at all well.

How would it affect his relationship with Morgan? Would Jack push his son away for fear of being hurt more? Or would they come together with a closer relationship in shared loss?

"Akira!"

Akira snapped back to reality to see Morgan standing in front of her with a worried expression. "What? Did they find Pat?"

"No, not yet. I was standing here in front of you and you didn't respond when I said your name three times." Morgan kneeled down in front of her. "Are you all right? Should I call for Heidi?"

"I'm fine. I was just lost in thought. About Betty and Pat."

Morgan nodded. "Yes, I am worried, too. Father is getting impatient and I fear what he might do if things do not change soon. And the Fuzzies they sent out as bait have been picked up by the slavers. Little Fuzzy was among them."

"Oh, Great Ghu!" Akira cried. "I know that was the plan, but Jack is going to go nuclear if it goes badly."

"More like super-nova, I think," Morgan said. "He wants to activate the Fuzz-bot with the sleep gas now, while Marshal Fane wants to wait until more decoy teams have been picked up. Father knows that the marshal is correct and it, um, chaps his hide, I think he calls it."

Akira smiled. "Something like that. Morgan, you know way more about space travel and star ships than I do. How can you stop a hypership without destroying it?"

"Well, a near miss with an atomic bomb can knock out a ship's systems, though that is tricky. A collapsium shell fired from a magnetic launcher can pierce the hull of a ship. That is also tricky since you might destroy the Abbott drive and release lethal radiation. We are working on a safer way to disable a ship at the CZC, but that may not be perfected for several years."

Akira shook her head sadly. "This is going to end badly, isn't it? Even if we stop the slavers."

"Don't think that. Every right-thinking person on the planet with the ability to act is on the Fuzzies' side and working to help them. We must believe that they will win out over these *klintooks*."

"I hope so. And don't use that kind of language in front of Little John."

XLI

"I will need you to send a cloaked shuttle to collect me," the hooded man said.

The man in the damnthing mask on the viewscreen nodded. "I will arrange for a pick-up after dark, after the raids commence. It won't take long for all of that to draw attention, so we should be able to come in and get you without being noticed. In fact, I will collect you personally. My other business here is going badly and I would like to be away from this planet."

"Other business?"

"A conversation for another time. It is enough to say that I will not be securing the additional partner we had hoped for."

The hooded man nodded. "Understood. What time can I expect you?"

"I will be coming over from Mallorysport after I finish my business here," the damnthing said. "I cannot be certain how long that will take, so let's shoot for midnight Zeta time."

"Good. I'll set up a beacon away from the campsite where you will be able to land unnoticed. Be careful of the Zeta inhabitants. They are very insular, though they are taking steps to aid in the loss of one of our personnel here."

"Hmm...I will return to the mother ship and swap my cruiser for a cloaked shuttle."

"Excellent. I will see you at midnight."

* * *

Deputy Colonial Governor Juan Takagashi turned off the comscreen and leaned back in his chair. After rubbing his temples for a moment, he opened the bottom drawer of the desk and pulled out a bottle and a shot glass. He allowed himself one drink before returning the bottle and glass to the drawer.

When Takagashi took over for Ben, he knew he would be in for a long string of headaches. He also knew that there would be some advantages and liberties he could take that would forward his plans in the future. Ben was starting to see the light in setting term limits, even if it would force him out of his position. Takagashi intended to be the next man to take the seat when Ben left. That meant putting in some time in the big chair to prove he was up to the task.

Now, he was not so sure. Plans he had made two years earlier seemed largely unworkable now. His side ventures had seemed to slip away from his grasp with all that had been happening of late: the problems with the Fuzzies, keeping the media ignorant of the Fuzzy slavers and the Fuzzy reproduction issues, the kidnapping and tiptoeing around Buck Trask in order to stay out of the veridicator...it was piling up.

Takagashi checked the clock and saw it was time to go. He had other things to do and couldn't stay in the office all night the way Ben often did. He hit the comm button.

"Francine, do I have any other meetings this afternoon?"

"No, sir. Your schedule is clear until 0900 tomorrow morning," Francine's voice said over the intercom.

"Very good. I am calling it a night. I will see you in the morning."

"Yes, sir. If there is an emergency, where can you be reached?"

"I'll let you know when I decide where I am going," Takagashi said. "Good night."

* * *

Clarence Anetrou waited patiently as his client was brought to him. He knew the corrections officers would take their time just to annoy him and his client so he decided in advance not to let it bother him. Besides, he had a lot of other things to think about.

Hugo Ingermann, visibly bruised, was escorted into the room and shackled to the table. Ane'trou looked him over and shook his head.

"What happened to you?"

Ingermann shook his head and winced. "Joe Quigley. He has it in his head that I tried to kill him back when he was doing some illegal prospecting on Beta. Somehow his mass-energy converter went critical and blew-up, killing his entire crew. He took the opportunity to extract some revenge on the way to the chow hall."

"I thought the two of you were in separate segregation units."

Ingermann shrugged and winced again. Apparently the beating he took was severe and extensive. "There was a foul up with the schedule. It also took the guards several minutes to realize something was happening when Quigley jumped me."

Anetrou brightened up for a second. "Is there any chance you defended yourself to his death?"

"None," Ingermann grunted. "Even with my medical enhancements, he's almost twice my size and strength. The worst I could do is make him sweat."

Anetrou sighed. "Too bad. Joe Quigley is the main witness against you, at least as far as your activities where Beta Continent is concerned. Even without your...allegedly trying to kill him there is a lot riding on his testimony. The Governor agreed not to pursue any charges related to harming Fuzzies if he comes clean. That drops the charges against him to illegal prospecting and collusion. He could be out in three to five years. Less if he impresses the parole board."

Ingermann swore. "So much for loyalty."

Anetrou rolled his eyes. "Yes, shocking. Well, I have more bad news. The trial starts on Monday. There is nothing I can do to get you another extension. The trial will be a short one and it will end badly for you, as we always knew it would. Sadly, I don't have the leverage you did when you were defending Thaxter and company."

"Leverage? HA! That went out the airlock the second that Fuzzy, Wise One, took the stand. If I hadn't skipped planet, I would have been named an accomplice after the fact for accepting stolen goods."

"Then why did you come back?"

"Why? Revenge!" Ingermann growled. "I wanted to set this whole planet on its ear for forcing me off of it. When I think of all the money and power I had to leave behind over a measly quarter-million in sun-stones, I want to vomit. Let me give you a little advice, Clarence. Avoid having anything to do with Fuzzies. Don't defend anybody that hurts them, don't try to use them to your advantage—and for damn sure don't try to adopt one! I think they are a lot smarter than they let on and they will bring you down every time."

* * *

"I do not care whose authority you are under, you will not put those ugly *things* on my ship!"

The Marine Gunny mentally counted to ten, while reminding him-self that he was under orders to be polite. However, he was also under orders to proceed with his mission and that took precedence.

"I don't care who ordered you to do what," yelled the elderly woman. "Do you know who I am?"

"I have no idea, Ma'am."

"I am Mariah Harcord-Lynchfield! My husband is the majority stockholder at BaldurTech Incorporated—"

"Yes, ma'am, that is very interesting. Now let me tell you who I am; I am Gunnery Sergeant Michael Glazier of the Terran Federation Space Marines. If you do not allow me to conduct a search of this vessel, and install these *things*, I will be forced to commandeer this ship and have you escorted off of it to the planet's surface. During that time, we will have to perform a health and welfare inspection. Should we find anything of a questionable nature, this ship will be impounded until a full investiga-tion has been performed, at which point it will either be returned to you, along with the impound fee, or confiscated as assets in the furtherance of a crime. The FBCI will be in charge of that investigation, though I understand that they have a significant backlog and may take a while before they can get to you.

"Of course," the Gunny smiled, "if you choose to cooperate, we can avoid a great deal of time and trouble."

"Well, your family must be very proud of you," the woman said acerbically. "Searching a ship without a warrant. And installing the gods know what...?"

"They are. My grandfather, Gerald Lippincott, is especially pleased with my career choice. And space, even in orbit around a planet, falls under Federation military jurisdiction. We can search any ship at any time with or without your permission, as cited by the anti-piracy act of 389 A.E., Ma'am."

"Gerald Lippincott? Jerry? From Odin Foods?"

The Gunny feigned indifference. "Oh, you have heard of him?"

"Uh, yes. Yes, of course. Do what you need to do, Sergeant."

"Thank you, Ma'am. Please clear the area so my men have room to work."

Mariah Harcord-Lynchfield left the area in a subdued manner. One of the Lance Corporals came over to the Gunny. "Guns, I thought you said your family hailed from the soil reclamation project in North America."

"Really? I must have gotten confused while speaking with Lady Harcord-Lynchfield. My mistake, Lance Cooley. Let's keep it our little secret."

The Lance Corporal smiled knowingly and returned to work.

*　　*　　*

"...and we will tell you when it is safe to leave orbit, sir."

"Ve haff limited ship's stores, here," Rheiner countered. "Do ve haff any idea how long ve vill haff to stay up here?"

"I'm afraid not, sir. I cannot give you any specifics, either. We will be in touch."

The image on the comscreen vanished in a splash of color and Rheiner shut it off. "Vell, it looks like ve vill be up here for a while." Rheiner checked the helm controls and gauges. "Ve may haff to put der ship in power-saving mode."

Cinda looked at the gauges though she had no idea what to look for. "Why?"

"Dese shuttles haff limited range. Dey are not meant for extended trips in orbit. Der nuclear batteries haff to be changed often. Ve vere fortunate dat ve had fresh batteries vhen ve started. Ve should be gut for six more hours at our present rate of energy consumption. If I cut der artificial gravity, ve vould be gut for almost tventy-four hours. Der are a few ot'er t'ings ve can shut down to extend die time."

"Is that what you meant by limited ship's stores? I thought you meant food and water."

"Nein. Ve haff food enough for a veek. Die vasser, uhh...vater, ist recycled so effectively endless."

"Recycled? Ugh!"

"It ist qvite okay, *Fräulein,*" Rheiner said with a wide smile. "Herr Morgan bought only der best filtration systems. Der vater is cleaner den vhat you drink from dein faucet at home. Ve Freyans are very picky about dat sort of t'ing."

"Um, okay...just don't use the facilities until after I fill a pitcher of water. I was going to do that anyway and keep it in the refrigerator, but I won't be able to drink it with the mental image of you...um...."

Rheiner laughed out loud. "Ja, I feel die same." He got up and opened a cabinet near the back of the shuttle living quarters. "Dat ist vhy I brought t'ree cases of bottled vater."

Cinda looked at the plastic bottles then laughed. "Were you going to tell me about that before or after I filled the pitcher."

"Vell, I chust did, so I guess before."

Cinda considered giving the Freyan a playful punch, but then thought better of it. Rheiner's rock hard musculature might hurt her more than him.

"You should take a seat, *Fräulein,*" Rheiner said as he returned to the helm. "I am shutting die gravity off und I don't vant you bouncing off der ceiling."

The gravity went off, yet Cinda didn't move. She could feel that nothing was pulling her down, while nothing actually pulled her up, either. "Why aren't I floating up or something?"

"Heh. You haff vatched too many old movies," Rheiner explained. "In a veightless environment you don't chust start floating. You haff to push yourself up for dat, but you vill hit der ceiling if you do."

"Oh...an object at rest will remain at rest until acted on by an external agency," Cinda quoted from one of her old physics texts. "So, if I try to take a step, I might push myself upwards?"

"*Sehr gut!*"

"Then how are we supposed to move around in here without banging our heads?"

Rheiner turned to a drawer near the helm and pulled out stretchable boots with a strange tread on the soles. "Pull dese on over your shoes. Die soles vere designed to catch die carpeting on der floor."

Cinda examined the boots. "Like Velcro!" She quickly pulled on the boots, then took a step. "These are great. Why didn't they have these on the big ship I came to Zarathustra on?"

Rheiner shrugged. "Der gravity on a hyperspace ship uses different dynamics, maybe. Basically, anyt'ing dat could kill der gravity vould also destroy der engine, und by extension, der whole ship. No point in vasting die money, I guess."

"Humph...comforting thought. Do you have something like this to keep my backside on the chair?"

Rheiner shook his head. "Nein, but dat is an excellent idea. I vill mention it to Herr Morgan."

Cinda started for the chair, then changed her mind. No gravity meant her legs didn't have to work to keep her up, and wouldn't get tired. "Well, now we just need to find a way to occupy our time while we wait to be allowed to return to the surface. Do we have any cards?"

"*Ja.* Vhat games do you know how to play?"

"Poker, solitaire, spades and gin rummy. You?"

"Ah, chust some Freyan games you vould not know and poker."

Cinda walked over to the small table near the kitchen and sat down. She bounced a little off the seat and her torso started to float up a bit until she forced herself back down. "Poker it is."

Rheiner joined her. "Vhat vill be der stakes? I did not t'ink to bring money."

Cinda shrugged. "Neither did I. Have you ever heard of Strip Poker?"

"Nein. Vas ist?"

Cinda winked. "We play for each other's clothing."

Rheiner seemed dubious. "I don't t'ink your clothes vould fit me very vell."

Cinda laughed so hard her boots lost traction and she floated up until her knees banged on the bottom of the table. "Ow! Oh, you must be putting me on. I am either going to fleece you or get hustled. No, we don't trade the clothes, we just remove them when we lose a round...a piece at a time."

"Och! Like *slummire*. Dat ist a game our *jung* play. Freyans are not so inhibited as you Terrans. Ve also haff fighting games vhere die vun who loses his *hosen*...pants is die loser of der fight."

Cinda paled a bit. "Well don't start thinking about playing that game here!"

"Nein...ist only for men. Vomen haff der own fight games."

"Don't tell me about them! I will look it up later on the datastream. Now, you deal first."

Rheiner shuffled clumsily with his thick fingers. "Vhat ist der ante?"

They learn so fast, Cinda thought. "Um, my socks."

"Och...dat might not be so gute. My feet sveat a great deal."

"Great Ghu! Thanks for the warning. You can just set them off to the side. Make sure they don't float around the room!"

*   *   *

Victor Grego watched intently as several men and women worked on something that looked like a cross between an old-style lightning rod and three radar dishes pushed together at right angles to each other. With him stood Commodore Napier and Captain Greibenfeld.

"How fast can your people build these, um, devices?" Napier asked.

Grego grimaced. "At top speed, six per hour."

"That's all!" Greibenfeld said without thinking. "We will fall well short of what we need at that rate."

"Maybe," the Commodore said. "We really don't know how long we have. For all we know these Khooghras have already spaced out. I doubt it, but we can't be sure."

"The problem is that we don't have the machinery geared for mass production. It would take at least a week to crank these out by the hundreds. Until then, we are stuck with manual labor to put these together. Then, there is the problem of getting the materials. I have teams scouring Mallorysport for usable parts we can cannibalize from other machinery. We will have a hell of a time rebuilding everything after this is over. It would help if we knew what we were building, Commodore."

"My apologies, Mr. Grego," Napier said. "I can't give out that kind of information. Classified."

"Really? Isn't there some sort of regulation that allows the company building the whatzis to be read in?"

"There is," Greibenfeld said. "FSN Regulation Manual page 86, paragraph three. To summarize, Commodore Napier can read you in if he deems it necessary. However, it is a very large pain in the posterior justifying such an action to the higher-ups."

"I realize this puts you at a disadvantage, Mr. Grego—"

One of the workers interrupted, "Mr. Grego, Abe thinks we could speed up production of these gravitic-beam generators if we switch out the R2 regulator units and replace them with the J3 and attach a secondary booster. We have about a hundred of those lying around...um...is something wrong?"

Grego laughed out loud. He couldn't stop himself. When he recovered himself he nodded and said, "Go ahead, Manning. Tell Abe to get on it." He turned to the Commodore. "Can you read me in now?"

Napier reddened a bit, then chuckled. "Well, this particular feline has made his escape from the sack, so I might as well. Someplace more private perhaps?"

Grego escorted his guests to his penthouse office and poured some coffee. He knew better than to offer a stronger beverage while Napier and Greibenfeld were on duty.

Napier took a sip, then a large swallow. "You get coffee all the way from Imhotep?"

"Homegrown. I simply imported the beans to start the plantation," Grego explained. "This is from our first crop. Now, about the grava-whatsis?"

"Gravitic-beam generators," Captain Greibenfeld said. "I imagine your people would figure out what they are for quick enough, so I will save you the trouble. The purpose of these devices is to create a sort of gravity net around Zarathustra with as few as one hundred ships."

Grego's brow wrinkled. "Where are all these ships coming from?"

"They have been here for months. Those tourists up there have been pressed into service. We have Marines overseeing the installation of the equipment even as we speak."

"Interesting? How does it work?"

"Ah, well, I lack the technical proficiency to really understand that," Captain Greibenfeld said.

"They create an energy mesh that fools a hyperspace engine into thinking it is entering a gravity field well in advance of the planet's actual gravity well," Napier explained. "A hyperspace ship coming in would bounce back thousands, even hundreds of thousands of miles if it left hyperspace too close to the field, for example."

"That is a big advantage when faced with an invading force," Greibenfeld said.

Grego still looked confused. "How does that help us here? These slavers are already planet-side."

"It also keeps a ship from entering hyperspace," Napier finished.

Understanding dawned like a flash in Grego's mind. "You are trying to keep the slavers from escaping. Brilliant!"

"Not quite," Greibenfeld said. "We don't have enough GBG units to completely cover this world. At best, we can cover sixty to seventy-five percent of the planet, depending on how fast your people can supply us with more. Then we still have to get them up in the air and install them."

"Hmm...I'm afraid I have cracked all the whips I can, gentlemen. My people are good, but they have to leave miracles to Ghu. Say, what if the slavers simply coast through your net on Abbott lift and drive?"

Greibenfeld smiled. "Navigation is very tricky in the GBG field. Their sensors will read each line of force as gravity sources and significant mass. Trying to maneuver through all that sensor noise would test even the best helmsman. In that case, we might have a chance to visually spot them and force them down."

"Even if they get through, they have to travel an extra 32,000 miles before they can enter hyperspace." Commodore Napier added. "It would still be best if we caught them before they hit the sky."

"Naturally, we can't be sure to accomplish that objective, so we are covering all our bases," the Captain added. "We still do not know how many boats they have. Best guess right now is two or more, though I lean towards three."

Grego thought for a moment. "And if you can't force them down?"

"We cannot allow them to escape, Mr. Grego," Napier said. "No matter what the cost."

XLII

The man in the damnthing mask watched intently as the wall chronometer made its way up to midnight. Forgetting that the clock was set for Zarathustran time instead of T-standard, he almost jumped the gun. Instead, he waited for the sixty-first minute to pass, digit by digit, until 2400 was properly displayed.

"Now," he said into the microphone he held in his left hand. Within the yacht he could not feel any sensation of movement as it ascended into the night sky. On his comscreen he watched as the captains of the three other yachts gave their commands to their crews.

Next to the damnthing-masked man stood Captain Shade. Unlike many of the men who used various aliases, Shade was his genuine patronymic. He watched the screen intently, decided they all acted correctly, then nodded. He took his position as senior captain seriously.

"Captain Shade, I will be taking the cloaked shuttle to collect Mr. Hood," the damnthing said. "Move the ship to hover above Zeta Continent and wait for me there. I do not anticipate being long."

"Understood, sir."

Mr. Damnthing took the lift to the shuttle bay and removed his mask after looking to see if anybody was around. It was a remarkably uncomfortable disguise and would be unsafe to wear while piloting the craft.

It would not matter if the man wearing the hood saw his bare face; they already knew each other. The disguises on the comscreen were simply for additional security. Screen signals could be misdirected and end up who knows where, so they decided to keep all of their transmissions as secure as possible, even when using scramblers.

As Mr. Damnthing headed down to the planet's surface, he

considered removing Mr. Hood and taking over the operation on his own, and not for the first time. It would be simple enough since nobody else knew Mr. Hood's identity. However, the hooded man was still useful and had access to resources Mr. Damnthing knew nothing about.

Better to wait until all of Mr. Hood's secrets had been laid bare. He could always be removed later on. It would have been so much better if he had been able to procure the other partner and win him to his side.

* * *

Steg moved the ship into position above the Reservation school. On the screen he saw very little movement below. The infrared images showed numerous small creatures, Fuzzies, most likely, and several larger ones that were most likely humans. There were also a couple blips that showed to be cooler than the surrounding area.

Steg checked the screen for any dirt, then ran a diagnostic on the surveillance equipment. After a moment, the blips faded. Steg shrugged and nodded to T-Rex.

"All teams, prepare to go," T-Rex said into his microphone.

Steg watched another screen as groups of men scurried into the various shuttles. "Why are we sending live teams instead of the robots, this time?"

"As you pointed out before, robots are slower than people. This time we want to hit and get, and I mean get fast. Hopefully, we can catch everybody off-guard and get out before we take any fire."

Steg nodded. He didn't want to stay this close to the school any longer than absolutely necessary.

* * *

"If I catch you adjusting that cold suit again I'll feed you to the bush-goblins!" Staff Sergeant Boulder barked at four of the Marines. "The enemy can spot you by a cold image as well as a hot one, damn-it. Are you trying to blow this operation?"

"Sir, no, sir!" shouted the four Marines in unison.

"The next one of you to screw up is not going to like what I do next,"

Sergeant. Boulder continued. "One more screw-up like this and I will personally gouge out your eyes and stick—"

"Sir! We have a visual sighting of a bogey," Private Haggerty yelled. "Hanson spotted it with his light amplification goggles."

Sergeant Boulder followed the pointed finger to the black dot in the air. It would have been completely invisible if not for the fact that Darius was behind it. He didn't waste any time. "Positions, now! Haggerty, call Holloway and give him the skinny."

"Sir, yes, sir!" Haggerty used his radio to relay the information to Piet Dumont. "Sir! Chief Dumont says he is ready to back us up, sir!"

"Good. Now shut up and get into position. MOVE!"

*   *   *

"I thought Fuzzies were on a diurnal cycle like most of the animals on Zarathustra."

Charlie Wilfong grunted at his shipmate. "Fuzzies are people. People don't hold to any schedule but their own. Why?"

Tanner, the signals and detection tech, pointed at the screen. "There is a mass of Fuzzies down by that lake. I thought Fuzzies hated water, too."

"You might be confusing them with cats," Wilfong said dubiously. "What are they doing?"

"Nothing much as far as I can see. Sitting around in small groups, mostly."

"That is odd. Well, maybe they picked up some bad habits from their Big Ones. Do you see anybody else?"

"One sec." Tanner reset the screen for infrared. "No humans near the Fuzzies. They all seem to be in that building."

"The Science Center." Wilfong gave it some thought. "These Fuzzies might be taking part in some sort of experiment. That would explain why they are out this late at night instead of asleep. Take us in slowly. I don't want to alarm the creatures before we can gas 'em."

Tanner nodded. "Should I send out the shuttles?"

Wilfong looked at the screen. "No...not yet. We don't want to attract any attention from the building, either. The cloaking doesn't block the noise of the contragravity engines so we have to be cagey."

* * *

"Sir, the Fuzzies say something is approaching, sir!"

The Gunny put on his goggles and scanned the horizon. Sure enough, a giant ball of obsidian slowly moved over the lake towards the Fuzzies by the shore. He turned to Gerd van Riebeek. "Sir, the hostiles are moving into position. We may have caught a break."

"Good. Joe, are you ready with that thing?"

Joe Verganno nodded as he adjusted a dial. "Just give the word."

Gerd turned back to the Gunny. "Your call, Gunnery Sergeant."

"Sir, yes, sir." The Gunny turned back to the window and watched as the ship drew closer to the Fuzzies.

XLIII

"Big One, wake up!"

Clarke blinked away the sleep in his eyes and sat up. It took him a moment to remember that he was in the *Jin-f'ke* village and why he was there. He looked over at the Fuzzy, Spear Thrower, one of the gang that finished off the bad Big One that he had shot.

"What is it?"

"Hear sound, like melon-seed made-thing that fly," the Fuzzy reported.

Clarke cocked an ear. It took a minute before he could hear the faint whine of a space yacht. He learned the difference the year before when Morgan Holloway brought his yacht full of Fuzzies up to the *Jin-f'ke* territory to rescue Jack Holloway.

"Good job, Spear Thrower," Clarke said as he ruffled the Fuzzy's fur. "Make run fast, tell other Big Ones. Time to get ready for trouble."

The Fuzzy scampered off while Clarke stood up and stretched to work the kinks out of his muscles. Wide awake and ready for action, he collected his rifle and headed over to where the Marines were situated. There, he saw several Marines also waking up and preparing for battle.

"I hope you had a good rest, Officer Clarke. You may not get another for a while."

There was no note of recrimination in the Master Sergeant's voice. Any experienced soldier knew to get as much sleep as you could when possible; you may not get another chance for a long time. Clarke knew that from his time in the Army.

"Do we have a twenty on the ship?"

"Coming in at four o'clock. How do you think they will proceed, sir?"

Clarke tried to imagine how he would act if he was a Fuzzy slaver. "They'll come in shuttles, gas the area, then collect as many Fuzzies as they can before drawing any attention."

"They are cloaked and this is a remote area, sir," Master Sergeant White pointed out. "What kind of attention could they draw?"

"Satellite feed," Clarke replied. "I heard Commissioner Holloway talking with Victor Grego about surveillance feeds from the satellite net above. Those yachts are invisible to everything short of actual eyes on them, so we might be able to get a video feed in the moonlight."

"Sir, the Fuzzies say the boat is getting close. They can see it in the darkness."

"Positions!" Master Sergeant White ordered. "Officer Clarke, please pull your hood up. You would stand out on infrared right now."

"Yes, Sergeant!" Clarke said as he pulled the hood over his head and covered his face. In the heat of the moment his old Army training came to the fore. He hoped his reflexes were still up to snuff. More, he wished his old commanding officer, Major Steefer, was with them.

*   *   *

"Biggest damned bunch of Fuzzies in one place I have ever seen, Sal."

Salvador Andreyev appraised the image on the screen and nodded. "Any sign of ZNPF officers?"

"Two, at the trading post slash guard shack on the other side of the ridge. Not enough to threaten us," said the other man. "Should we send out a hit team?"

Two men against his forty-man assault force was a small risk. Besides, the last two-man team that tried it ended up dead. He also considered launching a missile at the shack and dismissed that idea as well. Missiles were expensive and the explosion could scatter the Fuzzies.

"Ignore them until they become a nuisance. If that happens, do as you think best."

"You got it boss. The gas cartridge is cocked, locked and ready to be deployed on your word."

Sal smiled and cried out, "Do it!"

*   *   *

The shuttle came down in the small clearing just wide enough to accommodate it. The hatch opened and Clarence Anetrou poked his head out. Out of the foliage the hooded man appeared.

"Why aren't you wearing your mask?" Mr. Hood demanded.

"It's just you and I out here, and we already know each other," Anetrou said. "Now get in before somebody comes along."

Mr. Hood jumped in the shuttle just as bullets pinged off the hull. "Damn-it, didn't you scan for people?"

"With what? These shuttles never had the infrared gear installed." More bullets pinged on the shuttle, one of them came in and narrowly missed the hooded man.

"Close the damned hatch before whoever it is gets lucky!"

Anetrou closed the hatch and started ascending. More bullets struck the shuttle with no effect. The collapsium lamination easily dismissed such light weaponry.

"You're safe, now. Didn't you see anybody following you?"

"Through that jungle? Hardly."

"They could have spotted you heading out, whoever they are," Anetrou deduced. "They must have figured out who you are by now; if not, being the only other person missing from the campsite will give you away, regardless."

The hooded man removed his head covering and wiped his forehead. "You may be right, but there is damned little they can do about it now. Besides, I used an alias. A little cosmetic surgery on an out-of-the-way planet and I will be scot free."

Anetrou nodded. "I'll have to go the same route. I imagine they saw my face when I looked out from the hatch. Pity, I always liked how much I resembled my father."

*   *   *

"Do you think you hit one of them?"

Gilbert shook his head in disgust. "Only if I got lucky and pegged one of them with a ricochet. Come on, we have to call this in."

Sullivan looked up into the night sky and could see no trace of the departing shuttle. Even the whine of the Abbott drive had faded. "Max isn't gonna like this."

"Got away in a black shuttle?" Marshal Max Fane roared at the screen. He took a moment then calmed down. "Well, did you get a good look at either of them?"

"The man in the hood is Gregoire Rutherford," Sullivan reported. "He was the one we followed into the forest and is the only member of the expedition missing, aside from Cinda Dawn."

"What about the rest of these scientists? Anybody seem off to you?"

"Nah," Gilbert said. "Just eggheads with a puzzle to play with. If not, they are better actors than Darla Cross could ever hope to be."

Sullivan agreed.

Max nodded thoughtfully. "All right, what about the shuttle pilot? Did you get a good look at him?"

"I would know him if I saw him again," Sullivan said. "It wasn't very bright out, but I think I have seen him before, though I can't place where at the moment."

"Really? Now that is interesting. Any idea where?"

"It had to be in Mallorysport, Marshal Fane. I'm pretty sure he isn't a perp or I would know him right off. Somebody I bumped into off the job, maybe."

"Head back in first thing in the morning and see the graphics tech," Max said. "Maybe he can build a face from your description."

"Will do, Marshal."

The screen went dark and Max leaned back in his chair. It was a little after midnight Beta time, and after three a.m. in Mallorysport. He was dead tired and ready to go to bed when the screen beeped again. Max opened the connection to see Jack Holloway's grim countenance looking back at him.

"It's started," Jack said. "These bastards waited for midnight West

Beta time to start their attack."

Max snorted. "Somebody has a sense of the dramatic. A military man would have waited till three in the morning when people are at their lowest ebb. Well, I will alert Napier and Grego. Is Damien Panaioli on the job?"

"Yeah, he seems to think this is all some great adventure," Jack said. "Did you know he was in prison before going to work for the CZC?"

"Yup. Fourteen months for simple theft. Although I don't know what he may have pled down from."

"Humph. Well, he is trying to access the...uh...asset, now."

Smart, Max thought, *Jack knows the line might be monitored.* "Okay, I'll spread the word. Go get some bad guys."

Jack's image darkened and Max pounded out the screen code for Commodore Napier. When the connection was made it was not the face of the Commodore that appeared. It was an ensign Max had never spoken with.

"Commodore Napier's quarters. May I ask the reason for this call?"

Of course the Commodore had somebody to screen his calls, Max realized. "Tell him it is Marshal Fane and that the excrement has struck the wind generator."

"Understood." The ensign's face vanished from the screen and was promptly replaced by that of Commodore Napier.

"They went for midnight Beta time, didn't they?" the Commodore asked.

Max told him that was the case.

"I expected some idiocy like that," the Commodore said. "That means they don't have any military veterans calling the shots. I took my nap earlier to be ready for something like this."

That explains why the commodore looks so bright-eyed, Max noted. "Wish I had been able to do the same. You said you might have something in place to keep these mutts from escaping orbit—"

The Commodore grimaced. "Only about seventy percent in place."

Max shrugged. "Beats nothing."

"Maybe. It depends on the Dillingham models they are using and the quality of their sensors and detection gear. I can't go into specifics, Marshal."

Military types think everything has to be classified, right up to what they had for breakfast. "I understand, Commodore. Frankly, I don't care if it's a web of rubber bands as long as we catch these mutts."

* * *

Jack watched intently as the black ship hovered over the Reservation school area. Shuttles descended heading for the ground for a purpose Jack knew only too well. It was all he could do to keep from running out and taking shots at them. He knew it was useless to fire on anything covered in collapsium, of course, and taking shots too soon would only alert the invaders that they were expected.

Instead, Jack turned to the young man in the sensor helmet working controls in front of him. He was heavily adorned with tattoos of every type almost to the point of completely obscuring his natural skin color.

"Making any progress?"

Damien didn't turn to the sound of Jack's voice. He remained intent on his job. "Almost. I can only access one Fuzz-bot at a time. Cool name, by the way. Your sister thought it up, I heard."

"Yeah. She's good with nicknames like that."

"Aaaand, I'm in." A picture came up on the viewscreen in front of Damien. Fuzzies milled about looking for something, most likely a way out. Jack spotted Little Fuzzy and his heart skipped a beat. "It looks like they are all in a cargo bay. They didn't even bother to put the Fuzzies into cages."

"That cargo bay is one big cage unless you can get them out of it," Jack said irritably. "I should have anticipated something like this."

"No problem. Mr. Grego and Morgan Holloway—your son, right?—thought of this." Damien thumbed a control and the scene on the screen shifted. Jack could see that it was moving towards the bay door. "Mr. Morgan suggested a lock scanner and remote control be installed in the Fuzz-bots to jimmy any electronic locks the Fuzzies might end up stuck behind. Cargo bay door locks are pretty simple devices and easy enough to beat as long as these schmucks didn't upgrade the security. I don't know a lot about Fuzzies, but I heard that they are really smart, so these creeps may have done that."

The screen showed a Fuzzy hand reaching up to the lock control. It didn't quite reach. It didn't matter.

"Yup. They upgraded. That just means it will take a little longer. Don't worry, Mr. Holloway, I'll get through this thing before long. I've had a bit of practice at this."

Jack found himself grateful for Damien's criminal past. Sometimes, to get a job done, it takes a thief.

* * *

Major George Lunt adjusted his night goggles to better see the ship in the night sky. His stomach twisted into knots as he observed three shuttles moving away from the yacht and headed for the school area. He couldn't be sure, even with the goggles, that something had been ejected from one of the three shuttles. Then he saw the faint explosions and the billowing clouds of what he assumed was gas.

"All units, engage the shuttles," Lunt yelled into his radio.

He watched intently as the military fighter craft exploded out of their camouflaged positions and flew up to the sky. On the ground, men in cold suits and gas masks invisible to infrared, moved out to meet the shuttles with heavy gunfire. Shooting at a collapsium-plated shuttle was little more than an empty gesture. The rounds, designed to shatter on impact so as not to hurt anybody with a ricochet, were also treated with a low level radiation signature. If the slavers managed to get away, the shuttles could be tracked.

The shuttles, while virtually impervious to battle damage, could still be forced down by fighter aircrafts. Protected by a collapsium cover, the ships were free to bring their weight to bear on the shuttles. The shuttle engines, able to handle a full shuttle, were not necessarily up to taking on the additional weight of another collapsium-encased vehicle.

While the impact damage on the outer casings of such craft would be virtually nonexistent, the interior was a different story. Sudden impacts

Carr & Diehr

could jar the occupants and equipment significantly. For the pilot, this meant difficulty in maintaining control of the vessel. Even if there were no upsets within the cockpit, the addition of several tons striking the outer hull could overwhelm the engines and even tax the contragravity matrix. These were the problems Bront faced as the attack craft collided with his shuttle.

"What the Niflheim was that?" Allo yelled from the back.

"We have company," Bront yelled back. "Marine fighter craft. He's trying to force us down."

"Marines? To Niflheim with the Fuzzies. Let's get out of here!"

"What do you think I am trying to do?" Bront shouted. "I've got one on top, one on each side and one on my ass!"

"Then dive!"

"I can't, damn-it! We're too close to the ground. If I try to dive, we'll crash before I can pull up."

Allo swore luridly in Sheshan as he checked the screen. He looked over the fighter craft and said, "Then try to outrun them. That model has a limited fuel supply. They are faster, but can't run as long."

"I'm not even going to ask how you know this." Bront increased speed hoping that Allo was right. He never had the chance to find out. The shuttle shook, then started losing speed.

"What happened?" Allo screamed.

Bront desperately checked the readouts on the console. "Something is blocking the exhaust ports and thrusters. We're dead in the air. Contragravity will keep us up and momentum will keep us going forward for a bit, but for all intents and purposes, this is a lighter than air brick."

"Warn the others."

"No good," Bront said, shaking his head. "We're all being jammed. We're got and got good. All I can do is shut down the contragravity and go down."

"What is the penalty for kidnapping Fuzzies?"

"A whole lotta death for everybody involved," Bront said. "That doesn't even include the lesser charges of gassing them, forcibly removing them from the planet, exploitation...and no discretion of the court, either."

Allo thought it over. "I'd rather crash than be taken in."

"Then we are agreed." Bront shut down the contragravity. "Nice knowing you, Al...."

* * *

"...yes, shuttles. Right, Gerd, spread the word. The other teams need to be ready for that. Good luck!"

Jack put down the radio-communicator and turned his attention back to the viewscreen. He wanted to go out and join the fighting though he knew he would be more in the way than helpful. *Let the Marines do their job*, he decided.

"We're out, Mr. Holloway."

Jack watched the viewscreen as the door to the cargo bay opened, allowing the Fuzzies to run loose through the ship. He saw Little Fuzzy yeeking something and the other Fuzzies rallied around him.

"It looks like one Fuzzy is taking charge. Is that Little Fuzzy?" Damien asked.

"You bet it is," Jack said with pride. "He'll keep the others in line so they don't get caught again."

"Good on him. Um, should I release the gas now, or wait until the Fuzzies find the control room, Mr. Holloway?"

"Bridge," Jack corrected. "I think now would be a good time. And call me Jack."

* * *

Steg watched the viewscreen in horror as one by one, the shuttles were brought down. "The s.o.b.'s were waiting for us!"

T-Rex grunted. "Either somebody squealed or they spotted something during one of the raids. They're down and there's nothing we can do about it. We have to get out of here. Call Captain Anklo and tell him to make for high orbit. We space...space... (yawn) ...space out...soon's we clearrr...."

Steg turned to see T-Rex collapse to the floor. "Rex? Are you okayyy...?"

*   *   *

The Fuzzies followed the fuzzy robot through the corridors of the yacht. Jack watched as Damien guided the robot.

"How do you know where you are going?" Jack asked.

Damien tapped his helmet. "You don't see it on the viewscreen because that is what the Fuzz-bot sees. In my VR helmet I have a secondary display showing me the standard layout of a hyperspace yacht."

"They aren't all the same, you know," Jack said dubiously.

"Close enough," Damien countered. "All hyperspace ships are modeled along similar lines. I looked it up when Mr. Grego tapped me for this job. I understand you have been in space quite a bit, so you know that the Abbott Lift and Drive, along with the Dillingham and gravity generators are all located in the center of the ship. Next level is storage and crew quarters and so on. The outermost levels are cargo bays, shuttle bays, luxury suites and the con...bridge. Shuttle bays and cargo bays are always contiguous for simplicity and ease of access. The bridge is at the dead opposite side of the shuttle bay. I don't really know why...something to do with the captain going down with the ship, I would guess."

"Actually, it is so that the bridge crew won't be distracted by the vibrations of the shuttles coming and going," Jack replied.

"Really? I didn't think collapsium transmitted vibrations. Anyway, I am guiding the Fuzzies to the bridge based on that design."

Jack nodded, then remembered something he saw on Morgan's yacht. "You do know that the shuttle and cargo bays take two levels each, right?"

"What?" Damien adjusted something on the helmet then swore. "I see that, now. I'll have to have the Fuzzies take the lift up." He grumbled something about 2D schematics as he worked the controls in front of him.

Jack's radio beeped. "Yes?" It was George Lunt.

"We got the shuttle, Jack. Only two casualties."

"Us or them?"

"Them," George said. "They cut their contragravity off at about a quarter-mile up. Made a bit of a mess coming down. At least we had already chased them away from the school."

"Do you have a visual on the ship?"

"Can't help but see it now," George said. "We have it lit up with every light source we could get. Right now it is just drifting a bit. It's like the contragravity is on, but nobody's home."

"The Fuzz-bots deployed the gas. Is there an open bay you can get those Marine fighter craft into?"

"No, sorry. They're all buttoned up. They probably closed it as soon as they saw the fighter craft. A couple Marine pilots are circling it and are looking for a way in. No luck so far."

Jack expected no less. "Well, just keep at it. Mr. Panaioli is working on it from this end. Out."

"Call me Damien, Jack. And the Fuzzies are on the bridge. Do you want me to try and land the ship?"

Jack looked at the screen. He could see people asleep at their stations all over the place. "That might be a bit tricky and we don't want to take any unnecessary chances. Just open a shuttle bay and let the Marines take over."

"Will do," Damien said as he manipulated some controls. The Fuzz-bot scanned the control panels on screen until they found the right one. "Shuttle bay is opening. It's a shame we have to let the Marines do it."

"Why is that?" Jack asked.

Damien removed his helmet and turned to Jack with a grin. "How cool would it be for the Fuzzies to land the ship and for us to say we were there when it happened?"

Jack laughed. He had to admit it would have made for a good story to tell his grandson someday.

XLIV

Gerd van Riebeek put down the radio and rejoined Joe Verganno inside the Science Center. Joe was making some last-minute checks as he prepared to activate the weapon.

"Hold off activation, Joe," Gerd said. "I just learned something that might help."

"It has to charge up first, anyway," he replied. "Later on, if this works out, we can install a mass-energy conversion unit or a series of nuclear power cells. For now it runs on the building's power supply and takes about ten minutes to charge between uses."

"How long will it hold the charge before it has to be used?"

"Oh, indefinitely, I would normally say," Verganno said. "I can't be sure about that, though. On something this early in the development stage there are always a few bugs to be dealt with before going to market."

"Well, company has come and we need to be ready, so charge her up. Just hold back until either I or the Gunny gives the signal."

"Will do," Verganno said. *Wonder if I'll get hazard pay for this?*

Gerd moved over to Gunny Fitzpatrick's position. "I just received word that these slaver ships have a small complement of shuttles."

The Gunny nodded. "A craft of this size generally carries two to four shuttles. They haven't launched, yet, if that is what you are asking."

Gerd was relieved both by the information and the fact that the Gunny had stopped book-ending every sentence with 'sir.' "How long does it take to open a shuttle bay portal?"

The Gunny thought it over. "Best guess: five seconds if the ship is in good repair. Another five for the shuttle to lift out and reorient itself, assuming the pilot is highly skilled, then five more to close the bay doors."

"So fifteen seconds at best."

"I doubt they will be that quick, sir. Pilots that qualified are hard to come by, and highly paid. They wouldn't need to throw in with a crowd like this."

Gerd hoped the Gunny was right. From behind them he heard Joe Verganno say the weapon was ready to deploy. "Gunny, I don't know a whole lot about hyperspace ships in general, or the weapon we are about to use on that one, but I think it will be more effective if we catch it with the bay doors open."

The Gunny nodded. "I would think so. Collapsium is hard to get through with energy or physical bombardment. An opening in the hull would be very helpful."

"So, we have to hold fire until these Khooghras come out to play," Gerd said. "I'm curious as to why your men haven't done anything, yet? I thought there'd be all kinds of noise about this time."

The Gunny suppressed a chuckle. It wasn't Gerd's fault that he had never been in a firefight before. "War is ninety-eight percent boredom spattered with two percent horror, sir. Waiting is always the hardest part. It is natural to want to start shooting at a threat even when it would be useless to do so.

"Right now we have attack craft sitting under camouflage waiting to pounce. While those bay doors are closed, there is nothing they can do against that ship. If we did go out now, they would be very likely to just run away. I would guess that they are scanning the area looking for targets and hostiles. Our men in cold suits will be invisible to infrared, and their auto-shifting camouflage makes them effectively invisible to the naked eye. They won't spot our people."

"Wait, we aren't wearing cold suits," Gerd countered.

"We are in a building with a staff of about seventy-nine people," the Gunny replied. "If they didn't register some heat signatures coming from this building, it would be suspicious. Even the armed guards won't raise any eyebrows, which many of my men are dressed as."

Gerd saw the Gunny's logic. "Okay, how do we know they will be sending out shuttles, then? You obviously anticipated that they would."

"They have no choice." The Gunny nodded at the black ship. "While a craft like that can make a soft landing on the ground, it is difficult and time-consuming. Normally they would just cut everything but the contragravity and have the shuttles guide it down. At a spaceport, tugs would do the job. Then a gangplank would have to be extended and the men would rush out to snatch the Fuzzies. A team of Girl Guides could take them down in that case.

"Shuttles are faster, more maneuverable, and provide protection. My guess is they will come out, drop some gas canisters that will detonate several yards above the ground for maximum dispersal, then grab up as many sleeping Fuzzies as they can before drawing too much fire."

"So, they are expecting trouble, you think?"

"If they don't, they are complete idiots, sir," the Gunny said. "This close to a CZC building? Your boss has a certain reputation in how he deals with attacks on the Company."

Gerd had to admit that the Gunny had a point.

* * *

"I don't like it," Tanner said.

"Again? I thought we were past that," Wilfong said. "Look, there's nobody but Fuzzies down there. The infrared shows that."

"Infrared can be fooled," Tanner shot back. "When I was in the Army they were experimenting with camou-suits that would automatically blend in with the surrounding area and block infrared signatures."

"And you think they would have something like that on a backwater planet like this?" Wilfong laughed derisively. "On Thor or Odin, or even Baldur—maybe. Here? I very much doubt it. Even if you are right, how could they know we would be here? Now? No. We move forward. Prep the shuttles for launch. It's time to collect some cargo."

"Sir, the bay doors are opening," the Gunny reported. He put down his field glasses and stepped away from the building's edge. "I hate to be dramatic, but we might only get one shot at this, sir."

"Hell, this entire situation is dramatic, Gunny," Gerd said. "Joe, hit it!"

"One second, Mr. van Riebeek. I have to aim it better. Just a little more..." Verganno slapped the big red button on the console. The lights flickered, then nothing.

"Joe, I said hit it!"

Verganno started checking the gauges and readouts. They were all dead. "It's down, Mr. van Riebeek. Nothing at all."

Gerd swore. "Gunny, what is happening out there?"

"I don't know, sir. My field glasses have failed."

Gerd was on the verge of tearing his hair out. "What else can we do? We can't just let those Fuzzies get snatched up."

The Gunny tried his radio. It was also dead. He said as much and Joe Verganno slapped his own head.

"Of course! It worked! The EMP gun did discharge. Unfortunately we, or rather our equipment in this room, isn't shielded. Neither was the gun, it would seem. R&D will have to do something about that little flaw."

"Wait," the Gunny said. "If the gun worked, what all will be affected?"

Verganno thought quickly. "Everything in the immediate area and in line of fire with a dispersal pattern of, um, one to twenty."

The Gunny tried to follow Verganno's line of reasoning. "Then, for every twenty yards, the beam gets one and a half-foot wider?"

"Something like that," Gerd said, the relief in his voice apparent.

"Then what's going on in that ship?"

Wilfong collapsed to the floor. Tanner spun his chair around and went to assist the fallen man. All around him the panels went dark. Only the emergency lighting worked, along with the artificial gravity.

"Wilfong, what is the matter?"

Wilfong pounded on his chest. "Arti...ficial...heart—" He expired before he could finish his statement.

Tanner quickly returned to the control panel only to find that it was still dead. He tried to leave the room without success. The doors, designed to open electronically, failed to activate.

"What's going on?" Tanner yelled.

The shuttle pilots suffered much the same difficulties as the mothership. "Control! Control! I can't move. Everything is dead except for the contragravity, damn-it! Come in!"

Aaron French pounded uselessly on his control panel. All he could see was the night sky and Darius through the tempered glass of the shuttle. A streak of light shot past the nose of the transport. A moment later he felt a jarring and could see that the ground was rising to meet him.

"The bastards've got me," French thought aloud. "I don't know how, but they fried the controls and got me." He thought about the trial to come, the time in Prison House and how the other inmates would treat him; many inmates treated Fuzzy abusers much the same as child molesters—very badly. And at the end of the trial the best he could hope for was a bullet in the head, or maybe a firing squad. French knew about the last batch of Fuzzy slavers to be caught and how they ended up. He wouldn't even be able to plea bargain for life in prison.

"What do we do?" asked one of the men with him. French told them what they could expect. "I'd rather crash."

The others agreed.

"But, we can't crash. The controls are dead and the contragravity is locked on. To hell with this."

Pulling his pistol from the holster, French checked it to be sure it was loaded and the safety was off. He weighed his chances against fighting his way out. He gave up on that idea when he saw the Marine fighter craft. A Marine could wound him, take him into custody, then he would go through everything he already imagined.

"To Hell with this!" he repeated to himself.

When Lance Corporal Kelso finally opened the shuttle hatch he found four dead bodies; three shot in the chest, one with the top of his head missing.

Gunny James Fitzpatrick watched with interest as the shuttles were forced to the ground. He couldn't make out how many people were captured without his field glasses; he wished he had a pair of low-tech binoculars at that moment. Using simple flashlights and Morse Code, he did learn that all three shuttles were down with their personnel either dead or captured. Gerd accepted the news with great interest though something had him confused.

"Joe, if the EMP cannon worked, why didn't the contragravity cut off?"

Verganno nodded thoughtfully before answering. "I'm no expert in this area, though I imagine it must be the way the generators are designed. Contragravity takes a lot of power to keep running. That means nuclear batteries, as we all know. Well, the engines and batteries are shielded by collapsium and only have the tiniest access points to and from the control panel. Unless the EMP projector hits it at exactly the right angle, the contragravity simply loses connection to the controls and stays at its last setting. The same would be true of the artificial gravity generators."

Gerd thought it over. It made sense. "Okay, next question: How long will the systems be down?"

"That I can't say," Verganno admitted. "This is a prototype based on First century designs. I'm just the software expert. It may be a few minutes, it may be never."

Gerd spun back to the Gunny who was already signaling his men with the flashlight.

"I am sending the fighter craft into the ship before the enemy can power up. Hopefully, the doors have manual overrides; not all yachts do. If not, we'll have to cut our way into every area that was closed off before we disabled the ship. Ah, one of the fighters was caught in the blast. We will have to leave him floating until we secure the ship."

"I'll send somebody after him," Gerd said as he picked up his radio. He pressed the button, only remembering it wouldn't work when it failed to come on. "Ah, I'll make the call from downstairs. Hopefully the EMP field didn't extend that far."

XLV

Officer Clarke watched in silent rage as the shuttles came down just outside the Fuzzy village. As he had been warned by Jack Holloway, the slavers had gassed the *Jin-f'ke* Fuzzies, then settled down to collect them. It took all of his Army training to keep from shooting the lot of them.

Instead, Clarke moved slowly and carefully to the shuttle hatch. The plan was to get as many Marines into the shuttles unobserved as possible. It was slow going. While the cold suits kept them invisible to infrared detection, and the self-adjust camouflage made them practically invisible, sudden movement could still draw the eye. Moreover, the camouflage was less effective up against a mono-colored surface, like the black paint of the shuttle, or the painted walls within, and useless against a foe within ten feet without a lot of something behind the suit.

Clarke's size also worked against him. He couldn't scramble into the shuttle hatch as quickly as a smaller man, and his footsteps tended to crunch twigs and leaves beneath his boots. He wondered how the Marines managed to move so silently.

The hatch was wide open with one of the slavers coming out for another armload of Fuzzies. Clarke froze as the man walked passed him. If the man hadn't been so intent on his job he would have noticed Clarke, camouflage or not. Clarke breathed a silent prayer of thanks to Ghu and scrambled into the shuttle, careful not to step on any Fuzzies.

* * *

"What are you doing?"

Omar looked up and grimaced. "I'm trying to get these weapons away from the Fuzzies. I can't believe how hard it is. The gas must have seized the muscles. I hope it doesn't cause any heart attacks."

"Forget about that," The other man said. "We can take their toys away after we get them on the ship. We don't have time for that now."

"All right, Hank, if you say so. I think it's a bad idea letting them keep the weapons."

Hank snorted. "How much damage could they do? Once we have them in the cargo hold we can strip them of their goods easily. Now get that bunch into the shuttle."

* * *

Private First Class Reeve wasn't as lucky as Officer Clarke. One of the slavers tripped over him as he went for more Fuzzies. Lacking for an alternative, Reeve drew his knife and stabbed the man at the base of the neck. Thinking quickly, he looked about, saw that nobody was nearby and dragged the body behind a bush. There, he quickly stripped off the man's pants and jacket and pulled them on over his own clothes. His relatively slight frame, compared to the dead man's larger build, allowed him to do so without too much trouble.

Cutting power to his cold suit and adaptive camouflage, he put on the dead man's hat and joined the collection team.

"What do you think you are doing, Private?"

Reeve's heart skipped a beat as he recognized the Master Sergeant's whispered voice. "Sir, this man discovered my position and I was forced to put him down before he could warn the others, sir."

"And his clothes?"

"Sir, I suspect they will be counting bodies, so I am taking his place for as long as I can to give the rest of our people a chance to infiltrate the shuttles, sir."

Master Sergeant White thought it over and decided Reeve had acted correctly, not that there was anything he could do about it now. "You do realize that they will recognize you as not being one of their own when you get on the shuttle, right?"

"Sir, yes, sir."

"That means we will have to eliminate that possibility."

"Sir?"

"Just keep doing what you are doing. I will handle it. And you did right, Reeve."

Sergeant White quickly faded into the scenery. A few minutes later Reeve noticed a man go down, then another.

Oh, that's what he meant.

* * *

"The shuttles are returning, Captain."

Captain Scalia left the command chair and went to look over the signals and detection officer's shoulder. "Very good. Send the request for the call signs, Mr. Cushing. I think we can break radio silence."

The officer nodded and tapped out the request. Behind them a man in an expensive suit entered the bridge.

"Shuttle Two, *Abnegazar.*"

"Shuttle One, Belphegor."

The third shuttle only transmitted static.

"What is that? Static? Where from?" demanded the Suit.

"Sir, one of the shuttles appears to have radio problems," Scalia said. "I advise that we do not allow it to return without some means of verifying who is on it."

"Can we access the interior cameras of the shuttle?"

Cushing tried, getting a static-heavy picture. They could just make out four humans and what looked like a large rumpled rug.

"How many men are supposed to be on that shuttle?" the Suit asked.

"Four," Cushing answered. "And at least a dozen Fuzzies."

The Suit turned to the Captain. "Any trouble reported from the surface?"

"No, sir."

"Then let them in. Take whatever precautions you believe necessary."

"You can count on that, sir."

* * *

Red Fur continued to feign unconsciousness as the bad Big Ones opened the hatch to the shuttle. He couldn't understand why they couldn't see the good Big Ones in the back of the shuttle. Red Fur could see them easily. Perhaps the Big Ones had bad eyes?

Through barely open eyes Red Fur could see more Big Ones with the big gun things that could make even large animals make-dead. The other Big Ones, the Mah-reens, said that this would happen, and to pretend sleep when they took his people off of the flying made-thing. It took considerable time and effort to grasp the concept of *pretend* for the *Jin-f'ke*. It was a not-so thing used in strah-ta-jees, the Mah-reens said. Now Red Fur could see the wisdom in such a thing.

"Any trouble, Chuck?" a Big One asked.

"None. The Fuzzies took a nap and we just picked them up."

The Big One eyed the Fuzzies dubiously. "Then why do they still have their weapons?"

"Alex figures it's muscle spasms from the sleep gas. It would have taken too much time to pry the weapons away from them, so we figured we would deal with it after we got back. How much trouble can they be, anyway? You have those tranq-guns to deal with any early risers who give us trouble."

"I don't like it," The Big One said. "Let's strip the weapons now."

Red Fur didn't know what 'strip' meant, but he knew the word 'weapon' very well. It was time to act. He yeeked out the command to attack.

The Fuzzies leapt to their feet with amazing speed. In seconds they had spread out so as not to be caught in a group. Red Fur yeeked something to the Fuzzy in front of him. The Fuzzy, called Jumper, quickly crouched down to form a launch point for Red Fur. The Fuzzy chieftain lurched forward, leapt onto Jumper's back, then launched himself into the air directly at the Big One called Chuck.

It looked like Red Fur would miss his target as he started to sail past the Big One. At the second he came into range, he swung his chopper-digger, one of the metal ones from the trading post, at Chuck's neck. The Fuzzy didn't have the power to completely decapitate the Big One. He didn't need to. The blade cut easily through the soft tissue surrounding the carotid and jugular veins.

Chuck dropped his tranq-gun in an attempt to staunch the flow of blood from his neck. It was to no avail. He dropped first to his knees, then fell forward on his face in a most undignified position. Another Fuzzy, seeing the elevated posterior of the dead Big One, used it in the same manner as Red Fur had with Jumper and launched himself at another Big One. While his aim was not as precise as his leader's, the Fuzzy still managed to cut the Big One's throat causing him to die choking on his own blood.

By this time the Marines had joined the party aiming and shooting at any humans not already being swarmed by Fuzzies. While limited to .22 rounds—heavier ammunition could damage the interior of the ship where collapsium was not as heavily used—their expert aim more than made up for the low stopping power. Bullets entered eye sockets, struck throats and even severed main arteries, bringing men down left and right.

Armed only with tranq-guns, the bad Big Ones were quickly overpowered. Realizing this, the survivors rapidly surrendered. Master Sergeant White took a quick accounting of his men and the Fuzzies—no significant injuries.

"That went very well," White said. "Shackle the prisoners and put them back in the shuttle."

"Sir, did you see how fast the Fuzzies worked, sir?"

"Yeah, MacTavish. They didn't come up with that fly and cut maneuver overnight."

MacTavish nodded. "Sir, they've had bad feelings towards Big Ones since day one. I guess they decided to be ready for us if things went south. Sir."

"I think you are right, Corporal. I am too impressed to be worried about that right now. I think I will worry later, though. A lot."

The second shuttle bay saw activity much like the first with the same results. Things didn't go quite as well in the third. Clarke waited impatiently for the hatch to open. He knew that he and the Marines beside him would have to rush out and take down the slavers in the mother ship straight away or be found out. Unlike the other two shuttles, this one was piloted and crewed by Marines since the original members of the shuttle party had all been killed. As luck would have it, he flew in with them. The Fuzzies didn't need to pretend to sleep, they were up and ready to go. The hatch opened halfway then stopped. Something was blocking it.

"You, inside. Throw out your weapons."

Reeve, who piloted the craft, swore under his breath. "The static trick didn't work. We'll have to give up so they don't shoot the Fuzzies." He looked at Clarke and shook his head. Then he made a motion as if he were pulling something from behind his head over it. Clarke understood and pulled his camou hood up and over his face. "All right, we're coming out."

The hatch opened the rest of the way and the Marines filed out one at a time with their hands behind their heads. It didn't take a psychologist to see that it chafed their warrior pride. Behind them the Fuzzies came out all in a bunch. They were gathered so close to each other they almost looked like a single organism.

"Dolph, Henri, check the shuttle. Feel the walls, check everything. If anybody is left in there, they might have some sort of stealth suit. In fact, just spray the whole shuttle with bullets. The .22 rounds won't do as much damage as a hidden Marine."

The two men did as ordered and emptied their machine guns into the shuttle compartment. Then Dolph drew his sidearm and checked the load. He fired a few shots just to be sure. When finished, the two men left the shuttle and reported to the captain that all was clear.

"Very good." Scalia turned to the Marines. "Gentlemen, would you be so kind as to tell me where the original shuttle crew got to?" Nobody spoke. "Then I shall assume that they are dead or captured. Pity. I am very much distressed to admit this, but we have no need of you. Perhaps if these Fuzzies see how we deal with you, they will choose to be more cooperative. Dolph, Henri, have you reloaded yet?"

They both nodded.

"Then please be so good as to empty your weapons into these un-wanted guests."

The two men moved to comply when a burst of gunfire stopped them in their tracks. Clarke, who had hidden among the Fuzzies in his adaptive camouflage raised himself up on his knees and fired all around him, being careful to avoid hitting the Marines.

The Marines needed no instruction: without hesitation they moved as one to attack the men who had held them at gunpoint.

Reeve took three rounds to the chest and one to the arm. His fibroid weave vest under his uniform easily protected him from the .22 slugs, though his right arm bled profusely.

His left arm shot up sending the heel of his hand into his attacker's nose, splintering the maxilla and sending shards of bone into his brain. The man died instantly.

The Fuzzies were not idle during the gun play. Two, using the same method previously displayed by Red Fur, slashed the necks of two men while several other Fuzzies simply swarmed over two more, hacking and stabbing their way past them.

Captain Scalia, sensing he would not be able to win, made for the entry door. He was brought up short when he slammed into something as big, if marginally softer, than the door itself.

Drawing his camou hood back, Officer Clarke smiled widely at the prone captain. "I am afraid it distresses me greatly to inform you that you are under arrest."

"Sir, we have the enemy subdued," Reeve said. "What are your orders, sir?"

Clarke was surprised to find that the Marines turned to him for orders. Then he remembered that these men were part of the detached element working with the ZNPF.

"First, attend to that arm. Have the corpsman check the Fuzzies, too. Next, try to stop the Fuzzies from killing the prisoners. Shackle the prisoners and stuff them into the shuttle. We wouldn't want them to bump into a comscreen somewhere."

Clarke looked about the bay. There was blood everywhere and two Fuzzies were either dead or unconscious. "Contact the others and see if things went at least this smoothly. If so, we take the ship. Where is the

Fuzz-bot? It was supposed to activate if we ran into trouble."

"Sir, it went with team two, sir."

"Please stop sir-ing me to death! I'm ex-army, only officers are called sir. I work for a living. Ask Master Sergeant White what we should do—"

Clarke heard the door behind him open and he spun around ready to deal with whoever came in.

"Stand down is what Master Sergeant White wants you to do." White surveyed the shuttle bay. "Humph. While you goldbricks were having a party, we took the ship. Reeve, you should be ashamed of yourself for letting your uniform get damaged and dirty like that. Go see the corpsman and get that patched up. He is in the next shuttle bay over."

"Sir, yes, sir!"

"Everything went well for you?" Clarke inquired.

"So well we were in danger of getting bored," White answered. "I guess they got suspicious about the static, eh? Well, looks like you handled it well enough."

"I am curious about something," Clarke said. "These four men were about to be shot and just stood there. That was dangerous, even though they had bulletproof vests on. Why?"

White turned to Private. Emerson. "Explain, Private."

"Sir, Reeve suggested we risk being shot and play dead, then take the enemy by surprise at the first opportunity, sir," Private. Emerson explained.

"And if they had aimed at your heads?" Clarke asked incredulously.

"Then we would have acted sooner, sir. We hoped to also give you the chance to act, which you did, sir."

Clarke turned to Master Sergeant White. "You Marines are crazy."

"Sir, thank you, sir!" White replied with a smile.

XLVI

The ships had spread out from the orbit of Darius into orbit around Zarathustra itself. Situated at the edge of the ionosphere, the *F.S.N. Hikaru Hatori* directed the orbital traffic. While Captain Ralph Osborne and his bridge crew supervised the placement of the civilian ships that had been pressed into service, Commodore Napier and Captain Greibenfeld watched the screens intently.

"Do you think it will work, Captain?" Commodore Napier asked.

Greibenfeld suppressed the urge to shrug. "Every single ship, military and not, in orbit around the planet has been equipped with the gravitic-beam generators, and as many of the satellites as we could. We don't have enough to completely cover the planet, as you know, so we concentrated mostly on sealing in the space above Beta Continent. I figure the slavers would just try to shoot straight up until they could go into hyperspace, Commodore."

"That isn't what I asked."

"I just don't know for sure, Commodore. I do think we have a better than even chance of it working, though."

Napier nodded. He thought much the same thing. "Well, at least we have the pinnaces cruising about to improve our odds. They are in as high an orbit as possible without running into the GBG web. Sensors won't spot the slave ships with that cloaking goo on them, but they have a chance of spotting them against the backdrop of the planet."

"Ah, against the daylight side, sir," Greibenfeld pointed out.

Napier let out a long breath. "Yes. Unfortunately, against the night side the bastards will be effectively invisible. Damn them to Niflheim! Still, we could get lucky, and, if we do, the pinnaces are ordered to paint the slave ships with a tracking beacon. Once that is on them, they won't be able to hide even in a black hole."

"Sir, word just came in that the ship attacking the Reservation school has been brought down," Captain Osborne announced. "No casualties on our side."

The crew let out a brief cheer, then went back to work. Napier smiled wolfishly. "If they didn't wipe out the enemy, we'll have people to question. I'm getting a good feeling about this."

"Sir, two of the civilian craft we pressed into service have just gone dark," Ensign Taylor reported.

Osborne went to Taylor's station. "Destroyed?"

Taylor looked over his sensor screens. "Negative, sir. Mass analysis reads that they are intact. Just no power except for the gravity."

Osborne turned to the Ops station. "Send emergency crews with back-up generators to those ships. We need those GBGs back up five minutes ago. Send a security detail with them." He turned to Napier. "This might be the result of enemy action, Commodore."

"Already on the way, sir," Lieutenant Evens reported.

The Commodore walked over to Taylor's station. "What happened to those two ships?"

"I have no information, sir. They just shut down without warning."

"Sir, Science Center Beta reports that they took down a second ship with an...E-M-P cannon?"

Captain Greibenfeld's jaw dropped. "The EMP Cannon," he said. "It must have a lot more range than Grego's boys realized."

"The wave must be pretty dispersed this far out," Commodore Napier said. "We are lucky it only caught two ships."

"They may have caught more," Osborne said. "Remember all the traffic we halted? There are several shuttles, and our own pinnaces, floating around out there. Taylor, plot a trajectory from Science Center Beta and estimate the size of the wave field based on the two ships that were caught in it. Then send out lifeboats to collect anybody who's lost power."

"Sir, won't the lifeboats be powered down if they enter the wave field?"

"Damn, I hadn't thought of that..."

"No problems there," Greibenfeld said. "The EMP is a short burst weapon. It dissipated almost instantly after being fired. Your men will be safe." He caught Napier's quizzical expression. "I do still have some spies in the CZC, sir."

* * *

"*Ich verstehe nicht*," Rheiner grumbled as he tried to power up the shuttle. It was getting chilly and he wanted to start the heating system back up. When that didn't work, he tried the engines.

"Why are we losing heat?" Cinda asked. "This vessel has collapsium shielding on it, doesn't it? I read somewhere that a collapsium-lined freezer could keep food frozen for decades even if the power was shut off."

Rheiner said something in either German or Sosti. Cinda didn't hear it well enough to decide which. "A freezer on a planet vit' a temperate climate is very different from die vacuum of space. Outside it ist absolute zero...or close enough for our situation. If ve vere in direct sunlight, it vould be different. Darius is in der vay. Also, der shuttle is not completely covered in collapsium. *Die Fenster*...uhh...die vindows, for example, und die telemetry gear needs connection into der ship dat cannot be covered vit' collapsium. So, ve are losing about vun degree centigrade per half hour. If der power does not return soon, ve could freeze to deat.'"

Cinda pulled the blanket tighter around her. "What do we do?"

"I am trying to get der emergency beacon activated...och! Is so. Now, ve vait for help to come. Der are many ships in orbit. Vun should come soon."

"What do we do until then," Cinda asked.

"Ve share body heat."

* * *

Tension mounted on the bridge as the communications technician tried the connection for the *nth* time. Finally, he closed the circuit and shook his head. There were whispers and swearing in the background as the captain took his seat.

"Monitor the news services," Captain Shade ordered. "If they were taken down, the marshal and the governor will be crowing about it. And call the bosses. They'll have to hear this whichever way it goes."

"Sir, I am receiving a distress beacon. It is fairly close."

Shade wrestled with himself mentally. The last thing they needed was to get involved with somebody else's problems when there were so many difficulties of their own to address. On the other hand, traditions dating all the way back from the first boat to float on Terra demanded that a distress call be answered. Whatever else he was, Shade was the captain of a ship.

"Helm. Plot a course to the distress beacon. Do we know what we will be looking for?"

After a moment the signals and detection officer answered. "A shuttle from the space yacht *Adonitia*."

Shade thought a moment. "Ah, the private yacht owned by that Freyan half-breed. We'll clear shuttle bay four and collect the craft. Nobody talks about what we are doing here. If possible, I want to drop these people off safely. No point adding to our list of infractions. Plus, if we are detained by the Navy, we can just say we were rescuing the crew. We have no Fuzzies or anything else aboard the ship to say otherwise, except the hostages and they will be kept out of sight. Speaking of which, I think it may be time to dispense with the cloaking paint. It's come to the point where it makes us conspicuous."

Eric Stamp, the security officer, looked hesitant. "If the operation is blown down on the surface, wouldn't we be better off with the cloaking screen?"

"If the operation is blown, and they manage to find us like this, they will know for dead-bang sure that we are part of it. If we lose the cloak, we will just blend in with all the rest of the ships up here. That will be a better shield than sensor invisibility at this point."

Stamp nodded, then said, "I have to agree. We're so close to the edge of the Zarathustra gravity well that we can space out within fifteen minutes after notification."

"What is this about spacing out?"

Shade turned to the owner of the voice and found Clarence Anetrou accompanied by the man in a black hood. "No such order has been given. Yet."

"What is our status, Captain Shade?" the hooded man asked.

"No contact with the ships planet-side, sir. All three have missed their check-in. We are currently monitoring local news broadcasts," Shade summarized as he drummed his fingers on the book that lay on the arm of his captain's chair.

"Not the police bands?" the hooded man asked.

"On this world they are all encoded and work on a variable frequency," Shade replied. "I believe this is something the local marshal instituted prior to the Fuzzy trial a few years ago."

Anetrou nodded. "A couple of the Mallorysport cops were involved in a fiasco involving a ten-year-old girl in an attempt to make the Fuzzies less sympathetic. While they were looking for the rogue cops, Fane ordered the police bandwidth to be scrambled so they wouldn't be able to evade capture by listening in. This has also kept the news services from running stories about active cases as well."

"There is something odd going on," Shade said. "All the ships that were in orbit around Darius have moved into geosynchronous orbit around the planet." Shade tapped a few keys on his command chair console and the screen changed. "This screen shows the current locations of those ships."

The hooded man and Anetrou studied the image for a moment, then Anetrou spoke. "Is it just me or do those positions seem a bit regular, like a pattern?"

"Very much so," Captain Shade confirmed. "Staying clear of the satellite zone makes sense, yet the positions these ships have taken would require more power to retain their places. And they are all as exactly distant from one another as they can get."

"Is it like that all the way around Zarathustra?" the hooded man asked.

"We cannot scan past the planet itself. However, I see no reason to suppose it will be any different there," Shade said.

The man wearing the hood fidgeted a bit. "And still no contact with the other three ships?"

Shade looked at the communications officer who shook his head. "None."

The hooded man shook his head slowly. "Time to scram. Prepare to make for Terra with all due speed—"

"We cannot."

The man wearing the hood turned to the captain. "What?"

"We are rendering assistance to a distressed shuttle. The rules of space are very clear on this."

"Are you nuts! We're all looking at a bullet in the head, and you want to play hero for some idiots who got themselves' what: adrift, holed by a meteorite, or are in some other trouble…?"

Captain Shade stood and faced the hooded man. He picked up his book as he did so. "Sir, while my record was far from spotless during my career as a ship's captain, which led me to my current position, some rules are simply not to be broken. There is a vessel in distress, and we will be rendering aid." Shade smiled and waved a hand at the bridge crew. "You are within your rights to discharge me and appoint another captain. I suggest you make certain that they won't follow my example."

The hooded man looked around the bridge. Every person on it quickly turned to look at something of great interest at their stations. Even the security officer managed to busy himself with something. He turned away, and stormed off the bridge followed by Anetrou.

Captain Shade fought to keep his relief hidden. "Thank you, gentlemen. No matter how this turns out, know that you have acted in the best tradition of spacefaring vessels." Shade returned to his seat and set his book down. "Now, let's burn off that cloaking cover and rescue some people. And I hope to Ghu that they are worthy of our assistance."

XLVII

"I think the...air is getting...stuffy," Cinda gasped out. Her face was pale and her lips were beginning to turn blue.

Rheiner cursed his own ignorance in Sosti. "Vit' die...power off, die...air scrubbers are not...vorking. Ve haff an...hours vort' of...air left, I t'ink. Ve vill pass out...in about fifteen minutes...den slowly die of hypoxia. Dere are vorst...vays to die."

Cinda snuggled closer to Rheiner under the blanket, as much to comfort him as to keep warm. "Maybe the...beacon will work...and bring somebody...to help."

"Maybe."

Cinda looked out the forward window. "At least we...have a ...great view."

Rheiner smiled and looked out at the stars. Then something drew his attention. "*Was ist das?*"

Cinda tried harder to focus. It took a moment before she could distinguish the white ball growing larger from the stars. "A ship!" Cinda jumped up, only to become dizzy and fall back into Rheiner's arms.

They watched in hopeful fascination as a bay door slid upwards, relative to their perspective, and swallowed the entire shuttle. It was a disorienting moment as the shuttle turned and aligned with the internal gravity of the ship.

"Wait...how will they...open the hatch?"

Rheiner didn't have time to answer. The hatch was opened from the emergency manual controls outside. As fresh reconditioned air swept in, Cinda felt giddy. She stood up and let the blanket fall away.

"Ah, Cinda—"

Cinda was ready to run forward and give the man at the door a hug until she noticed the look of surprise on his face.

"Cinda. Your clozing," Rheiner said.

She looked down and was reminded that she and Rheiner had stripped down to their underclothing beneath the blanket to better share their body heat. Rheiner quickly wrapped the blanket around her, giving no thought to his own state of undress.

"Mein Herr, a moment please?"

The man at the hatch smiled as he removed his protective gloves. "Take your time, sir. I quite understand. Be careful exiting the shuttle... the exterior is still dangerously cold."

Rheiner thanked the man and went back in to gather his clothes. The man at the hatch turned to his fellows. "Whew! Remember our orders; we play nice and don't abuse our guests. Nobody talks about what we are doing out here. Captain's orders."

"Whoa!" agreed the second man. "I'd like to abuse her a bit, but not with that gorilla she has with her. My momma didn't raise no fools."

The other two men also nodded to that sentiment. When Cinda and Rheiner stepped out of the shuttle, they were met by four very polite men ready to escort them to guest quarters. They started to the door that led to the main corridor when it opened from the outside.

"Cinda!"

Cinda screamed, more in surprise than fright. "That's him! That's the hooded man I saw in the woods."

Mr. Hood did some screaming of his own. "Grab her!"

Before their sense of self-preservation kicked in, the four men attempted to follow orders. They were met by an angry Rheiner. Seizing the first man with one hand, the burly Freyan threw his hapless victim into a second. The next two attempted to grab him only to be thrown back several feet.

Rheiner spun around to face the hooded man. He felt something sting him in the shoulder and chest. It took a moment to process that he had been shot. It didn't stop him.

"Dat's a twenty-two, *nicht wahr*? All nice and safe for use inside of a ship." Rheiner smiled menacingly. "Not so gut against muscles designed for heavy gravity."

The hooded man stepped back and took two more shots. They struck the Freyan in the chest and leg. Rheiner just moved forward.

"All right," he said, shifting his aim to Cinda. "Shall we see if your girlfriend is as resilient as you?"

Rheiner stopped. Fast as he was, he couldn't move to block the shot in time. He let out the breath he hadn't even been aware he was holding. "I surrender. For now. Hurt her und not'ing vill stop me from ripping your head right off your neck."

"I believe you," the hooded man said. "Now back up and allow my men to restrain you."

Cinda watched with a mix of anger and horror as Rheiner was shackled. One of the men actually apologized for it. Cinda turned to the hooded man. "He needs a doctor!"

"Humph. He'll get one...as long as he behaves." The hooded man ordered his men to double the shackles. One man argued that even a Magnian couldn't break out of the chains. "Best not to take any chances with that one. We'll put them with the others."

* * *

Patricia was putting the final touches on the scarf she was knitting when the door opened. She cursed under her breath for not being ready. Betty looked at her and she shook her head.

"Ladies, we have some more guests. I do hope you will make them feel welcome."

Betty looked at the hooded man and broke out with laughter. "Look, Pat, it's Halloween. Who are you supposed to be? The Lone Ranger?"

"Wrong kind of mask, dear," Patricia corrected. "You'll need to know the difference if you keep dating Jack. He takes his old Westerns very seriously. This,"—Patricia pointed at Mr. Hood—"would be the big boss, too worried about his underlings being put in the veridicator to let them see his face."

"Very good, madam," the hooded man returned. "You should be grateful for my cautious nature. If you could identify me, I would have to remove you from my list of worries."

Rheiner and Cinda were pushed into the room. The Freyan collapsed on the floor and Cinda rushed to help him. Betty also moved to assist.

"What did this man do?" Patricia asked. "Insult your fashion sense? I think he has a point."

The hooded man chuckled. "Mrs. McLeod, I think we could get on under different circumstances. I will be sure to send a medic for our injured friend."

"And something to eat would be nice. I have low blood sugar and it has been a while since the last meal."

"I will see to it personally." He nodded politely and left.

After the door closed Patricia joined the others in tending to Rheiner. "Good God, son. What did they do to you?"

"He's been shot," Cinda sniffed. "Several times."

"Shot?" Patricia looked over the wounds. There was blood, but not much of it and the wounds looked minor. "With what? A BB gun?"

"A twenty-two," Rheiner corrected. "Da bullets didn't penetrate far into mein muscles, but it still hurts like all of *Grenwor.*"

Patricia didn't know what Grenwor was and assumed it was Freyan hell. She could well believe it. "Lucky for you your body was built for hard labor on Magni. Four of these wounds would have been fatal for anybody else."

"*Was?* How did you..."

"I met Johann and Heidi," Patricia explained. "I think you know Betty, here."

"Only by reputation...as Herr Hollovay's close friend."

"We need to get these shackles off of him," Cinda said as she choked back her sobs.

Patricia dug through her purse. All she had was an old style ink pen, her medication, some cosmetics, a comb, brush, cash card, and other odds and ends that only made sense for a woman to carry. "Hmm. They let me keep the knitting gear but confiscated the sewing kit. We might have been able to pick the lock with the sewing needles."

"Only one of these shackles uses a key," Cinda pointed out. "The other has a mag-lock."

"We'll deal with them one at a time," Betty said. "Pat, does that pen have a spring in it?"

"Yes. This is an antique I picked up on Baldur on the way here."

Betty took the pen. "I'll have to get you a new one. This one is about to get damaged." Betty disassembled the pen and straightened out the spring as best she could. "I used to pick the lock on my older sister's diary with something like this. Hopefully the lock on this thing works the same way." After ten minutes of cursing and struggling with the lock, it finally came off the left wrist. "I can't do anything about the mag-lock, I'm afraid."

Rheiner sat up and tried to break the remaining shackle to no avail. "My vounds haff veakend me. Und I can't bring mein full strengt' vit' mein hands behind me like dis."

"Let's get you on your feet," Patricia said. "Okay, Cinda, come over here, Betty you take the other side. Now grab the cuff...not his wrist... and when I say 'go,' Rheiner will try to pull the chain apart while we help. Maybe two young girls and an old lady is all he needs to get the job done. Now, ready?"

"Go!"

It took several seconds of effort, then a link in the chain cracked open. Patricia was dizzy and had to sit down, but the job was done. Betty maneuvered the opened link off the chain and Rheiner was free to move his arms.

"*Danke schoen.* Ah, dis may be a bit unpleasant to see." Rheiner pinched the flesh around the wound on his shoulder and the bullet popped out amid curses in Sosti. He repeated the action on his leg. "Och, dat helps a bit. I can't get die rest out dat vey, t'ough."

"Where is that damned medic Greg promised?" Cinda cried.

Patricia, Betty and Rheiner all spoke simultaneously. "Greg?"

Cinda sat down next to Patricia. "Yeah. Greg Rutherford. I recognized his voice. Oh, well, at least it isn't Dmitri."

"Whatever you do, do not say his name again!" Patricia warned.

"We will have to hope this room isn't bugged. Just call him Mr. Hood... or something less pleasant if you are of the mind. Now, let us talk about how we are going to—"

The door slid open to reveal a man in white medical gear accompanied by four armed men. Rheiner leaned against the wall with his arms behind his back.

"Oh, good," Patricia said. "Rheiner is getting weak from blood loss. Can you help him?"

The medic nodded. "If you'll lie down...."

"Dat is very uncomfortable vit' mein arms shackled. I vill stand vhile you take out der bullets. Dey are not deep."

The medic looked squeamish as he worked.

XLVIII

"The beacon is gone, Commodore," Captain Osborne reported, with a worried expression.

Napier wanted to say something vile and restrained himself. High ranking officers didn't show frustration in front of the men. "Do what you can to find that vessel, Captain."

Osborne gave a 'yessir' and went to the signals and detection station to relay the command.

"It's my fault all those shuttles and yachts are in harm's way, damn-it!"

"Sir, we are limited by what we have. This is a backwater planet five hundred light-years from Fleet Command. Our nearest back-up is on Gimli, a four-month round trip away." Greibenfeld pointed to the viewscreen. "Those civilian ships out there are all we have. As for the shuttles and cruisers we ordered to stay in place, well, how can we know which, if any, have those sons-of-Khooghras on them? Each and every one has to be inspected. We have done nothing outside the scope of our authority."

"Shuttles, small ones, anyway, have a limited power supply," Napier said. "That beacon could have come from one that ran out of juice."

"I sent out pinnaces with portable generators to repower any drifting shuttles," Greibenfeld said. "They may have already found and assisted the source of the beacon."

"Then why haven't they reported it?"

Greibenfeld had no ready answer for that.

* * *

The globe blazed a bright red. Below the globe sat the man called Steg, squirming uncomfortably. Before him stood Jack Holloway and Piet Dumont. Behind the commissioner and deputy stood Little Fuzzy,

Emily, Mike, Koko, Mama Fuzzy, Baby Fuzzy, Mitzi, and Cinderella. None of them looked happy.

"I don't know, Piet," Jack said. "Maybe we should just let the Fuzzies handle it."

"Hmm...technically, this is Fuzzy land, hence their laws apply," Piet said. "Red Fur up north has shown he can handle dispensing justice. You think your gang down here could be trusted to do the same?"

On cue, Little Fuzzy started yeeking, quickly joined by the others. There was also a great deal of waving of chopper-diggers and pointing at the prisoner. Steg seemed to shrink into himself a bit.

"Alright! I'll talk!" Steg screamed. His terror was genuine, as the globe above revealed with its bright blue glow. Stories about what had happened up north had made the rounds.

"I still think we should let the Fuzzies have him," Piet Dumont said.

"It's still on the table," Jack followed. "Now, state your name for the record."

"Stephoni Costner." Blue.

"How many other ships are there?"

"I dunno. Four is all I know about. There could be others." Blue.

"What is the name of the top boss?"

"I don't know that either. One wears a damnthing mask, the other a black hood. There is another guy in a suit, but I don't know his name, either." Blue.

The questioning went on for a while. Jack would ask some questions, then Piet took his turn. Little Fuzzy and the rest watched the entire time with their weapons at the ready. Finally, Jack decided he had enough for now.

"We'll let George Lunt handle the rest," Jack decided. "Better let Agent Trask have a go at them as well."

"Where are we going to put all these Khooghras?" Piet asked.

The local lock-up, originally designed to handle six prisoners, had been expanded to hold up to a dozen two years earlier. The complement of a space yacht was a minimum of twenty, and there were the crews of the other two captured ships to be detained.

"We'll let the Marines on loan from Napier handle it POW-style until we can get some transports in from Mallorysport," Jack decided. He threw a meaningful glance at Steg. "If we are lucky, some of them will do something stupid and save us the cost of a trial. I just wish Pat and Betty had been on one of the ships we captured."

Piet nodded. "Well, the Suit he mentioned would have to be Spike Heenan. Officer Clarke's team grabbed him up north on that third ship. I'll wager he knows more than this mutt."

Steg knew he was already dead for his involvement in the Fuzzy slaving operation. All he needed to do was put on a good suit and lay down. Still, he wanted to delay the inevitable for as long as possible. Cooperation seemed like the safest way to go.

"Mr. Holloway, I do know one other thing and I will tell you in exchange for a deal."

*   *   *

"The fourth ship should be in orbit around the planet," Greibenfeld reported. "According to one of Jack's prisoners, they will try to make a break into hyperspace the second they know for sure what the statuses are of the others."

Commodore Napier thought about it. "We could staff the captured ships with our people and try to rendezvous with the fourth ship...if it really exists."

"Why would you think it doesn't? The prisoners were questioned under veridication."

"They could have been given misinformation."

Greibenfeld shook his head. "These people would say they have fewer ships, not more. We captured three ships. It is to their advantage to say there are no more in the hopes that the fourth ship could stage a rescue. In a war you want the enemy to think you are stronger than you are to keep them from attacking before you are ready. This is the reverse; by us thinking they are weaker than they are they could pull some sort of surprise attack on us."

Napier thought it over and had to agree with the captain's logic. "Do you think that they will?"

"Not a chance," Greibenfeld said. "The second they know for sure that the operation is blown they'll space out for parts unknown and go to ground. The Navy is still the greatest force on this world and these bastards have to know that. That bunch Jack and the rest captured are all whistling in a graveyard hoping for a dawn that will not come."

Napier was about to say something when Captain Osborne approached.

"Sir, we have an anomaly on the sensors," Osborne said. "A ship in the general area of the beacon we were tracking."

"One of the tourists?" Greibenfeld asked.

"I don't see how," Osborne said. "We tagged and pressed into service every ship in orbit."

"Is it possible our people missed one?" Napier asked.

"Doubtful, sir."

Napier turned to Greibenfeld. "Our fourth ship?"

"Maybe, but why are they visible to sensors? Did they remove the cloaking paint? If so...?"

"Why would they do that?" Napier finished the question.

"Reverse camouflage," Captain Osborne said. "If they know we captured the ships on the surface, then they know that we know about the cloaking paint. It would be to their advantage to blend in with the locals. They have no way of knowing that we pressed all the other ships into service."

"I think he is on to something there, sir," Greibenfeld said.

"Captain, I think we should pay a social call on this anomaly."

"Commodore, there is one other thing," Greibenfeld said. "Jack's sister and lady friend have to be on this ship, if these are who we think they are."

Napier cursed.

* * *

"I gave those men strict orders that everybody on that craft was to be treated as respected guests!" the Captain shouted.

The hooded man took a step back from Captain Shade's verbal assault. Then his own anger flared up. "I'm the bloody owner of this ship and my orders supersede yours. Besides, one of them was the girl who spotted me speaking on the portable back on Zeta Continent. She is dangerous and needs to be dealt with."

"You were shot at leaving the planet," Shade countered. "If they don't already know who you are they will figure it out once they start counting noses and find yours absent. The girl can't do you any more harm than has already been done."

The hooded man crossed his arms. "Very well. Recharge her shuttle and send her on her way. She hasn't seen too many of us...."

Captain Shade glared at the man wearing the hood, "You know I can't do that now. Her companion has been shot several times. He might die of his injuries. Great Gehenna, I am amazed he hasn't already! What was intended to be a rescue, has now turned into an act of piracy. Guess what piracy earns you if convicted? Death by hanging for every member of the crew! I swore an oath to treat fairly with these men and women under my command. You have placed them all in jeopardy. By rights I should have you spaced."

Shade raised his book as if to throw it at the hooded man, then set it down carefully. The hooded man noticed that it was an ancient copy of *Moby Dick*.

"Seriously? Enslavement doesn't bother you but you draw the line at accidental piracy?"

In the background of the captain's office Clarence Anetrou watched the display before him. It was never good when partners or clients fought. It often ended in a division of assets in his experience. Something would have to be done and done quickly.

Anetrou left the loud 'discussion' and headed down the corridor. By the time he reached his destination, his decision was made.

* * *

Rheiner finished his sixth tin of Terran Federation Space Forces Emergency Ration, Extraterrestrial, Type Three with some distaste. Nobody but a Fuzzy liked the stuff. Rheiner, with his extreme bulk and high metabolism, needed more food than his captors were prepared to provide so Betty managed to sweet talk one of them into bringing the Extee Three. While unpleasant tasting, there was no denying the nutritional value.

Patricia idly noticed that the maker's mark on the bottom of the tin proclaimed it to be a product of Odin Dietetics. She absently dropped the tin into her knitting bag.

"I know this isn't something you will like to do—"

"Relax, Pat. I do racier stuff at the clubs," Betty said. "At least I used to before I met your brother."

"I'm up for anything that has a chance to get us out of here alive," Cinda added.

Patricia nodded. "Okay, then. Rheiner, get back up against the wall so they won't see that your arms are free. Great Ghu! I should have realized that is a two-way mirror. Hopefully, they haven't been watching us. Ladies, get ready. They could show up at any time. Rheiner, don't let yourself be distracted."

"Mein oat' to Gormond, god of battle, I shall be prepared," Rheiner said. "Mein last meal has set me in die right mood even vit'out die danger to all of you."

Betty laughed. "After six tins of Extee Three, I imagine you want to kill a lot of people."

"Chust our captors," Rheiner said. "Und maybe die people who make dat stuff."

* * *

"Remember, our story is that we are escorting them to their shuttle and letting them go," Anetrou reminded his men. "Once we get them to the shuttle bay, it's out the airlock."

One man shook his head. "Seems like a damn shame. The dark-haired one seems like she would be a lot of fun. The redhead ain't bad either. I was here when Nick opened the hatch and we all caught an eyeful."

Anetrou rolled his eyes. "Yes, such a shame, we are only thieves and murderers—not rapists." They came to the prisoners' room door. "Remind me to have some actual cells set up in the cargo hold in case this ever happens again."

"You think it could? I thought once we spaced out we were all going to separate and spread out."

Anetrou found himself wishing the men had a better sense of irony. "Never mind. Just open the door. Keep your tranq-guns handy. Hopefully they will be more effective against that gorilla in there than the .22s were. They only seemed to make him mad."

"Yeah, I was there," another man said. "I sure as Niflheim don't want him mad at me again. I still ache from that wall he threw me into."

"Yeah, no kidding," a third man said. "Where is he from, anyway? I've seen Magnians who weren't as buff as this guy."

"There are over five hundred colonized worlds in the Federation," Anetrou said. "There have to be a few with higher gravity than Magni settled by masochists with back braces. Wherever this guy is from, he's worth his weight in Thorans, so don't take any chances. I don't trust those shackles to keep him docile. Whatever you do, watch him closely and for the love of Ghu, don't get distracted by the women. They might try some phony fainting routine to give the gorilla a chance to plow into you."

Everybody agreed to be on their guard.

*   *   *

Captain Shade took his seat in the captain's chair. Once the shouting stopped, he and the hooded man agreed to simply leave the planet and drop their captives off at some random colony world. It was now six hours past the check-in time for the other ships, forcing them to conclude that they had been captured or destroyed.

"Helm, take us straight up and make ready to enter hyperspace," Shade ordered. "We're blowing this popsicle stand. Take her up nice and easy, no point looking like we are in a hurry."

The helmsman laid in a course for Vishnu while navigation worked out the path out of the atmosphere. Gimli was the nearest colony to Zarathustra, and the first place the Space Navy would search. It was necessary to get well away from any gravity well that might interfere with the Dillinghams before transitioning into hyperspace. Even a lunar satellite as small as Xerxes could disrupt the hyperspace matrix, preventing them from leaving normal space.

The viewscreen display showed stars moving downward. After several minutes the screens started to waver. The Signals and Detection Officer's fingers quickly danced across the console. The screen resolution continued to degrade.

"What the hell is going on?" Captain Shade demanded.

"There seems to be something scrambling all the displays. We are flying blind at the moment."

Shade knew instantly what must be happening. "It's the damn Navy. They are on to us. Can we hit hyperspace, yet?"

The signals and detection mate shook his head. "No way to know, sir. I can't even be sure the ship is still in motion."

Attempting to enter hyperspace too close to a gravity well could easily have unpredictable results. Those who had tried in the past variously underwent Dillingham failure, implosion, or just vanished never to be seen again. Shade balanced the possibilities against the certainty of what would happen if they were all brought in and tried for slavery.

"Let's try our luck. Transpose now."

Nervously, the helm officer tried. Nothing happened. The entire bridge let out a sigh of relief.

"Still too close to Zarathustra, sir."

"Damn," Shade said under his breath. "So, we are flying blind and can't enter hyperspace. Keep taking us up until we can. It is our only chance, now."

XLIX

"We are at maximum sensor range, sir," the Signals and Detection Officer reported.

Captain Osborne nodded. "Commodore, as we get closer to the mystery craft our sensors will become vulnerable to the distortion field created by the GBG. We will be as blind as they are."

Napier nodded. That was the drawback of the Gravity-Beam Generator Web, it blinded friend and foe alike. "Do we have any way of manually observing them?"

"One, but it isn't very efficient." Osborne nodded to the Signals and Detection Officer. A new viewscreen lowered over the first. "This screen is for the old-style telescopes. Regs require we still keep these operational in case the telemetry is destroyed."

Captain Greibenfeld raised an eyebrow. "You don't have backup telemetry?"

"Five units," Osborne replied. "In a battle or a debris field they could still all be destroyed. The telescope is behind durapane and better protected than the telemetry units. However, it wouldn't withstand a near miss from an atomic missile or a direct hit from a large heavy object like a meteorite or rail gun projectile. We also have a limited sight picture."

Napier shook his head and smiled. "It's never easy, is it? Well, let's get to it."

*   *   *

Rheiner stood with his ear firmly pressed against the door. His hearing, while not anywhere near as good as a dog's, was still at the uppermost range for a human or Freyan. The genetic manipulation performed on his people had raised not only their strength and endurance to the highest levels, but their sensory apparatus as well.

"Somevun ist coming, und I do not like vhat dey are saying about vhat dey intend to do vit' us," Rheiner said as he moved to the opposite wall. "If ve are to do anyt'ing, now ist der time."

Patricia pulled out her knitting needle while Betty and Cinda prepared themselves. Taking up a position next to the door, Patricia steeled herself for what was to come.

The door opened and the men filed in purposefully then stopped in surprise. Their eyes were locked on the two women naked to the waist. Patricia used that moment of shock to drive her knitting needle up into the soft tissue under the jaw of the lead man. More by luck than design, the needle slid up through the sinus cavity into the brain, killing the man instantly.

This added to the general surprise causing the men to hesitate further before acting. That was their undoing.

Rheiner rushed forward like an enraged bull. He plowed over the still falling first man into the others behind him. He wanted to roar in his rage as he punched and kicked his way through his captors. Instead, he kept silent, knowing that any noise could bring more men. He was still weak and sore from his injuries and didn't want to fight any more people than he had to in making their escape.

Behind Rheiner, Patricia grabbed up a tranq-gun and started shooting into the melee. She hit one man who was trying to stay out of the fray and he collapsed almost instantly. Betty and Cinda picked up two more fallen weapons only to find the fight was over.

"We need to shove these bodies into the room and lock the door," Patricia said. "We don't want anybody finding them too soon."

"I vill attend to dis," Rheiner said. It took more effort than he would admit. Nevertheless he threw all the men, dead and alive, into the room quickly.

"Thank you, Rheiner." Patricia turned to Betty and Cinda. "I think you can zip up, now."

Betty zipped up like it was perfectly normal to be standing in an open corridor half-naked. Cinda was a little more flustered. Rheiner kept his gaze politely averted as the women redressed themselves.

"The shuttle bays are that way," Cinda pointed. "We can take our shuttle out and—"

"Our shuttle ist disabled, Cinda," Rheiner reminded her. "Der is no reason to t'ink dat dey vould repair it. Ve must take a different shuttle."

"I need my samples," Cinda insisted.

"You need your life a whole lot more, young lady," Patricia said. "You can get more samples later. You can't get another life." *We should have worked this out before escaping*, Patricia thought.

Cinda grudgingly conceded the point. "Fine. Let's get the Niflheim out of here. And if they ever make a movie about this, they better leave the part about us exposing ourselves on the cutting room floor."

"Hey, do you think Darla Cross could play me?" Betty said, with a wink.

They moved down the corridor hugging the walls. Rheiner took point and listened for anything that might indicate more men were coming. Twice they had to shoot a tranq-dart into somebody in the corridor. Lacking the time to hide the bodies, they left them where they fell. After a few near misses they found the first shuttle bay. In it a shuttle covered in black paint sat hooked-up to several cables.

"*Scheisse*! It ist being recharged," Rheiner complained. "Ve haff no vay of knowing how much power it vould haff."

"Can't we just, I don't know, turn it on and read a gauge?" Betty asked.

"*Ja*, if you vant der bridge to know ve are here."

"We don't have time to look, anyway," Patricia said. "Let's just head over to the next bay and hope for better."

They arrived at the second bay without being noticed. This time the shuttle was not attached to any cables. Rheiner led the way to the hatch and used the manual release to open it. "Get inside. Be ready to close der hatch if I cannot get back qvickly enough."

"What do you mean?" Cinda demanded.

"Der bay door opens eit'er from die main bridge, or from der manual control in dat section over dere. It is closed off because die air must be sucked out before die doors open. Put on die protective suits und strap yourselves down. I vill open die doors und try to make it beck after die air ist removed. If I cannot, you must go vit' out me."

Cinda turned to Patricia and Betty. "Either of you two know how to pilot a shuttle?"

Neither did. "I can't either. No Rheiner, no escape."

Rheiner swore again, this time in Sosti. "Dis is turning into a terrible escape. Very vell. Put on der suits und strap in. I vill make it beck. I must."

The women complied as Rheiner forced open the door to the shuttle bay control room. He waited until Cinda gave him a thumbs up that they were ready, then activated the atmosphere controls. As the air was removed from the bay, he took a series of deep, controlled breaths. When the panel indicated that the air was gone, he toggled the door controls. The ceiling, relative to the shuttle, retracted to reveal the stars of open space.

Now comes der fun part, Rheiner thought. He grabbed a protective suit from the wall and removed the helmet. The suit would not fit him so he discarded it. The helmet would be useless for anything other than protecting his head from impact injury without the suit. Rheiner knew this and put it on. The part around the neck automatically formed a seal around his neck. Normally, it would have attached itself to the suit had it been present.

Grabbing onto the console panel as tightly as he could, and even bending the metal in the process, Rheiner opened the door. The sudden rush of air from the explosive decompression slammed Rheiner about as he hung on and exhaled all the air in his lungs. Once the air was completely expelled into the vacuum of space, Rheiner ran for the shuttle.

Each step was a study in agony. The sweat on his body froze instantly and even his genetically enhanced strength provided little protection from the forces working on his body. Halfway to the shuttle door he could feel the blood in his veins start to boil. Had he not exhaled all the air from his lungs he would start exploding from the inside out. The helmet allowed him to retain enough air so that his body heat kept his eyes from freezing in his head.

Just as he reached the hatch he felt himself starting to lose consciousness. He fought to keep his senses as he tried to climb into the shuttle. He heard the shuttle door opening and air rushing out....

"Sir, Shuttle Bay Two is open."

Captain Shade was about to issue an order when he was interrupted by the Signals and Detection Officer.

"Sir, I can't be certain...I think we have company."

"You think?"

"The scanners are still bollixed up, sir. I can only get a faint reading through all the noise. It looks like...I can't be certain. I think it is a destroyer-class ship, sir."

"Red alert," Shade yelled. "Battle stations."

Rheiner regained consciousness on the floor of the shuttle. First he was surprised to be alive. Then he became aware of all the pain he was in and considered the benefits of being dead.

"Rheiner!"

The Freyan managed to focus on the face floating above his own. It was Cinda yelling at him. He noticed that she was flushed, sweating and out of breath. Also, her helmet was off. Memories rushed back in a flood of the situation and he struggled to get up.

"Vhat heppened?"

"You collapsed on the hatch," Cinda explained. "We managed to pull you far enough into the hatch so that its closing would bring you the rest of the way inside, then pressurized the cabin."

"If the hatch hadn't closed upward and pushed you in, we would have never been able to bring you inside," Patricia added. "It was all the three of us could do to get you partway into the damn thing!"

Rheiner was unable to stand on his own. With great effort, the three women helped him up and over to the pilot's seat. Through the forward window he could see red lights flashing.

"I t'ink ve haff been found out. Dat is a red alert."

Patricia nodded. "Well, it has been a lovely visit and we had a lot of fun, but I really think it is time to go."

"I agree." Rheiner started up the contragravity and Abbott Lift and Drive and hit the power. The shuttle launched straight up so quickly that Patricia and Cinda were forced down onto the floor. Betty collapsed into a seat. "Mein apologies, *Frau* and *Fräulein*. Please mehke yourselves comfortable und strap in. It ist going to be a bumpy ride."

Cinda helped Patricia to a seat before taking one herself. "Are you okay, Pat? That was a bad jolt."

"Oh, I've survived worse. I am only upset about one thing."

"Only one?" Cinda asked.

"Yeah. I had to leave my favorite knitting needle behind."

* * *

Jack paced back and forth in his office in frustration. Communications had been lost between Xerxes base and the *F.S.N. Hikaru Hatori*. While this was anticipated as a possibility, it still chafed being kept in the dark.

Morgan walked in and narrowly missed being bowled over. "Father?"

Jack looked Morgan in the eye. "Pat's still missing, Morgan. Odds are she is on that fourth ship. If she is, and they start shooting at the Navy ship, Napier will have no choice other than to blow them out of the sky."

"I understand. Do we have a last known position of the *Hatori*?"

"Gerd's boys are tracking the whole mess from Science Center Beta. Whatever they are using up there that caused the communications blackout doesn't extend down to the planet surface. We know exactly where they are."

Morgan smiled. He looked even more like his father when he did that. "Well, with every other ship around the planet working with the Navy doing Gormand knows what, why don't we go up there and give Commodore Napier a hand?"

Jack's face wavered between confusion and annoyance. "How do we do that? Your yacht is up there with the rest doing Ghu knows what."

"This is true. It is also true that we have ready access to three more ships." Morgan glanced meaningfully at the window.

Jack looked and spotted the black slaver ship Little Fuzzy's team had captured. He smiled wolfishly. "So we do."

L

"Sir! We have a visual of the bogey," the Signals and Detection Officer cried out.

Captain Osborne tried to make out the ship on the screen. To his eyes it all looked like an unvaried starscape. After a moment he noticed one of the stars getting larger. He also spotted a small dark spot on the 'star.' "Is that it right there?"

"Yes, sir."

"What is that dark spot?"

"Sir?"

Osborne pointed to the viewscreen. "That spot right there."

Commodore Napier and Captain Greibenfeld stepped close to the screen for a better look while the Signals and Detection Officer worked to get a better view up. Greibenfeld watched intently as the growing 'star' resolved into a ship. The dark spot, he noticed, was lifting out of a shuttle bay.

"That has to be a shuttle with cloaking goo on it," Greibenfeld said.

Napier nodded in agreement. "I wonder why they dispensed with the cloak on the ship. They had us stymied pretty well with that."

"Until we caught their confederates and found out about it," Greibenfeld ventured. "Once we knew what to look for, the captain or owner of the ship may have decided looking like all the other ships made for better camouflage."

"And the shuttle?"

Greibenfeld was at a loss. "Maybe some of the crew saw us coming and decided to jump ship."

"Maybe. I want to talk to whoever is on board that shuttle."

Osborne didn't have to be told what to do twice; he was already in action. "I want a squadron of pinnaces out there to box in that shuttle and bring it in."

"Sir," the Security Officer spoke up, "It might be a trick. If we bring that shuttle in it might go nuclear."

"Damn. Excellent point, Baker. And we can't shoot it out of the sky because, for all we know, it might be filled with Fuzzies."

Captain Osborne thought for a second. "All right, escort the shuttle down away from the GBG web and try to raise it on the comm. If they don't respond, tell the squadron leader to do as he thinks best."

"Yes, sir."

*   *   *

Rheiner fought to stay conscious as he piloted the shuttle away from the ship. He felt severe pain in his shoulders, elbows, knees and ankles as well as itching around the ears, face, neck, arms and upper torso. His vision would become blurred for several seconds at a time and he would have to blink furiously to refocus.

Had their situation been less dire, Rheiner would have simply allowed the shuttle to drift until he could function. With the slave ship below he couldn't wait to recover, if he even could without medical attention. He needed a decompression chamber at the very least. He thanked every one of the gods of Freya that the controls were all on the panel and not on the floor; he could no longer feel his legs or move them.

Cinda came over to rub his shoulders. It hurt so much he couldn't help wincing at her touch.

"Are you okay?"

"I vill live...long enough to see you all safe."

Patricia came over and put a hand on his shoulder. "Tell me if this hurts or helps." She pressed hard against the shoulder joint.

"Och, dat vas better until you stopped."

"I'm afraid you have decompression sickness," Patricia said. "There are also signs of frostbite on your fingers, and I'll bet your toes as well. You need immediate medical attention. I don't care how tough you are, you're lucky to still be alive."

"What is that?" Betty said as she pointed out the window. Everyone looked to see six pinnaces surrounding the shuttle." Are those more of the hooded man's ships coming to get us?"

Patricia laughed. "Those are Federation Space Navy pinnaces."

"How do you know?" Betty asked.

"I was a Navy wife for fifteen years, dear heart. I even got to ride in a few of those things. Commodore Napier must have sent them out."

"Why are they surrounding us?" Cinda asked.

Patricia had to think a moment before answering. "Because this is one of Mr. Hood's...excuse me, Mr. Rutherford's shuttles, and those Navy or Marine pilots don't know us from a bush-goblin. See if you can raise them on the comm, Rheiner."

"*Jawohl*." Rheiner tried, getting only static for his trouble. "No *gut*."

"Then we just go wherever they want us to...wait, do we have a torch in here?" Betty, Cinda and Patricia quickly scoured the cabin for a flashlight. Betty found one and gave it to Patricia. "I hope I remember how to do this."

Patricia walked over to the forward window and flashed the light on and off. After several tense minutes one of the pinnaces moved ahead and spun around to face them head on. A light flashed back. After several exchanges, Patricia took her seat and dropped the flashlight.

"Follow the pinnaces to the Navy ship," Patricia said. "My Morse Code is rusty, but I managed to let them know who we are. I expect we will have an armed greeting party. I'm fine with that."

"*Ja*! I vill be happy to go vit' dem."

Patricia slumped in her seat and started to breathe shallowly. Betty noticed and became worried. "Better make it quick, big guy. I think something is wrong with Pat."

* * *

"The shuttle escaped with the aid of six Navy pinnaces, Captain."

"How do you know that?"

"Baldwin in shuttle bay three opened the bay doors and saw the whole thing through field glasses."

Captain Shade swore silently under his breath. It wouldn't do for the men to see him lose his composure. "There go our hostages. Oh, well, hiding behind women's skirts is no fit way for a man to act.

"Are communications still down?"

"Yes, sir, they are."

"Then it is time to make a break for it. Full speed away from the planet. The minute we can make hyperspace, do so. AND SHUT THOSE GHU DAMNED BAY DOORS! Tactical, arm the missiles. Signals and detection, get somebody to look out a portal as long as we are flying blind. Hopefully, the Navy ship is as bad off as we are."

Assuming they aren't the ones causing the comm failure, Shade added to himself. "If the Navy ship follows, be prepared to fire on my command."

Now to find out which of us is Ahab and which is the whale.

* * *

"Morse Code? That was brilliant," Captain Greibenfeld said. "I used to wonder why we still taught it at the academy. No more! I'm a believer."

"That husky young man is in pretty bad shape," Commodore Napier noted. "Decompression sickness, frostbite, numerous internal hemorrhages, several gunshot wounds, and yet he still piloted that shuttle like a pro...I would like to get a few hundred more like him in the Navy. What do we know about Holloway's sister?"

"She is unconscious," Greibenfeld said. "According to Miss Kanazawa—"

"Sir, the ship is starting to move off."

Osborne nodded and turned to Commodore Napier. "How do you want them, sir? Scrambled or hard boiled?"

"Scrambled will be fine, Captain."

Osborne took his seat in the captain's chair. "Send one across their bow. Let them know they are not going anywhere." On the viewscreen a missile shot passed the enemy ship, narrowly missing them, then exploding harmlessly in space.

* * *

"Incoming!"

Captain Shade had no time to react before the missile flew past the ship and exploded. "That was a warning shot. The next one won't be."

Greg Rutherford, having dispensed with his hood, and Clarence Ane'trou came onto the bridge unaware that the ship was involved in a battle.

"Why are we at red alert, Captain?" Rutherford demanded.

"The Navy has come calling," Shade explained. "They would like us to heave to and allow them to board us, I imagine. Shall we comply?"

"What? How did they find us?"

Shade turned in his chair and stared accusingly at Anetrou. "Somebody released the prisoners, or at the very least, allowed them to escape. Mr. Anetrou here was discovered inside the chamber we were keeping our guests in with three dead men and a couple more in serious condition. One had a knitting needle, or at least I think that is what it was, jammed up into his brain via the jaw. The rest looked as if they had ended up on the wrong end of a very large and very angry damnthing."

Rutherford turned on Anetrou. "You idiot! You went to kill them and got run over, didn't you?"

"I...I saw they were causing a rift between you and Captain Shade," Anetrou nervously explained. "I just thought—"

"And cost us our hostages, the one thing that might make the other ship hesitate to shoot us out of the sky," Rutherford yelled.

"But I was just—"

Anetrou never finished his sentence, or anything else ever again. The hole in his forehead, while small, was the entry point for a .22 round fired at point blank range. He collapsed to the floor where two men grabbed his arms and dragged the body away. Rutherford allowed himself a moment to be impressed with bridge efficiency before again addressing Captain Shade.

"My apologies, Captain. We had agreed to drop the captives off on an out-of-the-way planet and I had intended to honor that agreement." Rutherford gestured at the retreating corpse of Clarence Anetrou. "I dislike others breaking my word for me. Now, what do you suggest we do about our current situation?"

Shade nodded his acceptance of the apology. "We have three options; we try to run, we try to fight or we surrender."

"How do you rate our odds in each case, Captain?"

"That has to be a destroyer-class Navy ship to carry six pinnaces. It is faster than we are, although less maneuverable. Maneuverability means squat with those pinnaces to back them up. We might make hyperspace before they catch us: Maybe, maybe not? We are still flying more or less blind and can't be one hundred percent certain we are moving in the correct direction with the telemetry out. As for surrender, well, I think you know what is waiting for us after we are taken into custody."

"A bullet in the back of the head," Rutherford said.

"Or possibly a firing squad. This world's governor has a sense of theater, I understand. Still, a firing squad is an honorable execution to a former military man like myself."

"I would prefer to pass on that option," Rutherford said. "That leaves fighting. Can we?"

"We can. This ship has a complement of two nuclear missiles and a few other surprises. One dead-on hit and the Navy ship would be blown to cosmic dust. Sadly, it has to be right on target. While all spacefaring vessels are laminated with collapsium, Navy Destroyers have two to three times the layering of conventional ships. A near miss wouldn't even scratch the paint, so to speak."

Rutherford knew nothing of space battles beyond what he had seen on television as a child. "I think I have an idea. What happened to the shuttle that escaped?"

"Best guess is that it was escorted into the destroyer," Shade said. "We cannot be certain of anything with the telemetry compromised."

Rutherford had an idea. "Good. Let's send out another one with a special surprise inside."

* * *

"Sir, another shuttle is leaving the ship," the Signals and Detection Officer said loudly. 'This one has the *Adonitia's* registry on the hull. Sir,

I am getting three more bogeys coming up from the planet's surface on the telescope."

"Three?"

"Yes, sir. They are all black. I could only see them against the light side of the planet's surface."

Greibenfeld cursed. "The slave ships."

"We already seized those," Napier said.

"Maybe they found a way to—" Greibenfeld stopped mid-sentence. "Damn-it, it's Holloway! He got tired of waiting and decided to join the party."

"What? Where would he get the crew?" Napier commanded.

"His son's crew were all planet-side. Morgan allowed us to staff his ship with our own personnel as part of the GBG web. That leaves him sufficient personnel to put a skeleton crew into each ship."

"Shuttle still approaching, sir," Osborne said. "It could be a surrender vessel, or it could be a Trojan Horse."

Napier did some fast thinking. The GBG web was interfering with communications and entering hyperspace. That was a good thing when they were looking for the slave ship. Now it was working against the interests of the Navy.

"Cut the GBG web," Napier ordered. "Get Holloway on the horn and see who is piloting that shuttle."

The telescope viewscreen was retracted and Jack's face filled the primary comscreen. "Commodore, I brought you some backup."

Satan save us from well-meaning amateurs, Napier thought. He started to tell Jack to back off, then had another idea. "Jack, take those vessels and get between that ship in front of us and the edge of the gravity well. Find out if that craft has any weapons."

Jack turned and consulted somebody off-screen before answering. "Yes, we have a small nuclear payload and some missiles."

"Fine, if that ship tries to make a run for it, blast it to Em-See-Square!"

"Yes, sir! Wait, Pat and Betty might be on—"

"We already have them. There might be some Fuzzies on that ship, though."

Jack shook his head. "No, the people we questioned under veridication claim that the command ship didn't carry any Fuzzies. It was for cargo and supplies only."

Commodore Napier smiled. "Well, that makes my job a lot easier."

"Shuttle point-five miles and closing, sir."

"Any answer to our hails," Osborne asked.

"None, sir."

"Trojan Horse! Get that shuttle out of my sky," Captain Osborne ordered.

The weapons officer acted quickly and a missile could be seen striking the shuttle on screen. There was no noise or sense of impact from shockwaves as there was no atmosphere to speak of to carry it. The viewscreen automatically darkened to compensate for the intense flash of light.

"That was a thermonuclear device," Osborne said with forced calm. "Deploy secondary telemetry and hail that ship. It is time to let them know we are done playing nice."

The image of Captain Shade filled the main comscreen replacing Jack Holloway. He looked calm and composed sitting in his captain's chair holding his book. Before Captain Osborne could demand his surrender, Shade said one word, "Fire."

Two missiles launched from the enemy ship.

In a calm, almost casual voice, Captain Osborne said, "Countermeasures."

Though not visible against the blanket of space, thousands of iron balls were launched at the incoming missiles. The magnetized balls formed a barrier between the *Hatori* and the missiles. The double flashes of light proved their effectiveness.

"That was rude," Osborne said. To the Weapons Officer he added, "Explain it to them."

Commodore Napier watched Captain Osborne with interest. "He doesn't rattle easily, does he?"

Captain Greibenfeld shrugged. "I never saw him under combat conditions. I have to say his calm demeanor projects confidence. His men are picking up on that and acting the same. If this ever gets turned into a film, the actor playing his part will have to be a lot less reserved."

"Everybody wants a movie made about them," Napier said, which he followed with a string of curse words. "First we have to survive this conflict."

"You think the resolution is in doubt?"

"Yes. Which is why I have lived to see my current lofty age and rank."

*   *   *

"We're hit!" a crewman said unnecessarily. The impact of the missile shook the entire ship.

"Losing power, sir."

"Weapon control is down!"

Captain Shade drew a long breath and released it quickly. Their only real chance had been the Trojan Horse play, and that hadn't worked. Even the most heavily armored and equipped yacht was like a flea to an elephant compared to a fully functional Navy Destroyer. He opened his book to the page he had marked well in advance.

"I always knew this day would come," Shade said softly to himself. He stood up to address the crew. "Gentlemen, we are now defenseless and losing power. If we are taken in, it will be a short trial and an even shorter execution. I am willing to suffer that fate if all of you choose to surrender."

"And if not, sir?" the Weapons Officer asked.

Shade smiled with genuine humor, "Well, there is always that last great act of defiance."

As one, every member of the bridge crew cheered.

"What do you mean, Captain?" Rutherford asked, his voice trembling.

"We can't win, we can't run and we can't surrender," Shade said evenly. "So, we ram them."

"What?" Rutherford was dumbfounded. "That's suicide!"

Shade shrugged. "If you have another option, I am all ears."

Rutherford had nothing. He turned and left the bridge.

"Baker, eject my personal log with a beacon. We should leave a record of this for posterity, and I want people to know we weren't just bloodthirsty slavers. Helmsman, target the destroyer's bay doors. That will be the weakest point on the ship. Lock onto it and full speed ahead."

Shade tapped his book. "It would seem that we are Ahab about to meet his whale. Communications, please reestablish contact with our esteemed opponents. I want to go out with style."

*   *   *

Captain Osborne stood up from his seat to face the comscreen. "Captain, your ship is damaged and you have no chance of escape. Stand down and you will be treated fairly."

Captain Shade raised a hand to his forehead. "I salute you, Captain, and your valiant crew. I fear your assessment of my situation is accurate. Sadly, it is not in me to simply surrender."

The Signals and Detection Officer spoke up, "Sir, the ship is coming forward and gaining speed."

"What are you doing, Captain?"

"Shade. For the record, my name is Captain Shade of the *Pequod*. I am coming to meet my whale."

"Your what?"

"To the last I will grapple with thee...."

Osborne didn't bother trying to act cool this time. "All batteries, fire!"

"From Hell's heart, I stab at thee...."

Captain Shade did not get the chance to complete his quote. The full force of four atomic missiles converted almost every molecule of his ship into rapidly dispersing energy.

Greibenfeld swore as he watched the glow fade from the viewscreen. "Dramatic son-of-a-bitch, wasn't he?"

LI

Patricia McLeod awoke amid the sounds and smells she recognized as a hospital. She looked around her with blurred vision trying to get a better idea of where she was. She expected to be in a ship's infirmary given the fact that when she passed out she had been on a shuttle. As her vision cleared she knew that couldn't be the case.

The room had to be a private one on a planet-side hospital. Spaceships, even the really big ones, simply didn't have the liberty of private rooms given the limited area within the ship. She had to be in a hospital on the ground.

Well, if I made it back in one piece, the rest must have, too, she decided. She looked about and found the nurse's call button. A moment later the nurse came in. "I take it my brother is outside waiting for me to wake up."

"Yes, ma'am," the nurse answered. "Shall I show him in?"

"Yes, please."

Jack, with worry lines furrowed on his forehead, came in and sat down next to the bed. "You gave me quite a scare, you know."

"Sorry about that," Patricia said. "Where is Betty?"

"She's out buying a bulletproof vest," Jack said with a smile. "Actually, she is still being deposed by Gus Brannhard, Agent Trask and Captain Greibenfeld along with Miss Dawn. Rheiner is in the room next to yours."

Jack glanced around the room. "Say, this is the room I was in after Morgan shot me. Don't eat the food here; I'll bring in something safe to eat."

"So, Betty told you?"

"Not directly. You passed out on that shuttle and she had to tell the medics everything she knew. As next of kin they had to fill me in so I could make the decisions you couldn't while you were unconscious." Jack shook his head. "You should have told me yourself, you know. Betty took you pretty seriously when you said that you would shoot her for spilling the beans."

"Oh, she did not," Patricia argued. "Where is she, anyway?"

"Like I said; she is being deposed by the cops. She and I will be having a long talk afterwards. About us and where we will be going."

Patricia smiled. "I think that is overdue, little brother."

"Pat, how long have you known that—" Jack choked before he could finish.

"That I am dying? About six months...oh, wait, with the time dilation effect in hyperspace I guess that would be about a year now. That was why I decided to make the big trip and visit the family on Odin and Thor and so on. I suspected Zarathustra would be my last stop."

"Can't you get another heart? An artificial one?"

Patricia shook her head. "By the time the doctors back on Terra realized the accommodation meds weren't getting the job done it was too late. I won't survive another operation. Rather than die on the table, I decided to make my good-byes to the family. So, I imagine you have been bullying the doctors enough to know how long I have left. Spill."

Jack took in a deep breath. "Anywhere from a few weeks to six months. Morgan has offered to take you home in his yacht if you prefer. A direct trip will take half as long in hyperspace as the trip out."

Patricia shook her head. "No. That would mean saying good-bye all over again to Wayne, Larry, Lori, Buddy and Daniel, not to mention my friends and the rest of the family on Terra. I won't put them through that. There is one thing you can do for me, though. See to it that my body is sent back home to be buried on the hill overlooking the farm."

Jack promised.

"Good. Now get me out of this damned hospital. This is a place where people are supposed to get better. That isn't in the cards for me.

* * *

Gus Brannhard poured another drink. Although he had cut down on his drinking since his liver replacement, this was a special occasion. He took a small gulp, for him, leaving the water tumbler half full and nodded in satisfaction.

"I don't know what possessed the Heimdall Distillery Company to name this stuff Old Atom-Bomb Bourbon, nevertheless it fits," Gus said holding his glass at eye level.

"No argument here, Counselor," Trask said after taking a somewhat more conservative sip from his own glass.

"I would like to propose a toast," Jason Roberts said lifting his own glass. "To Miss Cinda Dawn, who helped us break this case, and Captain Osborne, who saved the government a ton of sols by blasting a healthy number of those sons-of-Khooghras straight to Em-Cee-Square."

"And my apologies to her for the lengthy depositions we will be putting her through," Trask added.

"Hear-hear!" Captain Greibenfeld added. After he downed his drink, he continued, "That Captain Shade was a Fuzzy slaving son-of-a-bitch, but he had real style in the end. We collected his personal log after blowing him out of the sky. Did I tell you about—"

"Only three times," Ben said. "Say, where are Commodore Napier and Captain Osborne, anyway?"

"Paperwork," Greibenfeld said. "Every missile has to be accounted for and resupplied, the after action report filled out and sent to HQ on Terra, awards and citations reviewed and approved or declined...Ghu, am glad I went into intelligence instead of taking a field command."

"You don't have to fill out paperwork?" Gus asked.

"Oh, mountains of it," the Captain said. "However, I only collate data and reports from operatives. We rarely see any bang-bang shoot 'em ups that have to be justified to the top brass. That sort of thing only happens in the spy thrillers."

"In other words, if you told us you would have to kill us," Roberts said with a chuckle.

"Ghu forbid! The paperwork for something like that would bury Beta Continent."

Everybody laughed. Then Trask asked why Jack wasn't joining them.

Greibenfeld sobered a bit. "Well, first he has to wait until Commodore Napier gets finished yelling at him for sticking his nose into the Navy's business."

"I would like to be a fly on the wall for that scene," Ben said. "Last year Jack dressed down Morgan for practically the same thing. Played a rather nasty joke on him afterwards."

"I doubt Napier will be too hard on Jack," Gus offered. "He put those ships to work almost the second they showed up."

"True," Greibenfeld said, as he took another drink.

Ben sat in thought for a moment. "What are we going to do with those three remaining ships? Is the Navy going to keep them?"

"The only one the Navy would have had a legal claim on went straight to Em-See-Square," Gus said. "Those that were seized on-planet come under our jurisdiction, though the Marines were involved in that, too. That does make it a bit sticky."

"Ah...I have a couple ideas for that," Greibenfeld said.

*　*　*

It took a big lunch and a long nap before Cinda felt human, again. The last few days took a great deal out of her and she needed to recover before returning to Zeta Continent. The depositions seemed to take forever and taking them was almost as bad as being a prisoner.

The Navy Captain, Osborne, had been kind enough to send out a pinnace to collect more samples for her to have analyzed. Gerd van Riebeek offered to run the tests at Science Center Beta and Cinda accepted. She really didn't have much choice in the matter; almost everything science related went through the Charterless Zarathustra Company sooner or later.

With Rheiner still in hospital she decided to return when he got out. The doctors assured her that with his amazing vitality the Freyan would be able to travel in a day or so. Cinda dodged any questions about what planet Rheiner hailed from; that was his story to tell when he felt up to it.

Cinda examined herself in the mirror. Though she wasn't ready to leave for the campsite, she had still put on her field clothes. Her new khaki-colored bush shirt with the red pocket tops accented her hourglass shape. She adjusted the zipper down for a moment, then pulled it up an inch. *Too many people have seen too much already*, she thought.

She couldn't decide whether to go with the matching khaki shorts or the black ones for contrast. She was also debating the advantages of socks over nylons with the boots since she wasn't tramping out in the bush, yet. She had just decided on which boots to wear when the doorbell chimed.

Wondering who it could be, she went into the front room and opened the door. Her eyes went wide when she saw her visitor. Before she could scream, a large masculine hand clamped over her mouth.

"Hello, Miss Dawn," Greg Rutherford said as he forced her back into the apartment. "I'm afraid we have some unfinished business to conclude before I can leave this damned backwater world." He kicked the door closed behind him then forced her down on the couch. "Your interference has cost me millions of sols, little girl. I'm going to extract a piece of that from your hide!" Rutherford pulled out his .22 and pressed it against Cinda's stomach then removed his hand from her face.

"What are you doing here? I thought you were killed on that ship of yours."

Rutherford back-handed her across the face. "I nearly was, thanks to you. When it was apparent that Captain Shade intended to ram that Navy ship I got the hell out of there in my personal shuttle. I barely made it; the yacht disintegrated as I pulled out of the bay. Fortunately, the cloaking paint of my shuttle hid me from the Navy's telemetry. Now, I am all set to leave on the next ship out for Gimli. That is, after I have dealt with you."

Cinda thought quickly. "You may have a problem with that."

Rutherford snorted. "Oh? Are you going to call your dog or something?"

"Rheiner!" Cinda shouted.

Rutherford turned to shoot the man he remembered from the ship. The memory of the incredibly strong and resilient Freyan was still fresh in his mind. When he shot at him this time, he was going to aim at the face.

When Rheiner failed to appear, Rutherford became confused. That is, until a boot struck him in the groin from behind. Rutherford bent over in pain though he still held onto his pistol. Then something heavy caught him in the head and he lost consciousness.

Breathing heavily, Cinda grabbed up the pistol as two Fuzzies and their dogs ran into the room. James Hutton and Sarah Balfour, her Fuzzies, saw the strange Big One on the floor.

"Mumy Cinda, is Big One sick?" Sarah asked.

"This is a bad Big One, Sarah. Make run fast and call for police to come on the comscreen."

James Hutton, upon hearing the Big One was bad, moved back and held his chopper-digger at the ready. The dogs sensing something was wrong growled at the prone body. Sarah came back in and said the police were on their way.

Cinda sat back down on the couch holding the gun at the ready. "Thank you, Sarah. Now stay away from the bad Big One. I wouldn't want you to catch something nasty from him."

*   *   *

"Do you know what this means?"

Victor Grego leaned back in his chair and picked up his highball. "Not really, Gerd. I am a businessman, not a scientist. You'll have to explain it to me with as many small words as you can manage."

Gerd's face looked somewhat dubious on the comscreen. "Well, we tested those samples that Miss Dawn brought to us. At first it just looked like simple anaerobic bacteria, nothing special. Then Tim Gordon took some initiative and ran some other tests. He found that these bacteria, two different kinds, by the way, had some unusual properties. One sampling absorbs radiation and converts it to light energy, which raises the temperature of anything it hits like the ground."

"What, like tiny living suns?"

"Exactly! The other sampling does much the same thing, only instead of feeding on radiation, they absorb particulate matter from cosmic debris. Much like the rock-eating bacteria on Terra."

Grego tried to follow Gerd and failed. "That is interesting, but I don't see what…?"

"These are two types of bacteria that are working in tandem to raise the temperature of this planet!"

It took a second, then Grego caught on. "This is why Zarathustra isn't a big chunk of ice-covered rock? My god! This is huge. If they can be introduced to other planets that are considered too cold to be inhabited… this would be a giant leap in terraforming! We need to get the—"

"Hold on, boss! Cinda Dawn has to be credited as the discoverer, and that expedition she was with also has to be included. We wouldn't have discovered this without them."

Grego had a larcenous gleam in his eye. "Did she sign papers that allow us—"

"Afraid not, boss," Gerd said. "My fault on this one as I didn't know it was a requirement. I may not be the right Division Head for this center—"

"Nonsense. It would have been tossed out in court, anyway. Get with whoever is in charge of that expedition and work out a deal. I want the CZC to have at least a part interest in this discovery. Terraforming frozen planets could make the Company a fortune."

Gerd shook his head. "It's not going to be that easy and it's going to cost a fortune. It could take decades of research to determine how to introduce these bacteria onto new worlds effectively. We also have to work out its effect on the living organisms of those worlds."

"What do you mean?"

"Haven't you ever wondered why there aren't any blood-sucking insects on Zarathustra?" Gerd asked. "I think the light thrown off from these bacteria does something to make exposed blood toxic, or at least non-nutritional once removed from the living body it comes from."

Grego flashed back to a meeting he had some years earlier with Leonard Kellogg. Kellogg explained that the blood banks had to take extra steps to insure the viability of drawn blood. They had never found out why.

"Run more tests on that. If there is anything to it, make sure the

CZC has the rights to it. There might be military applications we could sell. Get with Leslie Coombes to make certain we're on firm ground. What about the science expedition? Have you told them the good news?"

"Yes, but only because one of their people, a Dr. Dmitri Watson, was here waiting for the test results. I haven't said anything about the possible blood effects, though."

"Then don't, not until after you speak with Leslie. And send them a case of good Champagne. We will want to be partnering up with them. We might as well start out on the right foot."

*   *   *

"Cinda caught the boss?" Jack asked.

Marshal Max Fane smiled so wide an observant person could see his wisdom teeth. "Beat the hell out of him, too. That's one little lady you don't want mad at you."

Jack smiled back from the comscreen. "That's wonderful! Pat will be pleased. We're taking Pat on a whirlwind tour of the planet. Please ask Miss Dawn and her Fuzzies to join us. How did Gus take the news?"

"He put down his drink and practically purred like a big cat," Max said. "Five will get you ten he will be prosecuting this one personally."

"No bet. I will lay odds that Ned Foster will be his second chair. I haven't met him personally, but Gus speaks highly of him."

Max nodded. "Highly enough that Foster is prosecuting Hugo Ingermann."

"What?" Jack's eyes almost popped out of their sockets. "Gus isn't going to reel in the most hated man on the planet himself?"

"Nope. He said if he takes all of the big cases his people will never learn how to handle themselves after he is gone. Between you, me and the wall, I can't imagine that anybody could lose this one. Too much evidence, too many witnesses, and his lawyer has vanished."

"His lawyer? Think he skipped planet?"

Max shrugged. "Maybe. It would be poetic justice if he did. However, two of our officers identified a man matching Clarence Anetrou's description as the pilot of the cruiser that collected the hooded man,

Greg Rutherford. There is a good chance he is just so much radioactive dust floating in the ionosphere now. We will know more after we put Rutherford in the chair."

Jack chuckled. "I needed some good news. Thank you for the update, Marshal. I have to be going, now."

They said their good-byes then cut the connection. Max wondered idly what Jack had to hurry off for.

LII

The verdict came as no surprise to anyone at Central Court in Mallorysport. Chief Colonial Prosecutor Gus Brannhard was quoted as saying: "This is a victory not only for the people of Zarathustra, but for the entire Federation." The newscast went on to praise the work of Ned Foster who prosecuted Hugo Ingermann.

Jack turned the sound down on the viewscreen. "History has just been made, everybody: Zarathustra's greatest criminal has got his just reward!"

The room exploded with cheers. Everybody was there in Morgan's reception hall. Jack had wanted to host the party at his home, but the guest list proved too long for his homestead to accommodate.

Gus Brannhard walked over and stood in front of the six-by-nine foot viewscreen. "I would like to tell everybody here that Mr. Hugo Ingermann, Esquire has already been sentenced to death and will be executed by firing squad tomorrow at noon. The drawing for positions on that squad will take place tonight at 2300. Please get your tickets by 2100."

There was some light laughter and polite applause.

"I want to thank Ned Foster—take a bow, Ned—for his excellent work in prosecuting the case. Frankly, he brought in so much evidence and worked the case so well I feared that everybody who even looked like Ingermann would be convicted."

"I would also like to thank Patricia McLeod, Betty Kanazawa, Cinda Dawn and Rheiner Sostreus. Their testimony will put another...ah, I can't voice my opinion of this person as I will be prosecuting him shortly. I wouldn't want to be accused of having a prosecutorial bias."

A burst of laughter greeted this pronouncement.

Gus went on for a while then stepped down. General conversation broke out among the guests. Jack and Patricia walked among the crowd catching bits of conversation as they went.

Gerd spoke with Grego about the results of the EMP cannon test. "It was both too effective and not effective enough at the same time, Victor," Gerd said. "It knocked out the main controls and such all the way out to the upper atmosphere. We were lucky only one shuttle was adversely affected, and fortunately they were rescued."

"After significant drama, I understand," Grego said as he finished off his highball. "What do you mean by not effective enough?"

"Contragravity and artificial gravity remained on. Shuttles continued to stay up and nobody floated around or fell down relative to the planet's gravity. Joe Verganno has a long winded explanation as to why...."

Off to the side, Cinda Dawn and Rheiner Sostreus spoke with Dmitri Watson. Cinda and Rheiner had been invited by Jack, and Dmitri came as their plus one.

"You'll be in every scientific journal in the Federation, Cinda," Dmitri said excitedly. "The woman who cracked the Zarathustra climate mystery. You will need to write a paper on this immediately."

"The entire expedition is entitled to credit, isn't it," Cinda asked.

"Oh, how I would love to say yes," Dmitri said. "Never share credit unless you have to. Your impressive friend here should get an honorable mention as he was there when you made the breakthrough, and the CZC Science Center as they did the analysis, but the lion's share goes to you. I took the liberty of filing for a patent on the discovery and its applications the second I received the test results. In your name, of course. Rico is already talking with the CZC about further testing and application. You will be a very wealthy woman."

At the bar Agent Trask and Jason Roberts downed their drinks with reserved gusto.

"So, headed back to Terra? The case is broken, the bad guys all either dead or on their way to getting there and you have a rather sizeable feather in your cap."

Trask shook his head. "No, there will be follow-ups, trials, testimony, depositions and credit to be shared. The Navy and Marines did most of the heavy lifting, anyway. I'll just stick around for a while, whip the local bureau into shape and just generally enjoy the lower background radiation. You?"

"Well, I didn't really have a part in this," Roberts said, as he signaled for a refill. "I just found a lead while working another case. I doubt I'll even get an informant's fee. Don't even care. My partner is safe and that is all I need."

"Partner?"

"Mike Hammer. A Fuzzy. Earns his keep, too."

Trask found himself thinking about something, then shook his head.

"I will bet the next round that you were considering bringing Fuzzies into the Bureau," Roberts said.

"What are you, a mind reader?"

"A face reader. You should do it."

Trask didn't try to hide the surprise on his face. "What? A Fuzzy working for the FBCI? Are you smoking chuckleweed?"

"My first case on Zarathustra was broken by Mike," Roberts explained. "Everybody who has ever underestimated a Fuzzy has done so to their detriment. Fuzzies are smart, and learn fast. Oh, they have a lot to learn where Big Ones are concerned, but some of your cases will involve Fuzzies. You might as well have some on hand because nobody knows a Fuzzy as well as another Fuzzy."

In another corner, Marshal Fane spoke with Chief Carr and Juan Takagashi.

"That tin of Extee Three that Jack's sister brought us turned out to be a godsend," Marshal Fane was saying. "We pulled all kinds of prints from it telling us who they were buying from here on Zarathustra."

"One of the speculators was buying up all the Extee Three after the Fuzzy Trial," Chief Carr amended. "The Odin Dietetics imprint was a dead giveaway since all Extee Three on this world is now produced by the CZC."

"How does this help?" Takagashi asked. "There's no law against selling the stuff, though there should be. If only for humane reasons!"

"Oh, we can't arrest the seller for that, to be sure," Chief Carr said. "However, we questioned him under veridication and he identified the buyers. Another nail in the slavers' coffin. And, as an extra bonus, the CZC is buying back all the undamaged Extee Three from any and all speculators at a five percent markup."

"That will reduce the possibility of anybody trying this in the future," Marshal Fane added. "If they do, they will have to get their Extee Three off of Zarathustra to avoid detection. To stop that we're sending packets to all off-world distributors to let us know about any large non-military orders."

Chief Carr downed his whiskey sour. "You better believe that from now on, we will be watching for anything like this happening again."

Marshal Fane shrugged. "As long as there's big money involved, it'll start up again. Unfortunately, a *lot* of these off-worlders want their own Fuzzies." He pointed upward, reminding the Chief of all the ships in orbit around Zarathustra, most of them holding owners wanting to adopt a Fuzzy.

"What about that cloaking stuff they used?" Takagashi said, broke into their conversation. "Do we know where the slavers got it?"

"Commodore Napier is handling that," Fane said. "It's all supposed to be very hush-hush stuff, so we will let him have it. The paint is being stripped off of the remaining slaver ships even as we speak."

Jack and Patricia moved on before they heard anything sensitive. A few steps more brought them to Dr. Hoenveld, making a rare appearance outside of his lab, and Darla Cross in a stunning black and red gown was speaking with Johann.

"And you were all genetically manipulated for strength and higher perception?"

"Ja, Herr Doktor," Johann said before taking a huge swallow from his stein. "Ve also heal very qvickly. Rheiner ist almost completely recovered from his inchuries."

"I do not wish to be indelicate, but I would love to get some blood and tissue samples from your people. I might even be able to find a way for your young to be born more...um...."

"Normal, Herr Doktor?" Johann made an odd choking sound. It took a moment for Darla and Hoenveld to realize he was laughing. "I t'ink ve could verk somet'ing out."

Near the back of the room Morgan, Ben and Heidi waved Jack and Patricia over.

"Father, Governor Rainsford has some news for us," Morgan said.

"First, get your son to call me Ben when we are at social functions, Jack," Ben said. "After all, he is about to become a head of state."

"Head of state?" Patricia exclaimed.

"Herr Morgan has been made, ehh...I t'ink dat is der best translation from Sosti, Arch-Duke of Neu Freya," Heidi explained.

"Arch-Duke? What will the King on Freya say about that?"

"We should know in about four to five months," Ben said. "I sent a diplomatic packet with the documentation stating that the government on Zarathustra recognizes his claim to the title."

"Zeta continent has more land than any duchy on Freya," Morgan said. "As the chosen administrator I qualify for the title, though nobles are not elected as a rule. And by going with Arch-Duke instead of Prince Regent, I will offend fewer members of the nobility."

"Der ist a precedent vhere lower nobles rise in rank vhen dey acvire more lands, so der king must recognize der title or face trouble from ot'er nobles who may vant to also improve der station."

"What about the Federation," Jack asked. "Will it be accepted on Terra?"

"The Federation has no say in the matter," Gus offered, as he joined the discussion with a stein in his hand. "This is Zarathustra, and we are a sovereign world. As long as we adhere to Federation law and don't try to secede, we run this planet any way we want. On Freya Morgan's title is that of a noble station. Here on Zarathustra it is just another fancy way of saying regional administrator. Freyan law applies if the people of that region vote it in. Morgan can even set up his own parliament, much like each state in the old United States of America was able to have its own senate, before the great wars." Gus took a hefty drink from his stein.

"Ahh...anybody who can make ale like this can run things how they like, in my opinion."

"And if the King on Freya doesn't like it, to Niflheim with him," Ben said. "Hey, Morgan, if you are the Arch-Duke, what does that make Jack?"

"The Native Affairs Commissioner," Morgan said. "There have been rare occasions when a low-born man marries into a noble house, but he is never recognized as a noble himself. And you cannot buy a title, as one could back in Old England. You are born noble and that is it. However, on very rare occasions, a noble can be stripped of his title and his lands forfeited to the crown for some serious offense. I think the king will recognize my title just so he can keep that option available. Not that he could do much with it from Freya."

"Are you going to run things from this castle?" Ben asked.

"Nein. Herr Morgan has appointed mein vater der Bürgermeister," Heidi said. "He vill administer t'ings in Neu Freya. Ve haff already commissioned a castle to be built dere."

"Another castle?" Jack asked.

"It is traditional, father. Besides, the administration will have offices in it and run things there. It might also become a tourist attraction someday, if we ever reduce travel time from one world to another."

"So, what do we call you?" Patricia asked. "Your highness or something?"

"Just Morgan, Aunt Pat. We will leave all that 'Your Grace' stuff back on Freya."

Patricia smiled. "Good to know all this won't be going to your head. I need to lie down, Jack. Could you walk me to my room?"

"Of course," Jack said. "I can get my old contragravity chair if you like."

"I'd rather keep my boots on. Congratulations, Morgan."

"Rest well, Aunt Pat."

Patricia leaned on Jack as he helped her down the corridor. They took the lift up to the next level then down to the first room. Morgan had had the room cleared for Patricia's convenience. The bed, a monster that could hold a sizeable family, was equipped with wireless sensors that would monitor the life signs of the occupant. Most of the equipment had been used by Akira during her pregnancy.

"You should make the next family reunion, you know," Patricia said as she lay down on top of the covers.

"It would take a couple years just to get the time and place worked out," Jack said. "All that traveling between worlds, and the time involved—"

"Afraid to let them all meet your hot young girlfriend? When are you going to make an honest woman of her?"

Jack smiled. "We had a long talk after she got rescued. We are still proceeding slowly. I guess you would say that we are engaged to be engaged. As for the reunion, well, I have a lot to do here...."

"You're making excuses. I'll bet Morgan would love to meet everyone. You and Betty could just pile into his yacht and collect everybody on your way to Terra. All of our generation except for you and Dean are retired, now; so there wouldn't be any conflicts, there."

"All of the next generation are still building their lives, families and fortunes," Jack countered. "How many could take up to a year away from their homes and jobs? Oh, Niflheim. I'll see what Morgan and I can work out."

Patricia nodded. "I would like a drink. Could you get me a German Coffee?"

Jack searched his memory and recalled that Patricia and Leila had cooked up their own little brew with a teaspoon of instant coffee, a tablespoon of cocoa powder and a shot of Peppermint Schnapps. "Are you sure that is a good idea? Caffeine and alcohol don't mix well with the accommodation drugs."

"It doesn't really matter, now."

Jack called down to the kitchen and it arrived within minutes. While they waited Patricia asked him to put on one of her Jim Reeves recordings.

"This next song was rediscovered in a buried archive in Texas the same year Wayne shipped out with the Navy to deal with the Isis Insurrection. It became my favorite song."

Jack listened to "Distant Drums" from the chair near the bed. Midway through the song Patricia drifted off to sleep. A few minutes later there was a polite knock at the door. Jack turned to see Morgan, Akira, Betty and his entire family of Fuzzies standing there. Jack made a shushing motion and got up.

"Pat's sleeping," Jack whispered.

Morgan looked uneasy.

Akira started to speak and was stopped by Betty.

"Father, she is no longer with us."

"What?" Jack looked back and couldn't see Patricia's chest rise or fall. "How do you know?"

"The monitoring station downstairs," Akira explained. Tears started to flow as she explained. "Nerroohilan reported...told me about...."

"I'm sorry, father...um...Pa," Morgan said. "What traditions do you wish to observe...or that Aunt Pat would have liked?"

Jack smiled even as his own tears started. He recognized Patricia's influence on Morgan in calling him 'Pa.' "We can do a Freyan ritual, if you like, then send her body back to Terra. She told me where she wanted to be buried."

There came a sound from behind him. Little Fuzzy, with Emily at his side, raised Patricia's hand and watched as it dropped limply down. Morgan started forward only to be stopped by Jack. The Fuzzies shook Patricia's body and waited. When it was clear to them that she was made-dead, they started rocking back and forth making a keening sound in their hypersonic voices.

"This is what Fuzzies do when one of their own dies," Jack explained. "Pat is way too big for them to carry her out and bury her, though. That will be our job."

"Is it permissible for the Thorans to do that?" Morgan asked. "They were very impressed with her and would consider it an honor to take her to the yacht. Captain Zeudin is already preparing the ship for the voyage to Terra."

Jack nodded. "A military-style send off. Yes, she would have liked that."

LIII

The Governor's Presence Hall was full to bursting even though everything was being telecast and fed through the datastream. Most of those in attendance were the off-worlders, as evidenced by their fancy formal wear and air of superiority, looking to adopt Fuzzies. The most strident among them had formed an advocacy group, which called itself the Fuzzy Adoption Alliance.

Gustavus Adolphus Brannhard looked out at the crowd through the great curtain at the back of the stage and made a low whistle. "We should have sold tickets to this, Governor. It would have kept us in the black for the next century."

"Maybe next time, Gus," Ben said. "Those people out there will not like what I have to say."

Jack nodded absently; he had other things on his mind. Next to him stood Dr. Hoenveld and Darla Cross. They didn't look at all happy. Victor Grego whispered something to Juan Jimenez while Juan Takagashi sat off to the side reviewing his notes.

Marshal Max Fane paced back and forth. Security concerns sat squarely on his shoulders and he seemed to be stooped a bit from the weight.

"Do you think Jack should be here, so soon after...?"

"No, I don't, Juan," Grego said. "But I don't advise anybody to inform him of that fact."

Ben checked the time. "No point putting this off any longer. Juan, are you ready?"

Both Juans turned to face the Governor, then Dr. Jimenez realized it was the Deputy Governor Ben had spoken to.

Juan Takagashi nodded and stepped through the curtains onto the podium.

The hall, which had been abuzz with low conversation, fell silent. Takagashi looked out at the sea of faces and took a deep breath. He reminded himself that it wasn't his first rodeo and plunged in.

"Ladies and gentlemen, for those who do not know me, I am Deputy Colonial Governor Juan Takagashi. For the last couple weeks I have been holding the office of acting governor while Governor Rainsford has taken his first vacation in three years. Let me start by saying that Governor Rainsford has returned to his duties as of 0700 this morning and will be addressing this audience momentarily."

A man stood up in the front row and took a step forward only to be forced back to his seat by one of the policemen surrounding the podium. It was the man whose nose had been bloodied by Jack at the Fuzzy Adoption Bureau.

"We will not be addressing questions at this time," Takagashi said. "Please be patient." There was a moment of grumbling, then silence. "Most of you here today came to this world in the hopes of adopting a Fuzzy, and then returning to your home planets. During the past several days we have had to shut down the Fuzzy Adoption Bureau and many of you want to know why. Some of you think we did it just to prevent off-worlders from adopting Fuzzies. I can now say that there was a greater, more pressing reason.

"We recently learned of a conspiracy to capture and enslave this world's native sapient inhabitants. These slavers attacked and abducted Fuzzies on and off the Fuzzy Reservation and took them to Terra, where the Fuzzies were forced to work as entertainers for self-indulgent, entitled humans who cared nothing for the laws against doing that very thing."

A few people looked irritated at the description Takagashi used. A few others had the good grace to look a little guilty at the characterization.

"I have since been assured that all of the humans involved in the Terra end of the operation have been severely dealt with. I have received recordings of those trials. Those involved in the Fuzzy kidnappings here on Zarathustra will be executed within the next week."

A murmur filled the room with that last revelation. Most of them in attendance knew the penalties for enslaving an alien race. The precedent

of "The People of the Terran Federation vs. Anton Garrit" was well-documented and is taught in middle school history classes. The more schol-
arly in the crowd would also remember how Garrit changed his name
to Steve Ravick and fled to Fenris where he was eventually apprehended
by Special Agent Bishop 'Bish' Ware. After being declared guilty by the
Federation High Court, Garrit had been returned to Loki where he was
tried, convicted and very publicly hanged. The Federation takes a very
dim view of slavers, no matter what species they go after.

"We have captured three of the slaver vessels, though we believe a
fourth may have escaped. Know this; no matter where in the Federation
this ship flees to, they will know no peace, nor find any safe harbor. We
are also fortunate in that we have solid evidence that suggests that there
were no Fuzzies on the ship that escaped."

Behind the curtain, Juan Jimenez was confused. "I thought that
fourth ship was blasted to radioactive dust."

"It was," Jack explained. "Commodore Napier is hoping to use a
decoy ship to draw out any of the slavers' surviving confederates. He
and Captain Greibenfeld are setting up an undercover crew and taking
one of the yachts back to Terra, stopping at every planet along the way
broadcasting that secret beacon of theirs. The second is being kept by the
Colonial Government and the third is being purchased from the government by the CZC. Victor mentioned that he always wanted a space
yacht, now he has one."

"I won't do that much traveling, though it is nice to have the option.
I also arranged to fill the holds of Commodore Napier's craft with Fuzz-
bots," Grego added. "Napier is sending Lundgren along to work at refin-
ing the software and make them appear more life-like. He also promised
to share the results with the CZC."

Juan thought for a moment before remembering that Lundgren had
been one of the Sinister Six, as Gus dubbed them, who were working to
take over the planet and sell ersatz sunstones. Lundgren was the computer savant that had managed to hack his way into the Navy's computers.

"...and now, let me introduce our Colonial Governor, Bennett
Rainsford."

"That's your cue, Ben," Grego said.

Three years as the governor of Zarathustra had done little to make Ben comfortable with public speaking. There was a smattering of applause as he stepped out to the podium.

"First day back at work and I am already giving speeches," Ben said. "I hope this doesn't mean that I have become a real politician." The joke fell flat. *It's the wrong audience*, Ben told himself. "Yes, it was a bad joke, and you will not like much of what I have to say any better. A short while ago it came to our attention that some Fuzzies were exhibiting symptoms of sterility. With the generous assistance of the CZC, and most importantly Dr. Hoenveld, we have identified the root cause of this malady. Since my field of study is outside of this area I have asked Dr. Jan Christian Hoenveld to come out and explain."

Hoenveld did not need to be prodded to go out. He and Darla Cross walked up to the podium, shook Ben's hand, then they took his place at the microphone while Ben took a seat next to Juan Takagashi.

"I will try to keep this as simple as possible for those who may not be comfortable with hard science," Hoenveld started. He took the air of a professor lecturing a college class, which he had done many times before. "The first member of *fuzzy sapiens zarathustra* to exhibit symptoms of sterility was Zorro, a Fuzzy I examined about a year ago for an unrelated issue. After that we found several more Fuzzies suffering from the same ailment. With the assistance of Ms. Cross, here," Darla waved briefly, "and Officer Ahmed Khadra of the Zarathustra Native Protection Force...."

Behind the curtains Grego sat up straighter in his seat. "Hoenveld is actually sharing the credit?"

"He has come to appreciate the contributions of others," Juan Jimenez explained. "And Chris, whatever his faults, never accepted credit that wasn't his due. Not that he would even need to, given the body of his accomplishments over the years."

"...what we determined is that Fuzzies are exceptionally susceptible to the effects of radiation. Zarathustra has the lowest background radiation of any Terra-like planet. The Fuzzies evolved with a low tolerance as a result. Now, Zorro was never taken off Zarathustra. He had been X-rayed last year when we were doing a full medical workup on him. I, personally, ordered the X-rays and bear the responsibility for the results.

"In Zorro's case, fortunately, I have good news. The damage done by simple X-rays are temporary, provided the Fuzzy is not exposed to too many doses. His last sperm count is up to five times what it was a week ago. He is recovering and we can expect he will be providing more tangible evidence of his recovery soon."

A few people laughed, some cheered and several more applauded briefly.

"Next, we examined numerous Fuzzies who had been taken to Terra, most of whom had been abducted by the slavers Deputy Governor Takagashi spoke of. I am afraid the news is far less positive in their cases. I tested each and every one, all with the same results: total sterility. Terra has the highest background radiation of any Terra-like—the irony of this is not lost on me—planet in the Federation. This is due to the extensive atomic and thermonuclear bombing that left most of the northern hemisphere's landmasses irradiated wastelands. Even Terro-human births are affected by this, giving our homeworld a much higher rate of fetus malformation than any other known planet. Fuzzies taken there are simply, and permanently, rendered infertile."

"What about other low-radiation worlds?" somebody called out from the audience.

"Questions should be held until the end of cl...of my summation. However, I will answer your question, as I was coming to this point anyway. Worlds with lower background radiation such as Freya, Poictesme and Heimdall may not result in total sterility like Terra. Unfortunately, prolonged exposure to these worlds could result in malformation of the fetuses. It will take significant time and research to determine the long term and overall effects on Fuzzy reproduction. Obviously, we cannot simply take a furry of Fuzzies to any of these worlds and wait to see what would happen. That constitutes a capital crime at this time. No. Testing will occur in the laboratory on cultured cells."

"How long will that take?" came another voice.

Hoenveld mentally counted to ten and reminded himself that he could not fail anybody here like he could have done back at university. "It will take as long as it takes. The Charterless Zarathustra Company has allowed me to head up a department dedicated to this issue. I can say in all confidence that ten years is an optimistic time frame. There is every possibility that this issue will still be studied long after I am dust. That is all I have for now. Darla, do you wish to add anything?"

"Yes. I wish to ask everybody here to contribute to the Fuzzy sterility research. The Fuzzies need your help if they are ever to safely travel out to the stars with us. Thank you."

Dr. Hoenveld and Darla Cross stepped away from the podium and took a seat while Ben returned to the microphone.

"I have one last speaker, and then I will entertain questions."

Jack hated public speaking. Not that he was afraid. He just knew some idiot in the press would quote him out of context. He took Ben's place and cleared his throat. "For those who are unfamiliar with my face, I am Colonial Native Affairs Commissioner Jack Holloway. I will get straight to the point. A lot of people in this room came here hoping to adopt a Fuzzy. Let me say this: a Fuzzy is not a pet you can buy and dispose of when you are tired of it. Fuzzies are sapient beings protected by Federation and local laws.

"Anybody who doubts this is invited to stick around for the trials we will be holding for those men and women who kidnapped and enslaved Fuzzies and took them off-world. I expect the trials will be short, and the sentences dramatic. If you do not care to wait around, there are tapes of the last trial concerning Fuzzy slavers, and the executions that followed.

"Given what we have just learned, taking a Fuzzy off Zarathustra will be considered reckless endangerment and treated as such. On this planet a conviction earns the perpetrator a very large hole in the back of his or her head. We will not discriminate. We will not offer a plea deal. If convicted, we will shoot you and stuff you in a mass-energy converter. I have been assured that legislation preventing the transportation of Fuzzies off this planet will be passed by the end of the week and amended to our Constitution. So, anybody here wanting to adopt a Fuzzy better plan on making Zarathustra their new home."

Jack turned and waited for Ben before taking a seat. Ben fielded several question, most of which had already been answered by Dr. Hoenveld and Jack.

"Now, I have one last speaker," Ben said. "Please welcome the Chief Executive Officer of the Charterless Zarathustra Company, Victor Grego."

This time there was no applause at all. Grego simply wasn't well known off-world.

"Thank you, Governor." Grego turned to the audience. "All Fuzzies will be staying on Zarathustra for the foreseeable future. There is nothing we can do about that at this time, although we are working on the problem. None of you will be allowed to adopt a live Fuzzy unless you make Zarathustra your permanent residence," Grego reiterated. "Speaking as the *de facto* parent of two Fuzzies, I know what you are missing. I am here to offer an alternative."

Grego nodded to Juan Jimenez. "Here at the CZC R&D we have built what is being called Fuzz-bots." Several Fuzzy robots walked out onto the stage and formed a line in front of Grego. 'These robots are virtually indistinguishable from the real thing." Another nod and Juan toggled a switch on a small remote control unit. The Fuzz-bots began to move around and act like real Fuzzies to some degree. "These robots will walk, talk, be equipped with the most sophisticated artificial intelligence ever installed in a robot and can be taken anywhere in the galaxy. They will not eat or excrete, requiring only a small nuclear battery with a run time of over ten years. They can follow simple commands and even be used in a domestic capacity.

"You can't have a real Fuzzy, so consider purchasing an artificial one. I suspect that in a year or two they will become the latest status symbol."

The audience watched silently as the Fuzz-bots romped about the stage. Somebody in the audience asked how good the programming was.

"It is still in the early stages, I admit. That said, free software upgrades will be available as we create them, and sent out to all Federation-occupied worlds. Over time we hope to make these Fuzz-bots indistinguishable from the real thing. By the way, one of these Fuzzies *is* the real thing. Can you tell which one?"

After a moment, Diamond stopped and turned to the audience and waved. There was some applause. "At worst, these will be the greatest automated toy ever made. For those of you in attendance here, these Fuzz-bots will be available at cost. We will consider these units as advertising and will even give a discount for bulk. We can also supply any color exterior you might like…."

* * *

Red Fur made his mark on the strange skin that Little Fuzzy had brought him. Little Fuzzy, who could understand the strange shapes on the skin had told him that it was an agreement between the *Jin-f'ke* and the Big Ones so that no Big Ones would be allowed on *Jin-f'ke* lands unless invited.

Sitting with Red Fur was the Big One who had been hurt by the bad Big Ones and fought to protect the Fuzzies. Officer Clarke wore the fur of the People around his neck to show that he had been accepted into the tribe. For a Fuzzy this would not have been necessary, but Clarke was as hairless a Big One as any Fuzzy had ever seen.

"Now we all friends with Big Ones," Little Fuzzy said. "Get estee-fee, shoppo-diggo an' lots of good things."

"What do Big Ones want," Red Fur asked again. "More fur? More shiny stones?"

"Big Ones only want to be friends, Red Fur," Clarke said. "We want to teach you many-many things, and learn from you as well."

"Big Ones in the Wonderful Place teach many-many new things," Little Fuzzy added. "An' maybe can help Makes-Things with noise-in-ear."

"An' skin with strange spots says this is so?"

"Yes," Little Fuzzy said. "Good Big Ones like Pappy Jack make bad Big Ones go away. Not take Fuzzees away."

Red Fur was forced to agree with that. Around them were many of the People that were thought lost. They had all been returned safely and with *shodda-bags* and new *shoppo-diggos*. All had said that the good Big

Ones had been very nice to them.

"Is good thing," Red Fur declared.

The Fuzzies around them cheered in their hypersonic voices. Food was brought out and prepared by Little Fuzzy's clan. Red Fur's clan could not be trusted to control fire, yet.

Little Fuzzy gave the signed document to Officer Clarke and smiled. Then he turned to Emily, saying that it was a good thing that all the Fuzzies and Big Ones would be friends. There was a lot that the Big Ones could teach the *Jin-f'ke*. And there might also be things the *Jin-f'ke* could teach the Big Ones as well. There were so many things everybody could learn from each other.

The End

ACKNOWLEDGEMENTS FROM WOLFGANG DIEHR

Patricia Barr Montrose—She gave me encouragement and useful information about farming and guns. She is also my mother's 2nd eldest sister and I was her first nephew. If I did something stupid, she let me know it. If my writing was no good, she would be the first to point it out. Everybody needs a person in their life like her.

Robert R. Smith II—He didn't help with this book, but he was overlooked on *The Hos-Bletha Affair* and I would like to correct that oversight. His contribution to the wedding scene really made the story pop. He is also my brother (for real) from another father. And he will be performing the wedding of my son, Damien, and his future mate, Courtney.

David "Lensman" Sooby—For his pointing out certain technical aspects in the Piperverse. Everybody needs help, now and then, and he provided it.

Mallory Crowe—For helping with a scene in the story and suggesting a minor change.

Cinda Leech—For her assistance in filling out the character of Cinda Dawn. Any resemblance between her and the character in the book was purely intentional.

Peter Cwienk—For his invaluable assistance with the German language and accents, and his editing on the manuscript in English. We are old friends who also worked on The Devil Whiskey computer game together. In fact, we became known as Peter and the Wolf.

Mike Robertson—Fellow writer in the Piperverse. He is far more knowledgeable about space battles than I.

David Bailey—An admitted non-scientist who is amazingly knowledgeable. He provided the explanation for why Zarathustra is livable when it should be a frozen wasteland.

Michael Salinas—A Marine veteran who assisted me with Marine chatter and protocol. Without him, all the military types in this book would have sounded like they were in the Army, my former vocation.

All the guys and gals in the Piper-Worlds discussion group. Their dissection of Piper's stories and technology have been helpful many times.

DEDICATION

In memory of Patricia Barr Montrose (Feb 6, 1939 - Dec 16, 2013)
My first fan and biggest booster

CPSIA information can be obtained
at www.ICGtesting.com
Printed in the USA
LVOW01*0332060517
533487LV00018B/335/P